THE ELECTRIC OATH

AARON COLE WILLIAMS

PROLOGUE

He'd seen it a dozen times before, the charred remains of a comely old town, and sensed something wasn't quite right. The once esteemed order called Vigilant had become a joke in the modern age. After a decade of trying to prove otherwise, Gregory Pavane abandoned all attempts. Gregory, who preferred Gregor after discovering the name in an old fantasy novel, made a life as the Witch Hunter.

For over fifteen hundred years, Vigilant had protected the nation from threats foreign, domestic, and unnatural. The order existed to enforce the laws of the Compact, which regulated technological evolution, lest the world again fall to ruin as it had two millennia before. Sentinels were the highest officers in the order, each presiding over a region of the country. To the average person their exploits were fantastical tales of monsters and magic, much better than the lackluster reality. Though on occasion the order encountered foes worthy of the books.

For twenty years Gregor reigned over the northern branch of Vigilant and served as a crusader for twenty years before that. Gregor and his estranged brother, Matthew, were the order's shining stars. Though his brother abandoned the order, Gregor clawed his way to the top position. He pined for the times that he'd slay evildoers to glorious fanfare, however few of his days were spent living the life romanticized as monster hunting. Most of his jobs had him killing fools, unearthing long-dead machines, or destroying tech not yet allowed by the great law. It was seldom glorious and often rigidly cruel, but it was a calling he yearned for since the days of his misbegotten youth.

At the ripe age of sixty, he was a capable leader, but his body lagged behind his mind. The wear and tear from the job was finally starting to show. Broken bones and torn muscles no longer healed at the rate required. Gregor could still fight, but he had to be more careful while his wits were within the acceptable parameters of a leader. Gregor knew it was time to groom a new leader, and the only ones worthy were not much younger than him.

Gregor adjusted the chainmail armor under his white robes, while the other members under his command scoured the areas for clues of the Grey Sisters. The Grey Sisters were a pervasive cult that worshipped the outlawed technologies of the Old World, ranging from robotics to genetic modification. Over the past few years, these cults had grown more numerous and dangerous. Gregor removed his simple bucket-shaped helmet and ran his fingers through his white beard. A few flecks of snow landed on his hair, a last defiant stand of nature before the emergence of spring.

He tried to recall the name of the town, but he came up short. The village was abandoned back in his days as a young mercenary, before his capture and conscription to the order—a fate he had come to appreciate only after an exceedingly long time. Abandoned towns served as little more than gang hideouts. They littered the upper reaches of the continent, and for good reason: the brutal winters of an untamed wilderness.

This town was nothing special, nor had it ever been from what Gregor could tell. These remote places had gained infamy over the last few years for one distinct feature: a single, metallic cylinder jutting out of the ground with a glowing red light at the top.

The cylinder was thirty feet high and fifteen feet wide,

completely smooth. With its glowing eye, it gave the appearance of an otherworldly lighthouse. The machine stood among the devastation, mocking the smattering of humanity that once fought to carve out a life in the untapped potential of the north. Civilization died around the bizarre structures, and their numbers were growing. When Gregor moved close to the device, it whispered in his head—languages and numbers he could not even begin to process. His body grew feverish, followed by crushing pressure on his temples. Gregor dreaded their purpose. He had no name for them, but his men had taken to calling them Hell Gates, believing that evil emerged from them.

A Hell Gate meant his targets were near. Gregor's men surrounded the metallic construct, which thrust up from what appeared to be the center of town. Vigilant encountered many bizarre forms of tech, forcing them to always develop tools to destroy it, advancing their own tech in the process. Using newly fashioned superheated torches, they sliced through the obelisk halfway up, at the structural weak point where the pieces connected—an arduous process, but eventually the tower came crashing down with a final flicker of red light. With the gate deactivated, Vigilant could worry about the rest a bit later.

Vigilant had dealt with their fair share of these monoliths over the past few months but failed to discern their purpose. Hell Gates sprouted up with alarming frequency all across the Northern Frontier, the uninspired name for the nation's northernmost state. Gregor turned to face the mountains under a starless night and reflected on the sad state of the once prestigious order. Often, he needed to convince himself of Vigilant's relevance; it took moments like this for the convincing to stick.

He left the obelisk to scour the area for clues. Walking through the town, he found evidence of his prey. Foot imprints in the snow and mud, burned logs, and the signature electricity rippling through the air told him he was on the right track.

"Lord Sentinel!" came a voice from inside a dilapidated church. Gregor rushed toward the call with a speed surprising to the younger members. Inside the church, his men stood over a young woman in tattered clothes, whimpering and bleeding out amid the rotted pews. The damp wooden beams of the church gave off a rancid odor, only slightly better than the corpses he expected to find. Large icicles hung from the ceiling, dripping through to the cracks in the floor. The woman was beyond help. Lacerations trademark of a wendigo attack covered her arms and torso, though the lack of precision suggested something else—something had wanted her to suffer. She had light olive skin, auburn hair, and dull blue eyes. Gregor put her age at around seventeen. She had an air of innocence about her, the disenfranchised type cults attracted. She bore no markings or evidence of body alterations. He got down on one knee and gave the woman a warm smile. One of the brash young soldiers cried out, drawing his sword. Gregor raised his hand.

"Fetch the medic." Gregor usually executed those who abused technology, as the Compact dictated. Not everyone or everything he hunted deserved to die; yet regardless of their intentions, disaster often followed. Seeing her shredded body, he pitied her. He placed his hand on her chest, feeling her faintly beating heart. His stern demeanor grew welcoming and grandfatherly.

"What happened?" he asked, with one hand firmly gripped on his blade, just in case.

"I tried to flee from them… I… couldn't let—" She forced the words out as she fought the drowsiness of encroaching death.

"Where are the others, witch?" an overzealous soldier growled. He stood close to Gregor and received an elbow to the groin. He fell to the ground, whining. Gregor made a mental note to reinforce the groin area of the armor should this happen to him someday.

"Shut it!" Gregor bellowed. The other crusaders moved out of groin-hitting distance.

"I took it. They… found me and took it back," the woman said. Her words grew faint. Gregor hurried the conversation along. "What?"

The woman fought to move her hands up, mimicking the shape on an orb.

"The Eye."

Gregor thought about the timing, realizing it to be no coincidence. *Spring is almost here*, he thought.

"Where?"

"The mountain, the one with the tower. Bal… Balder's—"

"I know it," Gregor said. Vigilant interrogated sisters before, most never caved even under pain of death. Gregor wanted to know. "Why are you helping me?"

"They weren't what they said. Friends… died—" Her words came out slow and choppy. She opened her mouth for more words, but they never came. Gregor inspected the body for any other clues, but he possessed the intel needed.

"Burn the body; be quick about it. We move out as soon as you're done."

With the town scrubbed, body burnt, and the base of the gate dismantled, the crusaders marched toward Balder's Bane resting at the top of Mount Caellic. Through the forests and fjords, Vigilant made its way to the Jotun Mountains in the northwest region of the country, a few hours ride from the ruined town. The mountains peeked out over the forest ahead. Vigilant had traversed and scouted these mountains thoroughly in the past, reporting Old World technology still functioning in the heart of the mountains.

The horses grew increasingly agitated as they approached the mountain but pressed on after stopping to feed. The Jotun Mountains dominated the horizon, reminding Gregor of serrated blades. The group marched on parallel to the river, toward the mountain.

At the base of Mount Caellic, Gregor and his crusaders hitched their horses at the old station to finish the journey on foot. He kept focused on his mission. This was no simple group of tech abusers breaking the law, and reports from other branches suggested it wasn't isolated to the Northern Frontier. On rare occasions, violators of the Compact had the ability to become a serious threat, capable of war and death. He knew this was one such time. The last time strange events of this scale happened was centuries ago and resulted in fire consuming a large chunk of the nation's east coast that took over a decade to recover from. Gregor had to stop whatever threat to the nation this cult posed, and he'd kill any that got in his way.

Donning thick furs, the crusaders trekked up the mountain. Remnants of stone walkways and cracked bridges snaked up its sides. Snow began to fall more steadily as they climbed, bringing light to the oppressive blackness. Gregor let out a breath and watched it spirit away. The small bridges that snaked up the mountain were crumbling, pieces falling off along the way. Centuries of neglect reduced the splendorous creations of the mighty Blackthorne Empire to little more than expensive rubble a thousand miles away from anything that mattered. Despite ruling the country, the Blackthornes had almost no presence up north anymore.

The snow fell harder as dawn approached. Gregor sent a scout to go on ahead. Snow turned to a wintry mix that impaired the already poor visibility. He waited for nearly an hour for the scout to return, fully expecting to never see him again. Near the top of the mountain, the scout finally came into view. He approached the group with a face wrinkled in confusion.

"No sign?" Gregor asked. The man didn't respond, only stared at him with glossy eyes. The scout stopped just in front of Gregor on the narrow path overlooking the chasm below, jagged rocks descending like rows of monstrous teeth awaiting a meal. Gregor had seen this sort of thing before.

Gregor spoke in a soft, relaxed tone. "I'm going to wake you up." The enchanted scout remained as still as the dead, the pupils of his eyes gigantic. "I'm going to count backward from five. As I say the numbers, you will become more aware."

"Five, four," he began. The scout did nothing.

"Three." The scout twitched and mumbled. Gregor braced himself for the worst.

"Two." The mumbling continued, and the enchanted man's eyes began to roll around wildly. Gregor's hand gripped his blade.

"One," he said using a louder, more assertive tone. The convulsions ceased. He waited; the enthralled soldier glanced over the path and down the mountain. Gregor took a defensive stance.

"You're fine now," Gregor said. The scout's head turned slowly and met his gaze.

"I'm afraid he's not," the man said, the voice not his own. "Just another little soul you let down." Without warning, the scout hurled himself down the mountain. The other soldiers watched the scene in shock.

Gregor looked back at the soldiers behind him.

With hastened steps, the group continued to move up the mountain. Thunder roared above, and his men huddled together. Events like this happened few times in Gregor's life. He watched cities driven to murderous frenzy and nightmares prowl the dark of the woods. Cults like this possessed the ability to transform scraps of discarded machinery into walking instruments of death. Gregor would kill and die to preserve the law and expected no less from anyone that dare call themselves Vigilant. Gregor addressed his men.

"I'll keep it short and sweet. You know why we're here. We follow the balance of the Compact. Any who threaten that balance must face justice. The Old World must remain dead. Ever vigilant," Gregor said.

"Ever vigilant," the crusaders roared back. The tension rose sharply when they peered up over the rocks. Outside the redoubt walls, five figures stood, covered head to toe in dark robes. Gregor scanned the snow-covered rocks for possible traps. Vigilant saw the targets through the holes of the walled yard of an old fortress serving as the northernmost structure in the country. Fortresses like these once honeycombed the expanse of the mountains, though he was yet to find any that were more than a pile of rocks. In the back was a fat, stubby tower not meant to house more than a few people that spied on travelers coming from the neighboring countries. There was a single hole in the side of the tower, giving it the appearance of a rotten tooth. The group watched in nervous anticipation, seeing the hooded figures standing in a circle. The figures had yet to notice Gregor and his men. An impatient soldier grew antsy and inched in closer. Gregor placed his hand on the boy's shoulder and pulled him back as quietly as possible.

At the ritual site, one of the hooded figures facing away from them stepped to the center of the circle and placed a large green orb on the ground. Atop the crumbling tower, another figure emerged wearing crimson robes. Using his binoculars, Gregor got a better look at the figure.

"Sisters," the leader cried out. "The time has finally come. Our faith and loyalty shall be rewarded at long last! We've paid a heavy price to see this day. We have been ostracized, betrayed, tortured. Yet we remain. We have survived the corruption and failures of this wretched world. This world is now nothing but a half-remembered dream, one that ends now! Awaken!"

The leader removed her crimson robes, exposing her naked flesh and bald head. Her body consisted of pieces of metal embedded in her arms, abdomen, and chest—a twisted symbiosis of metal and flesh. Gregor watched the scene to study his foes. All forms of body modification Gregor encountered provided enhanced strength, speed, and reflexes. Her followers did not possess modifications, making her the only true threat among them. The woman's eyes turned from hazel to ethereal green. The orb flickered to life, turning the same green as the woman's eyes. He remembered what the dead woman from the town said.

"Eye," he muttered. The orb rose slowly from the ground like a miniature moon rising to replace the one obscured by blackening clouds. The icicles in the tower began to melt. The orb spun around as if looking at each of the figures.

Faint words stirred in Gregor's head. The words were beyond his comprehension, no more than hellish rattling in his skull.

"Lord Sentinel!" a crusader said, giving Gregor a push. The push jolted him from the trance.

"We have done all that you asked. Now we call upon you!" the leader cried out. Gregor had heard enough. The crusaders leapt over the rocks and rushed the cultists. Their leader did not seem surprised and continued chanting. When their gaze met, Gregor's head throbbed, and his body went numb. He closed his eyes and ordered his men to avoid her gaze.

The sisters fled toward the center of the yard and the crusaders followed suit. The archers maintained their distance and pelted the old ruins with arrows, none of which hit the leader. Inside the fortress walls, the witches kept their distance, brandishing daggers.

They slashed blindly at the soldiers moving in on them. One sister screamed out, and a shot rang out from the gun in her hand. Her bullet hit nothing. An archer landed an arrow through her wrist, and the gun fell from her hand and off the tower. A thunderous roar cracked the sky, forcing the attackers to pause. The thick wintry mix grew denser, and electricity surged around them. The orb flew into the crumbling tower and vanished. The order took a defensive stance quickly, forming a shield wall. The tower filled with green light. Mist started to form inside the tower, seeping out over the mountainside.

The strange mist moved like a phantom snake, winding and zipping around the peak until it wrapped around the sisters and enveloped them. Peeking through the shield wall, Gregor watched as the sisters appeared to vanish inside the serpentine mist, disintegrating into nothing. The mist zipped up toward the top of the tower and circled around the coven leader. She closed her eyes for its divine embrace. Then the mist flew out over the sea and dissipated. The leader was now alone and surrounded by enemies.

"I am worthy!" the woman screamed at the sky in vain. "They have forsaken me," she sobbed. Her sorrow did not last long; the sight of the crusaders filled her with intoxicating rage. "Defilers!" she roared. With the fury of a lioness, she dived toward them like a javelin.

"Hold," Gregor said. The wall held strong as she came flying toward them. Her eyes burned with green fire, which now surged through the metallic parts of her body. She hit the shield wall with the force of a cannon ball. Soldiers, swords, and shields went flying in all directions, some straight off the mountain. Gregor flew backward, landing mere feet from the thick walls of Balder's Bane. The enemy rose to her feet, using her green eyes to enchant the soldier rushing at her, who, without hesitation, ran his blade through his own unarmored neck.

Gregor scrambled to his feet and grabbed the closest tower shield. The sister pulled the sword from her latest victim and pointed at Gregor with it. He moved in to prevent any further casualties. The woman tried to enchant him. He shook off the mental attacks by dipping behind the shield. Numbness crept up his arms. He shook it off, running into her with his shield. She stumbled back but rushed again and raised the bloody sword to meet his. The swords clashed again and again, her inferior combat skills evident. But fatigue soon set in. Gregor's attacks became clumsy. She overpowered him with the sword. His sword arm went numb. He threw all his weight into one final shield attack. The impact knocked her backward.

"You are not the first witch I've killed," Gregor shouted. The metal weaving through the woman's arms like veins glowed with inhuman power. She slammed her fist into his stomach. Gregor flew backward, bouncing off rock and sliding back through the snow.

Frantically he scoured the snow for the sword and shield. Finally spotting the shield, he crawled toward it. The witch sprinted now, cutting down another soldier. Gregor's whole body ached with pain. He flipped the shield over and grabbed the handle.

Pushing himself up, his shield crashed hard against the attacker, knocking her off her feet. On the ground she accepted defeat.

"The past will never stay buried," she said.

"Maybe not, but you will," Gregor said. He drove the blade straight through her heart all the way through flesh, muscle, and bone to the cold, snowy ground beneath. Her very human blood spilled out onto the snow. The battle was over. Of the twenty men sent on the mission, eight were dead and five were missing.

Bruised and broken, the surviving crusaders made a hasty yet thorough search of the tower, finding nothing of value. Vigilant claimed the body of the sister and began the climb down the mountain. Gregor would send scouts to track the missing soldiers, however after 72 hours they would be declared dead. As Gregor made his way down the broken mountain path, he gave one last look at the Frozen Sea in the direction the mysterious mist had gone, seeing nothing.

Gregor pondered the situation. He killed the threat, but couldn't be sure what happened to the others gobbled up by an unknown force. Perhaps like so many others that came before them, the remaining cultists were destroyed in their own quest for ascendancy. He feared these witches may not have failed in their plan. This mist, and whatever horror lay within, warranted investigation. The nagging inside told him this was far from a victory.

ARIC

ARIC BLACKTHORNE COULDN'T travel anywhere in the country without running into trouble. Aric's long black hair was a shoulder-length veil of shadows among the starry backdrop. He wore black ceramic plating emblazoned with the emblem of a sword wrapped in thorny vines; under this, he sported a mauve colored gambeson with black pants and leather boots. Aric held the prestige of being one of the first in the country to wear ceramic armor, slowly replacing its cheaper metal cousins.

When a member of the royal family arrives in a city, usually the people fall in line. Yet Aric knew a few pesky revolutionaries scurried about. He needed to be out in the field; he had no intention of being an armchair king. Sitting in the kitchen of the country home of Harold and Anna Davidson, he nibbled on a pork sandwich and sipped a glass of wine before getting down to business.

"Delightful," he said between mouthfuls. "Nice break from the unpronounceable nonsense back home." His hosts laughed nervously while he ate. Anna and Harold were in their late sixties, an unassuming couple that lived in between the city and the farmlands. Harold, a portly man with a buzz cut, scratched his hairy left forearm repeatedly. Aric had learned through the years how body language could identify guilty parties.

The modest fieldstone cottage didn't classify as a luxury home, but a decent enough place for an out-of-work coal miner and an ex-teacher. The interior was designed to look like cut logs, with vaulted ceilings, a cozy sitting room, and a brick fireplace. A kitchen suited for a family of four lay adjacent to a half-finished sunroom. Aric nonchalantly eyed the area for any unwanted surprises, though feared little with guards outside.

Harold went through water like a man dying of thirst, losing most of it through his chest and armpits. The wife hid her emotions much better, flitting about the kitchen in a vain attempt to avoid Aric's line of sight. Aric did not fail to notice the shiny new refrigerator, one of the newer models only recently delivered to the region. With her back to him, the woman's graying hair wrapped up in a bun, her head reminded him of a cinnamon roll. Her demeanor suggested it was time to act.

"I hear you're wine enthusiasts. Might I peruse your collection?" Aric asked. The two looked at each other, still unsure what game he was playing. Aric leaned forward and rested his arms on the table.

Harold had scratched his left forearm red and raw. "It's not worth one of your stature." He tripped over his words.

"I insist," Aric demanded. He stood up and walked over to the kitchen counter with the wine bottle and corkscrew, cutting off Anna before she could get to it. Aric stared down both Anna and Harold with a predatory gaze. He could feel the rising tension, which gave him much needed excitement in his otherwise drab life.

"I'm also a gun enthusiast. A little birdie told me you are distributing to some upstarts that have been killing my friends, and that just won't do," Aric declared. His hand slid toward the corkscrew. Picking it up, Aric walked over to Harold and rammed it down through the flesh and bone of Harold's left hand. Anna lunged for the nearest knife. Aric quickly disarmed her. A few hard fists to her face sent her crashing to the floor. Harold's hand shook wildly as he pulled the corkscrew from his hand. Aric grabbed his plate from the table and shattered it against Anna's head as she came up from behind. He tore the corkscrew from Harold's grasp and rammed it right back down into his hand.

"That goes here," Aric chided. Half-dazed, Anna made a break for the door only to run headfirst into four soldiers with rifles pointed at her face. Aric pulled out his own pistol. Aric placed the barrel up against Harold's temple and addressed Anna. "Now why don't you be a doll and show me that cellar, eh, love?"

Defeated, the couple led them outside to the musty wine cellar after grabbing the key. Aric yanked the bloody corkscrew from Harold's hand, lest the man attempt to use it against him. A bitter wind swept through, winter's last hurrah before the coming of spring rains. Patches of snow clung to the trees and formed a polka dot pattern in the dead grass. *Spring always brings the rats out,* Aric thought. His soldiers stood guard outside. He addressed them on his way to the cellar.

"See the trucks?" Aric asked. Each man scanned the area and shook his head. Aric gave a glance out to the dead woods where a few of his snipers lay hidden. He thought about the possibilities from the laundry list of enemies plotting against his family. Aric took risks, including putting himself in situations that would test his abilities in the field and on the throne. Faint lights burned through the lifeless glen separating the ample cottage from the forest. Branches from the last round of ice looked like severed fingers from skeletal hands called trees.

Harold's hands trembled, causing him to drop the key; the resulting groan from the prince increased the poor man's anxiety exponentially. A successful click signaled the fifth attempt to be the last.

Slowly, the couple opened the cellar door. Aric gave Anna a swift kick in the back as she climbed down, sending her and her husband crashing to the cellar floor. Aric's soldiers were on them a second after. Aric stepped over the two to find empty crates once housing rifles, pistols, and various other military hardware stolen from the Blackthorne army. Aric moaned his displeasure. Anna and Harold crawled forward. A few corkscrew jabs in Anna's legs got her screaming. Harold wept at the sight. Neither of them revealed any of those involved in the arms ring, despite shallow cuts along the Anna's arms and legs. Aric suspected the two were just middlemen. Harold's uncontrolled blubbering disgusted Aric.

He spent the next few minutes interrogating the couple. More cuts, beatings, and a few crushed ribs got them no closer to the rebels in the region. Two of his men hovered near the couple with guns ready. The soldiers placed the blades under their throats. Harold and Anna looked at each other and mouthed the words "I love you." With a nod from Aric, the soldiers opened the couple's throats, leaving them to die face down in their own blood.

The four knights stared at the bodies while Aric paced, fuming over the people working against his family. The dank cellar they stood in smelled of mold and blood. The victims weren't rich yet possessed a decent wine collection. One soldier rummaged through the collection. Two of the other men tore open crates and barrels, and red liquor spilled out over the floor. The last man ran his hands along the uneven walls being chiseled out for further expansion. Aric pulled one of the bottles of wine from its rack and opened it with the bloody corkscrew. He took a few sips before pouring the rest on the bodies, discarding the bottle, and jamming the corkscrew down into Harold's skull.

"Finish up," Aric said. He gave one last sneer before scrambling up the stairs. Aric pulled a stolen cigar from his pocket, lit it, and took heavy drags, waiting for his mission to conclude. Unreliable officers left Aric taking on more and more assignments for those that lacked the will to do what Aric was convinced needed doing. The pale moonlight seeped through the openings in the curtained windows and illuminated the black metal armor of the men. He stood a good distance from the porch, scoffing at victims' home as well as the soldier's sleuthing ability. The quaint little family house was about three miles from the city of Greenfield, the central hub of the state known as Heartland. A few moments later, Aric's men emerged outside.

"Anything?" Aric asked.

"Nothing," said Thompson, the longest serving of his personal guard.

Aric puffed on a cigar, keeping his anger in check. Threats to his family required smoke and drink to cool his boiling blood. He smoked and drank quite often. Aric waited for his backup team.

"Our business is done," Aric said. He threw his cigar to the ground, not bothering to stomp it out. He turned to face his men, his thin, pointy mustache accentuating the condescending smirk on his face. He felt joy in protecting his country. It made being away from the capital so long easier to bear.

Aric walked toward the horses and motioned for his men to follow. Next time, he would take the family car, whether his father consented or not. Silently, they rode across the moon-drenched landscape to their destination, the city of Greenfield. Surrounded by grassy hills on each side, the town certainly didn't win any award for creativity. Aric had seen better, sure, though not many around these parts. The men reached the top of the western hill, and before long they saw the lights of Greenfield. Aric wanted a break and a nice drink. Aric knew as bold as the rebels were, they wouldn't dare attack him in the city. The intimidation satisfied him as much as any drink.

The nation's generals, advisors, and even Aric's parents begged him not to go to Heartland, yet he refused to listen. Aric understood the concerns and wasn't blind to them, but he believed that the last few centuries of leadership forgot how to prove they were to be respected and be feared. When leaders gave an issue personal attention it made the people re-evaluate things. To Aric, a leader could not afford to get comfortable or they wouldn't last long in the face of actual conflict. A strong king in the field showed the people actions had consequences.

Greenfield didn't have quite the electrical power system Kingsbury did thanks to Lake Thaxter, however it got by from nearby wind, solar farms, and massive generators in each hub of the city. This town held so much importance to New Prosperity, and that vexed Aric terribly. It started as a small community founded by Thomas Green just after the collapse of the Great Empire. Thomas Green had been among the first sent out by Alexander II to go rebuild the continent, transforming the small surviving communities, lawless settlements, and scattered tribes into a cohesive kingdom. This town and its outlying farms provided the majority of the food for the entire nation, courtesy of influential families like the Averills. Greenfield was the largest city in Heartland and the rebel's primary target. Since the founding of New Prosperity nearly two thousand years ago, the Blackthornes ruled this land, and this arrogant bunch of revolutionaries sought to end that. Agricultural centers like Greenfield had grown more important as the populations became as massive as they were during the Old World. Populations had multiplied tenfold since the beginning of the Second Dark Age. The idea that a bunch of farmers held the nation's balls in a vise made Aric livid. Aric almost dared his enemies to attack, giving him the excuse to bring his fist down hard on the region. He needed to prove he was not afraid of upstarts arrogant enough to topple a 2000-year-old dynasty. Aric made haste to the tavern.

Big Jack's Tavern lay at the northwestern edge of the town, an ironic name taken from its dwarfish owner. It was somewhat of a tradition and business strategy to lure people to town and get them hammered before they realized what a massive disappointment the place was. The tavern had been converted from an old run-down whorehouse and had been up and running back when Greenfield was nothing more than dirt road with a few houses and grocery. Aric's snipers took positions around the tavern while the other men entered the back room. The bulk of Aric's forces vacated town days ago to calm the alarmed locals.

Several dozen remained in town, though outnumbered, if anyone grew bold enough to attack. His own troops masked their anxiety and held up under pressure. He and his men all realized that they had a duty to stay here, even in the face of a threat. Any attack on the soldiers in town would set the entire Heartland army on Greenfield. With superior firepower and the risk of igniting full blown war, Aric saw his foes anxiety to be much worse. A show of force quelled malcontents for now. When the rebels made a large move he would prove to be a king not to be trifled with.

The waitress approached them for round of free drinks, courtesy of a terrified barkeep.

"Whiskey, strongest you got," Aric said, staring down at the table. The rest chose Greene Ale, a local apple-flavored beer. Aric downed a few shots of whiskey. The door to the back room remained open. Out of the corner of his eye, Aric noticed a vaguely familiar shape. The figure wore a sage gambeson under a Kevlar vest, the attire of a Knight-Ambassador. Knight-Ambassadors were the problem-solvers of the kingdom, independent agents that traveled to troubled areas to resolve problems as diplomatically or violently as they saw fit. Aric's suspicion proved justified when the shape took the form of a young Native American man with shoulder-length hair. Native Americans were a rarity anywhere on the continent, which meant the knight could only be Drake Hale.

"I just can't get away from you. Come to lecture me again, Golden Boy?" Aric said venomously. The young man scowled.

"Heard about your little stunt tonight," Drake said.

"Of course, you did," Aric hissed. Drake wore the stern face of disappointment often reserved for parents and teachers.

"Did you even have proof?" Drake asked.

"I only kill the guilty. And I'm doing your job I hope you know," Aric said, motioning for another drink.

"That wasn't the way to handle it," Drake replied.

"It is no longer your concern!" Aric stood up and threw the shot glass into the wall. He approached the young man and stood inches from his face. He didn't care that Drake brazenly provoked him.

"You're his favorite little student, nothing more. You work *for* us. You get that, right? I make the hard choices and pay for them daily!" Hot, whiskey breath rolled out into Drake's face.

"You kill suspects, which is everyone to you," Drake said flatly.

"Those bastards gave out intel on Outpost 15. Every man and woman there is now dead. They steal our weapons and use them against us. You should be thanking me."

"I'm not. Our job is to keep people from escalating violence, giving criminals due process," Drake replied. Aric smirked, continuing to stare young Drake down. "All I'm saying is tread carefully," Drake said.

Aric turned back to his men, fighting the rage bubbling up inside. The waitress slinked in to bring Aric a second bottle of whiskey, this time he chugged it straight from the bottle.

"The job's done. We'll be heading back to the fort at sunrise. If there is no more trouble afoot, I'll remain there until I'm called home. Run along," Aric said.

"Gladly," Drake said, taking Aric's new whiskey bottle from the passing waitress. She ran back for another.

With that, Drake walked out. Aric turned his bitter gaze to the waitress who promptly returned to give him a third bottle. She cowered under his predatory gaze. As the whiskey bottle hit the table, Aric immediately snatched it. The burning liquid washed down. After the spat, the men continued drinking, hoping to avoid Aric's anger now that Drake had riled him up. The soldiers around Aric braced for action. Aric's lips curled up in a nasty sneer.

"Don't worry about him." Hate dripped off every word concerning Drake Hale. "He'll stay out of our way for the time being."

"Leaving?" Jarod asked. The soldiers doubted anyone would move against them, but they didn't need the prince to give them reasons.

"No," replied Aric. He turned to the waitress. "Keep 'em coming." He relished the dark thoughts formulating in his head. "I'll have to arrange an accident for the golden boy… if the rebels don't get him first."

GREGOR

GREGOR SAT IN his old study, sipping Frostpeak rum. He both loved and hated the drink. It helped soothe his aching body, though it played roulette with his emotions. Three weeks' recuperation mended some of the damage done by the mountain battle; he counted himself lucky that all his injuries were minor for someone his age. Gregor spent his time recovering in Vigilant Tower. The tower stood at the northwestern edge of New Prosperity, a few miles from the neighboring country of Gloire in an area once called Ontario, Canada. Outside Gregor's window, the Frozen Sea lay beyond the ice plains to the north; to his south the Boreal Shield stretched out endlessly. The troops stationed outside his room did not hear his demands for more liquid comfort. Gregor hobbled over to the door. "Drink. Fire. Now!" he yelled and slammed his fist on the door. Pounding on the door woke the guards from their groggy half sleep.

Troops hastily restocked his fireplace with wood and cup with rum. Gregor grumbled his approval as the two soldiers ran back out. His lieutenant stepped in as they left. Gregor sat in silk robes, showing more of the pickled commander than anyone cared to see. The lieutenant picked a spot just above the commander's head to focus his eyes.

"It's uh, time for lessons." The lieutenant braced for an earful from Gregor.

Gregor took another swig of the bitter drink and limped over to the dresser for more appropriate clothes. Donning a cotton doublet and combat fatigues, he stumbled down the tower and out to the courtyard. Vigilant Tower had once been part of a magnificent fortress that existed many centuries ago during the War of Lords. Now the tower, servants' house, and cellar were all that remained. He requested funds annually, though his home repairs never made it onto the royal budget. He had often caught a few stealing the stones from unused areas for who knows what. A few rays of sunlight beamed down through the dense grey clouds like holy beams. He ignored the soldiers practicing outside and made a beeline for the classroom.

Lights dangled from the ceiling, unable to defend from melting snow dripping down through the cracks. Heads lined the walls; one skinless with an exposed brain three times the size of a human's, another resembled an infant with hundreds of serrated teeth, and one adorned in metal and wires. At the front of the room, preserver bags contained hand-sized rectangles with black screens strewn across the teacher's desk. In front of each student, leather-bound textbooks chronicled the known history and technologies of man from the last 2,500 years.

The three recruits jumped to their feet and saluted Gregor, who nodded in return. Moving to the head of the room, he cleared his throat with a few disgustingly unpleasant coughs. He saw the revulsion in their faces, and it amused him.

"It's all downhill from here," Gregor coughed. He inspected each of the three recruits, studying their body language. He learned to gauge a person's character from the simplest of things: posture, tone of voice, personal hygiene. Upon his initial go-over, two of the three held potential; the other one he placed under the dubious category of *probably not.*

"I apologize for not meeting you sooner. It's been an eventful few weeks." He introduced himself, and they responded in kind. Gregor did not recognize any of the last names, which meant they didn't belong to more famous—and infamous—families that often brought him grief. He paid little attention to the rest, not a fan of the backstory spiel. Slipping his hand under his desk, he pulled out his hidden flask of rum and added it to his mug. He drank the whole thing, wiped his mouth, and got to business.

"As you know, New Prosperity has not always been. It is a collection of most of the eastern third of the United States of America, which at its height also contained the assimilated countries of Canada and Mexico. Together they became the super nation called United North America, more commonly referred to as the Great Empire – though not the only such empire of the time. Two thousand years ago, this country had reached heights we can only dream of, using technology we still barely understand." He recounted the fragments of knowledge from that time period: genetic modification, digital books, moon colonization, body alteration, electronic drugs, resource generation to accommodate a growing population, weather control, animal hybridization, and small personal devices that people used to harass strangers with pictures of their genitals or attack each over trivial comments. Of course that wasn't the true lure of the job; it was the hunting of the monsters that came from the abuse of this ancient and forbidden technology. Gregor scratched his beard and made eye contact with each student.

"There are three different types of monsters in the world," he began. Pulling out his own personal leather-bound book from his desk, Gregor tossed it onto the desk of the closest student. The students gathered around and looked through the journal at the collected bestiary. They flipped through the pages.

"The first group is called Machina." Gregor walked over to the surgical table and picked up the bag containing the mechanical hand. He careful removed the hand from the bag. Without warning, he tossed it at the recruits. It landed in the lap of the closest one. The fingers twitched. The recruit screamed and leapt back. Gregor guffawed. He went on to cover the machines of the Old World, weapons and artificial life-forms outlawed by the Compact. "Some resembled humans and led to decades of debate on the nature of consciousness. In the current age they serve as bodyguards for rogue scientists, dubbed witches and warlocks."

Gregor then moved on to mutants: beings, both human and otherwise, that have been experimented on. With hesitation he moved on the third and most vile category.

"Last are the demons. These creatures are the physical manifestations of the sins of humanity through technology. They defy all explanation. They are born from technology yet are not machine. They're as alive as you and me. Each technological sin creates a new unique type of demon. Some demons are conscious, capable of complex thought and speech. I pray you'll never meet one."

He noted the disgusted faces of the students as they viewed the image of a spymaster: an infernal ball of eyes varying in size, with six slender human-like arms and long nails on each hand. "The creature uses its limbs to move at incredible speeds. It was born from those that used technology to spy on their fellow men, often corrupt leaders and faceless organizations. It watches its victims from afar, tormenting them from distance. When it's had its fun, it eviscerates the target," Gregor said. He glanced up at the tattered flag on the wall adorned with sixty-one stars, one for each state. Gregor went on to describe the history of the continent.

"Our world is built upon the ruins of the United North America. Despite the ups and down the country did well for centuries as a constitutional republic. By the start of the twenty-second century, however, it was the furthest thing from that. Once the United States assimilated the other nations of the continent, it changed dramatically. It began the downward spiral as all the empires before it. Other nations of the world quickly followed suit, becoming continental empires as well. While the specifics were lost during the collapse, we know that over time a few families, and their weaselly friends seized absolute power of the government, business, media, and virtually every other aspect of the nation." He explained how these elite wielded the power of gods. "They engineered wars, controlled economies, stripped away freedoms under the guise of security, used politics to divide the masses, stoked the fires of civil war, and exploited the common people for their every whim. In the final decades of the empire, wars were not fought over ideals but were more like business transactions, playing groups against each other the same way they did with their so-called 'stock market.' And the commoners they ruled over allowed it all to happen. Technology became a weapon of silence, censorship, and destruction. The populace grew too fearful of challenging those in power. In time their voices disappeared completely. People became too reliant on that same technology, unable to do even basic math or have social interaction without it. Then they lost it."

Gregor bent over behind his desk and grunted loudly. He lifted a projector onto the desk, mumbling about how this should've been done already. He pulled down a projector screen behind him and showed the recruits images of wars over ideals, land, and just about anything else.

"These wars culminated in a few powerful families gaining complete control of North America. Images of nuclear explosions set the sky ablaze before them, attacks designed to nullify the enemy's technology. Flying machines fell out of the sky. Neighbors butchered each other for basic amenities. Rising tides drowned the coastal cities after weather machines ran amok. Skies darkened as year-long storms tore the world asunder. Out of a world population of 10 billion, only a quarter of a billion survived on North America, with still no contact from the eastern continents. The artificial humans of the world went extinct, but their synthetic bodies remained to serve as mindless tools for those savvy enough to use them. Human knowledge was stored in machines instead of minds. The machines failed, leaving the world in utter ignorance. For whatever reason their technology didn't come back on. And thus began the Second Dark Age."

He cleared his throat and took a sip of lukewarm rum before continuing. Gregor walked over to a stand with ancient armor fashioned from repurposed automobile parts. He returned to his desk.

"When the world fell, the families split the UNA among themselves, becoming the nations you see today: Highland, Gloire, Toth, New Prosperity, and the rancher-controlled Badlands. The Blackthorne family is descended from the head of one of those very families, conquering the eastern half of the continent and calling it New Prosperity. Likewise, his advisers take their title from this time as well: the Board of Directors." Gregor pulled out a fat binder full of papers from the desk drawer. He held up this item and called it by its name: the Compact.

"The Compact served as rule book for the new nations. It lays out the controlled evolution of technology. Through the Compact, the nations evolve in a way designed to avoid further global catastrophe," Gregor said. In his own lifetime, Gregor saw the institution of automobiles, cancer treatments, ceramic plating, and less restriction on civilian ownership of firearms.

"Our job is to destroy any who violate the Compact. There is no better cause."

Pride swelled within Gregor. The non-potential recruit gave him a smug look and opened his mouth.

"So why are we out in the middle of nowhere?" he asked.

"Not everyone sees the value of our work," Gregor replied. His mouth grew dry. A few more swigs of rum warmed his belly. He recanted his own adventures, to his dismay there were not as well-known as he believed. He was particularly saddened by the lack of awareness of the dreaded wolfmen he killed in this very room.

"What about the aurocalypse?" said one. He raised an eyebrow in confusion.

"The what?" Gregor said in surprise. He had never heard of such a thing.

Another one of the recruits spoke up. "Oh yeah. They attacked farmers and drank their blood."

Gregor stood for a moment, absorbing this tall tale about vampire cows that made his order seem like a joke. For a moment Gregor considered giving up completely.

"Where did you hear this story?" Gregor asked curiously.

"So, did it happen?" he asked.

"No!" Gregor yelled out. His vision blurred. In a rage he threw the robotic hand at the cadet, connecting right with the boy's face. He muttered an apology then sat down, demoralized. The recruits murmured to each other.

"Class dismissed," Gregor said, utterly defeated.

The recruits rose to their feet while Gregor pouted, not acknowledging them. He sat alone in the schoolhouse for nigh an hour, when a man in his early forties with closely cropped black hair barged in. This was Cedric Wills, his second-in-command. The junior sentinel tried to cheer up the commander, though such a task fell beyond the scope of his expertise. The sour thoughts clung to Gregor.

"The world survives because of us. Well, not the cows," Cedric comforted.

"Don't you start with that shit," Gregor said. Cedric grinned.

"Gotta have fun somehow. Anyway, we're ready," Cedric said.

Gregor shook off the despair and followed Cedric through the door behind the surgical tray to the dungeons. A winding stairway spiraled down to Cedric's lab. Bits of earth peeked out from spots of missing stones. The two men reached an iron door with the faded words keep out plastered on it. The guards outside the door saluted Gregor and Cedric.

Gregor and Ceric opened the door that led to underground chambers of the complex. The aroma of tomato soup and warm bread seeping from the guards' lunch aroused his taste buds. The surviving iron bars of the cell rusted to the point of crumbling like crackers. The expansive dungeons of the ruined castle held no prisoners, instead serving to further Vigilant's research. Tables adorned with bone saws, needles, jars of formaldehyde, and technical documents on robotics cluttered up the halls. A synthetic heart hooked up to a motor pumped beside severed artificial limbs in one cell. Two green eyes in the next cell followed his movements. Across the hall, Cedric's queen-sized platform bed added a spot of pleasantness to this ominous place. Gregor often wondered if he allowed Cedric too much freedom with his experiments.

The two made their way to the cell in the northwest corner where the cult leader's body lay. Inside the "Chop House," Cedric immediately resumed poking and prodding the woman's body amid the white glow of electric lanterns, a cackle away from a mad scientist. Gregor had spent most of the last three weeks recovering from his wounds, and only now devoted any quality time with this cadaver. Cedric paced around the table where the body lay, clearly showcasing his frustration and excitement.

"This one's something special," he said while anxiously pacing. The rumbling of Gregor's stomach forced numerous stops and hateful glares during Cedric's analysis. Cedric opened a journal and scribbled notes at breakneck speed.

"It always disturbs me how excited you get examining corpses," Gregor said. Cedric continued to bounce around with childlike wonder.

"You know the old saying, Dead men tell no tales? Not true at all. They never shut up if you know how to listen." Cedric examined the lifeless sister; her body was a patchwork of metal and meat. Even so, she had been an attractive woman, not the normal cult types discarded for some deformity. Gregor already planned out the disposal of the body in his head, regardless of Cedric's upcoming objections. "When you're done, I'm destroying the body," he added. Cedric gave a begrudging nod.

Cedric made a series of grunts, showing admiration for this strange technical marvel. "I don't think I've ever seen body modification like this," he said. He reached over to a loaf of bread sharing a spot with his surgical tools. He tore a piece off with his teeth then swapped it for a sternal saw. He pulled the rolled-up gloves on his hands. Cedric sliced through the torso, grinding against metal interwoven through muscle and bone. He stopped sawing, losing a few saw teeth for his efforts. Switching to reinforced shears, he cracked through the troublesome bones and the metal inlays laced through the marrow. He pulled open the torso and motioned Gregor closer.

Inside the body, organic tissue mingled with the artificial. Nearly all of the woman's nervous system and non-vital organs were mechanical or made from a filmy substance that imitated organic material. Most curious was the lack of human heart, in its place a pale synthetic one still warm to the touch. A mixture of veins and arteries both real and fake ran through the body. Gregor stepped back at the monstrous sight.

"Perhaps she slowly replaced her failing parts to prolong her life. It would explain how they seem to be living so long. She must have been a scientist—or the victim of one," Cedric said. Neither of them could deny the impressiveness of the woman.

"From what I gathered her body modifications were to appease something… something that consumed the others," Gregor stated. Whatever happened up on the mountain terrified him, and he knew it would happen again.

"That's absurd," Cedric replied.

"The whole world is," Gregor countered. Cedric responded with a grunt.

"We need to access the king's resources," Cedric said.

"Then I must go at once." Gregor sighed.

Cedric picked up a small instrument on the nearby metal tray with tongs that measured electrical output of machines. He moved in over the heart and it beeped in response. The machine parts still hummed with life. A thunderous lightning crash outside startled both men, causing the device to fall inside the open corpse. Cedric fumbled for it. His gloved hand brushed against the exposed faux heart. Energy rippled through the room. Heat snaked in between them, creeping toward the corpse. The lantern lights flashed, then burst. The humming coming from inside the body grew louder. The corpse's eyelids flung open, and the body sprang up from the table. The eyes again burned green, and Gregor immediately turned from the enthralling gaze.

Cedric cried out in terror, drowning out his superior's own curses. Fear paralyzed him, leaving Cedric to watch helplessly as the corpse stumbled to its feet. Gregor backed out of the room and sprinted toward a weapons stash in the adjacent cell. A collection of old swords, axes, and maces hung on weapon racks inside; a few guns were stored in a locked safe aboveground. Gregor lunged for the first sword within reach. The body moved robotically, bereft of human consciousness. It hobbled around to face the cowering Cedric.

Gregor darted back into the room and sliced at the body's neck. Its mouth moved, trying to speak, though only screams and blood came out. The head slumped back from the open gash. Electricity shot from the artificial veins and arteries in the open neck. The body stumbled, knocking over the surgical tools with clumsy swipes. Cedric jumped out of its path. Gregor chopped away at the neck until the head rolled off. The body shambled around a few moments, until finally collapsing on the floor in front of the High Crusader. The head stared up at them with eyes still full of jade fire. Gregor's eyes met hers, and paralysis set in.

Gregor forced the words out. "Cover… head!" Cedric did not move. Gregor's body went limp.

"The head!" Gregor yelled. The High Crusader gathered his wits and threw the sheet from the table over the head. Gregor felt the control of his body return. The two waited until their hearts stopped beating at hypersonic speed. The green eyes could not penetrate the sheet. Gregor gave the head a nudge with his foot so it faced the cell wall.

"I think I kickstarted the battery," Cedric said, ashamed.

"Finish destroying the body and be quick about it."

"What about the head?" Cedric asked, still shaken.

"I'm taking it. They won't be able to ignore me anymore." Gregor picked up the cloth-covered head and tossed it in a small doeskin bag. Cedric followed him, watching him don his armor and pack a bag of supplies. Gregor didn't relish going to the capital with the possibility of civil war erupting at any moment.

"You're going now?" Cedric asked, confused.

"We both are. Gather the troops," Gregor said. His stomach growled again. He stopped Cedric. "And get me some damn soup."

THOS

Walking over to the closet, Thos Averill pulled out a pair of jeans and an old tan jacket. He muttered a curse. It was a bad start to what he knew would be a bad day, already behind schedule to boot. With an electric razor, he evened out his beard hairs as much as his patience allowed. A few stray hairs thrust out longer than the rest, reddish strands among the dark brown mass. In the mirror he gave himself one last look over. He dreaded the trips to Greenfield. Every February 18, the official first day of spring in the New Genesis Era, he made this trip. He hated the date. Thos owned the largest farm in the region, providing meats, produce, furs, alcohols, and tobacco to the people of New Prosperity. Once a year, he hashed out the new trade agreements with the businesses and supply lines across the nation. These negotiations were often tedious, painful, and put him on the radar of rebels wanting to bring down the Blackthornes.

Beads of sweat ran down his face and into his beard as he hastily prepared. An eerie silence permeated the walls of his Gregorian home. The family Estates and lands the Averills called home were the rewards for his grandfather's service as a Blackthorne knight, most notably in preventing an assassination of King Aldous. Thos fumbled down the steps into the kitchen. He moved over to the sink and ran his fingers behind the pipe to make sure the wedding ring remained undisturbed. He peered out the window and spied his girlfriend Cassandra Lewis tinkering on the rusty green tractor that always failed at the start of spring. The oversized coveralls she wore hid the feminine curves of her slender form. Her tan skin fared much better outside than his pasty complexion. Her silky brown hair ran down her shoulders. She usually ignored it until some accidental pulling encouraged her to opt for a ponytail. He considered proposing right at this moment, yet once again let procrastination get the better of him.

He threw open the doors to pale blue morning blanketing the fields gearing up for a lucrative year. Before him stretched out the 150,000 acres of land that belonged to his family, along with the houses and stores of the families that worked it. Averill Estates also employed a few hundred workers from around the region throughout the year, making it one of the largest businesses in the area. Workers already toiled outside, tending to sheep and cattle with his marshmallow-fluff Great Pyrenees dogs. The automatic seed planters chugged away, filling the ground for the growing seasons. Workers hauled the mobile irrigators into place. Containers of water and chemicals lay in position to be loaded. The automatic tractors hummed with life, a sight to behold when they worked properly. Technical hiccups notwithstanding, Thos felt good about the coming season. He could smell it as clearly as the morning damp. He beamed with confidence that this year would more than make up for the mediocrity of the last harvest.

Cassandra turned around and blew a kiss his way. Being as intentionally silly as possible, Thos responded with an equally girly kiss of his own.

"That's a good look for you. Maybe you should wear one of my dresses next time," Cassandra said with a smile. Thos smirked.

"They cut me across the bust," he remarked. He approached

her and wrapped his arms around her. He waved at men staring, until they went back to work.

"All set?" Cassandra asked. Thos slapped the pistol in its holster.

"My charm and my gun—all I need." He grinned. His lips met hers. He'd come to love the smell of grease that adorned her clothes in brown-black patches. Thos placed his arm over Cassandra's shoulder, and the two watched the workers toiling. The sun beamed down uncharacteristic warmth for the first day of the wet season.

"Beautiful day. All we need is a little breeze," she said. Thos pursed his lips together and gave a hard blow. She shot him the look; the lovable-fool look that let him know that he was the only man in the world for her.

"You need to be going," she said. His lips met hers. They kissed again and again, each one making the departure more excruciating. She was his great addiction, the terrible itch that was heaven to scratch.

"I always show up a few hours late just to annoy them, and you're a damn good reason to be tardy." Thos smiled.

"Keep this up, I may keep you here all day," Cassandra said. Her loving embrace was magnetic, and he never minded its pull.

"Hurry back," she said, leaving him with one last kiss. Thos jogged over to the stable where his trusty steed snorted his delight. Officially, the horse was known as Ol'Nag when Thos didn't have other cleverer equestrian-themed puns to call him.

"How's my mane man?" He laughed, the only person to ever laugh at that joke. The man in the stable rolled his eyes. He saddled up the horse and Thos hopped on. Thos made a quick stop at the family cemetery to see his brother, parents, and grandparents, as had become his tradition. White paint peeled off the wooden fence, leaving discolored black spots like an old banana. The oldest tombstones veered too far to the left, in danger of falling over again. He made a note to add cemetery repairs to the mounting list of renovations. Thos walked over to the gravestones of his father, mother, and brother.

"Wish me luck, guys." This spring was his sixth as the sole surviving member of the Averill family.

He gave one last wave to Cassandra before vanishing into the thick wilderness of Old Man's Woods. Patches of greenery formed in the dead forest, giving it a sickly quality. A few globs of snow clung to thin branches cracking overhead. At the entrance, flyers were nailed to the trees depicting a poorly drawn Anselm Blackthorne with the word *TYRANT* surrounding the figure. Other flyers said TAKE BACK YOUR HOME. Thos tore the propaganda from the trees and crumpled it up. The last thing he needed was for Aric to think he colluded with those on the hit list.

Thos scratched his head, cursing upon the realization he had forgotten his favorite duckbill cap. Dense forests served as the natural defense for both his land and the city of Greenfield. From the position of the sun, he gauged the time to be an hour until noon. He was a little slower than usual on this trek, though being the top businessman of the region meant that the Merchants' Union had to wait on him. He slowed his pace. Thos loved helping people, but after a few minutes of dealing with Greenfielders, he relished the miles of forest between him and them.

Nothing particularly interesting had transpired in the woods since his brother's untimely death a decade ago. Thos reached the end of the stream and experienced the oddest sensation. He shrugged off the feeling at first, until he heard voices coming from the direction of the abandoned cabin often used by reclusive hunters or sometimes reclusive fugitives. His gut reaction had him reaching for his revolver in case snallygasters or something worse lurked nearby. Thos paid local hunters handsomely to reduce their population, yet the population always came roaring back.

He veered off course toward the dilapidated cabin a half mile to the south. The roof clung to the front of the collapsed front wall, just a hard snow or gust away from sliding off. Downed trees from the fall's merciless windstorms lay piled behind the cabin, more evidence of unwanted activity. An ax and run-down generator lay beside the cabin, indicating recent company. Green light pulsated inside the old cabin. Quietly, Thos slid off his horse to get a better view. Against his better judgment, something urged him onward.

Thos came within a few yards of the cabin. He stopped when he noticed a line of figures standing in front of the ruined cabin. The figures were human, three male and three female. The men wore expensive suits of dull blues and blacks. The women wore green, red, and purple Victorian dresses, at least that was his guess based on the number of ridiculous frills. Few people in town wore such attire, and none he knew paraded around as such in the middle of the wilderness. Thos maneuvered himself behind thick trees and watched the strangers.

Wordless and unmoving, the six figures stared, fixated on the old cabin. Another burst of intense heat shot through the air from inside the cabin. Snapping twigs a dozen feet from him caused Thos's heart to pound so hard he felt it in his head. In unison, the six figures turned toward the direction of the sound as one. Each person wore metallic comedy masks of polished silver, all with the same lifeless expression. The eyes burned an intense emerald green, far brighter than any normal human eye. Beads of sweat dropped down onto Thos's jeans. His raised his gun to fire. A deer darted past them, bringing their attention back to the cabin now filled with mist. A strange humming sound hammered at Thos's skull, making him queasy. He fought through the nausea to see the cultish behavior play out, waiting for an opportunity to slink back to his horse.

The figures lined up, forming three couples, one male and one female. The women extended their hands and the men took them as in the beginning of a ballroom dance. One by one, the couples entered the cabin. After the last couple entered, the mist instantly flew back inside with them. Thos waited a few minutes to see what happened next, but nothing did. Crouching down, he moved toward the cabin. Thos hesitated but felt compelled to uncover what transpired a stone's throw away from his land. Faint scratching noise from within stopped Thos in his tracks. Heat rippled out through the holes and cracks of the cabin, coupled with the dew it gave Thos a blast of swampy humidity. Thos steadied his breathing, he couldn't tolerate any threat to his people. He mustered bravado and crept up to the door. The scratching ceased. When he made it inside, he found an empty cabin, devoid of furniture, decorations, and masked people. An eerie silence permeated the air.

Thos had heard nightmare stories of creatures across the land. He cringed when he heard about bumpkins, deformed feral children occasionally born to an unlucky family, supposedly because of a parent's infidelity. They made a skittering sound, much like what he heard from the dark corners of the cabin. In the dark, he spied knee-high animals, bipeds with fat bellies and heads just as big that spilled over the neck and down the back. Thos squinted and saw the humanoid faces grinning at him through four rows of sharp black teeth. Animal terror washed over him. Three bird-like talons protruded from each of their four limbs. The demons giggled and lunged at him before he could get any shots off. Kicking wildly, he kept the three of the little creatures at bay. However in doing so, he lost sight of the fourth. Tiny teeth clamped down on his calf. Instinctively, he turned to the attacker and threw the pinkish imp into the wall.

The ceiling above him creaked and splintered. Thos dashed out of the house seconds before the roof came down, sliding down the rotten walls with it. He jumped aside, landing face down in the dirt. Letting out a nervous laugh of victory, he picked himself up from the ground. When he stood up, he jumped back at the sight of a man in a three-piece white suit a few paces in front of him. A hot mist surrounded the figure, moving around him with a disturbing level of awareness. The man wore a golden mask, which grinned from ear to ear; his green eyes burning through Thos. The figure's skin was pallid and waxy, more like an imitation of skin. Thos felt dozens of eyes upon him. To his horror, he looked around to see scores of bumpkins surrounding the destroyed cabin. All of the demons' faces were contorted in terror at this new nightmare. Clicking and murmuring erupted from their lips. The figure casually waved his right hand, and the murmuring ceased, as did all traces of the little demons. Paralysis took hold of Thos, accompanied by mortal dread. Metal scraped inside his head.

"You're a curious little one," the man said. His thunderous tone echoed inside Thos's brain.

"Who… the hell are you?" Thos asked. The figure leaned on a cane of shimmering obsidian, studying him.

"Merely an observer, nothing to concern yourself with." His tone disturbed Thos.

"A bunch of masked assholes with demon babies in the woods outside my home is actually something I should concern myself with." Choking heat rolled off the strange man. Thos's anxiety rose sharply.

"Big changes are coming to the world. Can you feel it?" the man asked.

"Can't say that I do. I may shoot me a weirdo though. Can you feel that?" Thos shouted back, trying to bury his fear under shaky voice and hands. Even Thos knew at that moment he possessed the intimidation factor of a cricket. The aura rolling off the man made Thos feel powerless and small. The man laughed an inhuman laugh. Thos readied the shot. "I think it's time for you to leave, fella."

"Indeed," the masked man said. "I'm just a bad dream anyway." His green eyes flashed. Thos lost control of himself.

The man gave a friendly bow. Scorching mist rose from the ground, crackling with electric energy. The mist enveloped the figure. The man disappeared and the mist dissipated, leaving Thos standing alone and dumbfounded. A few more trees crashed down, finishing off the hunters' cabin for good. The next thing Thos knew, he was on his horse plodding along toward the city. He eventually formulated words.

"That's a terrible way start a day," he muttered, still in a state of shock.

ANSELM

"Welcome home, your majesty." The golden knight opened the rear left passenger door to the king's ebony car. Rows of silver and black trucks, cars, limousines, and boats on trailers filled the gargantuan room that served as the underground garage for the Blackthorne family. White lights illuminated each of the magnificent vehicles, which the king seldom used. The king liked to say he didn't use them to be more like the common folk, though it had more to do with a phobia he'd developed after a dangerous wreck left him needing anxiety meds for his travels.

The moment he stepped out the car, the gathered soldiers saluted him. Dressed in a black suit with bronze-colored tie, Anselm Blackthorne emerged with crown in hand. He ran his fingers along its surface, feeling the many jewels embedded in its golden frame. Thanks to the tinted windows he'd managed to sleep through the town procession. The king ran his hands through his graying hair, making a note to have his barber add brown to it tonight. He straightened his beard and checked his suit for visible wrinkles. He adjusted his tie and placed the crown back on his head. He nodded and dismissed the soldiers. After months of touring the country, all he wanted to do was see his family;

unfortunately, meetings came first. A knight—a short, joyless man named Frederick—approached him.

"The meeting has started, sir," Frederick said.

"Of course it has," Anselm grumbled. Frederick led him to the elevator. He hit the button beside the door, and the two awaited the agonizingly slow descent of the elevator. Once the elevator arrived, the soldier hit the button for the floor with the offices. The two ascended the glass elevator on the side of Blackthorne Castle, an Old World skyscraper repurposed to serve as the seat of the nation's capital. The metal behemoth thrust up from largest hill at the back of city. From the elevator, Anselm looked out over the city. Smokestacks from the industrial sector rose in the distance, wearing rings of light for the unfortunate workers on top. Bathed in neon light, the city's beauty amazed him. Below him, a million people carried on with their lives, all relying on their king to keep the nation strong and secure.

With a ding, the doors opened.

As Anselm left the elevator, he noticed fifteen men and women in dark suits hovering outside the meeting room, vultures over a carcass. These individuals were all members of the Board of Directors. The Board served as the king's advisors and the second most powerful group in the nation, though they were quickly becoming the first. Each member of the Board came from one of the elite families of the nation, some families that had held their status since before the fall of the Great Empire two millennia ago. Every aspect of country could be traced to the elite families, from industry to commerce to medicine and everything else. In most cases, the eldest member in each family served as a member of the Board, though the occasional up-and-comer sometimes found himself or herself as family representative. The purpose of the Board was to assist the king in running New Prosperity. However, Anslem knew that all they really did was push him closer and closer to the edge of madness and accomplish great heaps of nothing.

Although there were fifteen families, five held more sway than the others: the Derbins, Whitehalls, Campbells, Droullins, and Westerfields. These families each served as captains of industry. The Derbins were the premier weapons and armor manufacturers, a business in perennial high demand. The Whitehalls controlled the finance industry, responsible for First Prosperity Bank, the nation's largest (and quickly becoming its only) bank. The Whitehalls also once held power in Heartland, with the eldest son Victor commanding the state military until an event left him severely brain damaged and abandoned by his own family. Anselm believed Federal Prosperity Bank to be the most worthless institution in history, its sole purpose to give jobs to its leaders' incompetent friends and family. Anselm once recalled touring the main building incognito, watching employees spend much of their overpaid day discussing their favorite sandwiches, trying to get people they didn't like fired, and bleating incessantly.

The Campbells ruled the energy business—involved in wind, solar, hydroelectric, nuclear, and fossil fuels. They had a hand in nearly every oil rig, dam, and wind farm in the nation. The Droullins ruled over the alcohol business, tracing breweries back to pre-Prohibition era America. Last came the Westerfields. The Westerfields controlled the entertainment industry and the nation's media. The family of actors and newsmen also decided what plays, books, and news stories made it out the public. Anselm hated actors; he only enjoyed them when they were found at the bottom of Lake Thaxter. These families were the ever-expanding and increasingly poisonous thorns in Anselm's side.

"The tour went well?" Mr. Droullin asked.

"As always," Anselm replied, "though Westerbrooke seems to be having a problem with their sewage facilities, an issue of its integration with the new Xenos Management Systems. Also, the Kerr brothers are gaining support for their revolution further north it seems."

"About your son," Mr. Whitehall chimed in.

"I've been back ten minutes," Anselm interrupted, not hiding his dislike of Mr. Whitehall. Mr. Whitehall's pudgy frog neck spilled out over his collar like a gut for his head. Every time he talked, he made an audible gasping sound as if each sentence was a desperate cry for air.

In silence, Anselm walked to window that looked down on the courtyard where the statue of his ancestor Alexander I stood. The monument represented the glory of everything that the Blackthorne family had accomplished over the past two millennia. Roughly thirty feet tall, it showed Anselm's ancestor just days before he unified New Prosperity. In classic fashion, the statue revealed no physical flaws about the exalted ancestor, certainly not his testicle issue, which Anselm had regrettably learned about from historians.

Without talking, Anselm moved back to the people hunched over the circular table in the center of the room. He approached the table, removed his crown, planted himself firmly on the throne, and awaited the others. With the board members seated, the more serious discussion commenced. John Derbin toyed with his pocket watch. His thin vulture-like face stood out among the more bloated members around him. His sunken eyes and sullen face gave him a deathly quality that might give even the Grim Reaper pause. The middle-aged Ben Campbell sat in place of his father, Adam, who seemed to always have some new ailment only during meetings. The group droned on about the increasing violence in the nation, largely blamed on the king's eldest son. Anselm listened as long as he could.

"Heard enough. I've been gone for two months, and I'd like to see my family. I'm retiring for the evening. Good night, gentlemen." The stress of ruling nation for the past twenty years wore on him constantly, instantly exacerbated when dealing with the Board. Vacations and days off no longer helped. All the pressures of the world bore down on his chest, pushing until every breath hurt. The anger started welling inside. Each meeting with the Board only further convinced him they were no longer useful.

Without another word, Anselm made for the elevator, not bothering to notice the other members still seated. He didn't need to wait to hear the scheming fools bickering with each other for the thousandth time. Anselm quickly pushed the button that took him to his family and away from this nonsense.

The clang of rusted metal signaled that Anselm had reached the top floors of the makeshift castle. The top five floors of the structure served as the private residence of the Blackthorne family. The top floor consisted of a bedroom, fireplace, small library, a menagerie of artwork, and a trophy room—an impressive collection, but at the moment all the treasures and accomplishments of the bloodline were trivial things. Anselm entered the sitting room. In the center of the room stood his greatest treasures, his wife and youngest son, Edgar. Without a word, Anselm embraced Abigail and Edgar. The sweet vanilla-like scent of perfume had been the sign that he didn't have to keep an entire country from collapsing for a night.

"At least I still have you," Anselm said warmly. He placed his hand on young Edgar's shoulder. The boy's shaggy bowl cut and brown small clothes made him look like a mushroom. "Your mom and I have matters to discuss. Why don't you go to your room?"

"Yes, sir," he said.

"*Dad*," Anselm corrected. He gave Edgar a big hug and watched as the door closed behind him. Anselm turned his attention to his wife. Abigail's soft smile, coupled with the red silk dress with gold trim, lent her an angelic demeanor. Her honey-blonde hair flowed down her back in one serpentine braid. This place hadn't worn her down as it had done to him. He knew well how his enemies underestimated his wife, despite her ability to rule in his stead. He dreaded the conversation they were about to have.

"Edgar isn't doing any better, is he?" Anselm asked. When he said those words, she could keep it in no longer. He didn't want to hear the words. They somehow add finality to a situation he desperately tried to remain hopeful about.

"The medication is no longer helping. His dosage has doubled," Abigail said.

"Doubled? I don't enjoy the thought of my son turning into a zombie; the doctor needs some *encouragement* to get better results."

"I'm not sure what else to do. The only alternative is—"

"The first brain surgery in… Mercy knows how long," Anselm said.

He had buried his rage and frustration for years—keeping his anger in check only made it burn stronger. He kept calm. His head began to throb; just hours back, and it was already becoming more than he could bear. Despite everything crumbling all around him, he refused to let it get the best of him.

"Aric left for Greenfield two weeks ago," Abigail said. Anselm clenched his fist, trying not to decimate the closest wall.

"He should've waited. I doubt they could even organize a luncheon, let alone win a war. If only I didn't need—"

"But you do need them," Abigail reminded. Anselm ignored her comment, removed his suit, and tossed it carelessly on the floor.

"Enough politics. How's Percival?" he said changing the subject, stroking his graying beard.

"Well. Spending a lot of time in one of the taverns. Got so good at disguises, I mistook him for a thief in the courtyard one night. When he's up here, he spends a good deal of time with Edgar. A few times he even spoke on your behalf at one of the Board's impromptu meetings. A capable leader," Abigail said. Anselm thought about Aric's growing jealousy of his younger brother.

"I hope my children can avoid this mess. Politics is poison," he said. Pangs of hunger directed him toward an overdue family meal.

"So, I take we have a glorious feast planned for tonight?" He said as he stretched out his arm. Hand in hand, they walked to the dining hall. Anselm drowned out thoughts of rebels, poison, and aging parasites.

"Fit for a king."

THOS

In a daze, Thos came to full awareness atop his horse at the edge of the woods. He tried to recall the events that had led him here. Images of masked figures and pink demons popped into his mind and vanished just as quickly. His right calf ached. His ran his finger along it, feeling only a minor injury.

"One hell of nightmare," he said. He tried to think on it again, this time remembering nothing. "Something bit the shit outta me." He looked at his calf closer this time. The puncture marks were not deep enough to be severe. He pulled some bandages out of his bag and dressed the wound, making a note to add antibiotics to his shopping list. Exiting the woods, he passed his nearest neighbor's house, a place choked with overgrowth.

Nick Johnson lived in the collapsing home on his own, a lonely widower for as long as Thos had hair. He felt sorry for the man, decaying at a rate nearly as fast as his home. The old man sat on his porch in his bathrobe and gave Thos a friendly wave. There were other threats, besides Aric. Occasional brigands liked to rob solitary travelers. Thos kept a gun handy should a dicey situation arise—namely, a heavy, magazine-fed .44 magnum his father called a "Desert Eagle." The gun had been custom-made for his grandfather, with a grip made specifically for him, yet had worked well enough for his son and grandson.

Making the journey from the Johnson house, Thos headed to the city of Greenfield. Another half hour saw him at his destination. The town had a surprising charm about it during the warmer months, counterbalanced by the company he had to deal with. Many of the houses and buildings were wooden and cheap thanks to the plethora of trees that covered most of the state. Some of the wealthier residences and more important facilities got constructed out of brick, metal, or stone, but the vast swath of the city was a wooden landscape.

The city stretched for six miles, forming five rings around the big hills that stood at the center. The largest and outermost ring made up the middle- and lower-class residential districts, along with a few bars, two large schools, even a brothel, or so he had heard. The commercial district lay beyond the outer layer, an entire district full to bursting with shops, vendors, a few restaurants, and his destination: the Ag Centre. Past the markets lay the more lavish side of town where the well-to-do lived. Past the nicest area of town, the government area could be found—where all the people that kept his empire rolling awaited his arrival.

A man dressed in black drove a truck past him, human forms beneath the red-stained cloth in the bed. The mortician touched the tip of his wide-brimmed hat. His sullen eyes told Thos that these were unfortunate victims of the prince's wrath. An old woman in a shroud mourned at the front gate, refusing to let the bodies go. A man placed his arm around her and escorted her from the dismal scene. Two soldiers wielding pistols watched the pair until they vanished from sight.

Thos made his way up the hill and past the tavern. Sitting on top of a horse for half a day had left him restless, so he decided to walk his horse the rest of the way. Thos did a little people-watching on his way to the Ag Centre—old men standing on the street corners discussing trivial matters, young men chasing after young women, children running and laughing.

A blinding light down a small alleyway caught his attention. The light hadn't come from the sun; it had reflected off the armor of more Blackthorne troops. He certainly didn't have a problem with the knights. However, most people seemed anxious when they saw the metal-clad warriors carrying guns and swords. He spied a few more people in the market district. None of them seemed to be doing anything but walking around, chatting up friends, and casting more than a few glances at the troops. Whispers of murder grazed his ears. Thos kept his head down and focused on the task at hand.

The Ag Centre took up and twenty percent of the market district. The name often led traveling merchants to assume the Centre was a gigantic building. Reality was quite different. It was a simple white office building no bigger than a school, right beside the livestock exchange pens. Here, Thos, the most prized calf, came to make lucrative deals to supply nobles, troops, grocers, the impoverished, and anyone else deemed necessary. Thos Averill was the main event in these parts. He puffed out his chest as he thought about it. *Good to be the belle of the ball,* he thought.

Near the entrance of the office building, a small group of people in suits prattled endlessly about projections, objectives, and humdrum business stuff he always ignored. They noticed him and waved him over.

"Your salvation has arrived!" Thos exclaimed. They weren't fans of his humor, which only encouraged him to use it more. Officials representing various businesses, including delegates from Kingsbury, chattered among themselves as he approached.

"Now we can get underway," one said.

"Yes, let's. I assume our deal is the same as usual?" said Thos. *I doubt they've even seen crops,* he thought.

During his brief greeting, a silver-haired woman in her sixties began rustling through papers on a clipboard. He recognized her as Elise Jenkins, Blackthorne liaison.

"Actually, we have a change in orders this time. Most of your goods are going north, forty percent increase in demand this year," she said. "Why?" he asked.

"I can't say, and please leave it at that," Elise insisted.

Thos dropped the subject. He looked around a bit, processing the coming arguments with investors and the smaller farms that made up Averill Estates. It had to be important if an official from Kingsbury was here, and even he knew better than to reject an offer from the capital. He hated the thought of his goods being used to supply a war against his own state. He held no love for the upstarts, but he sympathized with their plight. Poverty had risen steadily nearly all his life for many reasons, though at this point, most were just looking to cast blame on any with success. All across the nation tensions boiled, and it looked as if the kettle was about to blow.

"I suppose your contributions will more than make up for the business I lose. Send the squad on Monday and we'll hash out the details," Thos said.

"Good," Elise said with an impersonal smile. "Here's your pay. I'll send the men over at first light Monday. We appreciate your support."

With a handshake, the woman vanished into the bustling market crowd. Thos returned his attention to the members of the Heartland Farmer's Union.

"That has to be the record deal time. People from outside the Heartland actually have schedules," Thos joked.

He kept the rest of his jests internal to avoid upsetting the rest of his clients. Despite what others might think of him, he had some business sense and he knew how to play this game well.

"She hijacked our meeting, been sending everything up north. Everything," said Jacob Walker, owner of the local grocery chain, Down-Home Country Store.

"Explains the nerves," Thos said. Working with the Black-thornes may earn him a few dangerous enemies today. However, getting in good with the army provided serious advantages. Besides supplying the other regions, Thos also helped feed the city, as well as offering the chance to invest and expand to other farms. Every season, Thos kicked it off by providing a meal for the less fortunate in town. Out of the corner of his eye, he noticed soldiers carting away a man spewing insults directed at Prince Aric. As always, Thos stayed out of it.

Grabbing hold of the reins of his horse, he made his way to the Grand Royal Hotel. The hotel was complete with restaurants, a small theater, and a fighting pit. Every trip to Greenfield ended with Thos unwinding at the Grand Royal. His father and older brother always had a meal and watched the fights. It had brought him such joy as a kid, though now it was almost pure nostalgia with his family long gone. Hitching the horse, he noticed a packed house with the outdoor area filling up quick.

Thos worked his way to a small table near the fence that over-looked a large, square pit. There were tables surrounding the pit, but most spectators preferred to lean on the railing around the pit to catch every second of the action. Thos took a seat and placed an order with a passing waitress. The usual: seasoned bison steak smothered with onions, a loaded sweet potato, and a frosty mug of the Green Ale. A half-hour passed, Thos's stomach roared in disapproval at the lacking service.

Thos saw the announcer on the other side of the pit, and the other patrons began to crowd around the fence. A serving girl handed him his second mug of frothy beer. The mugs at the Grand Royal were glass and shaped as if chiseled out of a block of ice. It took mere seconds for him to finish his drink. Another half hour passed while Thos waited on his food. The announcer began to rally the crowd for the event.

"Did the good folks of Heartland come to see a big empty

pit? Or did you come to see the world's toughest cock!" he said. The audience began to respond with intoxicated burps, grunts, and yells.

"Lemme down there, I'll fight!" cried local butcher Robert "Bull" Diggler. The announcer held up his left hand to silence the crowd, and then pointed at the gates opening below. Robert was a hairy, barrel-shaped man that looked the part of escaped rodeo animal. The people began to boo the man as he showboated. Some of his more colorful gestures weren't exactly tailored for the children in the audience and even seemed like personal attacks on a few of spectators. He grinned with yellowed teeth at them. The gate on the other side opened slowly and dramatically. In came "Big Red" Ronald; a tidal wave of cheering washed over the audience.

The waitress arrived, and Thos noticed the shock on the faces of the kids who'd never seen Big Red before. The creature had reddish-purple skin, a long cylindrical body with no feathers, and two tiny undeveloped wings. Most people believed Ronald to be a mutant, while others called him a cockatrice.

The beast stood at nearly seven feet tall and bobbed his head back and forth when not lunging at the challenger. The fights were staged and non-lethal, but convincing enough that you couldn't tell most times. Somehow this beast became trained and knew exactly what it needed to do to earn delicious rewards.

The challenger made a feeble attempt at dodging, catching Ronald's face in his shoulder. His lightly armored tunic and some padding provided a comfortable, albeit humiliating, defeat. The man rag-dolled around the arena to the amusement of the onlookers. The gate opened, and some people came and dragged the unconscious gladiator away. Thos savored every bite of juicy meat as he watched the spectacle. The new challenger, a wiry-muscled man called Axel, charged headfirst into Ronald and collided with him. Thos watched while whiskey-laced barbecue sauce ran down his cheeks.

As always, Thos finished his steak before touching the rest of the meal. With fork in hand, he skewered his onion strips and put them into his hungry maw. A balding, gray-haired man approached him and took a seat at his table. Thos recognized the woolly-worm mustache a mile away. Thos debated ramming his knife through his own skull to avoid the pain of enduring Joseph Kerr.

Whenever Thos left the comfort of this spacious land, Joseph tracked him like a vengeful spirit. Thos distanced himself from the man when he could, however, Joseph's constant presence made it impossible. Thos knew he was already guilty by association to Joseph and would also gain the ire of his rebels should he flat out denounce him. The nearby men eyeballing him from other tables coerced him into talking. Joseph's recruiting strategy became increasingly aggressive. Thos always made it a point to be around others when he told Joseph he was happy to be involved in nothing but giving people their meat and potatoes. Thos had a gut-sinking dread he would have to pick a side, and unfortunately Joseph was the better option.

Worse yet, his financial costs were outweighing the benefits, with his goods no longer reaching the entirety of the country. With hungry competition eager to shut him out, he felt way too many people had him over a barrel. Even so, he was not ready to commit to Joseph's rebels. He braced for the eventuality that one side would force his hand. Thos answered the man's question before it was even spoken.

"No. Good day." Thos performed a backhand wave as if swatting a fly, but Joseph didn't leave. He ignored Joseph and watched the next fight, one that actually involved fighting. Joseph decided to get straight to the badgering.

"Well, a pleasant howdy to you, too," he said.

"Why don't we just skip to the end of this dance, shall we?" Thos said as he continued to watch the fight.

"We need you. The Blackthornes are after our heads now."

"Throats actually," Thos said with a mouthful of marshmallow and sweet potato. "I want no part of your so-called rebellion. I ain't trashing my future for you guys. I value it too much."

"Things may be great for you now. Unfortunately, your case is rather rare nowadays. I'd rather be home with my son, but men like us have to fight men like Aric." Thos rolled his eyes at the guilt-trip lecture Joseph liked to use. He ran his finger over the top of his glass, frowning when it didn't make a noise. "Y'all think that starting bloody conflict will somehow fix it? I know selfish creeps run this place, but not every rich person is a villain. I'm not."

"You think we're stupid?" said the man, growing increasingly agitated. "This isn't some attempt to kill the rich and take all their money. We've simply had enough of leaders playing with our lives. Time power was back in the hands of the people."

"Yet, without them, there wouldn't be a country, so unless you have an idea for some damn good replacements, things won't change," Thos stated, matter-of-factly.

"Things don't get better on their own, people make that happen," said Kerr.

Thos didn't like the direction the conversation, so he decided to end it.

"I'm sorry, but the answer is still one big, fat, unambiguous *no*. Go home and spend some time with your son before you get us both shish kebab-ed," Thos said. Joseph sighed and stood up.

"Very well, but trust me when I say you will come around to our side." Joseph motioned at another man, who began to tail an older woman Thos recognized as Elise Jenkins. Joseph stood and walked away. Thos didn't know what they were planning; however, he paid it no mind given the military presence. There was a creeping fear that some rebels were extremists with their own aims for power, another reason not to join them. Joseph always seemed surprised when Thos turned him down. Things were changing, though. He was right. For the first time in his life, Thos seriously considered selling out the Averill Estates and leaving this powder keg before it was too late.

They want the soldiers to see me with him. It'll force me to join, he realized. Thos watched Joseph leave and meet up with another one of his colleagues who was emerging from an apartment at the end of the east alley. Thos assumed it was safer to go to him than talk here. He gave Thos one last look. The kind of look that told Thos he had overstayed his welcome.

DRAKE

DRAKE CLUTCHED THE gold insignia of the Knight-Ambassador as he thought back on the day, eight years ago, when he became a travelling peacekeeper for the king. Now, he used that power to undermine the king's own son.

"Congratulations, son," Anselm had said. Kneeling, Drake looked up at the king. Anselm wore a slate-gray suit and silver tie, looking almost metallic in the sunlight. Anselm opened a tiny box in his hand to remove a small golden-sword pin wrapped in thorny vines, gently pinning it to the right breast of newly appointed Knight-Ambassador. The king extended his hand, and Drake Hale did the same to the thunderous applause of officials, officers, and civilians gathered in the courtyard. Soldiers dressed in blue uniforms stood beside nobles in their finest formal attire. The crowd gathered around the pregnant queen and her youngest son. The white outfits of the royal family blinded the young knight. Other Knight-Ambassadors, clad in green, watched the knighting alongside Prince Aric, Knight-Lord Jerrick Hart, and his young boy Jaren. Shiny colors from the metal-plate armors created a shimmering rainbow under the merciless rays of the summer sun. The statue of Alexander cast a large shadow over the crowd. It served as an impromptu sun dial marking the time: an hour past noon. From this moment forward, Drake Hale would begin a new life.

Drake bowed his head and embraced the king. "I'm proud of you," Anselm said with a smile. Drake beamed with joy. Years of rigorous training had culminated in the moment he had doubted would ever come. Fitted with a sage-green gambeson, he squirmed under the thick coat in the blistering heat.

"T-Thank you, s-sir," Drake stuttered. He scratched his head, not yet used to the shaved sides and short slicked-back top of his new haircut.

King Anselm leaned in. "Breathe easy. You only have to wear it on today. You'll get a better one later," he whispered.

Drake spied his parents behind the royal family. He was genuinely surprised to see them in a mood other than sullen. He wiped away the tears welling up, assured his family finally saw his worth. A courier approached Anselm, forcing him away from the event. A path opened up in the middle of the crowd, allowing the new, shimmering silver Blackthorne car to drive up.

Aric moved up behind Drake and placed a hand on his armored shoulder. "Don't get too cocky now. The arrogant die first," he cautioned. He gave Drake a pat on the back.

"Yes, sir," Drake replied. Aric smirked.

"Only one other person younger than you has ever become an ambassador. Nothing to scoff at. You've earned this," Aric said.

At the age of twelve, Drake now held the title of Knight-Ambassador. In that role, he would soon be free to travel the country and solve problems however he saw fit, though for now had been personally chosen for Aric's elite squad. The daunting authority of the job finally dawned on him. "Come on," Aric said.

Aric led Drake over the royal car polished to a mirror sheen. Blackthornes replaced the royal car every two years or so. Drake secretly hoped the king might send this one his way when that happened. The retired cars were repurposed, spending their golden years as luxury community transportation vehicles. Drake and Aric looked back to see the king scowling at them.

"He still hasn't gotten over that wreck," Aric said. Soldiers opened the doors for them. "I'll drive," he told the soldiers, catching one mid-plop in the driver's seat.

Aric drove through the city streets and out to the country. Traffic from the nobles' vehicles clogged the major streets. Aric grimaced while navigating the traffic of Kingsbury's elite. Drake paid the other cars no mind, focusing his attention on the crowds of people resuming their daily lives. Despite its numerous shortcomings, Drake loved the city. He reminded Aric that only a few bad apples spoiled the bunch. He glanced over at the prince. He had noted that Aric's behavior had grown increasingly morose as of late.

"Can you feel it?" Aric asked.

Drake raised an eyebrow. "I don't... what?" he replied.

Drake did not like the darkening mood from his friend. "The people are turning against us. Economic depression now in full swing."

"We had a few mills close down and some layoffs at the refinery... I didn't think it was that bad," Drake said, surprised.

"It's getting there. Our money is practically worthless. We are taxing everything just to stay afloat. Damn bankers have squandered away our coffers, the trade agreements are breaking down, people aren't spending wisely, and a dozen other things on top of that. We are on the verge of a paradigm shift." Aric lost his train of thought and laughed. "Sorry, didn't mean to shit on your big day."

Outside the metropolis, Aric pressed the button on the side of his door, rolling down the windows. The soothing breeze made the summer heat slightly more bearable.

"Where're we going?" Drake asked. Over hills, Aric drove them to a remote outpost a dozen miles outside of the town, a small fortress covered in scaffolding. Cranes and trucks renovated the dilapidated parapets protecting the southeastern watchtower which served as a checkpoint for the important road into the capital. At the base of the crane, soldiers pointed guns at three men in jeans and cotton shirts. The men got down on their knees after a warning shot. Aric stopped the car and the soldiers saluted. He stepped out of the car and approached the figures. Drake went over to the prisoners while Aric gathered intel from the captain, then hastily broke off the conversation. The place smelled of wood and gas. The cranes and crew toiled on while the others focused their attention on the prisoners. The ebony cloaks revealed the soldiers to be Royal Agents, the secret police of New Prosperity.

"Plotting to kill my father. Almost got me back in Cypress, a mistake on my part," Aric said. He pulled out his standard-issue Derbin M10 pistol. Aric sauntered over to the prisoners, hiding his true emotions beneath a tough façade that would come to devour the once kind young man. He raised the pistol up to the first prisoner's head.

Drake saw the hesitation from the prince. Tears began to stream from the prisoner's eyes. A dark trail ran down his pants and onto the ground.

"Please, no. It wasn't me!" he pleaded. Aric's hand began to shake, clearly no executioner.

"Is this a good idea? Violence often only inspires more violence," Drake advised, surprised at himself for speaking up. He could see Aric considering his words.

"We need to put a stop to it now. What kind of ruler would I be if I don't respond? They need to know the price of treason." Aric showed visible signs of some great anxiety preparing for his first kill. The prince closed his eyes and took a deep breath.

"Maybe there is—" Three shots drowned out Drake's words. Aric's hand trembled. The figures slumped over, with their dead eyes now fixated on Drake. Aric started panting, his hands on his knees. The black-clad warriors maintained an icy calm behind him.

"Ship the bodies back to families. Let them know the truth and what will happen if they retaliate," Aric said. The agents nodded and carried out his orders. Aric walked over to Drake, visibly frazzled.

"Why did you bring me here?" Drake asked.

"To show you what our job really entails. I want you to be sure you're ready for it." Drake didn't respond. Aric stared down at the pistol a moment before finally placing it in his holster.

"Let's get back. Time to celebrate. This is your day, after all."

Drake returned his thoughts to the present. He chose each action with the utmost care—actions that now involved working against his former friend and CO to avert a rebellion that might bring the entire royal family down. He had followed the prince down to the city of Greenfield to broker peace between the locals and the government. During his time in the city, he'd seen the rising tension, but no violence. However, watching government representative Elise Jenkins powerwalking while periodically look-ing over her shoulder suggested it was about to become something much more serious.

Years had passed since Aric's warnings, and there had yet to be a full rebellion. Drake liked to think himself partly responsible for that. As the setting sun painted the city in blood-orange, he once again took up the cause of peacekeeper. As the economic situation worsened, crimes had increased through the country. Suspicious commoners were rounded up, while successful businessmen were harassed and even murdered. The declining state spiraled toward war, but Drake believed things could still turn around. He knew right away Elise was in trouble.

Elise spent much of her time traveling from city to city, handling business for the government, and she never exhibited paranoia before. Normally, no one would dare assault a government official, knowing full well of the capital punishment that ensued. He thought to call out to her at first, however decided against it. He kept pace, while trying to stay far enough away to catch whoever stalked her. Dipping through alleys, Elise tried to lose her potential foe, zigging and zagging so much Drake nearly lost sight of her.

Her pace quickened. She threw trash cans down to slow those that followed. Drake leapt over the obstacles. The piss smell of the alleyways overpowered his nostrils; it was always worst around sunset when the shops closed. Elise's dipping and dodging proved useless, given Drake knew her goal was ultimately the Grand Royal Hotel after she lost her stalker.

Eventually she arrived at the hotel and Drake watched as she contacted other soldiers, who immediately began patrolling the area. Drake arrived soon after Elise, stopping to make a note of the people in the area. He slipped on spilled beer decorating the gray stone floors just between the restaurant and the lobby, managing to catch his balance at the last minute. He saw Thos Averill, the most successful businessman in the state chatting with Joseph Kerr, an outspoken critic of the government, inciter of violence. Drake made a note to speak with these men after interrogating whoever hunted Elise, if she was truly in danger.

Elise dipped inside the elevator. The gates closed right before she saw Drake. Drake hurried up the stairs to the suite on the top floor, reserved for government officials. At the top, he peeked around the corner for any signs of danger, finding only the hypnotic pattern of the brown-and-yellow checkered carpets. Quickly and quietly, he moved down the hallway toward Room 10. He knocked and identified himself.

"Ms. Jenkins? It's Drake Hale. I need to speak with you," he said. Elise did not respond. He knocked again. He heard muffled cries inside. Drake rammed the door open with a couple of swift boot kicks.

In the darkened room, Elise lay on the floor, fingers wrapped around her opened throat. In an instant Drake realized another person lay in wait for him. Before he could react, the figure was on him, a black-clad intruder brandishing a still bloody dagger. The attacker was a beast of a man, with a barrel-chested physique more common in a bull than a man. Thick blue-black hair converged in a long, braided ponytail out of the back of his head. Drake didn't know or care who or what this was, more than likely a hired killer. Drake knew if he could subdue the killer, he would gladly sell out his employers to avoid any punishment himself. With a swift kick to the sternum, the attacker fell back. Again the attacker lunged at him, slashing at Drake's thinly armored legs.

"Should've stayed home, boy," the man said. Drake avoided his attacks with ease, wearing him down with quick volleys of punches. The man shrugged off the attacks with an arrogant bellow. Drake paid him no mind, giving a hard kick to the man's ankle. He reached for his sword, only to be pushed back by the man's tree-trunk arms. The man darted for the window. Drake grabbed a chair and threw it at the killer, who cursed loudly as he hit the ground. Drake ran up on him, however, the intruder jumped to his feet and turned around just in time to grab him. The man picked Drake up and slammed him down, breaking a table.

"Come on, little dragon, show me that killer instinct," he said. He apparently knew about Drake's bloody past. Unfortunately for him, though, not enough to keep his mouth shut. Drake kicked the man in the groin, repeatedly. The man staggered, giving Drake time to get to his feet.

"You might regret it," Drake growled. The dagger whizzed by his face. He focused his attacks on the killer's right arm, softening it up. Drake grabbed the attacker's arm and bent it back with all his strength. The armed cracked. The man howled in pain. He looked back toward the window.

"Oh, you want out, huh? I can help with that," Drake said. He tackled the man. With his good arm, the attacker pummeled Drake's back. Drake pushed on tackling the man straight through the window. He landed on top of the attacker, who crashed on the ground with the bone-shattering crunch. People below quickly scattered. Drake pushed himself off the large man, drew his sword, and pointed it at the man's throat.

"Talk," Drake said. The man breathed heavily.

"Fuck… you."

"Tell me what I want to know, and I will get you help," Drake said.

"All right, I'll tal—" Without warning the dart-like sound of a silenced shot put an end to the assassin. Drake switched to his pistol and aimed in the direction of the entry wound. Blackthorne troops and onlookers rushed onto the scene, allowing whoever fired the shot to get away unfettered. Drake pushed through the crowd to no avail.

He cursed under his breath. The soldiers approached him. Drake explained the situation. The soldiers proceeded to disperse the crowd. The locals looked at Drake with disgust. His mission to keep Prince Aric under control just became a race against the clock to prevent a war. Someone ordered a hit on a government official, right under the prince's nose. With the killer long gone, Drake followed up on circulating rumors of a man funding this planned rebellion: Thos Averill.

THOS

Thos watched while Ronald mowed over each opponent. He finished his fourth mug of ale and decided to cut himself off. He looked at his rust-bronze watch, convinced he should really be heading back home. While he waited for the tab, he scanned the outdoor eatery, thankfully finding no sign of Joseph Kerr or his cohorts.

He looked back down into the pit. The gangly monstrosity had begun a decent match and Thos felt compelled to stay a tad longer. Ronald bobbed his head side to side, then up and down. The purple-skinned, featherless, chicken-beast bore down on the trained professional engaged in the mock battle, carelessly slinging his plastic sword. The monster bird belted out a scratchy caw and flapped its undeveloped wings.

Thos plopped his feet up in the other chair and chose to enjoy the rest of the show. But soon, he felt the sensation of someone staring a hole in the back of his head. He turned around and prepared to chew out the recruiter, instead finding a woman that did not fit the rebel stereotype, attractive, around twenty years of age, with an athletic build and a fierceness more often found in soldiers. Her very demeanor gave him the impression of a "fish out of water." Her boiled leather and fabric ensemble seemed way too intricate and fashionable for simple country folk. Fine girl or no, he didn't like people watching him.

A loud crash from behind the hotel caught Thos's attention. When his gaze returned to the café's edge, the mystery girl had vanished. A sudden panic from over in the hotel took precedence. A soldier ran down the stairs.

"Murder!" cried the gasping man. He regained the calm soldier demeanor and gestured to some other nearby guards who circled the area. Thos stood and tried to make an exit.

"Nobody leave," the guard said with a failed attempt at authority. Thos didn't need to hear his botched dialogue to tell he was greener than moldy bread. The poor lad was obviously shaken up from seeing death.

"Aw, balls," Thos said.

He sat back down, keeping his feet away from the sticky beer-soaked floor. The matches ended, but they gave Ronald free reign down there for the time being. Thos looked down at the beast. "Now I know how you feel," he said. He leaned forward, resting his head in his hands while waiting for the interrogations to commence. He tried to lose himself in pleasant memories, but the stirring masses kept dragging him back. He looked up, and the stars were now out. He kept reminding himself that he should be home with Cass.

The Knight-Ambassador looked barely over eighteen and still needed to fill out the Blackthorne gear he sported. The man carried an impressive sword engraved with the Blackthorne insignia and polished to a mirror sheen. Knight-Ambassadors getting involved heralded that things were about to get interesting.

"Ladies and gentlemen, my name is Drake Hale. I apologize for this, I do. The officers will get the necessary contact information. Do not leave the premises. It'll only make things worse for all of us, me included. I promise you will get through this as soon as possible; justice will prevail," he said. He heard some murmurs casting doubt on just that.

The young swordsman spoke, keeping a calm demeanor, even surrounded by locals who clearly did not want any more soldiers here. The young officer walked toward Thos.

"For fuck's sake," Thos muttered.

"Good evening. Mr. Averill?" Drake said politely.

"For now. Maybe someday I'll finally be a missus," Thos joked. The man gave a slight annoyed chuckle.

"I see, you're just how they mentioned. Mind if I sit?" After Thos nodded, Drake took a seat. "I just want to ask you a few questions and I'll be on my way."

"Well, at least you're more genteel than my usuals," Thos said.

"I'm not one of the usuals," Drake replied.

It always bothered Thos that outsiders thought of Heartlanders as dumb hicks, now glad at least one bucked that trend.

Drake continued, "I've spent a few weeks in Greenfield, and the moment you stroll in, everything goes to hell. Sounds like you and me have that in common."

"Our burden to bear," Thos said, wiping his mouth. "Look, I know it means little, but I promise you I had nothing to do with this, and I just don't have the figure for being strung up."

Drake didn't laugh this time.

"I'm not accusing you of anything. We've been studying the residents for a long time, and you just chatted up one of our suspects. You're the, how to put it… the booby prize of Heartland."

"Wrong usage I think 'cuz everyone wants a squeeze," Thos grumbled.

"That may be true," Drake conceded. "I hope it is, but right now you're a person of interest. Protocol is to have you brought to Aric, and neither of us wants that. You could save us both the trip if you'd just identify the conspirators."

"Like I said, I'm not a part of it and I really want to keep it that way," Thos countered. "Please tell me," Drake said.

"I'd like to believe you, but it's really hard to. If… and most likely, when, I get shipped off to the fort, I'll be just another dead man," Thos said darkly. He re-evaluated his options, tiptoeing dangerously close to treason. Out of the corner of his eye, he saw twelve men stand up and confront the soldiers. Even with the weapons, the five of them were outmatched. The man turned, clearly in disbelief that the locals were standing up to the knights. Thos panicked. He still had the bottle he paid for on his table, his whole body now in fight-or-flight mode. He decided on a little of both.

"Sorry," Thos said. As the young knight spun around, Thos grabbed the bottle and slammed it into the knight's head. The bottle did not shatter.

"Ow!" Drake said. Thos looked at the bottle, bewildered and disappointed.

"It was supposed to break…"

"Ah," Drake responded, right before planting his fist into Thos's jaw.

He turned back toward Drake and raised his arm, preparing to return in kind. The knight anticipated this and covered his face, a little too early, receiving a fist in the gut for his miscalculation. Drake barreled into Thos, while Thos pounded on his back. The two collided with the pit fence. Neither expected it to give way. But it did. The two men tumbled down into the pit below. They both slowly rose to their feet only to realize Ronald was still in the pit. The monster bird had been trained to fight anyone who stepped into the ring. Even though it wasn't to the death, fighters ended up seriously wounded. Ronald cocked his head and charged at them. *Payback for all them chicken dinners*, Thos thought.

Before they could react, Ronald crashed into them, knocking the two into the hard dirt wall. Instinctively, the men rose, and Ronald cocked his head. The young knight pulled out his sword.

"Don't. He's pretty much the most important townsperson," Thos said.

"Have another plan?" Drake asked irritably.

"Throw the fight."

They could hear the commotion back up on the ground floor. The soldiers might be outnumbered now, but there were more in the city and the number would double by tomorrow night. Thos needed to get home as soon as possible. Right now, however, Thos and Drake faced a more pressing matter.

"He won't bother us if we keep our backs turned to him. Well… usually," Thos said.

"Usually?"

"Let's find out?" Thos gave Drake a hearty slap on the back.

The two inched toward the contender gate, keeping their backs turned to the freaky giant. The simple fact the two weren't getting viciously pecked proved the plan's success.

Thos squatted down and began to push up on the gate. The gate budged only slightly. Drake looked over at Thos and matched his stance. From behind, Drake could hear Ronald crowing. Pushing the iron gate caused their arms to burn. The gate began to rise, and they could feel Ronald edging closer. The gate rose to shoulder height.

Thos felt Ronald's gnarly breath rolling off the back of his neck. The gate rose over their heads now. They turned to each other again and gave a nod. Together they let go of the gate and slid under. They turned around to see Ronald indifferent to their endeavors. Thos felt relieved that the little stunt didn't get Greenfield's main attraction permanently retired.

"You didn't have to attack me," Drake said like a hurt child.

"Authority figures generally don't treat us well, and your pal Aric has a worse rep than most."

"He isn't my pal," Drake snapped.

"Whatever we do seems to incur wrath, even an ill-timed fart. You know what fate the prince has in store for me whether I'm guilty or not," Thos said. They walked through the dark tunnel and up the stairs back to ground floor. No one remained.

"You will be dragged off to Alexander," Drake said with certainty, a tone that seemed to confirm Thos's fears. Thos felt dread now, he had to get back home.

"Please, Drake, you have to let me go. I want nothing to do with Joseph Kerr. I'm just another guy caught in the shitstorm," Thos pleaded.

Drake cursed under his breath. "Very well. I do know where you live. I will show up and question you, if necessary. Just don't flee the state," Drake instructed.

"Thank you."

Thos felt like a simpleton asking permission from a guy over a decade younger to go back to his own house. He ran to his horse, unhitched it, and sped home.

DRAKE

Drake understood knight protocol. However, that did not always mean he agreed with it. The rioters had been carted off to the local jail for the time being. The jail lay on the southern edge of town, a miniscule, ramshackle brick building that looked more like a park bathroom. He made haste toward the prisons before the suspects met a sticky end up at the fort. Drake saw people gathering everywhere and already knew the main topic of discussion. He had studied the city well during his tenure here, learning its nooks and crannies, in case things turned dicey. He used them to avoid Aric's soldiers patrolling the streets.

When he reached the jail, he saw a lone electric light from within the window and five men through the bars. It took nearly an entire day for Drake to gain access to the prison. He shooed away Blackthorne troops and local law enforcement alike. That evening, he opened the door to a more receptive lawman, shuffling through a stack of papers. The man began to speak without looking up.

"Visiting hours are five to six." The man looked up and noted his error.

"Ambassador Hale! I thought you were—"

"A kid? Yeah, I get that," Drake said with a groan. The jailer waved him on back, reaching down into his left pocket and removing his key ring. He opened the door to the cells. The jailer returned to his paperwork while Drake walked to the first cell. Four of the men sat on the cot, but the other paced around nervously. The frightened man looked on the verge of shitting himself.

"I have some questions about the riot, and the murder," Drake said politely, yet stern. The man seemed a little old to be this terrified of a rinky-dink jail.

"I didn't hurt anyone," he whimpered.

"Tell me what happened," Drake ordered. One of the seated men responded. Drake hated the lack of etiquette.

"He's got nothin' to say, dog."

Drake admired stubbornness up to a point. He really got tired of the tyranny shtick. Too many people believed Blackthorne troops to be mindless killers for the government, and unfortunately Aric's men reinforced the notion. According to some locals, Anselm was a baby-eating lunatic and the Board members were malevolent squid from another dimension. Drake usually found the loudest voice often knew the least. He kept his attention on the scared man, who was now pacing.

"Why did you guys confront the soldiers?" Drake asked.

"They were going to arrest us. It was fight or die."

"Shut the hell up, Randall," said another cohort.

"We didn't kill that woman," Randall said.

"Shut. The fuck. Up!" the ringleader said, striking Randall.

"Touch him again, and you hang. Please, Randall, tell me," Drake asked. Randall burst into tears. This other man, who had so desired to interrupt, must be the instigator. Drake felt like giving the man a good thrashing, but the man surely wanted to provoke Drake to violence.

"Tell me or you'll have to tell Aric. Trust me when I say such a fate is bad for everyone," Drake warned. With a sigh of defeat, Randall divulged the information. Randall sniffled, wiping a glob of snot dangling from his nose.

"Edwin Whitehall and Joseph Kerr," he said.

Drake suspected the local power brokers were fanning the flames of war, especially a member of the Whitehall family.

"They still in town?" he asked.

"Edwin is. First house on Frankfort Street, on the left," Randall said.

"Thank you," Drake said. Drake looked at the jailer and the other members.

"Release this man and give him protection. If he is harmed I will hold you responsible," Drake threatened.

Without another word, Drake walked out of the building and headed for the Whitehall House—the air now chill and damp, the remnants of winter still clinging to land. Frankfort Street lay about a mile east, the edge of the nicest part of town. He followed the electric streetlamps toward his destination. Fog began to roll in, and he used the streetlights to navigate the obstructive muck. He could hear the indistinct sounds of the human chatter inside the fog.

Drake reduced his pace. He could see precious little in front of him. He heard the chatter all around. In his travels, he always found the impoverished areas of cities smelled of soggy garbage, and this place was no exception. As he walked, the sounds of the people became less audible. Drake kept his right hand on his holster, just in case.

He saw lamps in the distance, the fog a little less thick. The lights ahead signified the beginning of the nicer part of town. He kept walking and saw a rather large three-story home belonging to Edwin Whitehall. It wasn't surprising that the riot engineer who championed the poor wasn't one of those same poor. An armchair general—the thought of men like him made Drake sick. Most successful businessmen and women he knew were decent people.

He stood in front of the three-story house that towered over its neighbors. Before Drake stepped onto the property, the front door swung open and out came armed guards dragging a man. The man was rotund and wore a cranberry-colored velvet shirt with white trim and matching velvet pants. His clothing gave him the appearance of a walking cake, the smattering of white hair the icing. This man bore a striking resemblance to Thaddeus Whitehall.

ARIC

In his room at Fort Alexander, Aric Blackthorne stared out the small window overlooking the mist-kissed Appalachian mountain-side. He grumbled at the constant gray and damp of early spring. It reflected his glum disposition. The days crawled by, leaving Aric to find reprieve in the soothing grace of local spirits.

His mission down here was to quell unrest by simple intimidation, an Aric staple. Greenfield had become a hotbed of upheaval in the past years, culminating in its use as a potential staging area for nation-wide revolution. National discontent, political spats with the elite families, and an economic collapse found Aric drinking for avoidance when not out of boredom. He dreaded inheriting the throne. In the end, whatever happened, the Blackthorne family would take the brunt of the blame, he more than the rest.

The liquor warmed his belly and lifted his mood. Turning away from the window, he walked over to his sword lying on the bed. He picked it up and admired its craftsmanship, the icy blade unpleasant to the touch. Engraved at the hilt end of the steel sword, thorny vines wrapped around the blade, stemming from a brilliant crown at the base. The sword had two brothers, one for each of Anselm's sons, forged for each upon birth. Aric remembered his thirteenth birthday, his dad towering over him with this most precious gift. A fine gift, albeit purely ceremonial. With each gulp of liquor, fond memories turned as bitter as the drink. In Aric's mind, he was nothing but a disappointment to his father.

Aric's doubts slithered their way to his core. Aric fumbled his days on the throne during his parents' absence. However he handled things, something in him always said not good enough. Words of praise rung hollow. His mood darkened over the years, happy and carefree until the burdens of being a prince and king strangled all semblance of joy from him. Such negativity always sprouted up after encounters with Drake. Aric cursed Drake's name aloud. He heard the precise thump of soldier's footsteps outside his door.

"Sir, the men are ready," said a voice.

"I'll be down momentarily," Aric replied.

Walking over to the table, he picked up a half-empty whiskey bottle and drained the last vestiges of liquid. The stores of alcohol never got much use, and anyone other than Aric who drank on the job faced harsh punishment. He sheathed his sword and looked around the large empty room. He had left the room barren, never bothering to add his own personality to it. The spartan existence it represented matched him perfectly.

He opened the door and walked down the stairs to the war room, fighting the itchy sensation from drinking in so many layers of clothing and armor. The room stood empty save for the large table and an old map of Heartland upon it. A crude drawing of Drake Hale with a limp penis sticking out of his head added life to the corner of the map, Aric's own personal touch. Everyone waited for him in the courtyard.

Aric walked outside, instantly hit by the frosty mountain air. Within the walls of the fort were three large buildings: the main building with the officer's quarters, war room in the north, and barracks on the east and west side. The western barracks connected to the mess hall with the entrance just opposite the barracks. The empty southern area of Fort Alexander served as an area for drills and training. The silent army awaited him as he walked past the barracks. Blackthorne Knights were the cream of the crop. They rivaled any fighting force that had come before.

"Knights," Aric said. In unison, they saluted him. "I am proud to call you my brothers- and sisters-in-arms. You are a well-oiled machine. Shame we can't pay you your worth. We'd have no money. But I guess we already don't because our wise Board of Directors needed so much for their golden latrines and young whores." The soldiers laughed.

"Soon, your targets will not be dummies, well, dummies of a different kind, I suppose," Aric said with a smirk. With a nod, Knight-Commander Williamson began the daily drills. Aric desired to find some more delicious comfort, but more shouting quickly altered his plans. He ground his teeth to soothe his mounting anger and bit his lip to prevent an outburst.

"Sir!" the scout shouted.

"What is it, soldier?"

"Mrs. Jenkins, she's dead!" The news brought the fort to a halt. Aric's blood boiled at the thought of the death of a family friend. He needed something to hit. The courier stepped back, knowing that, too.

"How?"

"Murdered in her room. Throat cut," the man said still half-panicked. Two other soldiers hauled a cart carrying a lump of meat under a tarp.

"I told her to carry a gun. She used to bring me little chocolates when she'd visit father. She was one of the nicest people in the world. Tell me everything," Aric growled. He held up the tough façade as he had been taught, despite losing the closest thing to a grandmother he could remember. The soldiers brought the cart over to him and threw off the tarp. The corpse of Elise Jenkins lay before him. Deep cuts marked up her body, forming a pattern. He read the words aloud.

"No kings." The belly button served as the "o," somehow insulting Aric even further. Everyone understood the value of having the Averill Estates in his or her corner. However, Aric wondered if Thos Averill was truly so bold.

"Last night, she approached me outside the hotel, deathly afraid someone was after her. I told her not to worry and that I'd check in on her later," the scout said,

"But you didn't." Aric's eyes blazed like a cat sizing up prey.

"No," the man said, shame-faced. "Everything happened so fast. It's my fault she's dead." The man recoiled like a whimpered dog when Aric moved closer.

"What's your name?" Aric asked.

"Luke Dame, sir."

"It wasn't your fault," Aric said, putting his hand on the boy's shoulder. Aric's hand slowly crept toward the knife in his belt. Suddenly the hand came up, giving the terrified courier a pat. "They finally grew some stones." The soldier raised an eyebrow, seeing Aric apparently overjoyed by the news. "I don't suppose you noticed anything out of the ordinary?"

"I did see that Averill fellow talking to Mrs. Jenkins earlier, with a few other guys. One looked like Joe Kerr. I reported it to Knight-Ambassador Hale. He found her body and took down the killer. Someone shot him before he could talk." Aric grimaced at the mere mention of Drake Hale.

In his mind, the pieces added up. The rebels had managed to recruit Cynric's grandson. Whether he was coerced or not, if he was working with them, he was just as guilty in Aric's eyes. Attacking an official from the Department of Infrastructure was a slap in the face to the king. Aric would not stand for it. He knew the importance of the Averills and scowled. The Averill Estates provided supplies throughout Heartland and King's Crown, with a few more alliances and farms it could become the largest in the nation. Guilty or not, the man in question held the answers he sought.

"Return to your duties," Aric said. The soldier nodded and leapt out of Aric's sight. Aric knew the time had finally come. If they were brazen enough to go after Elise, they might target more important figures, perhaps even the royal family. If he could get the proof, father would let him crush these traitors. He cracked his knuckles, which boomed in the silence, relishing a chance to end the stalemate. *Time for a heart-to-heart with Mr. Averill*, Aric thought.

Aric felt the alcoholic temptation stirring within, but he denied it as best he could. He had an hour before the troops returned. Presently, he couldn't let himself get lost in the bottle. Instead, he paced around the yard, plotting his next move. He ignored his cracked, desert throat and formulated a plan. Anxiety reverberated through his bones. He steeled himself. Each unbearably eternal minute melted into another, and, at last, the sounds of the military machine signified the end of the agony.

As the gate opened, the sight of their dour leader filled all with dread. Aric held up his hand, signaling the patrol to leave the gate open. He focused his gaze on the soldiers.

"Brave and honorable defenders, the moment we have all feared is upon us. We are finally going to war. Elise Jenkins was murdered last night, in retaliation for the Andersons. The Andersons were working as middlemen for arms dealing throughout the south. We have yet to find all the families involved, but I've heard the names Kerr and Averill thrown around too long to ignore. We are unsure how many people are involved in this, so be wary of all locals. I'm sending the Knight-Investigators to Greenfield. These people are targeting my friends and family, that will not stand."

"Interrogate the locals. If Thos will not help us, then apprehend him and bring him here, either as a guest or prisoner. We have no time for diplomacy. If he sees you, he may flee, so be discreet. If he does discover our intent, head to the Averill Estates. He'll probably try to lose you in the woods on the other side of town.

Bring him back alive, or don't come back. If he causes trouble, lethal forced is authorized, but do not use it unless he leaves you no choice."

"Sir, are you sure? This is a violation of law… sir." A brave soldier brought up a question few dared ask. Slowly, Aric turned to face the objecting man.

"Our weapons are being stolen, our vehicles disappearing, and officials carved up. They're not playing by the rules, so neither will we. Putting an end to this is more important than what people think or some legal detail." He returned his attention to the investigators. Standing there, it brought him back to an image from that day eight years ago of an indecisive boy shaking wildly at the idea of performing his first execution. He never let his doubt show, just as his father taught him.

"Go with great pride and greater haste. By the way, if Knight-Ambassador Hale interferes, detain him. His interference will be tolerated no longer." Aric paused as if remembering another vital piece of information. "If there's trouble, conscript the nearby soldiers to aid you. It's time for the people to take sides."

The Knight-Investigators headed to the stable outside and mounted for the operation. Aric Blackthorne found that killing a certain few individuals to be the best way to make others fall in line.

"Maybe I'll get lucky and get rid of the golden boy, too." He smiled at the thought. "That I'll drink to."

CASS

"This is completely nuts, you know that?" Cass said, shooting Thos a sour look. Even after a chance to sleep on it, she couldn't help but run her hands over her face in an attempt to process all the information. Cassandra Lewis found Thos's tale rather hard to swallow, and most certainly not the way she had expected to start the day.

"You look haggard," she said.

"Frazzled, terrified, and fugitive are also good descriptors," Thos replied.

He had spun awfully bizarre tales in his life; however, taking on Ronald seemed a bit much. Thos ended up in delicate situations every so often, but he always tried to do what he thought best.

"I know," he said as if reading her thoughts.

"But—"

"I've been dragged into this war, and I intend to fight if I must. In the prince's eyes, I am already guilty. For all I know that asshole Joe framed me, but now he may be the only ally I got. I may not love farm life, but this is ours. I'll be damned if they're gonna tear it down."

Thos had slept about half the day, not out of the norm for him. The workers outside toiled diligently, oblivious to the unsettling developments. Cass tried to chalk this up as one elaborate dream, but no matter what she told herself, she knew the truth.

"So—" she began, still trying to accept it.

"We need to be ready tonight," Thos interrupted.

"If it comes to that. Just remember not to shoot unless absolutely necessary," she said. She scowled at the notion of war on their doorstep. "I'll gather everyone. We'll have a meeting out front. I hope you have plan."

Thos glanced anxiously out the kitchen window.

Thos and Cassandra snacked on over-sugared butter tarts and dark coffee, which gave them a temporary jolt of nervous energy. The two sat quietly at the dinner table. Cassandra never felt comfortable in a dining room big enough to seat the crew of a battleship. They continued to sit quietly, sipping on their respective drinks, not really knowing what to say. Cass looked at him and gave a slight smile; he didn't return it. Cassandra's mind raced with thoughts. Her body yearned for a cigarette. She started to believe selling off the farm wasn't such a bad idea after all. *Hindsight is always twenty-twenty*, she thought.

Cass fumbled around the kitchen for the smooth relief of tobacco, nearly putting her fist through a cabinet when no cigarettes turned up. As she began to leave the kitchen, Thos's mind jolted back to life.

"Don't forget to keep that gun of yours handy. Can you still shoot?" he asked.

"I can hit things," she said.

"Sounds like a yes," he replied. "We'll have to put guards across all our lands, but they'll likely come straight for me and bypass the other houses unless we attack first. If you see any of them government boys make a move, don't you hesitate to shoot, you hear?" he encouraged her.

Cass frowned. She wasn't sure she was capable of killing fellow humans.

"My little Casserole," Thos said. She smiled at his words in a way the emphasized her annoyance.

"I hate that name," she replied.

"I know," Thos said with a grin. Cass leaned in, kissing him one last time. She knew he found it funny, seeing her irritated. Thos sat quietly at the table, running his fingers through his pincushion whiskers, a clear sign of his taut nerves.

The lack of nicotine forced Cass up and out of the house. On her way out, she looked over toward the woods and thought of the numerous animals scurrying about after dark. She dipped back into the house, snatching up the lantern sitting on the small table near the door. In her mind, an internal explosion accompanied a eureka moment, something that devolved into an "oh, shit" moment the further away from the Estates she got.

The deathly chill of last night had lifted, yet the pleasant spring weather had not yet arrived. She passed by the horse, before opting to go on foot. She glanced back at Thos, seeing him playing with a cookie through the window. She curled up her lips and sucked in breath for a whistle, though only managed to spray spittle across the ground. Thos caught wind of her and hurried after her when he saw her unwavering determination. She went over the hazel barn with the door not in the center and came back out with one of the bulls.

"What are you doing, sweetums?" Thos asked.

"Something ingenious or moronic. Haven't decided yet. Go rally the troops," Cass replied. Thos nodded and sped off. The bull stared at the woods, completely apathetic to all around him. "Sorry, big guy." Cass turned on the electric lantern, tied it around the bull's neck, and gave him a hard pat on the ass. The animal ran deeper into the forest. "Give these fellas a proper Heartland howdy."

Fighting off the constant yawns, Cass returned to full consciousness on her way back home. Approaching the hill, she saw the familiar sight of Thos preparing to rally his men. Her loud yawning easily announced her presence to everyone around. During the speech, she bummed a few cigarettes off workers and found her rapid-fire mind slowing down from the tobacco goodness.

The two walked silently up the hill; he never liked being the center of attention, while she didn't mind so much. Thos continued the casual stroll up the hill, doing his best to ignore the glances. Cassandra wondered exactly what their chances were.

Thos turned toward a crowd of frowns and scowls. She knew Thos had been raised well and had learned much from overpriced tutors and his grandfather's extensive library. He stood above the crowd while formulating his thoughts in awkward silence, sucking in his gut for a more commanding presence. He cleared his throat.

"Uh, hello there, my fellow… crop… people," he said. "I know all of you are amused while I fumble as a wordsmith, but there is a rather dire situation heading our way." He paused to clear his throat again. "I have been… implicated in the local uprising against the Blackthornes and—"

Cass gave Thos a comforting pat on the back. "They are coming to interrogate me for the murder of a government official. Something I didn't do, but we are all guilty to the prince. I'm not gonna lie to you. Things may get ugly. Hopefully, they won't, but we need to be ready." The crowd buzzed with disquiet. Cass saw the other families quite upset and the workers afraid, their fear justified. Cass's eyes grew wide when the gravity of the situation finally dawned on her. There was no way they were walking away without a fight, and when she looked into Thos's eyes she knew he agreed. Her hand on him gave him that boost he needed.

"This… is our land. We work it, we bleed for it, and, if need be, we will fight for it. They could arrive around dusk. When this is over, I will have a nice little chat with Joe Kerr," he said, with an expression that showed as much dread of that as dealing with his own assassination. Thos turned to Cass. "And what about you?"

"I'm not going to spend what is likely to be a very short life running. Remember, it's you and me 'til the end," Cass said. Thos nodded. She saw him swell with pride at the thought of her fighting by his side.

"So what happens afterward?" Cass asked.

"If things really do get bad, we'll have Joe station men here. If we have to join his cause, he'll have to protect this place in return. I'll also call in some favors with the mayor as well. From there… well, we'll burn that bridge when we get there." She leaned him and planted a kiss on his flabbergasted lips.

"I'll help get everyone armed. Get the crack shots up in the house for sniping." Her fingers formed to hold a cigarette, disappointed she had exhausted her supply. Anxiety hammered away at her insides. Her bile-ridden stomach felt like the heart of a volcano. Thos turned to face the crowd once more. The workers approached him.

While Thos talked to them, Cass thought about the secrets between them. During his trip to Greenfield, she had stumbled across the bankruptcy letters he took great pains to conceal. She was no fool. She listened in on his phone calls the moment he thought she had left. Cass had a head for numbers, so she noticed the steady decline in business he hadn't the heart to tell her about. She had seen agents of the Rancher's Association skulking around their place with lustful eyes undressing it like a bride on her wedding night.

"I've done a little bit of reading on Blackthorne special operations. They'll send a platoon down here. We don't have a lot of guns. We do have swords. Do the other families have any arms? Anything you can kill with, use it." All at once, the crowd began a mass clockwise rotation to other owners all stationed behind the horde. Cass found their silence disturbing and grumbled at their inaction.

James Cranton, the Estates butcher, argued with the other five members of his family. Two nearby families quietly conversed with each other. Everyone else gathered at the event turned their collective gazes toward the silent debaters. The workers listed the number of knives, pitchforks, pans, pipes, boards, and the occasional firearm, ready to repel the invaders.

"They don't know how many of us there are. Hell, *I* don't even know how many of us there are, so that gives us an advantage. Guerrilla tactics will be our best defense," Thos said.

"How will acting like monkeys help us?" one man asked.

"Fight sneaky," Cass explained. Thos offered an irritated smile.

"They also keep the gun use to a minimum on these little covert missions, so the other locals don't join in," Thos assured. Cass procured a few rifles just in case, thanks to the Averills' influence. She realized that a few ranchers and farmhands could do little in a straight-up fight against trained soldiers; her backup plan, however, would even the odds.

"There's a little surprise waiting for them in the woods," she said. The collective mob looked over toward the direction of woods, where more than a few old-world creatures held sway. A few in the crowd nodded their heads, knowing what she planned.

"With some luck they won't even make it here. Some of you get up in the trees and pick them off."

The planning over, tonight the people of Averill Estates would face an interrogation at best, and death at worst. Thos addressed the crowd again.

"They're probably horsing their way down here soon," he began. "Take the day off. Kiss, hug, sex, do what you need to do cause, if we fail, we'll get crucified… maybe literally. I'm counting on all of you to make sure that doesn't happen," Thos said.

With a friendly nod, he and Cass walked back home. As Cass passed the entryway she hoped the old things and the poor bull in the woods did the job.

"This is the dumbest thing we've ever done," she muttered.

ANSELM

For many people, morning brings a feeling of refreshment and renewal; those people were not kings. Anselm lay in bed, staring at the ceiling, listless and slick with night sweat. He looked over and saw Abigail still peacefully resting beside him. She always told him how handsome he looked, but time and ruling had done him no favors. At fifty-two years of age, his brown hair had all turned a dull gray.

His day would begin like any other: meetings upon meetings, with some occasional meetings thrown in to break up the monotony. First a meeting with the Board, followed by a meeting with scholars from the Institution of Moral and Intellectual Affairs, followed by a meeting with Safety, Services, and Sanitation. Then he held court to address issues brought forth by the public. Finally, a meeting with the Office of Commerce, the proverbial cherry on top. He grumbled at the endless complaints chipping away his already weary soul.

His breakfast of runny quail eggs and toast roiled in his gut like a vomitous hurricane. The sunlight worming in felt harsh and unpleasant. Anselm returned to bed and sprawled across it, pulling Abigail's hair by accident. Time passed, and he valiantly tried to convince himself to face the day.

"I can't fathom how you can still be so kind and beautiful," he said softly to Abigail.

"I avoid politics when I can," she replied.

They shared a brief kiss, neither of them moving from the bed just yet. They stared into each other's eyes for the longest time, saying nothing. Anselm stoked her flowing ash-blond hair. He felt a tinge of nostalgia, wishing to be free of this cursed job. "Times like this I wish I had been the second son."

"You remember when we first met?" Abigail finally said. She liked to remind the king about his past to lighten his mood.

"How could I forget? Thirty-three years ago today if I'm not mistaken. Father intended for me to court the young Jenny Droullin, the harpy." Anselm gagged at the mere thought.

"She came down the stairs in a tannish velvet dress with white swirls. Mercy, the pattern almost made me collapse. When she finally reached the bottom step, she must've stepped on the back of the dress, because she lunged at me. I may have squealed, just a little bit."

Abigail laughed, and so did Anselm.

"I backed into those damn candles and, before I knew it, my pants went up. I ran screaming out of the house and into town. I threw the pants off and ran through the streets. Everyone just stared. Didn't expect a full moon that night. I ran to the fountain and dove in."

Abigail laughed, and Anselm's laughter faded at the idea that others still saw this image as their sovereign.

"My first encounter with the great king." She smiled.

"You got a few laughs in, more than the others now that I think about it. With a burned ass, sitting in the fountain in the middle of town. You asked me if I was okay, remember," Anselm said. His body grew restless, but he lay in bed, savoring the perfect moment.

"And you were, weren't you?"

"My memory is a bit fuzzy," he said.

"This'll help," said Abigail. The kissing became much more passionate than they had intended.

"You have work to do," she said, interrupting his advances.

"I can skip a few meetings," he said.

He threw the blanket from him and stood up. He put on some shorts and a button-up shirt, relishing a chance to enjoy the uncharacteristically warm early spring. With his wife and youngest son in tow, they spent the morning at the edge of Lake Thaxter, known as Lake Michigan during the time of the Great Empire. Unfortunately, a broken-down royal boat left them shore bound. As a consolation prize, he, Abigail, and Edgar spent the afternoon remembering just how subpar their fishing abilities were. Despite catching nothing and chilly gusts of wind rising, he relished his time away from the city.

Edgar doggedly pursued the fish long after his parents gave up. Abigail and Anselm held each other on the dock, sitting with closed eyes, listening to the gentle ebb and flow. Abigail gently ran her fingers through his graying beard. The air picked up, heaving like a lover in the throes of passion. Edgar yelled excitedly as he pulled in a small-mouth bass of no consequence to anyone else— however momentous a conquest for him. Edgar admired his catch for a moment before tossing it back in the water. Anselm never put much stock in simple moments like these in his youth. He regretted making so little time for Aric and Percival. He had vowed to not let it happen a third time. Anselm, Abigail, and Edgar lounged around for another hour before duty ripped the king away from what little still mattered to him.

After a blissful morning, Anselm braced himself for the mundane hell of the kingdom's bureaucracy. His first meeting always consisted of arguments that seldom accomplished anything. Anselm yawned ferociously. He felt assured that his work with the Board left him with enough experience to become an elementary school teacher when he officially stepped down.

As always, he'd wear a dark suit, dark vest, and a tie. He opened the house-sized closet and chose a custom-made black business suit, white undershirt, and a tan and navy striped tie. Slipping on his drakeskin shoes, he turned to Abigail, and with a bow, he entered the elevator. His good mood faded quickly. With a heavy sigh, he officially started his day.

After hours of contemplating throwing himself out a window, Anselm absconded back to the love and comfort of his family. The ping of the elevator heralded an unexpected stop. The elevator stopped too early, leaving him on the medical floor. He hit the button again, but it did not respond. The doors opened and a figure approached him, a young woman with a buzz cut, sporting the muted blue vest and pants of a scholar. Anselm rarely paid scholars any mind. However, one heading straight for him was hard to avoid. There were no other signs of life in the halls. As the woman moved closer, Anselm noticed markings across her face, what he believed to be scars. When she was upon him, he saw the markings were not of scars, but for surgery. Dotted lines ran down her forehead, past her nose, and down her left cheek. Red ooze trickled from the black pit where her left eye had once been. Anselm's face wrinkled in disgust.

"It's rude to stare," the woman said.

Anselm's posture remained corpse-stiff. "What's the meaning of this?" he asked. He made no movement against her. The woman immediately raised her hands in submission.

"I am here only as a messenger… for now, at least," she said.

"Then speak, while I'm still in a good mood," Anselm said.

"I've come to inform you that the masters wish to meet with you. They have taken a great interest in you."

Anselm guffawed.

"Masters? Of whom do you speak?" Anselm's tone grew strong and demanding.

"You will know soon enough," the woman said with a smile.

She pulled a green sphere dangling from a wire out of her pocket and placed it in her eye socket. Vile sounds of wires tearing through and bonding to flesh made Anselm take a step backward. The sphere burned bright, moving as naturally as her other eye.

The woman walked past the dumfounded king and entered the elevator.

"Important things will happen here. Soon Vigilant will arrive, and death will follow." Without warning, she doubled over in pain, clawing at her temples. She began to mumble as if talking to someone else. Anselm looked around bust saw no one.

"I've said too much. Perhaps you'll see me again if they demand it. Roof. Tomorrow. Midnight. Don't be late." The doors closed. He hit the button and the doors opened again. The figure was gone. Anselm cursed. He ran down the sterile white hallways of the medical wing, only to find workers and doctors all collapsed on the floors. He ran into the nearest room and placed his fingers on a man's neck, finding the faintest pulse of a still-living employee. Medical instruments and tools lay scattered among bits and pieces of gauze on the floor. Standing back up, he noticed a bloody scalpel and a sticky red orb attached to a severed cord lying on the table. He heard the stirring of the unconscious medical staff. Without a word, he hit the alarm. *Can't have a single day,* he thought.

With yet another group to battle and manipulate him, a second wall of stress slammed down on Anselm's chest. His body and mind couldn't handle any more of a life surrounded by schemers and fair-weather friends. Anselm's heart pounded to the point of bursting in his chest. Anselm stretched out his arm for the wall to support the weight of the nation strong enough to demolish the castle. Anselm hit floor.

Anselm despised his own mounting frailty, leaving him an anxiety-riddled shell of his former self. In the elevator, Anselm could be free to let the problems hit him. On the floor, he let out a series of deep breaths and after fifteen minutes got back up to his feet. The second elevator on the opposite side of the hall opening to a ding. Soldiers rushed to Anselm's side. Anselm adjusted his suit and filled them in on the psychopath rummaging through medical supplies. Anselm stepped inside the elevator and continued his journey to his private residence. The elevator moved again, this time opening to a wonderful sight. The visages of his wife and two youngest children filled the cold room with much needed warmth. Anselm waved his hands and assured his family the developing situation floors below would be handled. Only the start of the day, Anselm already need a reprieve.

"A joyous morning, indeed," Anselm said, distracted. Percival approached him first. He greeted Anselm with a handshake as strong as iron. Anselm saw the same political conditioning in Percival as he did in himself. Anselm found it a little cold and disheartening. Percival always kept things impersonal and professional. Being a future leader of a nation meant that every action he performed was raked over with a fine-tooth comb. As with Anselm, his private life would never truly be private.

Anselm's thoughts zipped back to the strange encounter. With hundreds scouring the castle, he tried to convince himself no one else might slip through the firm grasp of his military. The event left him rattled and checking the corners. With potential enemies nonchalantly waltzing through his home, he reflected on the fact he may need to take more drastic moves to root them out. He had options, dangerous and risky options but effective all the same. Like all leaders, Anselm followed the Compact to his best ability, but there were deadly temptations should he find more invaders skulking about. He realized that just one intruder could wipe out his family and the Blackthorne legacy itself.

Anselm shook off the mental fatigue for just a moment, knowing it wouldn't be long before the situation in the medical wing and dozen other things would pull him away again. Anselm moved alarmingly close to denial.

"I trust you're prepared for tonight's festivities?"

"I regret that I will not be in attendance tonight," Percival said.

"Anything serious?"

"No… festivals just aren't my thing." Percival was not as sly as he thought.

"Say no more. At least one person in this country should be able to have some secrecy. Just be careful, with people sneaking about we need to be aware at all times."

"Thank you, father." Percival nodded and hurried away.

Anselm saw Abigail straightening young Edgar's suit, Edgar hiding his embarrassment, though only his family and a handful of guards were present.

"Stop it, mom. I can do it," he said. They didn't mean to wound the boy's pride, but their laughter only furthered his emasculation.

"If you are a man, I'll let you handle these meetings, oh, king," Anselm joked. Edgar didn't laugh. Anselm turned his attention to Abigail. This morning had been the first time in months they had done anything passionate.

"Where'd all this energy come from, you old dog?"

"From you," he said.

"You know I'd love to, but we're not yet ready for tonight. A little later, maybe." He tried to hide the disappointment, unintentionally shooting her the big-eyed, sad puppy look.

"For the best," Anselm said. He forced a smile. "If the radio towers are working, I'll contact Aric. See how mountain life is treating him." Abigail's face soured.

"Don't bother. I tried the phone last night. Still down," Abigail informed him. Anselm sighed.

"Always reliable," he said.

As they reentered the elevator, Anselm noticed that Edgar was paler and more cadaverous than usual. He said nothing to Abigail. However, it couldn't be ignored. He wasn't one to throw blame around, but he knew that most of the Board intended him to have a violent, early retirement. He wouldn't be surprised if they had a hand in Edgar's condition as well. And now, someone new had eyes on him. His chest tightened at the thought. The fear and stress crushed him inside, leaving him drastic steps to fight back. Thoughts of drastic action and death only worsened the burden threatening to crack his bones under the weight.

Perhaps I should've thrown myself out the window when I had the chance, he thought.

DRAKE

Soldiers dragged Edwin Whitehall down the street for delivery to the prince, shredding his expensive silks. From a distance, the rotund Edwin looked on the verge of flooding the street with tears.

"Wait!" Drake hollered. The captain of the men, a gruff man named Daniel Cooke, acknowledged Drake.

"What's your business with us?" Daniel asked with an annoyed sigh.

"Why is Edwin in custody?" Drake asked.

"Treason. Some of the market folk worked for this little pig and sold him out for immunity. They told us about his smuggling operation," Daniel replied. Before Drake could speak, the frightened Edwin attempted to weasel his way out of trouble.

"We're just doing what Thos told us to do," Edwin sobbed. The color of Edwin's face matched his garish outfit. Drake believed Edwin's fear, but not his words. That the Whitehalls were involved with the rebellion was speculation, however Drake saw through Edwin's blatant attempt to make Thos the scapegoat. Drake shook his head, drawing the attention of the captain. Edwin pointed at Drake.

"He helped him escape! He hates the prince more than anyone!" Edwin cried. Daniel's scowling face and order to his fellows made his dislike of Drake clear. With his peripherals, Drake spied soldiers with itchy trigger fingers just waiting for an excuse to take him out.

"Lies… poor ones at that," Drake said. *The hate part is true,* Drake thought.

"We'll know the truth soon enough," Daniel said.

"This escalation will lead to war," Drake said. The captain motioned, and his soldiers escorted Edwin and his henchmen away.

"Aric doesn't want you involved in this operation. Our orders to detain apply to you as well," Daniel said.

Drake wondered if these men would really kill him if he interfered or what might befall Thos. Drake refused to let an innocent man die and ignite a full-blown conflict. He decided to make his way to Thos, threats be damned.

"Very well. Carry on, gentlemen," Drake said with a slight nod.

He set out immediately. He glanced around before entering the alley behind one of the small clothing vendors. The locals shot him vicious glares, a few pursing lips to spit at his feet. Drake headed westward and out of the city, avoiding the troops in the area. Checking the rooftops, he made sure no riflemen were present.

The alleys proved worse than the slums: rancid meat, pet dander, and all the rotting wood a termite could eat. The knights wouldn't see him, though they might smell him after the shortcut. The orange light of dusk bathed the land in a tangerine sheen. Even the back alleys of Greenfield seemed more pleasant in this light. Drake reached the stables. He considered himself fortunate the local depot couldn't spare any vehicles for Aric's troops, giving him a chance to beat them to the Estates. Creeping around the side, he scanned one for time for prying eyes. Being a Knight-Ambassador allowed him a private stable for his steed, Aeneas. The golden brown Aeneas stood regal among the drab browns of the horses in the other stables. It took only seconds to get the horse prepared. Drake took off without delay.

Drake found it hard to believe that even someone as ruthless as Aric would attack a person as influential as Thos Averill. It was possible Aric's troops may be frenzied enough to disobey him to kill what they believed was a terrorist. On the other hand, Drake knew how vindictive the prince could be.

Early on in Drake's career, before he proved himself capable of being on his own, he served directly under Aric. Drake killed numerous people over the years, most of those from the last few years. Bandits, murderers, thieves, and some purely in self-defense when they saw the prince's attention as a death sentence; some of Drake's kills were no older than he was at the start of his career. Drake killed his first man at age twelve, an execution to test his resolve. A hundred kills later he doubted every mission had to end with a bullet. After leaving Aric's unit, courtesy of the king, Drake opted for a less violent life. Drake received heaps of praise for being a peacemaker and negotiator. Drake wanted to prevent war, but it became clear that it may no longer be possible. He feared there would soon be red on his hands again.

Drake looked around the entrance to the Old Man's Woods before thrusting himself into the endless mess of barren trees. The wine-colored blanket of dusk gave way to the greys and blacks of night. He followed the winding trail into the endless, dead wood. Inside, he saw a light source. His eyesight adjusted in time for a thunderous boom, indicating his time had run out. He maneuvered the horse to a more heavily concealed area a few dozen feet from the trail. A bull cried out and a loud thud followed. Thunderous hooves now intertwined with human voices. Drake twisted and turned through the trees until he was sure he'd concealed himself. Drake peered out over his tree stump hiding spot and watched the cavalcade of troops passing by. The sound of dozens of scurrying tiny legs came behind them.

Drake followed the soldiers. A small light ahead danced wildly as the masses passed over it, then came screaming. He drew closer, noticing the distinct lack of clanging swords. One of the approaching men drew his sword as Drake's horse came upon him.

"You were told to stay away! Leave now! Final warning!" the soldier warned. Other soldiers rallied back to attack. Drake did not move.

The man charged at Drake, but before he could blink the man lay on the ground dead with finger sized puncture marks in his left gauntlet. The hole went through the soldier's armor and into his flesh. The soldier's body swelled, becoming grotesquely deformed. Drake saw the culprit: an eight-legged horror with a brown fiddle design on its back.

"A fucking brown recluse!" cried one of the knights.

Before anyone could react, more spiders were upon the soldiers. Half the men were down in seconds. Drake unsheathed his sword with the intent of striking the monsters while they were occupied. Drake ran toward the closest beast and thrust his sword down into the spider's head, which split apart, covering the ground in sticky goo.

As the spider died, it let out an unholy squeak. The other spiders pulled themselves from the soldiers to defend against the intruders. Drake eyed three of them directly in front of him. They moved in on him. Two of the spiders jumped. Drake threw himself to ground. The bugs sailed right over Drake's head, but in doing he came face to face with the third monstrosity. The spider raised its mandibles and lunged forth. Drake swung the sword at the beast, taking off its two front legs. The monster screamed in agony. Drake rammed his blade between its fangs.

Behind Drake came the pitter-patter of more tiny legs. With his sword still in the monster, Drake picked up both blade and beast, flinging the corpse at the oncoming spiders. The body connected with one but leaped right back without hesitation. Drake raised his sword above his head. When the creature was within range, he thrust his sword downward, catching the monster in the abdomen. The action pinned the monster to the ground. Twisting the blade around, Drake severed its abdomen.

The sound of a fleeing horse got his attention. When Drake turned around, he saw Aeneas bolting down the trail, a spider latched on the horse's neck. The monster sunk its fangs in. The horse galloped a few feet before collapsing. Drake gave chase but the creature fled deeper in.

Drake looked around to make sure no other spiders lurked about. In the distance, he heard the scurrying die down. A soldier near him stared right through him at the woods beyond. Drake remained fixated on the man in front of him. His face scrunched up in confusion when the man did not move.

"They're just spiders," Drake pointed out.

The soldier fumbled out incoherent noises meant to be words. Before Drake could form another thought, a weeping sound emanated from behind him. At that moment, Drake understood what the man had wanted to say: demon. Drake spun around to attack. To his horror, a grey mass rustled through the thick spattering of downed branches off the main road. Drake's tough demeanor failed him as he gazed upon the ancient evil. The demon had thin skin wrapped over a mass of bones and meat and that resembled a flayed bear. It shambled toward him and watched him with bulbous black eyes. The face reminded him of a man's stretched out to horrific proportions, with gaping black maw in a permanent frown. The creature had two thick elephant-like legs and two small, malformed arms resembling a newborn's. This demon was known as a shrill.

Seeing a demon in the flesh, Drake found it madness such a thing existed. He had studied demons back in Kingsbury for just such an encounter. According to Vigilant's book *Legacy: Demons of the Ancient World*, shrills were drawn to the sadness of humans and driven to consume it. Shrills were the result of Old World humans using technology to air their personal grievances for the world to see.

The lethargic demon roared to life. Drake leaped out of the way leaving the other soldier in the demon's path. The demon's baby arms stretched out, quadrupling in length. The tentacle appendages grabbed a hold of the traumatized soldier. The weeping came from inside the monster's gut. A line formed in its stomach revealing rows upon rows of jagged teeth. Drake pulled his gun and wasted no time firing at the demon. The demon's rubbery arms gripped the solider and pulled him toward his doom. It bit down on the poor man, devouring him headfirst. The soldier's gurgling screams were drowned out by the sounds his collapsing skull. Drake unloaded a round of bullets, tearing through the demon's frail skin. The monster faced him, with the soldiers dangling legs being sucked into him now. Drake quickly reloaded his gun, grappling with paralyzing fear.

The gaping mouth of the demon bared red-stained teeth, still crunching human legs. Shaking off his fear, Drake unloaded more rounds on the demon. A bullet ruptured one of the demon's eyes, shooting its tarry blood across the ground. The injury halted the demon's attack only for a second. The demon grabbed hold of him at the waist. Drake reloaded again as fast as humanly possible. The demon's arm retracted faster. Drake fired until he had no bullets left. Switching to his sword he prepared for the ravenous jaws moving ever closer. Drake gripped his blade and thrust it forward just in time to run it through the demon's second mouth. He stabbed the demon until it let go. It stumbled and fell a few feet from him. Drake looked down at the demon's weeping humanoid face. He drew his blade and slashed at the neck, hacking away until the head separated. Taking no chances, Drake chopped until the body ceased moving.

The rush of adrenaline left Drake as quickly as it had risen. With its passing came the realization this there was still another situation brewing at the Averill Estates.

THOS

Thos paced anxiously in front of the worker families that made up his civilian army. At the moment less than one-third of his lands were active while the rest were fallow. The Averill Estates produced crops of all kinds year-round, with fields devoted to each season and type of livestock. Thos's father had always told him there was something special about the soil here, but that downplayed how hard his family worked to turn this place into the business it was today. The fall fields were the focus of protection and the lion's share of Thos's revenue. The surrounding worker houses created a ring around the Estates, with Thos's home taking the mantle of the castle. He divided the workers into teams in the fields outside, away from the homes but not far enough to lose sight of them.

Thos took a moment to look at his workers and friends that may not survive the night. He saw the Bakers, longest serving of the worker families. The silver-haired matriarch, Janet, and her burly sons had been the first to join Thos's fight. Janet was a close friend of his father's, and the way they both spoke about each other, he suspected something more. Her sons, John and Judah, were among his best workers. Despite being wheelchair-bound, old man Mike Wilkerson sat with a repeater in his lap while his daughter prepared to defend her children. The young couple, Jill and Evelyn Dobbs, stood with pistols at the ready while their son took his position as sniper. Bob Masterson chomped at the bit to slice up royals, while newlyweds Gabriela and Glen Warwick aided Thos for the sake of their newborn. Some of the other families, such as the Fishers, had required a monetary incentive to maintain their loyalty.

At that moment, the one thing Thos knew was that he had no inkling how events were about to play out. He breathed deep the cool evening air. Thos realized it wasn't such a bad thing to die defending one's homestead.

Above them, the sky shimmered with silvery stars. Thos looked down at the sword at his side and the gun in his hand. Swords were the still weapons of the common man and foot soldiers, thanks to the rigid laws of the Compact. Nobility and high-ranking officers also carried them for ceremony and the occasional duel. Firearms required strict licenses and absurdly high taxes. The fact that Thos and his workers had a few unlicensed guns only made him an even bigger criminal after tonight, and the possibility increased he'd vanish without a trace like others that broke such laws. Thos raised his sword skyward to rally his workers. He ignored the nervous chatter of the anxious farmhands.

Thos rallying was interrupted by screams from the woods. He positioned a few gunmen near the edge of the woods to pick off any soldiers that survived the spider trap Cass set for them.

Thos imagined killing enemies to be no different than putting down a wild animal, and this line of thinking made it easier as he prepared to engage the enemy. He heard cries from behind. The stench of flames grew strong, too strong for it to be just torches. Upon turning around, Thos saw the fields ablaze.

"They really did it! Behind us!" he cried. All the workers turned and saw the blaze slowly consuming his most valuable plot of land. Amid the flames, he saw soldiers in armor coated with browns, blacks, and greens. He spied twenty of them, and he knew a few dozen more likely hid in the grass. The enemy moved to the easternmost fields and houses, taking three houses down before Thos's forces noticed. The farmer army held the line, though a few broke off to defend their respective homes from the conflagration.

The western workers charged into the oncoming attackers and halted their advance. Thos and his troops wasted no time using their guns. A handful of soldiers died in the initial volley. Jack, hidden in the grass, dropped a few more men with headshots. The troops emerged from the woods, sprinting toward them with reckless abandon. Their erratic and vicious condition suggested they were driven half mad from Cass's devious trap.

A few lightly armored troops slipped past the eastern defense and engaged the group nearest Thos. John Baker staggered back toward him with an arm dangling by little more than bone. John's brother screamed as he lunged at the attacker, tearing off his helmet and ramming his fingers down into the soft eyes. Evelyn bled out a few feet from the Baker men.

Thos panicked when a heavy armored Berserker zeroed in on him. Berserkers were heavy-armored troops sent to bull rush the enemy with plating resistant to all but powerful gunfire. Tanks and trucks very still heavily regulated in modern age, and Berserkers were the closest thing allowable. Thos was both flattered and terrified Aric sent tank-men after him. The Berserker ferociously slashed at him. Thos avoided the blow and attempted a few close-range shots. The bullets bounced off the Berserker's thick turtle shell plating. Thos switched to his sword. The Berserker forced him into a face-to-face confrontation. He hit the Berserker with his sword only to have it bounce off, nearly splitting his own skull. Thos heard laughter bellowing inside the heap of reinforced metal. The hilt of the attacking sword connected with Thos's stomach, knocking the wind out of him.

Thos's father had taught him how to deal with armored foes, as did his father before him. Heavy armored Berserkers usually didn't bother with under armor, leaving joints exposed. The hulking foe lumbered toward Thos, presenting a brief moment to strike. A thrust of Thos's blade sent it through the soft fabric between helmet and cuirass, causing a fountain of blood. The blood spurting from severed carotid artery sprayed all over Thos's chest and face.

Thos rushed over the help the eastern workers overwhelmed by the marauding force. He brought down two men with pistol shots. Judah Baker took a sword to his midsection, spilling his slippery entrails at Thos's feet. Bob rushed at a killer only to be knocked off his feet. Judah gave him one more desperate slash to aid Bob before succumbing to death. Thos shot Judah's killer twice in the back. One soldier ran directly at Thos, taking one of his bullets in the jaw. Thos reloaded. He made sure no forces moved on his home. Cass and the other worker's wives peppered attackers with shots from all floors of the house, felling a dozen men that slipped passed the militia defense. Matthew got off a few shots from a distance, wheeling around the fields like a madman.

The western farmers wiped out the men coming from the woods, though taking heavy casualties in the process. The eastern side fared worse, losing most of their forces to snipers. Jack prioritized the snipers, snaking his way through the grass after them. Between Jack and the snipers an arsonist prepared more molotovs. The arsonist saw Jack and readied another killer cocktail. A bullet from one of his sharpshooters hit the bottle causing a shower of flames. The man cried out in agony as the flames consumed him. Thos's riflemen brought down the other arsonist before he could scorch another field.

Thos ran toward his corpse and snatched up the ready-to-use Molotov. He lit the bottle and threw it at the field where the snipers hid, sacrificing his field for the greater good. The fire quickly spread, catching one of the snipers trying to roll away. Rustling in the grass gave away the position of the other, allowing Thos's riflemen to take him out.

Thos persevered until the survivors of the eastern wall pushed back the opposition. As he ran, he tripped over the dying, mangled bodies of his workers. Even at the ghastly sight, he refused to stop. He felled three more knights. Tonight was the first time that he had taken a human life, he kept forcing the thought from his mind.

Bob accompanied Thos, and before long he had cleared the east field of invaders. Bob grinned, showcasing how invaluable his days as an ex-raider had proved. Thos and company let out a cry to gain the attention of the southern attackers lead by three Berserkers. The knights turned toward the oncoming force. The last of the southern workers did not squander the opportunity and took four of them down.

Soldiers lacking night vision tech removed their obstructive helmets to get a better view of the battlefield. Thos capitalized on the opportunity and went after the exposed flesh. He swung his blade and connected with the tender flesh. One man's neck and chopped away at it like a tree.

Thos had lost many men, but so had his enemy. The slaughter continued an hour before the last of the knights were surrounded, however, the Berserker acting as commander growled his refusal to surrender.

Thos faced the final ax-wielding Berserker himself. He used speed to his advantage, chipping away at the opening above the shin. The berserker's attack grew sloppier with each hit. Bit by bit, Thos cut through the leg until it could no longer support the torso. The bottom of his leg gave out, falling sideways in a grim display. With the support of both legs, the heavy armor became too great of a burden. The Berserker collapsed and bled out.

The Averill Estates lost eighty-one workers and killed fifty-four soldiers. With the battle over, several survivors attended to the fire devouring the fields. A few smaller blazes sprouted in the north and south, consuming parts of Old Man's Woods before being extinguished. Exhausted and shocked from the event, Thos took a seat in the grass. Ten knights remained. Thos felt a crisis of conscience and mulled over their fate.

For the longest time, Thos sat there looking at the bodies littering his grandfather's land. He closed his eyes to block out the sea of death; the smells however he couldn't block. Thos turned to his side and threw up at the realization of igniting a war. Wiping his mouth, he stood back.

"That's enough!" a voice cried. The voice belonged to Drake Hale. The fact that Drake had not been implicated in the attack combined with the adrenaline rush from combat fading, Drake simply being a government agent made Thos hate him at that moment.

"Just in time," Thos grumbled. Drake fought his way to help Thos who responded with accusations. Drake did all that he could to remain calm and let the shaken farmer vent.

"I fought my way to help you, despite being attacked by a demon in the woods," Drake said.

"What?" Thos asked, looking at Drake as if he were an insane drunk.

"A demon," Drake snarled.

"That's nonsense. I've never head of a demon 'round here," Thos said. Drake waved his hand, irritably.

"Fine. Forget about that. Aric's men tried to kill me back there. We need to put a stop to this before it gets worse."

"Worse? It's already a titanic, flaming cloud of shit!" Thos shrieked. Drake grimaced.

"I know these people came to kill you. I also know that this is on Aric's head. I can appeal to the king—" Drake began.

"Against his own son? In what world?. And you think he'll overlook you helping me?" Thos reminded. Drake looked down at the ground and muttered a curse, relenting.

"I'm gonna talk to the rebels in Greenfield. I'm sure they're already planning to attack Fort Alexander. Killing Aric may stop this mess," Thos said, closing his eyes at the seemingly impossible choice.

"And incur Anselm's wrath?" Drake quipped.

"If the king is as reasonable as you say, then maybe he can understand why Aric has to die. Heavy casualties on both sides might get us a truce. Or maybe we can hold the prince hostage."

"There has to be another way," Drake shook his head. Thos doubted that. Wiping the bloody bits of flesh from his clothes he signaled his men to move in on Drake.

"We can't let you leave. I'm sorry, Drake, but you'll have to remain as our hostage," Thos said. Drake groaned and begrudgingly nodded.

"Guess I have no choice," Drake said bitterly.

"We have a guest room you can use for the night. We can both head to Greenfield in the morning. No one will harm you. We'll take these knights with us and some extra manpower too." Drake nodded again and headed up to the Estates with an armed escort at his back. Thos turned back to his men and prepared to bury the friends and workers he considered family.

GREGOR

"Ah, warmth," Gregor uttered, pleased to be free of the damnable cold of the Northern Frontier. The warmth lightened his mood, making the trip more bearable for everyone. Gregor and his troops avoided the well-traveled roads, only stopping to restock supplies and rest. The first stop, Fort Aldean, proved less than accommodating. The walls crumbled before Gregor's eyes as if breathing too avidly would bring the building down. A scout on the discolored rampart didn't give the new guests a single glance. Gregor mumbled a series of profanities as the gates opened.

"All of you, shut up. The army doesn't like us. I'll have to sweet talk 'em," he said. The fort commander casually walked over to Vigilant.

"Bad time for a crusade, Gregory," the commander said sourly. Gregor hated when people called him by his birth name. It sounded condescending, almost as much as when people used his middle name of Lynn. "We'll let you know if any devil cows are about," the commander said with a laugh.

Gregor bit his tongue, knowing better than to provoke a force that outnumbered his ten to one. He gave an authoritative grunt to keep his men in line. Vigilant spent the night in the stables, humiliated, though shielded from the spring rains. Rains pelted the fortress the whole night with unrelenting fury. Gregor slept sporadically thanks to the booming thunder.

At first light, Vigilant made haste through the state of King's Crown. Gregor missed traveling through the other states, but not when tensions were boiling. The country had teetered on the edge of civil war for many years now, and with Aric himself deployed to Heartland, the tipping point was here. Being down south meant he could also be a target for both anti and pro-government forces. Regardless of the political climate, Vigilant had a job to do.

"Stay frosty. Could be enemies all around us," Gregor said.

"We stay frosty. Let's stay toasty for once," Cedric replied. Cedric moved his horse closer to Gregor and leaned in. Gregor anticipated the coming words.

"No," Gregor said in a low growl.

"Don't you want to see your brother? It's been years hasn't it?" Cedric asked. Gregor grumbled.

"I don't associate with deserters," he said. A detour to the White Woods wouldn't take him that far off course. Gregor always chose duty first, even when it pained him to do so. "He chose to live with the Fey as a prancing ninny."

"We all deserve a little prancing every now and then. You used to be like that, if I recall," Cedric said. The words set Gregor off, his white flesh turned so red he thought he might pass out.

"I don't prance! We don't prance! No prancing!" Gregor roared, drawing odd glances from his companions. He lowered his voice and thrust his finger in Cedric's face. "No prancing."

"Can you blame him? Not a bad retirement, I'd say." Cedric mused.

"We don't retire," Gregor said.

"Don't give me that shit. You must get tired of visiting brothels… settle down before it's too late. Forgive your brother and go see him. You may not get another chance." Cedric gave Gregor a nudge.

"I do miss him," Gregor said.

Gregor's brother didn't deserve the hate lobbed at him. Matthew paid his dues more than Gregor and found love that the Sentinel wouldn't allow himself. Gregor couldn't allow himself to feel joy for his brother and condemned him for abandoning a job Gregor planned on doing until his final day. Technically, the job didn't forbid marriage or families, but it discouraged them for cases like Matthew. Gregor realized denying himself a life outside of the order left him, as one failed recruit once called him, "so sour he shit curdled milk." Gregor truly wanted to make amends with him running headlong toward the grave.

"Then make time," Cedric advised. Gregor considered Cedric's words.

"We still have to deal the cults," Gregor said. He held up the sack with the woman's severed head.

"Of course we do," Cedric began, "But we also have put some thought in what comes after; soon we will be too old for this job."

"We were too old a decade ago," Gregor said. Gregor imagined a life out in the wild with his brother, and it made him joyous, though he would never admit it.

"I called him a coward. I called him worthless. He was such a shit, but he was a damn good warrior, and a damn good brother too."

"But—" Cedric said, already anticipating the excuse.

"It can wait until after we're done in the capital. When they see this witch, they'll finally stop ignoring us. With more resources at my disposal, I'll be able to make time for it." he said, clinging to hope.

Vigilant reached their last stop before the capital. The town of Evansboro stood in the shadow of Kingsbury, a place straddling the line between town and city. Evansboro had only two claims to fame: spicy frog legs and a manor at its heart. The town had served as a plantation centuries before a community slowly rose around it.

Gregor chomped the bit for some frog legs. Gregor set aside dreams of a long overdue family reunion and eyed the throng of people lining up to greet their guests. A bevy of smiles greeted Vigilant, showcasing a disturbing and uncharacteristic happiness.

"Maybe they're just happy," Cedric said.

"Have you been in this city before?" Gregor replied.

"Maybe they just need some prancing," Cedric teased.

"I'm going to knock the shit out of you." Gregor put his hand around the cloth bag holding the sister's head and gripped it firmly.

"Welcome!" came a voice. A well-dressed man Gregor assumed to be the head honcho approached. He got titles mixed up more and more these days. He deliberately left out the title when he addressed the man.

"Pleasure," Gregor said. The well-dressed man wore a tight waistcoat under a long brown jacket, silken britches, a wide-brimmed hat, and the fine leather shoes. The man's smile perturbed Gregor more than anything else about him.

"Indeed, the name's Godric. I'll take you to your lodgings. You'll be well taken care of during your stay, I can promise you that," the mayor assured them. The soldiers grew excited at the sound of that, but their hopes fizzled when they learned of the town's distinct lack of a brothel. Godric gave Vigilant a brief tour of the city along the way to the guesthouses. Gregor tuned out the words, choosing instead to rest his eyes while his horse got him to his destination. A nudge roused him prematurely.

"No napping," Cedric said, mildly agitated. Gregor's face went red with embarrassment.

"You're almost as old as me," Gregor scolded. He said loud enough to get the attention of the mayor droning on up ahead.

"Distillery, nice," Cedric said. Cedric's attempt to cover his inattentiveness failed miserably, Godric frowned his disappointment.

"What brings you here?" Godric spoke with concern.

"An audience with the king," Gregor said. The mayor sighed

with relief. Gregor spoke no more during the trek through the town, delegating the speaking duties to his mouthy subordinate.

Godric escorted Vigilant past the splendid manor that years of decay had left anything but splendid. Time had chomped away at the building. Spots of rot and discoloration peppered the old structure, leaving it a putrid collage of green and white. Appearance wise, it gave off a vibe more ominous than beautiful. The manor windows were like a dozen black eyes that judged Gregor's every move. Gregor started to doze off again near the manor when something caught his eye in a window on the second floor. Vaguely white humanoid shapes peered out from inside the structure. The image caused him to snap to full alertness. He blinked and the figures vanished. *A little too cliché and perfect*, Gregor thought.

"Anyone live there?" Gregor asked. Godric laughed.

"That'd be our celebrity ghosts," Godric replied. "I'm surprised you haven't heard. Haunted the place before I was even born. Started out as guests reporting strange lights and shapes during tours, owners who vanished decades ago, so the stories go. It was a tourist hot spot years back, but not so much these days." As Godric spoke, his tone turned from amusement to disappointment.

"We could solve your ghost problem," Cedric suggested. Gregor recalled his time investigating a community during his prime with a similar history. In that instance, the wicked spirit in question was a buried Old World super generator that caused mysterious lights and noises. Gregor remembered that mission as the most disappointing of his career.

"I don't think there's really a ghost, just people with wild imaginations we make money on. I also know your reputation and would like to keep the building intact." Gregor couldn't deny urban missions often came with a hefty amount of collateral damage.

"Very well. We have more pressing matters anyway… like food. Let's eat, dammit," Gregor said.

"Aye," Godric said. "We'll cook you fellas up a batch of our famous frog legs and all the beer you can drink, or Prosperity's Finest Soda, if you'd rather." The men followed Godric and his militiamen to sweet amenities prepared at the rec center. Gregor and his men greedily consumed all food and drink in their path. Cedric burned his mouth on a frog leg much to the delight of his superior. Cedric savored revenge when Gregor choked on a sweet cake. The others drank their fill of beer, while Gregor drank only vanilla flavored soda.

His men enjoyed their night with wild stories and better rest than they'd ever find back up in the dingy tower. The desire to explore the old manor proved too great an itch for Gregor. He slipped out the back of the rec center and out into the chilly air outside. Cedric waited for him. Over the years the two had grown to know each other very well, coming to an understanding between the old men too stubborn for reason. Cedric did not stop Gregor, nor join him. Cedric offered only two words.

"Good hunting."

ANSELM

ANSELM COULDN'T STOP yawning. Constant meetings laced with veiled threats left him drained, and he'd only been back a few days. A large crowd gathered in the castle courtyard. Anselm tried not to be too contemptuous, yet he failed miserably. Sycophants, liars, and opportunists robbed of him of any hope to accomplish anything, and here they were, now all in one spot.

Anselm saw Percival and some other man slipping past the masses incognito. Anselm picked up his golden goblet and took a sip of wine, hoping to take the edge off his nerves and the night chill. After a sip, he turned the cup upside-down. An attendant rushed forward and apologized. "Tastes like fermented shit. Get something better," he commanded.

The king supervised the festivities while Abigail made the obligatory rounds to chat with the nobles. The server dashed away and brought the king a better vintage. Anselm sipped on his new, and much improved, wine.

His eyes bounced from one streetlamp to the next, which stretched from the castle courtyard to the city below. The lights flickered, showing the ever-growing strain on the city's power grid. After emptying his goblet and eyeing the many lights in town, Anselm's attention moved back to the crowd in expensive silks and furs moving around tables littered with the best foods the nation had to offer. A local group of musicians strummed on guitars as they prepared for a show that Anselm fully expected to be lackluster, as usual.

His gaze turned to the marble statue of Alexander, his mighty ancestor. Anselm thought about how Alexander would deal with this situation. During the last days of the Old World, Alexander had been the grandson of the most powerful family in the world. After the collapse, the advisors turned on the family, kicking them out to the angry mob. Alexander's parents survived and raised him in exile. Twenty years later, he'd make a triumphant return. He brutally slaughtered the traitors before establishing the nation of New Prosperity. Anselm realized he had it easy compared to his exalted ancestor.

He sat motionless in his chair, lost in pleasant thoughts. The nondescript prattle of the crowd faded from his mind. A state of peace washed over him like the soothing waters of a hot spring. He imagined running his hand through the flowing locks of dear Abigail. He began to smile at the world he wanted as this one passed him. He continued sitting in his own world, oblivious to the hands shaking him.

"Anselm, dear," came a voice. The clear skies and green country seemed so real. He felt the light breeze on his face and Abigail's head resting on his shoulder. Little Aric played in the fields with Drake, happy and carefree. Anselm kissed Abigail, relishing the honeyed taste of her lips.

"Anselm!" With a jolt, Anselm found himself sitting among chattering nobles. Abigail sat beside him, giving him a queer look. He managed to hide his horror and stared into her soft brown eyes.

"Daydreaming," he laughed.

"Sleeping," she corrected. Anselm's skin reddened.

"Perhaps I should turn in early," he said. He felt older than his years, constantly exhausted from ruling. *Old and weak, that's what they'll say.*

"Don't you leave me alone with these parasites," she commanded.

"We don't have to stay," Anselm replied. He gave her a slight nudge and placed his hand on top of hers. She accepted his invitation with a smile that brought his weary body back to life. The two walked hand-in-hand from the crowd, making their way through the serpentine gardens.

The hanging gardens at the back of the courtyard spiraled up, forming a miniature version of the castle. The gardens teemed with exotic flora from all corners of the continent. Two young lovers passionately kissed in the corner; part of him grew jealous at the sight. Suddenly remembering the midnight rendezvous he cut his stroll short, leaving a sullen Abigail to return to mingle with the nobility. Anselm smirked at the meeting on the so-called "witching hour."

He hurried back into the castle toward the private elevator. He paid no mind to the city as the elevator climbed to the top of the castle. With a ding, the elevator signaled his arrival at the roof of Blackthorne Castle. Many of his ancestors preferred watching the city from this spot, while others chose to end their reigns by flinging themselves from it. The doors opened to the stairs leading to the roof. Anselm attempted to pull a fast one on his blind date. Two AR wielding gunmen accompanied him to his destination with a dozen more a floor below ready to scale the building at a single shot or word. Anselm reached for a pistol he kept hidden under his jacket. Pistol in hand, he stepped outside seeing no one around, yet something alarmed him. Anselm looked back to his men, unmoving and unresponsive. He looked over the side of building to see no one else to aid him. Anselm turned to see a man in a white suit leaning on an obsidian cane surveying the electric world below.

"Punctuality isn't one of your strong suits, nor following orders. We applaud your effort, it's a smart if useless move," the man said, regarding him with an impersonal demeanor. The man didn't turn to face the king.

"I had prior engagements," Anselm replied.

"Placating the masses, yes, we saw. Just look at them all. They believe the world lives and dies by their whims. They are nothing more than insects oblivious to the boot coming down on them. You are all fools, squabbling over flags and chairs and dirt, accomplishing nothing. How does that make you feel, ant-king?" The man's condescending manner angered the king. Anselm proceeded with caution.

"Why have you summoned me?" Anselm asked.

"History is cyclical, an ebb and flow to it. Prosperity gives rise to corruption. Corruption leads to collapse. From collapse comes rebirth and, in turn, prosperity. It is an endless loop that no one has ever broken, an algorithm, the Great Equation—and it defines all." Anselm rolled his eyes.

"Did you bring me up here to philosophize?" Anselm asked, not hiding his irritation.

"You have been summoned because your kingdom is entering another phase of this loop, the time of correction has come."

"Correction?" Anselm mused.

"Your violations of the Compact have not gone unnoticed, they never do. You and your advisors bring ruin to this kingdom. Perhaps it's time we select new leaders," the man said.

Anselm knew that every nation violated the Compact at one point or another. He also recalled stories of those that used technologies not yet allowed by the Compact either vanished or met grisly ends. Anselm found this stranger's words threatening. His fingers tightened around his gun. Paralysis took hold of him. The figure turned to face him. He wore a golden comedy mask with a pointed nose, and eyes and grinning mouth of complete blackness.

In a flash, the man stood directly in front of him. He thrust his cane into the king's stomach. Anselm struggled in vain against the paralysis. He tried calling for help, but no soldiers answered his cries.

"They can't help you, none of them can. Make no mistake ant-king, your kingdom exists only because we allow it," the man said. Anselm's blood burned inside his body. He could only muster a gurgle at the agony. With an uncaring wave of the man's hand, Anselm flew backward. His body came to a stop at the edge of the roof. Anselm crawled to his feet, only to be lifted into the air by some otherworldly force. Out of the corner of his eye, he saw six other well-dressed men and women in silver masks. The figures studied him as if he were some scientific curiosity. The man in white held out his hand and Anselm's pain intensified. A million invisible needles stabbed at his insides. Blood ran out of his nose and mouth. The man in white stepped back as if surprised by this development. Anselm fell to the ground.

"You might be ready after all," the masked man said. The masked man waved his hand again and Anselm's pain stopped as quickly as it had begun. The figures stepped back allowing the king room to get to his feet. Anselm stumbled about, disoriented by whatever had just happened to him.

"A time of great upheaval is upon this land. We are anxious to see how the next iteration plays out. The algorithm is built on constants and variables, it's time to see which you shall be." The masked figures walked away from him and moved to the edges of the roof.

"What the hell are you talking about!?" Anselm cried. His head spun, and bile crawled up his throat.

"Soon you'll know," said the man in white. "Enemies are moving against you, some under your very nose. There's something that may aid you, a violation that we will tolerate. It is deep in your vault, your trump card. You know of what we speak of, forbidden tech. A gift left by Gideon Grey, and one that we have modified. We will allow you to use it."

"Allow it!? What about the Compact?" Anselm asked.

"We will handle that. It's your salvation. However be warned: salvation has a price." Moving to the edges of the castle walls, the masked figures outstretched their arms and threw themselves over the side. Anselm rushed to the edge to find no trace of them, only a strange mist rolling over the city. After taking a moment to gather his wits, the king quickly abandoned the rooftop. Anselm made his way to the royal bedroom, finding Abigail already in bed. Anselm washed all traces of blood from his face before climbing into bed. He turned his affections toward his wife, desiring a much-needed release after the nightmarish incident.

He woke Abigail with soft kisses, giving her the passions he'd built up during his travels. After a session of intense lovemaking, Anselm and Abigail lay wide awake staring and the large crystalline chandelier of the royal bedroom. Both of them were still sweaty, and Anselm threw the covers off to cool them down. They were rarely intimate anymore. Stress always left Anselm tired or not in the mood. Even in the bedroom, Anselm felt crushing failure, Abigail's fake orgasms only made him feel more pathetic. The failure gnawed away at him. He attempted to please Abigail again. He kissed her bare breasts; she began breathing heavily as they hardened. He ran his tongue gently over her nipples, hoping to get another erection. His valiant attempts failed. *Limp, weak and worthless*, he thought.

"I'm sorry," he said shamefully. After a few minutes of silence, Anselm switched to an unpleasant conversation.

"I fear there is a plot to destroy us. I believe the Board really will move against me. Only a matter of time," Anselm said.

"What do you suggest?" Abigail asked.

"Leaving myself vulnerable for an attack—with well-hidden agents, that is. If my foes learn about my solitude, they'd capitalize on it. They think I'm an arrogant fool," he stressed. Abigail frowned and turned her gaze to the aquatic spiral pattern forming a whirlpool amidst the white gypsum ceiling of the art deco royal bedroom. Anselm looked out the windows for any sign of the strange mist.

"Percival should avoid town for now," Abigail said with lament.

"Our agents will follow his movements," Anselm assured.

"My son has enough people doing that, as is," Abigail snapped back. Anselm sighed; the overwhelming pressure returned to squeeze his chest like an orange.

"I know. Finding the truth, we can show these villains for what they are. Then the people will see," he said. Abigail sat up and grabbed hold of the covers hanging off the side of the bed.

"We can discuss it in the morning when our minds are sharpest. Goodnight, love." She pulled the covers up over them, leaned over and kissed him, and closed her eyes. Anselm's thoughts turned again to masked figures and deadly plots. Anselm realized that new emerging forces had powers in clear violation of the law that killed paupers and kings with no exception. More and more, he found himself in need of an edge to compensate for his diminishing power, risking the possible damnation that came with it. He hoped it wouldn't come to opening the vault to survive, but deep down he always knew it would.

DRAKE

The midday sun radiated ungodly heat today, just in time for a long march.

"Cold every other day," Drake whined. Drake had a few risky opportunities to escape, but he chose to remain a hostage. Seeing the amateur nature of the group meant it should be easy to learn more of the rebellion and how to stop it. Thos and Drake rode through the woods, exchanging few words.

Drake periodically checked on his fellow prisoners, not trusting Thos's men to honor their word. He remained calm and focused. If he had to kill Thos or Aric to save the country, he'd do it without hesitation. Drake steeled himself to do whatever necessary to preserve the peace. *Taking one life to save many. I've done it before*, he thought.

Looking back, Drake saw Thos asleep on his horses, his drooling mouth agape. Emerging from the dense woods, Thos woke almost upon hitting the blinding sunlight of the open fields. He swatted at the brightness. Drake's horse moved closer to Thos, nearly catching one of his flailing hands to the face. Thos's monstrous yawn echoed like a thunderclap over the plains, as all sighed with relief that his noises did not attract any dangers. Thos wiped the sleep from his eyes, adjusting his greasy, matted hair.

"We there?" he asked, half-yawning again. No one answered.

Drake ignored the ever-increasing loudness of Thos's yawning. With a few quick breaths, Drake cleared his mind, keeping himself calm.

"You recover from tragedy quick," Drake said.

"Sometimes you got to," Thos replied. He leaned to his side and reached into one of the bags attached to the horse. Thos removed a pipe and a small pouch filled with tobacco. Pulling a match from his pocket, he began puffing on the scratched-up pipe.

"I used to smoke too, well, cannabis. Helps cope with the stress," Drake said. Thos's twitchy demeanor had worsened after the attack on his Estates. Drake gave Thos a look over, analyzing his new traveling companion. "Aric's the reason I smoke." Thos leaned forward and rested his head on his hands.

"Now he's the reason I'm here, too," Thos replied.

"You really mean to go through with it?" Drake asked.

"Mercy help me. I really do," Thos said.

The conversation brought them to Greenfield, where a thick blanket of soft white clouds hovered above. The men pulled into the stables and hitched the horses. Strangely there were no Blackthorne soldiers in sight.

"What're you gonna do if I let you go?" Thos asked. Drake turned his gaze to the ground, knowing what he planned to do was more than likely futile.

"I'll take some men to calm Aric down. Perhaps we can make some sort of compromise to avoid more bloodshed. I'll warn you now that this may require some of your friends arrested for treason," Drake replied.

Drake ran his fingers through his hair and smiled, ignoring the guns pointed at him. Thos moved his head back and forth, what Drake assumed to be him mulling the situation over. Thos advised the group he had business to settle, the man he suspected had roped him into this mess. Drake judged Thos as a proud man, not wanting to grovel at the rebels' feet on top of giving Drake the chance to learn anything that may be used against him. Drake laughed at the idea, given that Thos held hostage the one knight Aric was happy to let die. However, Drake understood his logic, he was caught between two leaders of questionable morality. The city streets were now bathed in the warm sunlight as the two men parted ways. Drake stayed where he was, surrounded by a host of angry rebels.

"I'll be here if you need me," Drake said with a bitter groan. Thos let out a loud, single laugh at the words and walked away. The other hostages were placed in the care of Thos's men. Drake leaned against the outer wall of the small jailhouse waiting for the proverbial epiphany that would set him on the right path. The heat bore down on him. He sweat buckets beneath his tunic. Drake closed his eyes and let out a heavy breath. A rebel fighter approached him.

"You're free to move around the city, but know that we're watching you," the man said.

Pushing himself off the wall, Drake walked with haste for the local knight barracks. The streets began to fill with people now, like ants drawn to sugar. Drake ignored the hateful murmurs from rebel agents examining his every move. He arrived at the southern watchtower on the edge of town, the structure that served as the army barracks.

The guardsmen on the tower hailed him as he approached, and he raised his hand in acknowledgment. Three low-ranking knights in the tower base played a game with provocative cards Drake didn't recognize. Their attention was drawn to him with a throaty cough. The man closest to Drake spoke first.

"Greetings Ser Hale. I'm Knight Mason. What is your business?" Judging from their demeanor Drake caught the trio in off hours. He made a little small talk before cutting to the chase.

"Tell me, what do you think of the prince?" Drake asked. As expected none of them responded. The raised eyebrows and crinkled foreheads told him such a query was out of the ordinary. Drake saw the thick grey piles of dust caked all around the wooden beams above. He fought to keep his allergies in check with furious nose wrinkling.

"I'm not here on his behalf. Everyone knows we loathe each other. I want to know honestly what you think. Strictly off the record," Drake said. At first, the knights thought this some sort of bizarre test until finally, one spoke.

"No man here supports Aric, but you didn't hear that from me," Mason said. Drake listened, occasionally peering out the tower window for eavesdroppers.

"I've heard there's a large contingent of men up at the fort that doesn't even support him. Talk of desertion if the rebels march on them." Drake's eyes wandered as he weighed his options.

"So if I gave orders that conflicted with his…" Drake said trailing off.

"You ask much, then. Do you expect war?" Mason asked, eyes widening.

"Most definitely," Drake said. He shrugged off the dirty feeling from scheming, more of a Board strategy. The knights looked at each other. Drake knew they saw the truth in his words.

"What do you propose?" Mason asked

"When Aric orders the attack, do not obey. Get as many people as you can on board." The other two men whispered to each other.

"You'll take full responsibility for this? We'll be blaming all this on you if it goes to shit," Mason said. The men focused their gaze upon the Knight-Ambassador, making sucking noises with his lips.

"You think Aric's defeat will solve everything?" said one of the other man, cards still in hand.

"No, but it will ease tensions. With him gone, Anselm can stabilize this country; perhaps force the government to work together and put down this rebel threat… or negotiate a peace. If we're lucky, Aric will change his tune and keep his head," Drake said.

"So it's settled," Mason replied.

"Gather the other knights tonight at ten o'clock in the market square." Each of the three men nodded. Drake considered their betrayal well beforehand and had planned for that, too.

JOSEPH KERR

Joseph Kerr felt this day coming for a long time. He could smell it as sure as the brush smoldering just outside town. He and his brother, Abraham, spent the better part of the decade trying to get this revolution off the ground. The Kerr family had never been anything special in the grand scheme of things, but that was about to change.

Before the decline, Joseph had a moderately successful automobile repair shop business in Greenfield, while his brother had left for Emerald Coast to seek a life in the political arena. Things went well until the government shut down Joe's business for selling old cars to unlicensed commoners, and a disgraced state regent tried to murder Abraham for criticizing the wrong people. Things only got worse from there. These events set the Kerr brothers on a path toward rebellion.

The rebellion was in full swing now, yet it didn't provide Joseph the satisfaction he craved, until he saw a certain man walking his way. He grinned from ear to ear as Thos approached him. Thos maneuvered his way to through the private room in the Grand Royal Hotel toward Joseph's usual spot.

Joseph sat in a booth by himself, sporting a khaki brown jacket and boot-cut jeans. Joseph combed his mustache, fighting his one stray hair that curled toward the heavens. Only a handful of people skulked around the restaurant since the ruckus following Elise's murder. Joseph gulped down his water and motioned for a refill. Thos noticed Joseph and grunted his annoyance. Joseph didn't like water, but he needed to kick his soda addiction. With his right pointer finger out, Joseph motioned Thos over. Joseph leaned back in his booth and thrust his legs up on the table. *Got you by the balls now*, he thought smugly.

"Drink?" asked the man.

Thos shook his head and sat up against the plain wooden back of the booth. Joseph saw the famed Mr. Averill as a dog with his tail between his legs. He could almost feel the pain it caused Thos to be here.

"Popular man these days. Didn't we just talk about this? Now here you are, hat in hand," Joseph said with too much elation in his voice. He considered himself a decent man, though one of his vices included proving his detractors wrong. A few of Joseph's friends sat a few booths behind them, guns at the ready. Thos's face scrunched up with rage and he clenched his fists. He avoided eye contact with Joseph, staring at a big hole in the table.

"You want—" Joseph began.

"I don't want any fucking… no thanks," Thos said, smiling at the approaching young waitress. Thos regained his composure, muttering a few more curses under his breath. Joseph followed the waitress with his eyes as she left, fearing spies belonging to someone other than him. He quickly gulped down the water.

"I told you, these things are as predictable as spring rain. Do you accept my offer now?" Joseph asked, repressing the urge to grin.

"I give you my full support," Thos said with a heavy breath. Joseph motioned to the waitress, who poured him a glass of water as Thos glared in annoyance. Joseph poured him some water. The light from the antler chandelier above reflected off Joseph's gleaming dome, furthering Thos's salty disposition.

"My offer stands," Joseph said.

"I ain't your little soldier boy," Thos said, pointing his finger at him. Joseph waved his hand.

"All we need is your voice and your supplies." Joseph reached for his wallet and removed a silver coin. He stood up, and Thos followed suit. Joseph handed the coin directly to the waitress, and the two men walked out. Joseph stopped, waiting to unveil this last surprise on the unsuspecting Thos. "Unfortunately though we… well…" Joseph said embarrassed.

"What? I'm not in the mood for this cocktease," Thos growled.

"You'll be coming with us for a while." Joseph scratched the back of his head while talked.

"Why?" Thos asked, fuming.

"Word is spreading fast about your deeds. You're a big hero now, and wars need heroes. Others will join with a big shot businessman hero on our side. We'll send some men to watch over your lands and your woman… if you accompany us. I have already sent agents to let Ms. Lewis know. They'll bring back a few clothes and essentials for you, too," Joseph said. Thos followed Joseph back out to the stables over to the white and brown paint horse. Thos ran his hand through its mane.

"Where are we headed?" Thos asked.

"You'll see," Joseph replied with a smirk. Thos cocked an eyebrow.

A few of Joseph's cohorts came over to Thos. Joseph started to climb on the horse before he remembered he had one thing left to do.

"I have some business before we head out. Wait here," Joseph said. He checked the pistol at his side and power-walked his way to his home, departing on one final task before kicking off the revolution in full. Something inside urged him to speak to his wife one last time. Joseph couldn't tell when it had happened, but it was far too late to repair the relationship. It wasn't his wife's fault; she was faithful and devoted. Though both had numerous opportunities to cheat on the other, neither ever did. Despite the fact, Joseph's marriage failed all the same, and he knew it was all his doing. *I sacrificed my family for my country*, Joseph thought.

Joseph and Margery did well for themselves in years past but were by no means rich. The one-floor house consisted of two bedrooms, two bathrooms, living room, kitchen, storage closet, and a 300-square-foot backyard. The house was the only thing Joseph had left, and that would end today. Now, the only thing Joseph had was the cause.

Opening the door, Joseph's chunky labrador jumped on his leg and barked excitedly in his face. "Good boy, Emmett." He scratched the dog behind the ears. The dog's right leg began to twitch wildly almost causing him to fall over. "Where's your ball?" The dog took off in a flash, tail wagging with such a fury it looked about to fly off. Emmett sniffed around the couch at first and then through the open door out to the yard in back. Joseph reached for his gun.

Noises came from the storage room, so he walked back toward a possible threat. Margery stepped out of the storage room at the same time. Joseph jumped out of his skin when she appeared. He cursed loudly, causing her to jump out of her skin as well. Her faded red hair went in every direction. She wore old work clothes and coveralls, giving her an uncharacteristically tomboyish appearance.

"Fuck sakes! You could've let me know you're here!" Margery snapped.

"Sorry," Joseph said, not meaning it. Margery stopped her work, clearly wanting this to be her final moments with Joseph.

"Another man showed up today. We're eight months delinquent on the house now. Our savings are almost gone," she said showing no emotion. Joseph hated being reminded of his failures, at least that was how he always interpreted her words.

"To hell with them, damn bankers devour everything. This broken system has limped on for far too long." The mere thought of the nobility sent him into an uncontrollable rage; Joseph knew Margery wearied of his constant jeremiads against people with power.

"And you think you can change all that?" she said, slightly condescending.

"I do. I can. The people need to stand up instead of being stood on. Violence is the only solution," Joseph replied. He picked up the broom and tossed it in the storage room, and she closed the door. The two went to the living room. Emmett shimmied through the door, his fat stomach swinging as he walked. Margery walked to the kitchen doorway when Joseph moved to close.

"Tommy stopped by this afternoon. I fixed him lunch, but he didn't eat it. It's yours if you want," Margery said. A cold roast beef sandwich and fried potatoes lay on a solitary plate at his spot at the table. Joseph picked up the sandwich and ate standing up. Margery went back to fiddling around the house. The dog watched Joseph's every move, occasionally inhaling a fried potato when he whined too much.

Joseph's body cried out for rest, the sleepless nights finally catching up with him. He told himself the people needed him. Joseph yawned and gave himself a moment to rest. Plopping down on the couch, the dog jumped up beside him, almost hitting him in the face. Joseph gently rubbed the old boy. Margery returned to the living room with a stack of papers and tossed them on Joseph's desk in the corner in the room.

"So you're going through with it?" she said, giving up on persuasion.

"I saw Thomas out in the field, said goodbye already." Margery didn't respond. He continued rubbing the dog for a time, delaying the inevitable.

"You didn't ask him to join did you?!" Her tone darkened.

"I don't want him involved," he said. Her constant busywork gave him the cue she just wanted him to leave. Joseph signed the stack of papers on his desk. "So this is it," he said.

"This is it," Margery said. "The divorce is final. Now nothing is keeping you here. You can go fight your war." He wanted to apologize for so many things. Once upon a time, Joseph had a happy wife and a loving son. He lost count of the times he came home and paid little mind to the two people always by his side. The last few years he spent backroom dealing and networking with the other like-minded individuals had left him with precious little time for family.

"I'm fighting for his future. He deserves better than slaving out there every day for scraps. If there is only one thing in my life I can do, it will be this," Joseph said. Joseph attempted speeches far too often. They never hit the mark. Another awkward silence fell upon them. "You haven't loved me in a long time have you?" he finally asked.

"No," she replied bluntly.

Joseph reminisced about the carefree ignorance of a youth that had gone by way too fast. He pushed himself up from the couch, no longer feeling welcome in his own house. Though Joseph no longer loved his Margery, her words hurt all the same.

"I'm going to let the bank take the house. Anything you want you better take with you. I'm giving Thomas the dog," Margery said.

"He'll take good care of him. I've already taken what I want." A few clouds parted overhead letting more light into the house. Joseph gave Emmett one final pat.

"Why didn't you just leave?" she asked.

"I… wanted to say goodbye. I owe you that much for sticking by me this long." She offered a soft smile and hugged him.

"I wish you the best, I do," she said.

With a final farewell Joseph left his house for the last time. He made a quick stroll through Greenfield to remind himself what he fought for. Recent years had not been kind to the city. Shacks and shanties grew in number every month. Joseph wondered if he and his cohorts could do anything to fix the problem. He knew that the problems of the country weren't simply rich versus poor, but if that got people fighting or even killing, he would use the sentiment to achieve his goal.

For the past two years, Joseph had talked and plotted with men from around the country, gathering soldiers to the cause. He and a handful of men across the nation lit the match, now came the fire. Soon, the streets of every major city would run red, he justified the carnage as best as he could. Reaching the end of the city he did not look back. Thos sat on his horse, fidgeting anxiously. Joseph knew Thos saw him as an opportunistic villain, but Joseph intended to show Thos the righteousness of his actions.

One of the rebel lieutenants paced impatiently by the western gate, clad in workman's clothes. The man perked up when he spied Joseph coming his way and saluted.

THOS

THE CRIMSON GLOW of dusk bled onto the open fields in front of Thos Averill and his rebel host. A light breeze blew over the grassy fields. Two hours of monotonous riding saw Thos farther from home than ever before. He reached in his bag for a cigar and clumsily dropped it to the ground, responding with a childish whine.

The rebels followed the dirt paths outside Greenfield for hours now while he visualized Cass's displeasure at his actions. It seemed to Thos that someone was always displeased with him. *Like a whore, I'm fucked no matter what*, he thought.

During the ride, he focused his mind on plans for future travels with his soon-to-be wife. Thos considered traveling after the rebellion had triumphed. He thought about visiting The Scar, the 300-mile-long chasm left over from the war and during the final years of the Old World. Thos imagined the towering mobile mining platforms repurposed into weapons of mass destruction responsible for The Scar. The repurposed machines were originally intended for use on other planets, turning what was once intended to be terraforming, into what came to be known as "terra-reforming."

A holler from Joseph brought Thos back to the task at hand. In the distance, Thos spied seven horses with riders surrounding a woman.

"What's going on up there?" Thos asked, squinting for a better view. Joseph's trigger finger moved toward his gun and as his riflemen did the same. As they reached the conflict, Joseph quickly brought his men into submission.

"Stand down! If she was with Aric, we'd be dead already," Joseph said. The seven men laughed as the woman's face contorted with anger. Her long auburn hair flowed freely over her reinforced leather armor adorned with nature symbols, including the sun, moon, and others Thos didn't recognize.

"Shouldn't be traveling alone. You need a warrior to protect you," one soldier remarked. She frowned.

"Let me know when one comes along," she snapped back. Thos laughed. Joseph leered at him.

The youngest of the men did not appreciate the woman's jest, although the other men laughed at their friend's humiliation. He raised his hand in anger. In the time it took him to raise his hand, she threw a small object at him, knocking him off his horse. She jumped on him and jammed her blade on his throat. The soldier's face shone beet red. His comrades reached for their weapons.

"Stop!" Joseph bellowed. "If anything happens to her, I'll hang those responsible by their guts." All clearly saw her fighting capabilities, though making an enemy of Joseph's forces was a losing battle.

"You must be Joseph Kerr. And that must be Thos Averill," she said. The man at Joseph's side reached for his pistol, but a whisper from Joseph stopped him.

"Indeed," Joseph replied.

Thos gave the woman a look over, and she responded in kind. Her hazel eyes regarded Thos staring at the symbols on her clothes.

"They're Greek in origin," she said.

He'd seen leather armor of all kinds often enough, but never so decorated. Underneath the leathers, she wore dark green chainmail in a leaf pattern. Her sword belt looked like twisted branches. Thos recognized her as one of the Fey, a name given to various ungoverned free tribes across the country. Thos recalled seeing this woman in Greenfield.

"Have your men had their fill of staring me down? I see you all have a few hidden daggers you neglected to mention," she said.

"Was that a boner joke?" Thos asked. He spun around and saw a few men nervous covering their privates. "It was."

"Identify yourself," Joseph said. She sheathed her sword after giving one more swing at an arrogant man getting to close.

"My name's Zora. I'm your Fey contact," she said.

"I knew the Fey would come around. To be honest, I didn't think your people wore such attire," Joseph said with a wry smile.

"We do. Your men better not try anything, just because you see no others don't assume I'm alone," Zora said, ignoring his comments.

"Noted," Joseph said. The air became crisp as the moon rose over the hill. Thos leaned over to Joe. "Where are we going?"

"Ellora, the city in Mammoth Cave," Zora replied. Joseph's eyebrows nearly shot right off his face.

"I thought that was an urban legend. This is becoming quite the learning experience," Thos said.

"It would seem so," Joseph said. "Anyway we can discuss my secrets somewhere that's not out in the open." Joseph looked over at Zora. "Best keep up," he said.

The group pressed slowly onward as the stars began to shine. It felt like hours crawled by as Thos, Zora, Joseph, and his rebel army made haste to the underground city of Ellora. Thos maneuvered his horse closer to Zora. She noticed him in her peripheral. While conversing with Zora, Thos kept an eye out for the biggest threat in the region: snallygasters. Snallygasters, also called drakes, were car-sized lizards that fancied snacking on runaway cattle.

"I didn't know we had a Fey community round here," Thos said, trying to sound casual. Zora looked at him and smiled.

"There isn't. I come from the woods south of Kingsbury," she stated with a mixture of pride and pain.

"That's a nice little walk from here," Thos replied. Her proximity to the capital gave him an idea of what her business might be.

"I haven't been back in some time. I've been living near Greenfield. They contacted me about requiring some aid. I'd rather not discuss it yet, if that's alright with you. I'm a little wary of large groups of strangers, you understand," she said.

"Yeah, you might get roped into a war, or something," Thos replied, gaining Joseph's ire.

Nightfall spread across the land. The sounds of the emerging crickets singing their amorous songs created a beautiful symphony heralding the five-week season of spring. Thos's father once told him how different things had been during the Old World. The seasons came at different times, and the weather patterns far less volatile until man tampered with weather control.

Hours passed, and at last Thos saw the gaping maw of Mammoth Cave. No lights or torches visible inside. Like the mouth of a ravenous monster, it was as far from inviting.

Upon closer inspection, Thos spied stairs descending into the darkness and barely flickering lights at the bottom. As soon as he blinked, the lights vanished. In unison, they all hopped off their horses and entered the cave. Joseph snatched an old electric lantern hanging from the cave wall. He flipped a switch and gave it a few hard smacks until white light burst forth. "Watch your step." Joseph ignited the lantern and the group followed.

"How come nobody found this place?" Thos asked. The lantern illuminated the grin on Joseph's face. He nodded toward the cavernous alcoves above.

"Snipers," Joseph replied. Joseph raised his lantern, and seconds later red dots peppered Thos's chest.

Thos and Zora looked around, soaking in every little detail. Running water flowed beside them and stalactites bore down on them like the fangs of a dreaded serpent. Electricity hummed faintly in the distance. The group entered a long tunnel leading to a small cart on the side. A couple of men stood watch, armed with high-powered rifles. Joseph seated himself in the front of the vehicle and motioned them over.

Picking up a key from the seat, he stuck it into the front of the machine, and it roared to life. Thos and Zora jumped a little from the sound, not used to seeing such a rarity. Zora walked around the machine, analyzing it as an animal would. After a few laps around the machine, she took her seat beside Thos. Joseph grabbed hold of the circular device on the front and turned it. The vehicle responded with a demonic screech. Thos and Zora instinctively gripped the sides of the vehicle. The motorcar took Thos, Zora, and Joseph through the tunnel while the rebel forces made the trip on foot.

"Dad always told me this place was full of freakish hillbilly creatures, guess he was right," Thos jested. Joseph stopped the cart and turned around to face Thos, staring daggers at him. Thos shut up, and Joseph started the vehicle back up.

The motorcar emerged into a large open area, and Thos's jaw hit the floor. The chamber in front of him stretched out in all directions. A large, natural, hole-filled pillar hung the middle of the cave, intense light poured out from inside. The cavern opened up into a honeycomb of tunnels. Buildings carved in the very walls filled the cavernous world around them, some even hung from the ceiling like the stalactites. Smoke rose and escaped through holes in the ceiling. People hurried to and fro the various houses while some sat around the small tables and stalls.

Small tents littered the main road making the place a makeshift metropolis, reminiscent of a city of dwarves in fantasy stories. As the motorcar reached the main path, they realized the pillar was actually a building carved from inside the massive formation. The structure did not touch the ground, A large stairway came out from the ground up to the odd structure.

"This is just one area; we have many more. The place is filled with a few thousand people, and we've barely even scratched the surface. There are generators in each area. We have a sewer and waste system running through the darker parts of the caves out to an opening about five miles from here," Joseph said, beaming as if he were the architect himself.

"So this is rebel HQ?" Thos said in astonishment.

"It is where the nation begins anew," Joseph replied. The motorized cart stopped in front of the second tower to the right side of the chamber. Joseph continued his brief tour of the place. "This apartment complex has some vacancies on the top floor. Food will be brought to you within the hour."

Joseph pushed open the large tube-shaped complex carved from the eastern wall. The middle of the building contained a spiral staircase connecting to six rooms, two on each floor. They reached the top floor.

"Someone will get you in the morning," Joseph said. "For now, rest up. I have men stationed outside should you need anything." Joseph reached into a box on a small table and handed a room key to both of them.

DRAKE

Among the moon washed streets of Greenfield's market district, Drake Hale awaited his backup. Howls of stray dogs echoed through the city intermingled with singing and shouting from the nearby hotel, all background to the aromas of bread and hooch. Drake's backup was already late. He flipped his pocket watch open and closed it furiously, a nervous habit. In his irritation, he dropped it on the ground. Locals gawked at him. Drake studied their movements obliquely, preparing to fight at a moment's notice.

He heard the clang of armor from the other end of the market. He counted ten knights approaching.

"Have you reached a decision?" Drake asked impatiently. The knights glanced at each other, and he could see the indecision in their eyes. Drake needed to be more persuasive this time.

"Aric will raze this state. When that happens, the people will turn against us. There'll no place safe for us. It pains me to say it, but the prince is a lost cause. We need to stop this war now."

He gave them a stern glare, expecting their support. He then tried to appeal to their sense of duty, of honor. "Don't you people have families here?" Drake asked. "Aric and the rebels will have no qualms going through them to get to you if it comes to that."

"We don't have families here so not really an incentive to risk our necks," Mason said, again speaking for the group.

"I bet we'd get a pretty penny for bringing in that Averill fella," said another soldier. Drake's gamble soured quickly.

"You choose to do nothing?" Drake said, finally giving up.

"Yep," the voice of the apparent leader rang through. "We'll pretend we didn't hear your treason if you just leave us be."

"Very well," Drake sighed. He turned his gaze to the moon and waited for the inspirational words to rally his fellows, but none came.

Drake heard the synchronized marching of troops behind him and noticed that the man in front wore dirty and slightly dented armor, the kind of wear and tear from a recent battle. Splatters of crimson painted the armor and weapons of the group. Leading the group was Captain Harlon, Aric's number one man in Greenfield.

"This man is working with our enemy! He attacked us in the woods!" cried the banged-up knight. The man unsheathed his sword and thrust the blade at Drake's throat. "By the decree of Aric Blackthorne, you're under arrest!"

The wounded knight nodded to his subordinates, who surrounded Drake. Trapped in the steel-clad circle, Drake knew his ability as a peacemaker was failing fast. Now Drake's very life hung on his next words.

"These loyalists will kill you too if Aric commands it," Drake said. The few city guardsmen that arrived tonight were now Drake's last chance.

"Will I get paid?" Mason asked. Drake realized his life had been exchanged for a fatter wallet. Mason looked at Drake and shrugged, a gesture that suggested this was nothing personal. The other knights didn't go with Mason's plan. "You sold him out to these… cowards?" said one.

"You side with him?" Harlon asked. The card-playing man now stood alone as the guardsmen threw up his hands and walked away.

Each of Aric's men unsheathed their swords and motioned Drake Hale to their personal stable. As they walked away, the card-playing man muttered something under his breath. In a single movement, Harlon spun around and thrust his blade toward the man's face. The card-man's eyes widened in terror, but after a moment of shock, he breathed a sigh of relief that he still lived.

"Aric would kill you," Harlon said. Drake played the part of the obedient prisoner, knowing it maneuvered him closer to Aric.

"Return to your duties, soldiers. We'll take him from here," Harlon said, sheathing his sword. Drake had no choice but to comply. As they walked, the knights kept a tight circular formation around him. The cadre of soldiers crossed through the market district to the stables. Drake weighed his options, including the risk of engaging his captors if they decided he was better as a corpse. Despite Aric's hate for him, Drake knew the prince lacked the gall to kill someone that Anselm considered his fourth son. Drake also considered being delivered to Aric personally an opportunity to eliminate him and prevent full blown civil war. Drake would surely die after, but it was a price he'd gladly pay to fix the country. Regardless of duty, he couldn't help feeling disgusted at the idea of killing his former brother and earning the hate of the man that loved him like a father. Disgust or no, he'd do what he deemed best for New Prosperity

The few stragglers of the night gave the passing soldiers a wide berth. The north quarter looked pleasant under the cool moonlight, but the smoke and sounds of metallurgy from the industrial district wormed their way in.

A nudge of the sword kept Drake moving to the stables, filled with Appaloosas, Choctaws, and Mustangs, none of which were for him. In front of the stable lay a small, uncovered wagon containing four shackles. Two of the knights grabbed hold of Drake and forced him into the wagon. Drake felt the deathly chill of the iron shackles licking his wrists and ankles. He lay face up watching the few shining stars glistening through the blankets of rainclouds.

"Charming," he grumbled. He could sense the rebel spies watching and could almost hear their laughter.

146

ZORA

Zora sat facing the open window looking out onto the bustling underground streets of Ellora. Heaters, streetlamps, generators, and a dozen other machines powered the hidden city. Apartments and homes snaked upward for hundreds of feet much like skyscrapers lining the streets of an industrious city.

Zora marveled at how people lived here, wondering how far down this world extended. The aromas of baked fish and sweet potatoes wafted up toward her. According to the small clock in the apartment, the midnight hour approached. Zora's limber muscles yearned for movement.

Her internal stirring rapidly turned to claustrophobia. Her breaths grew short and shallow. She picked up her weapon off the nightstand and proceeded to the door, grabbing the key carelessly laid on a wayward stool. She moved across the hall toward Thos's room. The guards monitored her movements yet made no move to stop her from seeing him. Zora knocked on the door. While she waited for Thos to answer, she noticed the lifeless faces of Old World people carved on the hallway. They gave her the creeps.

"Kiss my ass later," Thos said while opening the door. "Oh… hello. I thought you were literally anyone else."

"Hey, I don't like being down here alone," Zora said with an anxious smile.

"I get it, these faces are scary as hell. Come on in, mi cava es su cava," Thos said, waving her in. He noticed the guards at the door and jokingly invited them in too. He closed the door when they sneered at him. Zora and Thos took a seat at the small plain kitchen table where his half-eaten meal resided.

"Ya alright? Don't worry about those guys, we are their prizes for the moment," he said, as he forked bits of fried fish in his mouth. Zora picked up on his mounting anxiety. The two made small talk for a time.

"Homesick?" she asked.

"Absolutely. Wish I stayed home with Cass and let the workers take care of my problems," he laughed.

"There is an old creek just outside home, no matter what I did I always managed to end up there. I'd throw rocks in the water; about all there was to do most days. I grew tired of it. Now I just want to go back." Thos finished his meal and frowned.

"That's home for ya. Can't stand it 'til you leave it," Thos said.

"So is that why you're here, for protection?" she asked. Thos pulled an unlabeled glass bottle from his icebox.

"Yep. They hate me less than Aric, so here I am," Thos said, directing the comment more toward himself than her. Zora stared longingly at his drink. He sighed and handed it to her.

"A bad position to be in," Zora said. Thos cocked his head and stared at her, causing her mild irritation. She cocked her head to match his and responded with a large toothy grin.

"It's nice not to be the odd one, well not the only one," Thos said, tossing a crumpled napkin into a small metal trash container. He poured her another round and kept the bottle for himself.

The two chatted and drank, growing more loose-lipped with every sip. Thos's humorous persona vanished, and a more sincere one took over. "I'll be honest with you, I am a terrible farmer, and just about broke. I hate working that farm, and it's suckin' me dry. The rebels want to prop me up as some messiah, and those assholes put me in this position in the first place. The rancher's association has wanted my land for a while now, and if Aric doesn't get to me first, they'll be next in line. I need these bastards even more than they need me. If you're part of this, too, I imagine that you must be in a similar situation," Thos said.

Zora did not respond and Thos chose not to press the issue. Thos yawned loudly. The white light flickered. "I think it's bed-time," Thos said. Zora stood up and headed for the door. She didn't trust anyone, but she liked Thos Averill.

"I like talking to you. We'll have to do it again, soon," she said, opening the door.

"Sure… just don't tell Joe what you heard, all right?"

"Our little secret," Zora replied with a smile.

Zora heard raised voices and a commotion from the street below. She and Thos hurried to the window and peered out. A small crowd had gathered around a burly, bearded man with an absurdly large two-handed sword strutting about. The man thrust his blade in the ground. Behind him on a long cart laid the body of cow-sized lizard, a black-scaled snallygaster common in southern Heartland. The short, stocky hunter pointed at a woman in the crowd.

"Show some love for mighty drakeslayer!" he cried. The woman ran to him, wrapping her arms around him. Out of the corner of his eye, Thos saw Zora shaking her head.

"Does every town have a braggart?" she asked. Thos folded his arms and nodded.

"There was one in Greenfield a few years back. Tiny little fellow that carried a scythe and called himself The Harvester," Thos said.

"What happened to him?" Zora inquired.

"He was going to slay some fabled demon said to live around here. Ate some bad fish and shit himself to death."

"Ufff!" Zora replied.

After a few minutes of gawking, the crowd dispersed. Zora bid Thos goodnight and walked the cavernous halls of the city, easily losing the guards on her tail. She made her way from the hustle and bustle of the crowds toward the less populated areas. With some alcohol in her, claustrophobia posed less of a hindrance. She took in her surroundings to keep her mind off things. Drops of water echoed like gunshots through the dark tunnels. Hulking warriors carved in the walls decorated the tunnels going down toward catacombs that wrapped around a temple far removed from everything else. Beams of light poured out from the walls like eight orange eyes. The anxiety returned, and this time walking through the city didn't help. Her only hope lay in meditation.

She doubled back to her room. She sat on the floor and prepared "mind's eye," the hallucinogenic incense of the Fey. The incense calmed her nerves, and her body took on a buoyant quality. One moment she sat crossed legged in the underground lodging and the next she sat in the grove near her childhood home. The churning waters of Luna Creek filled her ears, causing her to lose herself in serenity. The giant Fey called Redwood scouted among the treetops while Skye fought imaginary monsters near the circle of stones.

The cloudless blue sky looked down lovingly upon Zora, but she suddenly sensed something was wrong. Zora floated effortlessly through the community. A steady buzzing sound cut through the silence. Soaring through the air, she scurried up toward the house of Venus, the highest of the treetop houses. Like a spirit, she passed through the door. The crimson-haired Venus lay in bed watching the birds perched on her window. The buzzing continued. Instinctively, Zora zipped around the trees for the origin of the noise. Reaching out to the closest villager, she pressed her smooth fingers onto the old crone's shoulder. Touching Wicca's flesh elicited no response. The buzzing grew louder, becoming a painful drilling in her skull.

Rubbing her temples failed to drive the buzzing out. Shadows danced in the distance. The buzzing grew louder until it reached its peak. Her head throbbed with pain. Her vision blurred. The world became a violent tornado of green and brown. The shadows moved with greater speed and ferocity. The buzzing stopped and simultaneously the black shapes vanished. Her heart sank. A monstrous black shape rose from the ground with burning green eyes. The titanic horror uttered sounds like the shredding of metal; the other black shapes fell upon her. The sounds in her head turned to words.

"She is ours."

Zora now sat cross-legged back in the familiar apartment complex, exhausted after her meditation. Her clothes were drenched in cold sweat. The thoughts weighed heavy upon her, as strong as they did when she first left home. Zora removed her clothes and climbed into bed, wrapping up in the cool, soft sheets. She hoped sleep would ease her mind. Before Zora drifted off into a dreamless slumber, she heard the terrible voice again.

"She is ours."

GREGOR

Under the cover of darkness, Gregor made his way to the crumbling manor at the heart of Evansboro. Blackthorne soldiers and Godric's militiamen patrolled the streets in alarmingly high numbers, courtesy of the looming civil war.

Though not the stealthiest person, Gregor eluded the patrols. The manor itself was unguarded, allowing Gregor to slip in the front door. The doors opened up to a huge entryway with carpeted staircase. A cocktail of dust and grime assaulted Gregor the moment he stepped inside. He waited for his eyes to adjust to the dark, then slipped down the hallways, moving from room to room. The decayed paintings disturbed him. The chipped paint and fading colors coupled with black pits for eyes and mouths gave the faces nightmarish qualities. Gregor looked for signs of Old World technology: light from unknown sources, areas with high heat, low humming, electrical surges, and headaches—these unexplainable phenomena appeared supernatural to the common man.

Dipping under the ropes that blocked off the back areas, he moved through the kitchens, careful not to draw the attention of the men outside. Light from the entryway caught the edge of his vision. He followed it taking in every detail of his surroundings, every object, every sound, and every rancid smell. From the corner of his eye, he noted a white shape observing his movements. He rubbed his eyes making sure it wasn't wishful thinking. The shape moved up the stairs. With his EMF detector drawn, Gregor scanned for any signs of the ancient world. The meter spiked with a rhythmic humming.

Gregor followed the light upstairs, as appeared and disappeared in each room. The light took the shape of a human woman. Gregor's heart fluttered, and the excitement started to bubble inside him. The light vanished in the room ahead. Gregor braced for a confrontation only to find another cold, empty room. He let out a disappointed sigh and walked to the window, not hiding when he realized no one paid the old house any mind.

The streets were quiet as a ghost town. A few people huddled near the mayor's house a few blocks away. A circle of men argued with Godric, while armored guards played keep away with civilians. Gregor made out a reflection in the window that was not his own. He squinted for a better view and saw a young woman's face. His heart stopped, and his sword fell to the floor with a loud clang. Gregor blinked and the face vanished.

A loud crash sounded from downstairs. He picked up his sword and followed the sounds, which led him to a roped off area leading downstairs. The detector started humming again, more intense with each step. Gregor stepped over the rope and moved down the steps.

A faint tapping sound emanated from the bowels of the house. The bottom floor was even worse off than the neglected areas shown to the public. The hallway to his right had collapsed long ago. Gregor saw through the wreckage the halls beyond, which smelled of rot. He went down the other way toward the cellar and saw a huge warning sign plastered on the wall about the patches of green mold. He thought about how many years he'd just lost inhaling a mold colony.

A sudden burst of heat smacked Gregor. He pulled a small light from his pocket. Light filled the dank cellar, revealing a brunette woman in a pale turquoise nightgown. Stumbling back, he cursed loudly. He gathered his wits and took a defensive stance. He blinked and again found the figure gone. Out of the corner of his eye, he spied three more pale figures moving down to areas he couldn't reach. He pushed aside the refuse blocking the hall and crawled through.

A ghostly shape walked ahead with a casual pace, and he followed suit. The bits and pieces of rubble crashed to the ground behind him. Judging from his experiences so far, he believed this place had an infestation of wisps. Wisps were a type of electrical energy that played back events that had occurred in a location. The light ahead took the form of a man sprinting. Gregor moved forward at an unchanging, cautious pace. Energy pulsated through the decaying hallways. The winding hallways lead to an iron door, rusted shut.

Using a Vigilant designed cutter, he sliced through the iron door. Pushing it aside, he stepped through to a massive entryway to another house hidden below the surface. A yellow chandelier flickered above. The hall had a lived-in feel, complete with two entwined skeletons on a hole-filled couch. A transparent man and woman argued in front of the fireplace. The female disappeared. The male figure doused himself in gasoline. He lit a match and became engulfed in spectral flame. Gregor crept closer, seeing a nameless black shadow rocking back and forth down the hall. The playback sequences were becoming stronger, too strong. *This isn't from wisps*, Gregor realized.

He followed the lights to the large bathroom at the back of the underground house. A skeleton lay crumpled in in the tub. A low hum filled Gregor's ears. When he blinked, the crumbled bones were replaced with a woman bearing a tired expression. The woman wept uncontrollably and swallowed a handful of pills. The image sped up. She held a knife in her hand. She dug the blade deep into her forearms and up her wrists. The blood flowed into the tub. The woman closed her eyes and lay back, assuming the position of the bones. The digital playback crackled, for a second, Gregor glimpsed the dead figure smiling at him. The playback fast-forwarded to the apparent father hugging the woman's lifeless corpse.

When the images vanished, Gregor picked up scratching sounds from somewhere else in the old house. Back in the hall, the father from his previous vision pointed a gun to his head and the splattered fragments of his brain flung toward Gregor. Gregor swatted at the fragments, the pieces disappearing upon contact. The EMF detector hummed wildly before exploding in his hand. All of the ghostly figures played out their last moments again. Gregor became tired of this game.

"Face me, demon!" The ghosts faced him and vanished, leaving a static howl in their wake. The walls trembled. A familiar voice came from behind him.

"Too late, brother, as always," came the voice. The ghostly apparition of his brother stared him down with hateful eyes. He knew at once this was a specter. Specters were a particularly nasty kind of demon. Like all demons, they were the direct result of abused technology. Specters fed off the electrical energy of objects, people, animals, and even wisps. They were the manifestation of those that used long-distant communication technology to torment others. Like their Old World counterparts, these demons could drive humans to suicide.

"You won't fool me!" Gregor roared. The imposter walked over to a skeleton crumpled in the corner, a pile of bones wrapped in the tattered robes of a Vigilant crusader.

"He died right here," the demon said, with a devilish grin. Another image of Matthew Pavane appeared over the corpse. The exhausted and terrified Matthew swung blindly at an unseen attacker. He cupped a wound at his side trying to keep from bleeding out.

"He just wanted a life beyond the service, and you disowned him for it. Years of guilt proved too much to bear. He heard about me and came to redeem himself. He wasn't worth my time," the demon snickered. The image of Matthew fell to the floor and assumed the position of the bones.

"He's not dead," Gregor snapped back.

"How would you know?"

Gregor's defense waned, and doubt crept in. In truth, Gregor didn't know the fate of his brother. Specters were sadists at heart, gaining pleasure from the pain of others. The specter leeched off Gregor's energy while he grappled with his doubts.

"You're not a satisfying meal. I suppose Godric grew tired of our arrangement and sent you to end it, finally grew a conscience," the demon said. Gregor noticed fresh corpses littering the back wall. Gregor humored his foe for a moment.

"Are you telling me the mayor gives you victims and you protect him?" Gregor couldn't trust the demon; however, he had dealt with humans more than willing to make such arrangements with one.

"Power does funny things to people, but it keeps me well fed." Gregor cut the conversation short when he realized the demon drew off other sources of energy besides his own.

"Let's hurry this up. I have things to do," Gregor said. The form of his brother convulsed violently, twitching and contorting in inhuman ways. The flesh peeled away, to an eyeless face with a freakishly large grin of jagged black teeth wrapping around its face. Fingers melted together, becoming large clubs of razor-sharp bones. The body grew bulky and became an image of electric static. Normal weapons didn't work on a creature without flesh, but Gregor's sword was no normal weapon. Vigilant weaponry utilized electromagnetic pulses, ironically one of the very things that started the Second Dark Age. Wires ran from inside the hilt of his sword and up through the blade. The wires connected to circuits that when switched on could harm such creatures. The charge itself was diminished due to the metal surrounding the circuit casings, however, he'd yet to face something capable of withstanding it.

Gregor charged at the demon, running straight through its static form. The demon roared in pain and took physical form. Gregor jumped back, narrowly avoiding a swipe from its clubbed hands. Gregor's sword went through the ghostly form, causing it to respond with cries of agony. The house groaned. Gregor caught one of the demon's electrostatic clubs to his chest. Energy surged through his body. His heart pounded, almost to the point of bursting in his chest. Gregor retreated from the fight in the hopes the arrogant monster would choose to torment him rather than kill him outright. He moved back through the hallways to keep a few rooms away from the static hum.

The images of the demon's victims wandered about the house looking for Gregor. The demon took the form of the woman from the bathtub with the split open arms. Sparks shot from the electric apparition.

"I've spent many centuries in this place," it said in a sweet, feminine tone. Blood seeped from the ethereal form only to disappear upon contact with the floor. Gregor crept from room to room, avoiding the demon in its human guises.

"I am in the very walls now. It's forgotten machines give me life," the demon said. The demon's voice grew deep, reverberating like a hellish bell. The words gave Gregor an idea, one with possibly disastrous consequences. The bleeding woman drew too close for comfort.

Gregor jumped up and moved to the curtain. The female figure reverted to its demonic form and walked toward him. Gregor sprinted to the main hall, avoiding the doors slamming behind him. The demon phased through the door, almost within reach of Gregor. Swooping up the gas canister, Gregor threw it to the ground in anger when he found nothing inside. He had one last desperate option. Inside his pocket, he had a few basic medical supplies, including a bottle of rubbing alcohol.

The monster took on a more corporeal form to consume its

victim. Gregor pulled out the rubbing alcohol out. With a simple twist, the top came off.

"Stay with me," the demon said.

Gregor flung the rubbing alcohol at the demon. He jumped back a split second before the liquid hit the sparks. A shower of blue flame shot forth from the entity. Gregor sprinted with all his might as the flames quickly engulfed the manor. He dashed out of the manor as fast as his body allowed. The demon, now in flesh, scrambled to catch him. The eyeless monster grinned at him with its jagged black teeth. Gregor ran through the door back up to the tour area. He darted outside and crashed to the ground just outside the manor, a few feet from a dumbfounded Cedric. His crusaders did not even get the chance to utter any words.

"Let it burn," Gregor demanded. One of his soldiers carried a bottle of vodka, courtesy of their house. Gregor snatched the bottle from his hand, growling back at the man when he whined about the theft. Gregor tore off a piece of his robe, making an improvised Molotov cocktail. Finishing his work, he barked for one of his smokers to ignite the thing. He tossed it at the building to hasten its demise.

"Eventful night?" Cedric asked. Gregor shook his head. Citizens of the town emerged from their homes screaming at the sight.

"Let's go, let's go!" Gregor said nervously, running right past his men.

"You realize you burned down a historical landmark, right?" Cedric asked.

He kept running as he talked, going straight for his horse. His crusaders followed suit after a moment of intense bewilderment. Gregor turned back to see the once proud mansion collapsing behind him.

ARIC

Screams of anguish reverberated through Fort Alexander and down the mountainside. The chubby Edwin Whitehall barely resembled a man now. The boastful mill owner that found himself born into one of the most successful families in the nation was now a quivering mass of blood, tears, and shredded meat. Aric himself whipped Edwin, finding the act intensely therapeutic. Aric's whiskey-laced breath wormed into Edwin's wounds, stinging his tender flesh. Edwin's cohorts were chained to the wall behind him, wearing despair on their faces. Edwin was Aric's best chance at identifying the revolutionaries; killing a family member of the Board of Directors was icing on the cake. Aric mocked Edwin's pleas for mercy.

"I don't want to hurt you. Oh, who am I kidding; yes I do," Aric said with a smile. A few precise jabs to Edwin's jaw shattered it. The Whitehall family had its fair share of blood on their hands, more than the Blackthornes if the rumors of them funding the gang wars in Mexico were true. Aric didn't feel a shred of guilt tearing Edwin apart.

Beads of sweat flew off Aric and onto the mangled Edwin, the white ceramic armor of Aric no longer perfect thanks to the streaks of blood. Edwin's head rolled across his fat neck searching for anyone sympathetic to his plight only to be met with pitiable responses.

"I know you're guilty." Venom dripped from Aric's every word. He sweetened his tone. Rain gently sprinkled down, helping wash the sweat and blood off the prince. Aric opened his cracked lips for a few precious drops. He circled his captive.

"Don't you care that people are dying? Your friends are slaughtering indiscriminately. Are you willing to trade thousands to oust a few?"

Aric enjoyed the damp smell of morning, the cool water made him feel alive. Edwin buried his head in the collar of his torn velvet clothes and attempted eye contact through eyelids nearly swollen shut. All of the other captives stared down in an act of noncompliance.

"I will sweeten the offer, help us and you will gain our protection. You may be loyal to your friends, but are they loyal to you?" Aric stuck out his pointer finger and thrust it into Edwin's stomach. He pondered his captive's uncharacteristic defiance. Aric ran his arid tongue against the roof of his mouth, itching for something stronger than rainwater.

He casually strolled off toward his private chambers, giving the soldiers the cue to take over. With a slam of the door, Aric withdrew from his fruitless efforts. He reached for one of his half-empty whiskey bottles decorating the floor of his bare room. The radio in his room provided the only long-distance communication in the area, though he wouldn't know since it seldom worked. He wanted to strangle the so-called telecom maintenance man, forgetting he had already done that. He slammed his fist into the broken radio, taking it out for good. Aric no longer had a radio or a phone.

He flung his sweat and rain-covered armor to the corner as if it was now forever ruined. Taking a swig of whiskey, he cursed himself for being so quick to hit the bottle. He scooped up the whiskey bottles and tossed them out the window.

The dreary fortress became a melting pot of despair and frustration at the heart of a burgeoning war. Nearly all of the soldiers stationed here came from elsewhere. Most of its occupants spent their lives shuttling back and forth between forts and outposts throughout the region. Aric longed for the comfort of Kingsbury. To his great dismay, Aric even missed his estranged wife. Despite it being a blatantly obvious political marriage devoid of love, he missed her. He imagined the radio working and the honesty flowed like his hidden stash of liquor.

"I have done nothing right, but I'm trying." His eyes grew moist with tears as the train of thought continued without having to be spoken. I never did anything to anyone that didn't deserve it. I… one day you will see I'm right. His thoughts grew muddled as the drinks continued. Heat surged through his body with just enough of a warning to make it to the bathroom to vomit. He poured his innards out for over half an hour. After sobering up, Aric steeled himself to do what needed to be done.

Thrusting the door open, he walked backed out into the courtyard. Edwin raised his head to verbalize his pain, but only produced spit. Soldiers in the courtyard took formation when Aric reappeared. The prisoners raised tired heads to meet his predatory gaze.

"Answer me or die," Aric said with sinister calmness. Gasps burst forth from some of the prisoner's lips while others closed their eyes to wait for the inevitable. Aric maintained his icy demeanor, approaching the bloody mess named Edwin. Edwin mustered up enough courage for one last ballsy comment.

"Your days are numbered," Edwin said, grinning through broken teeth. Aric sighed, and pulled a small knife from his sheath on his hip. He drove the knife into Edwin's waist and slowly pulled the blade upward.

Edwin's cries pierced their ears, like the yelping of a slaughtered piglet. The blood bathed Aric in a crimson glow as Edwin's guts spilled out over him. One of the other captives wept. Aric's eyes peered into his as he surrendered to base desires.

"They'll be here in three days," the prisoner said. Aric's teeth ground together and his vision blurred.

A few cannons lay in the underground chamber, and he decided that the rest of the day should be devoted to getting them up and running. Aric's body surged with heat.

"Get these cannons restored on the double," he said with cheer. He pointed at his scouts. "Alert all patrols to return here immediately." With his eyes he motioned for Edwin's corpse to be thrown down the mountain, two soldiers rushed to do the job. "We'll give our guests a grand welcome!" The prisoners stared lifelessly at the courtyard floor.

The rain began to fall in torrents, and lighting crackled in the valley below. The men outside took the prisoners to the chambers underground, leaving only Aric and his patrolmen outside. Aric did not move. He allowed the heavy rain to wash over him.

The raindrops grew too cold for Aric, forcing him to retreat inside. A soldier played banjo in a room just below him, stolen from one of the prisoners. Aric had trained his whole life for war, as did all in the Blackthorne family all the way back to Alexander I. He then imagined himself riding back through the streets of Kingsbury as the beloved hero.

"The Blackthornes will endure. We always endure." The lighting grew closer, zapping at trees down in the misty valleys. Aric could sense in his marrow his time at Fort Alexander was coming to an end.

THOS

Thos and Zora sat on chair-like rocks just outside the central building, awaiting their meeting with Joseph Kerr. Thos kicked the ground in front of him, annoyed at the early meeting. Without his nine-plus-hours sleep, he grew antsy. Zora and Thos inspected the cave walls adorned with the grim stories of the early years of the Second Dark Age. Strings of lightbulbs above illuminated the crude drawings of collapsing skyscrapers, tribal wars, and the emergence of demons.

Around the corner, the surly hero from last night approached in great strides, wearing leather armor covered in snallygaster bones. The warrior peeked around, clearly wanting the attention of his peers. The short, stocky figure puffed out his bulky chest to drive the point home. The obnoxious man slapped the ass of a passing woman, who responded with a slap of her own across his face. Thos couldn't tell which of them enjoyed it and which didn't. The attack did nothing to remove his wide toothy grin. The woman smiled. The man and the woman locked lips. The woman walked away.

"Glorious day, is not? You must be Thos and Zora. Melvin Shor's the name," the man said. Thos stifled a laugh, trying not to stare at the red hand engraved on Melvin's right cheek. Zora rolled her eyes. Melvin extended his hand in friendship and Thos responded after it was clear that the man wouldn't lower his hand until Thos did. Thos wondered how this man stood straight with that absurd greatsword strapped to his back.

"Nice sword, isn't it? I named her Elsa after my ex-wife because it's a huge bitch," Melvin beamed proudly.

The three received stares from the first shifters scurrying about the underworld community. Thos broke the awkward silence with a loud cough.

"How long is this gonna take?" Thos directed the question at Melvin.

"No idea. I'm just here to kill," Melvin said with a shrug and grunt.

Moments later, the chamber filled with the boom of the opening door followed by a man descending the rusty staircase. Thos groaned at the sight of Joseph Kerr. Joseph's mustache, Thos noticed, grew farther out on one side than the other; this vexed him terribly. Thos scratched the side of his face as if Joseph's asymmetrical mustache was his own.

"Come on," Joseph said. The three ascended the stairs and entered the lobby. Joseph closed the giant double doors behind them. The central lobby lacked the grandeur Thos expected, just a few simple chairs lining the walls. Idle chatter echoed from beyond the walls of the next room.

Joseph pushed open the wooden door, and the three entered the chamber. The chamber itself was cramped but made up for it in verticality. The room consisted of three floors overlooking a long table and a podium in the middle, like a classroom. A large chandelier made of dozens of deer antlers hung above. Thos counted at least 300 men and women in the room, all bitter, angry, and not likely to fight in the coming battles.

"Man they look like assholes," Thos muttered. Thos's words echoed louder than he intended. He felt Joseph's hateful glare burning a hole through the back of his skull.

"Hi," Thos said, with a wave and a stupid grin. Thos and Melvin took seats behind the lectern. Thos grew uncomfortable by the attention, while Melvin appeared re-energized by it. Melvin ran his fingers through the mass of tendrils he called a beard, knocking a few crumbs loose. Thos tuned out the rhetoric, only perking up when it concerned him.

"These two men to my right will play a major role in the battles to come," Joseph said. "Melvin will be leading the troops and Mr. Averill will be supplying our campaign. We march to the fort within the hour!"

Thunderous applause erupted in the chamber as Joseph thrust his arms into the air. Joseph relished the spectacle for a few minutes before exiting the stage to chambers further up the spire. Thos frowned at the thought of following an army campaign, but being an enemy of the state now meant he needed to follow orders.

"I better not have to fight," he blurted out.

"You join a rebellion and don't plan to fight?" Melvin asked.

"I'm here for moral support. Joe thinks a well-to-do farm mogul rising up against the crown will *inspire* everyone," Thos replied. Melvin grunted his displeasure. Thos wondered just what they had in mind for her and the Fey.

"What's gonna happen to her?" said Thos, asking Joseph directly. Zora looked at him, smiling at his concern. "She helps us at the fort, and then we help the Fey with their problems. That's all you need to know," Joseph replied.

The group continued the one-sided conversation as they walked out of the meeting chambers. Following Joseph out of the main cavern, the group moved to a tunnel dimly lit by wall sconces fashioned out of snallygaster bones. Joseph crouched as he entered the tunnel but not the half-asleep Thos, who bonked his head on the low-hanging ceiling. A menagerie of curses filled the dark chambers.

The quintet navigated the silent darkness of winding tunnels guided only by sparse firelight. Along the way, the tunnel opened into a large area with a stream cutting through it. Joseph pointed out the translucent blindfish darting through the murky abyss. No bridge crossed the water. Joseph hopped across effortlessly, as did the others. The group moved through the blackness by hugging the walls. The drips and drops along the way were oddly comforting to Thos.

The areas close to the city were deathly humid, while the dark tunnels were bitter cold. In the claustrophobic hallways, they were forced to slide through single file, lacking enough space to use of their long blades. Intense manmade light and human chattering permeated the chambers ahead.

A few hundred men stood erect in the next chamber, brandishing knives, swords, spears, cudgels, axes, and various firearms. Joseph passed them, yet no salutes were exchanged. An opening in the adjacent cavern led to a massive stable and an exit back to the surface near a small village. When Joseph stepped into the stable, all others followed suit.

Joseph and his rebels all saddled up and headed to the outside world. The cold, damp air hit Thos like a ton of bricks, jolting him out of his groggy state. Beside Thos, Melvin held his leather bag over his head to shield himself from the raindrops.

It drizzled throughout the trek, following them at every step of the way as their constant, unwanted companion. Every now and then, the guerrilla army veered off the roads to avoid heavy traffic areas. This zigzagging went on for a few hours until they arrived the Great Highway.

"The Great Highway. It stretches across the entirety of New Prosperity. They say it first began as a trade route from Kingsbury to the remaining towns after the war, built upon the remains of the Old World roads. Take it in because it'll be nothing but trees from here on out," Joseph said. Crumbling patches of road littered the ground ahead, more like giant stepping-stones for the world's largest kid. Some patches of road were large concrete islands among the seas of grass.

The highway itself was a monstrosity stretching across New Prosperity, connecting just about every important place in the country. Thos gave it one final look. With weapons at the ready, the group ventured off the beaten path to unfamiliar territory.

DRAKE

Drake Hale cursed himself for falling asleep but cursed the rain even more for interrupting it. He growled before spitting some rainwater out. Thick grey clouds whizzed by from what little he could see outside his mobile prison. His driver, a one-eyed man named Hadron, offered Drake his good morning.

"Morning, Little Dragon," Hadron said.

Drake grimaced. If there was one thing that really got Drake's blood up it was the nickname from his bloody past under Aric. Hadron told a little story about Drake's career, good and bad.

Drake struggled to break free of his bindings. Drake's head bounced off the cart, causing more laughter at his expense. The shackles around his wrists and ankles held firm and secure, this time captured by trained professionals. The little slack in the chains prevented Drake from slithering free, and a throbbing head discouraged any more attempts for now.

"Might as well get comfy," Hadron advised. Drake had an idea of how to get free using the rainwater to slide out of the shackles. It was a sound idea, until the rain stopped. Drake felt the inevitability of facing Aric, and relished assassinating him far less than he expected.

The cart stopped, giving Drake a partial view of a Blackthrone outpost with a few tents and scout towers. Drake remained shackled to the cart as his jailers ate and drank with the men stationed at the outpost. Drake smelled the roasting pork and fresh beer accentuated by the banter of off-duty soldiers. Heavy rain began to fall again. Drake suppressed the urge to piss as best he could. He heard the jaunty soldiers using him as the butt of many of their jokes. Fear of an imminent rebel attack forced him to act.

"The rebels will attack soon. I'm more use to you if I can shoot back," Drake said. The soldiers ignored him." Drake yelled. He repeated it over and over, forcing them to acknowledge him.

"I will get free you know," The squad leader walked over with a smug grin and a mug of beer.

"You need a drink," a soldier replied before dumping the mug of beer on Drake's face. "Looks like you made a mess of yourself. Let me help you with that." He kicked one of the poles out that held of the tarp causing it to fall down on Drake. The man threw the tarp off Drake, as he expected. Though not the best option, some rainwater was a way to help Drake slide his way out of the restraints.

The soldiers finished their meals, sat around a campfire, and caught up on current events. The topic turned to the end of their tours and pining for families long distant. Drake hated hearing about families, knowing how many soldiers would never see them again. Hours rolled by as the men chatted.

A crash in the distance brought the festivities to an instant halt. All soldiers sprang to their feet and drew swords. A single shot blew out the back of Hadron's skull. A volley of arrows and bullets dropped the soldiers near the campfire and on the towers, one hitting the wheel beside Drake. Rebels barreled into the camp armed with swords, spears, bows, and guns. The Blackthorne troops fell slaughtered in only a few minutes. The youngest Blackthorne man lay dying on the ground. One rebel kicked his face repeatedly until it caved in like a rotted melon. A well-placed shot connected with the gunmen at the top of the outpost sending him over the side. Drake finally managed to slip his hands out from the bindings during the massacre. Hands free, Drake unlocked his ankle shackles and dashed from the cart. A few stray arrows reduced the food cart once housing Drake to a pincushion.

Drake sprinted away from the outpost. A loud bang preceded a bullet nearly clipping Drake's foot that stopped him in his tracks. With all rifles pointed at Drake, he raised his hands.

The rebels lined up, taking up the position of a firing squad. Drake's heart raced. A voice interfered just in time. "Stop!" said the voice. The senior rebel approached him. The man had speckled grey hair and one dead eye. A scar from the side of man's right lip traveled up one side of his face over his ear, giving him a freakishly large grin. He wore a large camo jacket with the emblem of a blood-soaked devil. The man regarded the carnage with complete indifference.

Drake knew the meaning of the symbol. The Red Devils were a notorious mercenary band in the southern states with a cold-blooded reputation. Red Devils were just as much a threat to the common man should the price be right. The merc, whom his comrades called Keller, addressed Drake.

"You just can't get away from us," Keller said.

"Apparently," Drake replied.

"You're our hostage. You are free to move about the camp, but our eyes and guns will be on you at all times. Please run, we could use a little target practice." After making his threats, Keller dipped inside one of the tents. Rebel soldiers tossed the bodies into a pile and lit them on fire.

After relieving himself, Drake paced around anxiously and pondered why the rebels had spared him. He walked the burning corpse pile at the outpost's western edge to the scattered collection of gear pulled from the dead. He sifted through the goods for his most prized possession: the sword commissioned for him by King Anselm. At the bottom of the pile, he found his sword. Anxiety bubbled inside Drake when he heard the thunderous sound of an even larger group approaching.

THOS

GREEN SPECKS OF emerging foliage added a nice color change to the dismal march to Fort Alexander. Thos stirred restlessly on his horse, mumbling to himself about the increasing spring rain that only fell at the most inopportune time. Clouds lingered maliciously over the Appalachians. Melvin stretched, habitually gripping his sword while periodically glancing over at Zora.

"Want to hear of my snallygaster hunt?" Melvin said, announcing it more than asking. Everyone nearby responded with a unanimous "No." Melvin sulked.

"It could save your life," Melvin said.

"I know about snallygasters all too well. Lost my brother to one," Thos said darkly, then went quiet for a time. Thos scratched his head anxiously afterward, a telltale sign of emotions bubbling to the surface. Thoughts of Thos's late brother put him in a foul mood, why he steered clear of the subject completely.

Joseph raised his hand. His army replied with raised swords, guns, and any killing instruments on hand. A column of smoke rose up ahead. Nervous tension permeated the air as they approached. The rebels braced for combat. The army cautiously approached, and a voice rang out again. Upon calling back, men jumped out from behind the trees, blending in seamlessly with their surroundings. The camouflaged troops led the rebels toward the smoke.

At the top, the group found a series of tents and scout towers, formerly belonging to the royal army. On the left side of the road, men gathered around a fire. The army passed off their horses to a handful of wranglers and all headed to tables of salted pork, hot bread, and ale. Thos noticed a gathering of mercenaries all sporting the image of a blood-soaked devil, an image juxtaposed to the rebel's cause of justice.

Thos recognized the man clad in black standing alone.

"Son of a bitch," he muttered. Drake walked away from the fire and waved his hand in response to Thos's cries. Melvin followed the crowd toward the food lines while Zora and Thos approached Drake.

"How's my favorite hostage?" Thos asked.

"Peachy," Drake replied. Drake noticed the Fey scout. He extended his hand toward her awkwardly; she did not respond. Thos whispered something her ear.

"It's a handshake," he said. Zora raised an eyebrow.

"I know what it is. I've never had a man do that," Zora replied. Awkwardly his hand slowly fell to his side.

"Oh… uh… pleasure to meet you, I'm Drake Hale."

"Just kidding. I'm Zora," she said, brandishing an alluring smile. Thos laughed, having a little fun at the flustered man clearly attracted to the woman. Drake responded with a smile of his own, something he clearly needed to practice.

"Why are you out here?" Zora asked.

"Long story," Drake said tiptoeing around the truth.

"Got captured," Thos said.

"Okay, maybe not that long," Drake said with embarrassment. "Hey, Thos, perhaps you can use your good standing to keep these gentlemen from shooting me?" Drake asked not entirely in jest.

"Joe hates me… but I'll see what I can do. You should get

comfy though, I doubt we're leaving the circus any time soon," Drake groaned. He spent the rest of the time with Thos and Zora. The trio ate dinner together in a corner away from the rebel forces. Thos tossed sticks into the small campfire while the three recounted their separate adventures. Melvin joined them, sitting down between Thos and Zora. He spoke little now, focusing his efforts on pulling pieces of shredded pork from his beard.

"What's your story?" Drake asked, adjusting his boots.

"I'm the go-to fighter for this bunch, helping them with threats," Melvin said proudly.

"Like a Knight-Ambassador?' Drake asked.

"Eh… sort of. To have a woman in every city and the head of every beast on my wall… that's my dream." Thos saw Drake developed a dislike for the man.

"It'll remain a dream. Anyway, where did you say you were from?" Drake asked.

"Nowhere in particular, just all over Heartland. Had a family once upon a time but they left me to die, so fuck 'em," Melvin said.

"Family is always an interesting subject," Drake said. Thos speculated on some of Drake's own dicey family history.

"Aye, it is. It wasn't so bad, I guess. I found ways to stay fed. This bunch gave me steady work and I made a name for myself. Pretty good life now," Melvin said.

Thos found Melvin's evasiveness about Ellora amusing. He assumed Drake knew about it long before the rest of them did.

"What about you? I've heard you hail from the… Hale family," Melvin said, the sole person laughing at the pun.

"Indeed. We are the most affluent of the 'lower' noble houses, as my father liked to remind everyone at least once a day. I spent most of my time with Anselm and his sons. My parents mingled with the other nobles, angling for a seat on the Board. The king raised me while they were busy hobnobbing. He always said he saw something special in me. I heard many stories about the lofty accomplishments of my family. I hope someday I can get the family name back to that."

"What brought you all the way down here?" Zora asked

"I came here to keep Aric in check. It turned out, well, not as planned," he replied. Drake watched the crackling flames.

A cool breeze swept through the camp. The day dragged on, leaving eventually just the four of them, and a few watchmen, awake. The four of them, now buzzed, told stories growing less and less serious and coherent as the drinks continued to flow. Thos Averill didn't know what of think of these people yet, but he dubbed them as "potentials." Thos yearned for a few genuine friends. He'd need them in the days to come.

ANSELM

Beads of sweat rolled down Anselm's brow as he thrust his sword forward. Percival parried, and Anselm stumbled backward. *Old and weak*, Anselm thought. The words replayed over and over in his head.

"You all right, father?" Percival asked, not the least bit sweaty. Anselm panted heavily. He hunched over, heaved, and raised his arm for the universal "just a minute."

"Again," Anselm wheezed.

The practice armor hung loosely on him. The supple muscles of Anselm's youth had withered away ages ago, leaving him droopy and soft. Percival egged him on. Their swords clanged loudly when they connected. Percival's attacks decelerated over time, as did the king's from exhaustion. Sweat rolled down Anselm's brow like a floodgate had opened. Not long after, Anselm finally gave up and chose to hack away at the training dummies.

"I've really let myself go," Anselm said.

"You're busy leading a whole nation; that demands all your time," Percival replied.

"You and your brothers will all bear this weight soon enough. Aric will need you by his side when he becomes king. And not just your support—you must keep him in check," Anselm said sternly.

"Are you still retiring at year's end?" Percival asked.

"No," Anselm sighed. He ran his fingers along the edge the blade, blankly staring at his own reflection. "I love Aric, but he isn't ready. I fear I'll stay in this damnable job until it kills me." He laughed bitterly. With a vertical slice, Anselm's blade dug inside the neck of the training dummy. The two cleaned up and talked as father and son. Talk of Percival's travels through the city dominated much of the conversation.

"We need a vacation. We need get away," Anselm said. Anselm hated lying about a future he knew wouldn't come to the pass, but saying the words gave him a brief chance to enjoy the thought of a normal family life. Anselm had divulged all the necessary info about witches and warnings, still questioning his own sanity on some bits.

"It sounds nice, but it you know it won't happen. If what you were told is true, we have to be ready. We have people sneaking around the castle. You don't have to pretend things are going to be okay. I'm not a child anymore," Percival said.

"No, they won't, but it was nice to imagine," Anselm replied with despair. The conversation continued for a while longer. Even with thousands upon thousands of troops at his beck and call, Anselm no longer felt safe. Thoughts spiraled. Should the Blackthornes hide until things blew over? Be out in the public, not fazed but cautious? If witches and masked freaks could pop up anywhere, can anyone truly be safe? Percival grew antsy while Anselm's rapid-fire thoughts bounced off his skull.

"You have plans this evening. Go have fun, but be very careful. Never stray too far from your men," Anselm said, trying to seem cheerful.

"I won't take unnecessary risks. Thanks, Father. I don't think I'll make it to dinner tonight," Percival said, trying to hide his excitement so as not to disappoint Anselm further.

"I understand," Anselm replied. Percival threw on work clothes and fake beard and left.

Sore and exhausted, Anselm entered the royal bathhouse and threw off his clothes. The lure of the heated pool proved too great for the king to refuse. The entire Blackthorne family enjoyed the heated pool. Inside the royal bathhouse, servants tended the Blackthorne family's every need. One of the female attendants stripped off her clothes and approached Anselm. He motioned her away. *Too accustomed to Aric's needs*, Anselm thought.

Anselm sat in the warm water, nibbling on cheese and drinking the wine the servants brought him. Two marble lions sat on each side of the pool with chests thrust out and heads held high. Looking at the proud beasts turned Anselm's thoughts of his unsatisfactory performance in the training room.

Anselm motioned at another female attendant, wearing the swimwear.

"What do you need, your grace?" she asked.

"Just a back massage. Same as always," he insisted. In years past, he'd gladly seek release and solace in the arms of other women, but that changed when he met Abigail. "You're a rare man, my king," girl said.

"Not all royals are philanderers," he said. Anselm talked to the woman about life in the castle. The more she spoke, the more he caught the slightest hint of a French accent.

"From Gloire?" he asked.

"Oui. My name is Simone" she replied. He never realized how many of the maids, serving girls, and house workers were gifts from his neighbor.

"Do we take good care of you here?" he asked.

"Oui," Simone repeated. The massage worked all the tension out of Anselm's stiff, aching muscles. He grunted as Simone worked on his neck. Anselm's cock hardened beneath the waters.

"Stop," Anselm said. The bloated and skeletal faces of the Board bore into Anselm's brain, softening the problem. His chest tightened. "Please leave," he commanded.

Simone nodded and emerged from the water. Anselm looked away as she walked past the marble lions and out of the room. He noticed her there again out of the corner of his eye.

"I said leave," Anselm growled.

"I am not one of your caged whores," a voice replied.

Anselm glanced up to find a robed woman looking down at him. The right half of the woman's face appeared metallic and she now flaunted two luminescent green eyes. Anselm recognized the woman from the medical wing, now realizing what had become of his stolen medical equipment. Metallic wires protruded down her neck, running down beneath her robes. She noticed his eye movements and threw off her robes, showing the extent of her improvements. Thick plates replaced her abdominals. She turned around, revealing a sleek black spine. More surgical lines wrapped around her chest and major muscles, suggesting her next upgrades already planned. The faint hum of machinery emanated from inside her chest. Neon blue tubes ran down the right side of her head to her shoulders. Anselm's clothes and weapons were just out of arm's reach.

"We meet again, my king. Your... equipment is proving to be most helpful. I confess it's still a work in progress," she said. Anselm eyed the pistol lying with his clothes. She looked at him and sneered. "I still don't see why they chose you."

"Such flattery... especially from one wearing thousands worth of my equipment. What is it you want this time?"

"To help you. The masters believe we can help each other, and that helping you will help them. It's time we prepared for the future." The woman finally piqued the king's interest.

"How so?" he asked. The woman smiled.

ZORA

Zora awoke earlier than anyone else, as was always the case. She loved the smell of fresh dew and sight of the lavender sky peeking out from behind the trees; it made dealing with strangers and looming war easier. When no one watched, Zora snuck out of the camp to explore. She breathed in the morning air and found peace. A misshapen heart carved in a tree along the way made her heart soar.

She ventured farther from the area, double-checking on any eavesdropping scouts. Without the watchful eyes of the rebel host, she enjoyed nature. She delighted in walking in any given destination to see what she could find, especially the areas untouched by man.

She sensed another presence in the nearby treetops. Quietly, Zora's hand moved for her knife. She moved to adjust her boot, securely moving the dagger to her hand. She tossed the dagger with her full strength at the figure in the trees. With a clang, the dagger bounced off the figure, now wielding a curved blade. Dressed in forest camo, the figure scrambled down the trees, landing on the forest floor with feline grace. It threw off the camouflage revealing herself to be a Fey huntress. Hunters and huntresses were warrior-scouts that served as the communication lines among Fey communities. Her long, tripled-braided hair wrapped around her shoulder like a knotted serpent. Zora had seen this woman before during her last trip to the community southwest of her own. The woman was an expert archer called Notch. It did not surprise Zora that the Fey had scouts watching her.

"Zora," she said.

"I'm impressed. I didn't notice you," Zora replied. The huntress leaned up against her longbow made from a large antler.

"I've been watching you for many days now. It is good that you have contacted the rebels. We're pleased they've been honorable, but be on your guard, especially around those Red Devils." Zora nodded, irritated at Fey's attempt to babysit her.

"Are you keeping tabs on me?" Zora asked, a note of irritation in her voice.

"And them, it's good to know who our allies truly are," Notch replied. The huntress bobbed her head around to ensure no one spied on them. "Return home when your task is done. No one blames you for what happened."

Zora looked away. She still heard the screams and smelled the blood associated with her home. When she looked back, Notch was already halfway up the tree. Zora rushed back to the camp when she heard the rebel army waking, no one the wiser.

A crier went from tent to tent rousing the army for another day of marching. Out staggered the weary and poorly rested fighters not yet adjusted to the soldier life. The mercenaries doused the fires and cleaned up the camp.

Traveling with the rebel army made Zora uncomfortable. She never traveled in large groups, and certainly not with strangers. The rebel soldiers treated her well during her brief time with them, though some didn't seem too keen to have a lawless forest dweller in their midst.

At the edge of the camp, Joseph Kerr barked out orders. From behind him emerged the well-rested Thos Averill with coffee and bacon in hand. Joseph's eye twitched when Thos took another chunk out of quite possibly the loudest, crunchiest bacon in history.

"Dammit Thos, this ain't a vacation! Hurry up!" Joseph growled. He sneered at Thos. Thos waved his hand in annoyance and sipped his coffee. Zora noticed some Fey warriors from various communities had joined the ranks, per the agreement made with Joseph in return for his aid. A skeleton crew took up residence in the repurposed outpost. Melvin looked over some papers, squinting hard and repositioning them in the hopes the right angle would help him decipher them.

"I can't make out the numbers on this. I think they are Roman Numeros," Melvin said. Joseph immediately stopped what he was doing and turned to Melvin with a look of confusion, anger, and slight disgust.

"You know, Numero Uno," Melvin said, waving the papers to jog everyone's memory. Joseph walked over and snatched the papers from Melvin.

"Why don't you go do something else?" he demanded. The veins in Joseph's forehead pulsated as if he was on the verge of an aneurysm after the morning rounds with Thos and Melvin.

The stable masters brought forth the horses, and the war machine headed out. The rebels followed the old trails and passed glades and over the hills toward the remnants of the Appalachian Mountains, where Fort Alexander stood. A light breeze and rays of sunlight provided a tolerable climate for the slog ahead. Few words were spoken in the areas in which Blackthornes troops were reported to haunt.

When the whole of the army exited the woods, Joseph stopped and raised his hand. "Watch out, drakes have been spotted in the region. Keep your heads about you and they won't end up in one," Joseph said, trying to bury his own anxiety. Melvin perked up. Zora tracked the movements of animals scurrying through the underbrush. Melvin interrupted her train of thought.

"So, Drake, are you named after these things?" Melvin asked.

"We're both named for mythological creatures that aren't quite dragons, but close enough," Drake replied. Thos raised his hand and thrust his pointer finger into the air.

"A drake is also a duck," Thos interjected. Drake shook his head.

"Let's just call them snallygasters," Drake grumbled. Thos's jests did not distract the others from minding the surroundings.

Melvin's hands instinctively gripped the hilt of his sword. Zora had seen a few drakes in her lifetime and knew how dangerous they could be when startled or provoked. With permission from Joseph, she grabbed an assault rifle from the surplus cart and prepared for the worst.

The underbrush rustled off to the side followed by the loud thump of feet. The thumping sounds grew louder, joined by others, signaling to Zora a stampede headed their way. Without hesitation, a scout shot an arrow in the direction of the noises. A loud roar meant the arrow hit its mark. The group had only seconds to respond when an enraged drake charged at the archer. In a panic, the horses bolted in all directions, scattering from multiple snallygasters.

Covered in viridian scales and thin plates, the monstrous snallygasters were twice the size of horses, like gigantic versions of animals her father called "Komodo dragons." They were three feet tall and quadruple that in length, the perfect size for eating anything in the area. Zora quickly fired. One of her bullets popped the right eye of a drake. Zora's comrades panicked, worsening the situation.

The horses dashed as fast as their legs could move them. The massive lizards barreled into the stragglers. The force of the impact threw riders from their mares, including Drake Hale. Melvin's and Thos's horses ran from the largest, fattest lizards nipping at their heels. Zora fired at the biggest one, but its thick black plates deflected her shots. The beast puffed out its chest in defiance. She fired shots in the soft spots on the belly during its arrogant display. Melvin's horse made a desperate sprint back to the woods but caught the arrow-shaped head of the beast. Melvin hit the ground hard. He cried out in pain as he rolled to a stop in the grass.

It was up to Drake to save Melvin. Zora saw his hesitation when Drake saw a chance to escape. He made a movement toward the forest, but after belting out a loud curse, he turned back. Drake sped forth with sword raised at the black plated alpha slurping up the innards of Melvin's horse. It caught sight of Melvin's clumsy movements. Melvin clutched at his side, grimacing with pain. He had lost his gun in the attack, leaving him to rely on his giant sword. The beast barreled toward Melvin, abandoning the equestrian feast to get at him. Melvin raised his sword, shaking wildly. Zora covered them with gunfire.

The smallest of the snallygasters ran toward Zora, pulling her attention away from Melvin. The juvenile drake lacked the protective plating of adults. Shots in the legs, throat, and head slowed the beast but didn't stop it. A few shots through the neck sent it sliding forward, stopping a few paces in front of Zora's horse. Nearby, soldiers gathered around Zora in a vain attempt to shield her from harm.

"I'm fine. Help Melvin," she said. The soldiers refused to leave her side, so she rushed over toward the thick of battle forcing them to follow. Drake ran his hardest to reach his embattled comrades. Zora galloped toward him as well, using gunfire along the way to drive off one of the beasts. Melvin dodged the bull rush of the creature, swinging the blade wildly upon standing. The monster charged again, nearly connecting with Melvin's leg. Melvin dropped his sword while rolling out of the creature's way, leaving him an easy target. Drake ran up behind the beast. The beast moved to face Drake only to find a sword driven into its right eye.

The last thrash of the tail caught Drake's side, knocking him in front of the monster. Melvin picked up his sword and slashed open the monster's throat. Drake pressed his hand against his side. Melvin's face was flushed from terror and exhilaration. He howled like a madman. Drake's horse could not be found, so he ran toward the chaos, with Melvin in tow.

Out of nowhere, another drake burst from the underbrush, almost crushing Melvin and Drake. A loud bang and a shower of blood erupted over the two men before the dead monster slid right past them.

"Watch out," Zora said, holding the smoking gun.

Joseph calmed his horse, now too far away to help anyone. Zora counted four dead drakes. No soldiers had died from the ambush; however, a few horses lay mangled on the field. Captured horses cried out in pain and terror as hungry jaws wrapped around their soft torsos. Joseph lit another cigar and watched the battle wind down.

"Help anytime," Thos roared.

"It's under control," Joseph replied calmly.

Zora glanced back at the chaos over the western plains. She made her way back to the group. The living snallygasters dragged off the wounded horses toward their nesting grounds and vanished into the woods. After a few moments of shock, the army reconvened. Cautiously, the rebels pressed on to Fort Alexander. Arriving at the Appalachians, the troop noticed large craters in many of the mountains

"What happened up there?" asked one the soldiers.

"The Great Empire blew up the mountains for the resources. Some sort of botched mining," Drake explained.

No one relaxed in the thick woodlands at the base of the mountains. Scouts moved ahead, on the lookout for enemy camps and snallygaster nests. Melvin headed over to Joseph and spoke with him in private. From the glances and scrunched up brows of Joseph, Zora knew they spoke about the Knight-Ambassador. Through the trees came the dull lights of a sleepy town in the shadow of the dead Appalachians. The rebels stirred and murmured.

Armor-clad soldiers emerged from the nearby trees and bushes. The men panicked, quickly drawing swords.

"Everyone relax," Joseph said. "These are our guys. They look like the genuine article, don't they?"

The pseudo-knights led them into the quiet villages only a few miles from the base of the mountain. The term "village" was a bit of a stretch, twenty small houses with a stave church at the back. Rebels armed with shovels went off toward the edge of town. The armored men led the group to the center of town.

"At dawn we march!" Joseph declared.

After dispensing the orders and information, the formation of soldiers went in and out of the church that served as the dining hall. The rebels loaded up on chicken, fried potatoes, and various collections of non-alcoholic drinks. Thos ate like a man possessed, while Drake and Zora displayed more restraint. Melvin chatted up one the local girls departing for a house, despite Joseph's protests. Drake spent far too much time looking down at his gun. After the meal, the tables were cleared, and the church became sleeping quarters.

Thos, Zora, and Drake sat behind the pulpit under the cracked beams of the old church. The church needed major renovations; Zora half expected to see mice scampering across the rafters. Zora noticed Drake intently avoiding contact with the others.

"Nervous?" Zora asked. He looked at her with eyes full of regret.

"I'm wondering just what in the hell I'm doing here. I'm stuck between a rock and a hard place no matter where I turn," Drake said. Zora had learned body language well during her travels and, up to this point, Drake had hidden his anxiety very well.

"If it's any consolation I think things will turn out pretty well.

As long as good people take charge, things will get better. You seem like one of those people," she said warmly.

"Why do you say that?" he asked.

"The way you grapple with your decisions. Good people always question what they do, only villains are sure of themselves—what my dad liked to say, at least," Zora said.

"I've never really thought of it that way, but thanks," Drake said.

"You're welcome," she replied.

"The ice queens are melting," Thos laughed. A chunk of half-eaten chicken fell from his mouth as he talked. Thos returned his focus to his meal and avoided the chilling glares. Melvin yawned loudly, signaling bedtime had arrived.

"We ought to be wrapping things up. Helluva day coming up," said Melvin, tossing his plate and missing the trash bin. Melvin pretended to not see the miss and sat down on a nearby cot. Zora closed her eyes and again heard the ominous words. "She is ours." This time she would fight back.

Not for long.

ARIC

Aric's throat ached for drink. He tapped his fingers against the table bearing the map of Heartland. Banners outside flapped in the wind, slapping up against the walls outside. His lieutenant wanted to speak, but hesitated. Aric's temper steadily rose.

"Something to say?" Aric asked in his usual threatening way. His hands crumpled up the edges of the map. The lieutenant had developed a tepidness Aric couldn't tolerate. The officer stuttered a bit.

"Th… the rebels will march on us any day now. It's likely they are coming up the mountain as we speak. Our reports suggest they are much larger than we believed," Aric got the feeling his officers were looking for a way to abandon him at the first sign of trouble.

"So long as you do your jobs they won't breach these walls. I don't need to remind you what happens if they do. They are rabid dogs and we must put them down."

The officers looked up at him, some with respect and others with scorn. All of the commanding officers of Heartland gathered around the table were older than Aric and came off as condescending know-it-alls.

"You really mean to burn the city?" said Calvin Mets. Calvin, a balding man with fading red beard, was the senior-most field officer and Anselm's personal pick to oversee Heartland. A trusted friend of his father, Calvin was the true authority here.

"Nothing important. The Averill farms are the only things that matter here," Aric said. "As you have been made aware we have a list of all known conspirators in the area. We will seize their lands. A few executions will frighten the masses back in line," Aric said.

Aric made sure to look at every single one of the officers present in the war room. He imagined Drake's head mounted in the throne room when he returned home and it pleased him. "We're almost done here, gentlemen. Soon we will be going home. Dismissed." The men all nodded.

Aric left the stuffy war room and stepped onto the fortress wall, taking in the chilly mountain air. Everyone he passed saluted. Soldiers prepared cannons. Aric suppressed his desire for drink. He no longer smelled the dampness of encroaching storms in the air, enjoying the relief from the incessant rain.

The last of Aric's troops marched up the mountain path toward the main gate. His men brandished rifles, pistols, shotguns, and swords, ready to fight. Aric strode across the fortress walls, overseeing the last of the scouts speeding toward the fort. He did not recognize the scouts. He immediately sensed danger, and his heart sank.

The rebel army had attacked without warning. Fear took hold of Aric Blackthorne. "They're really here! How did we not see them?" A horn sounded in the southwest tower, and the soldiers poured out, archers scrambling to their perches. Bullets and arrows rained down on the fort. Aric froze at the sight, his assurance of victory evaporated with the dawn mist. He went deaf to the officers shouting at him. Aric panicked, unable to formulate a single thought. Officers marshaled their forces without him. Calvin shook him violently.

"Sir!" the soldier screamed. The roar of gunfire forced Aric out of his paralysis.

"Ready the cannons! Secure all entrances! Burn the whole forest down if you must!" Aric made a mad dash for the nearest rifle.

The skies darkened from the torrents of death. Aric's soldiers responded with a volley of their own, their arrows alight with flame. The flaming arrows bore down on the rebels igniting both man and land. The flaming landscape pushed the rebels into the path of the cannons. Rebel ladders banged up against the fort walls with invaders scrambling up.

Troops surrounded Aric at once to counter the phalanx formation of rebels. Aric's men led him toward the walls where he had a nasty surprise waiting for the rebels. Aric rallied nearby soldiers to his side and slowly pushed them down the stairs to the closest tower. The man inside the top dumped boiling oil on them. The armored soldiers were quickly reduced to a mass of melted flesh and metal. Firebombs smashed into the walls and down in the courtyard, forcing Aric back.

As they moved a safe distance away from the volleys, one arrow pierced the soft opening in the neck area of one of Aric's defenders. Aric had no time to fetch his helmet. Men hidden behind rocks further up the mountain shot at Aric. In his time here, none of his men had seen or heard of mountain folk organized into a singular group. He wondered how the rebels got them to stop the infighting. In fur and leathers with thick bushy beards and stocky frames, they appeared like bears. He realized just how organized his foes truly were.

Aric and his men rushed down the stairs to the center of the main yard of the fortress. Aric grabbed a helmet from a fallen soldier and hastily threw it on. Men screamed from behind him, quickly drowned out by the sounds of battle. Rebels arrived at the front gate, chopping relentlessly. "I can't die here. I won't!" Aric roared.

Aric killed five men with rifle shots as they climbed over the walls using siege ladders. With bullets exhausted, Aric switched to his sword. A runner headed for Aric. Aric sliced open his shins then stabbed him through the back of the skull before he could get to his feet. Aric heard more cries. "They're coming through the escape tunnels!" Aric's gut compelled him to flee.

Overwhelmed by panic, Aric fled toward his room. The noises grew louder; Aric fled so quickly his escort failed to keep up. From the tunnel doors near the back wall, the mountain men burst through, blindsiding the men inside the fort.

Aric sat in his room trembling as the battle raged all around him. The window provided him with the means to escape. Rebels hadn't yet surrounded the fort. Aric's bodyguards saw the fear in his eyes. The soldiers watched in disgust as the prince cowered. It took only a moment for them to abandon him to go help their brothers. Aric contemplated his decision from the safety of his private quarters. "I'm not strong, father. I was never the man you wanted. I'm sorry I failed," he cried. He thought of his family, defenseless and surrounded by enemies with him gone. Aric's hate overcame his fear. He berated himself. *I will defend them… to the last.*

Slowly, Aric rose and regained his composure. The gravity of the situation hit him in full force. The prince mustered all the courage he could as he recanted the oath of the Sons of Prosperity. "I am the sword of the nation," Aric said, voice shaky. He kicked open the door.

DRAKE

Drake prepared himself for the looming battle and the crippling anxiety that came with it. He breathed in the dew-covered forests as he headed up the Appalachians toward a man he had once loved like a brother. Drake spotted Joseph approaching out of the corner of his eye, stopping his plans at conception.

"We could've just killed you," Joseph told him.

"Likewise," Drake groaned. Breathing in the cool air calmed Drake's nerves.

"You think this rebellion is one big joke, I get it. You think we want this, but I assure you we didn't. Poverty led to this. Poverty is the parent to revolution."

Drake smirked, impressed to hear such a quote from anyone other than a pompous High Scholar. Drake didn't find Joseph's quote accurate. He knew this wasn't some rich versus poor showdown, and to classify it as such was to not fully understand the situation or how to solve it. People always wanted to lay blame on something or someone they hated. He found it all the more ironic since Joseph's revolutionaries were propping up the most successful businessman in the state as their hero against the elite.

"That's Aristotle. You are a well-learned man," Drake said.

"Fools don't change the world," Joseph replied.

"In my experience, they change the world more than anyone else… and not for the better," Drake replied.

"Maybe you're right," Joseph laughed.

"Why did you spare me? Do I make for a fat prize?" Drake asked.

"To be frank, you remind me of my son," Joseph said. Drake buried his cynicism and listened to the story. "He wanted to be a knight like you, a tireless defender thinking only of others. He found out that the bandit attacks a few years back were started by an aspiring crime family, the Parkers. The Parkers took power around the time Victor Whitehall was kicked out of Fort Alexander. Long story short, my son led the local militia, killed the bandits, and drove them out. He got the attention of the governor, and from there he was on the path to knighthood," Joseph beamed.

"Now that you mention it, I remember a young Kerr banned from joining," Drake said, well versed in the rank and file of his order.

"There's a reason for that," Joseph said, spitting on the ground. "Mr. Williamson's son Jacob was in town. Jacob took a liking to one of the girls who did not feel the same way. You can guess what happened," Joseph said, spitting on the ground. Drake cursed under his breath.

"My son found out and roughed the pig up. For his troubles, my son's title was stripped and he's lucky not to have been executed, all for punishing a criminal. I love my son. I've had to kill people to keep him safe—not all of them deserved it. Surely you can sympathize," Joseph said, reaching for a smoke. Drake begrudgingly nodded.

"My son's story is one in a pile. So many of us are crushed beneath the heel of people lucky enough to born into the right family or have the right friends. We will break this cycle," Joseph said. Drake couldn't deny the truth in his words.

"It shouldn't have come to this," Drake said.

"But it always does… and it always will," Joseph said.

"Violence only causes more violence. It's escalation that only stops when one side kills more than the other," Drake replied.

Joseph moved farther up the group and the rebel army prepared for the final leg of the march to Fort Alexander. After many long hours, Fort Alexander greeted them. The fortress walls commanded the mountainside. Drake grew nauseated at the thought of watching his fellow soldiers die. He forced the bile back down. Thos squirmed nervously on his steed, shielding his eyes from the bright sun burning in the cloudless sky. Melvin clutched his beastly sword.

The scouts ran off ahead of the group, soldiers manning the watchtowers glimpsed the inbound force. A hollering sound rang out on the other side of the fort. Joseph and his crew slowly crept toward the fort. The holler died down instantly. More screams echoed from the other side, followed by a hail of death.

"The mountain men came through. Maybe Abe will take me seriously now," Joseph muttered with amusement. Flaming arrows set the mountain pass alight.

Bullets zipped through the growing inferno, taking out a few of the rebels. Joseph kept Drake near him, ensuring the Knight Ambassador didn't do anything rash. Armored rebels carrying siege ladders raced toward the sides of the fort, while Thos and a brigade of riflemen protected them. The bulk of the army gathered around the fortress, either scaling walls or hacking away at the entrance. Soldiers atop the towers fired their cannons. Cannonballs plowed through troops of soldiers like bowling balls. Limbs and a shower of blood made the grass slick and red. With a sea of fire at their backs, the rebels had no choice but to press on with the attack.

Bullets hit near the feet of Drake's horse, forcing him to veer from Joseph's side. The man tasked with shooting Drake was preoccupied with enemy gunfire to focus on his ward. Drake calculated the risk of escape too great to make a move yet.

Rebels climbing up the ladders fell off one by one from rifle shots. The rebel soldiers came faster than the response and swarmed the walls. With a brigade at his back, Melvin diced up enemy forces, bragging with each kill. The Blackthorne forces held strong behind their walls, refusing to face the invaders on the mountain path. Rebel casualties mounted.

At Joseph's signal, Molotovs pelted the main gate; rebels at the gate braced for the flood of troops on the other side. The rebels surrounded the door and burst through as the Blackthorne soldiers scurried to intercept them. Joseph's men shot down the cannoneers. Soldiers dodged the arrows stepping over the dead to reach the canons, eventually taken out by the rebels.

Securing the cannons became the enemy's priority. Joseph remained a comfortable distance from the action, leaving Zora and Thos with the task of eliminating the shooters. Ascending the stairs came a rebel force hiding under shields, like a metallic beetle. Shooters mechanically shifted focus to defend rebel cannoneers from the attacks, skewering the neck of one soldier. Cannons and rifles kept Aric's forces at bay.

Kicking the body out of the way, the others arrived at the cannon. Joseph gave his horse a fierce kick in an attempt to escape the fire, mistakenly running into a volley of arrows. Joseph survived the maelstrom. The arrows separated Drake from his captors. In the chaos of battle, no one watched him. He maneuvered his horse toward the nearest rifle. Drake quickly hopped off his horse and snatched it up. With one shot he brought down Joseph's horse. *No more Aric. No more Joseph. No more war,* Drake thought.

On the fortress walls, Aric got behind a cannon while his bodyguards killed the rebel occupiers at the other. Aric loaded the weapon, narrowly missing a retaliatory strike. From up on the tower Aric saw Drake. Aric screamed at his former friend. Drake hightailed it out of the area. Aric followed Drake with the cannon, as he bobbed and weaved behind the rocks. Drake maneuvered too fast for him to follow. Aric abandoned his effort when he found the downed rebel leader.

Joseph leaped to his feet as fast as he could. He caught one glimpse of the rusty cannon before the roaring ball of doom burst forth. Joseph dove to the side, a ball that would've popped him like a balloon had it not missed. Joseph lost a dozen men to desertion after that, personally shooting two of them in the back. The mountainside glowed a brilliant orange with the fire spreading through the trees.

Inside the fortress walls, the local "Mountain Men" pummeled Aric's forces with reckless abandon. Aric forsook the cannon, leaving his underlings to man the station while he fled toward the barracks. A bullet scrapped Aric's shoulder. He ran into the courtyard, sending a small contingent of soldiers over the wall supported by arrows and cannons.

Wielding hunting knives and shotguns, the Mountain Men cleaved through waves of Aric's forces. Melvin and his men brought up the rear of the Mountain Men. Fifty of the prince's men lay dead feet from the doors of the solemn fortress. The other two cannons spewed forth death with remarkable speed. Mountain Men outside the walls died from cannon fire. Melvin and his group backed off when the forces ahead grew dangerously thin. The first wave of Mountain Men fought savagely, taking three for each man they lost. With all his outside forces dead, Aric screamed in anger.

Joseph divvied out orders. More waves of Mountain Men threw themselves at Aric's men, both dying in equal measure. Drake looked for a way out through the fire. Out of the corner of his eye, he spied rebel gunman lining him up.

Aric reined his troops in. Attacking rebels tripped over the corpses piling up near the gate. Melvin's team climbed over the bodies with the help of rifle support. Melvin dropped switched from a bulky claymore to a shotgun given to him by a Mountain

Man. Melvin brought down any soldiers forced outside the gate, firing his gun from point blank range.

Joseph sent his reserve armored division into the fray. The division formed a ring around Melvin. They entered the gate and veered up to the stairs. The armored shell deflected arrows, causing the gunmen to step in. Five guards surrounded the cannoneer on the tower. The reserve units killed the men while losing only one of their own. Melvin ran up on the tower guards, filling the heavily armored men with shotgun shells. The rebels grabbed hold of the cannon and directed it at the fortress walls. Soldiers loaded the gun. Melvin fired. Aric's eyes widened in horror as he turned to see a gaping hole in the old wall.

A rush of attackers pushed Aric's forces to the south wall. The rebel cannon decimated enemy troops. The guards around Aric scrambled to fight both forces, losing men to the rogue cannon all the while. Joseph, Thos, and Drake moved closer to the fort. The bulk of the rebel army gathered near the fort entrance. Aric sweat profusely as he braced for one final attack. Drake saw Aric turn wild from desperation. Joseph, Drake, Thos, and Zora pulled back too. Aric's frightened expression became a twisted grin.

"You want this fort? You can have it!" Aric screamed. He pulled a small object from his pocket with a tiny button on it. Joseph screamed for his men to open fire on the prince. Aric slipped to the back of his men.

"Everybody out!" Joseph screamed. Rebels darted out from the building, but the exits forced them into a bottleneck. Aric pushed the button. The front half of the fortress erupted in a shower of stone and fire. Bits and pieces of men and fort shot out in all directions. Debris nearly knocked Thos from his horse. The shockwave from the blast knocked both Aric's forces and the rebels back. Rebels burned and screamed inside the fortress. Aric and the others mobilized for a last stand, getting a few cheap shots in at the incapacitated rebels.

Joseph quickly rallied his surviving troops and attacked again. The two sides engaged in a vicious battle in the center of the burning fort. Aric killed a dozen men, slashing open legs and throats with sword and getting headshots with a pistol. Nearly all of the rebel gunmen were killed in the explosion, leaving Thos and Zora as the only two left.

Drake aimed his gun at the prince. His hand shook. Images of Drake with Anselm and the other Blackthorne children flashed through his mind. He recalled fishing on the lake with Anselm and Percival under the summer sun. He remembered mock battles in the halls back when Aric and he were not bitter enemies.

A shot rang out from Thos's gun, clipping Aric's arm and causing him to drop his weapon. The rebels enveloped Aric. With their leader surrounded, the Blackthorne soldiers froze. Red Devils mercilessly attacked the Blackthorne forces until Joseph stopped them, showing his disgust at the mercs' viciousness.

"The battle is over. Those of you willing to lay down your arms will not be harmed. Those that will not, will be executed," Joseph said, trying not to gloat.

"Don't listen to his lies!" Aric yelled.

"Lies?" Joseph snarled. "Does the crown take care of your families? What happens when people like the great prince takes a liking to your wives? What happens when you displease him? You are nothing but ammunition and targets to people like him." Aric stood unmoved by Joseph's little speech, but the rest of the soldiers were more easily persuaded.

"Your amateur speeches won't dissuade these men. You and your kind are trash," Aric screamed, turning to his fellows.

"You don't speak for us," said a soldier. One by one, Aric's men turned against him until only ten loyalists remained. Aric surveyed the scene, finding Drake in the crowd.

"Anselm would be disappointed in you," he snarled. Drake lowered his head.

The sickness in his stomach permeated Drake's entire being now. The hatred emanated from Aric like a tornado of fire. Drake turned away, hoping the guilt would subside.

"Look at me!" Aric roared. His eyes became watery with tears. The rebels laughed at him. Drake didn't meet Aric's gaze. The prince spit at Drake's feet.

"Enough!" Joseph shouted. "Those of you joining us step forward." The weaponless men stepped forward. Rebels escorted the captives to the southern wall. Joseph looked at the prince and gave out his orders to have the POWs thrown in the dungeon. Joseph looked at Aric and the standing wall. He decided the prince's fate.

"Prepare the gallows."

ARIC

ON THE SOUTHERN wall above the gate, Aric knew his ultimate fate neared. A surreal experience, waiting for death. First came fear, then bitterness, acceptance, and then fear again. The battle of Fort Alexander felt as though it happened years before. Anxiety soaked every fiber of his being, and he could barely suppress the contents of his kidneys.

Chained to the wall, Aric watched beetles scurry to and fro in his claustrophobic cell. They were now more fortunate than he was. Drops of water and blood from the leaky walls hit the ground like bombs all around him. Aric witnessed the execution of his loyal men through the cracks in the ceiling. He heard the hungry birds pecking at his comrades' soft dead eyes. The stench of charred and rotting flesh slithered down in his cell, filling his nostrils. Cries of torture reverberated further within the ruins, courtesy of the Red Devils working over Blackthorne soldiers promised amnesty. Red Devils shot some of the others that surrendered, already locking horns with new rebel forces. Aric fought off the tears, regretting a great deal of his life. His family needed him. As much as he feared death, the powerlessness to save them was infinitely worse.

During his final moments, Aric wished to have any sort of

company, eventually fate granted his wish—disheartened by the result. Down the hallway came the familiar sight of Drake Hale.

Aric laughed as Drake approached. "Is this some new torture cooked up for me?" Aric asked.

"You have no one else to blame," Drake said.

"They struck first. I simply responded in kind," he replied.

"Too many have been killed on your account."

"Not all of this death is my doing," Aric reminded him. Drake held back saying anything else, stopping a pointless argument.

"That's not why am I here," he said, switching the subject.

"Then, pray tell, why are gracing me with your presence?" Aric mocked.

"I wanted to say I'm sorry that it has come to this. I wished things could've been different. I do. I loved you once as a brother," Drake said. Each word stung with disappointment.

"And I you, once upon a time. We've done many horrible things, haven't we?"

"I did what I could for our country," Drake admitted. "I'll never forgive you for putting me in that position. Never forget his face or the others I killed for you." Drake threw off his linen shirt and turned his back to the prince. Along Drake's back was a crisscross of scars and the Blackthorne symbol burned into his right shoulder. "Your scars have never healed." Drake put his shirt back on.

"Doing bad things for good reasons is what we do," Aric said. "I did what anyone in my place would do, protect my family. We're all the same when enemies are at the gates." Aric's broken ribs provided constant agony—the words hurt coming out.

"Tell yourself whatever you need to," Drake replied.

"Remember what you promised my father?" Aric asked.

"I promised him to do whatever it takes to preserve peace and ensure justice," Drake said.

"Why the fuck do you think I'm here? All I've ever done is for them! I've spent my whole life doing that! Never a moment's peace.

Duty. Rebellion. Economy. The Board. Death threats. Assassinations. Trade agreements. Speeches. I watched as the job killed my father. I told myself I wouldn't let the happen to me. I wouldn't let it destroy my family. I ensure justice was done… to the last."

"Your father—" Drake barely got the words out before Aric exploded in a rage. Aric lunged forward only to be knocked back by his chains.

"He loved you more than me!" Aric screamed. "Everything thing I've done wasn't good enough. I could see it in his eyes. In all their eyes, when they see me, all they see is a drunk and a killer. Today I was going to make things right," Aric said, fighting the urge to weep. His attempts to hold back his tears failed. The pent-up emotions flowed forth.

"I'm just a man trying to do the right thing," Drake said. Aric forced his head up to look at Drake.

"The kingdom will be better off with me gone, won't it?" he asked. The truth hit Aric Blackthorne, stripping away his will to fight.

"It will," Drake said. Aric wept.

"Percival will be a good king," Drake's words provided some comfort. "I'll make sure of that."

"He will," Aric forced a smile, finding some comfort in the thought.

"I'll look after your family; I swear on my life. I will not let any harm come to them. I will end the rebellion," Drake said. Aric gave him a confused look.

"Can you really kill your new friends? Killing your own and them—you'll be hated more than I ever was. Perhaps the dragon is still in you after all," Aric smirked.

"Doing bad things for good reasons is what we do," Drake replied.

"You really do care about them, don't you? They'll need you… after…" Aric trailed off.

"Your father loves you. Even after all you've done. Find some comfort in that," Drake said. He turned from the prince and walked toward the stairs. Aric called out to him.

"You promise?" Aric asked.

"On my life. Find peace, old friend," Drake replied before vanishing from his sight.

A holler from upstairs signaled that Aric's time had finally come. Two rebel soldiers pushed Drake aside on the way to Aric's cell. They opened his cell and unshackled the prince, although not before giving him a few hard fists to the face and stomach.

"Rapists and killers the lot of you. Your cause is as false as you," Aric said, spitting blood in the man's eyes.

"Not your problem, anymore," the man reminded him with a hard fist to the jaw. More hollering roared from above. Aric heard Joseph's voice. "Time for the prince's coronation," Joseph boomed.

The two men on either side gave him a kick in the back each time he stopped moving. The stairs leading up the southern wall went on forever. Aric deliberately slowed his steps to agitate his abusers. The rebels made Aric watch as they prepared the noose. As the noose grew closer, Aric reflected on his life and the overwhelming regret of unfulfilled promises. On his way through the courtyard, the soldiers tossed Aric to the floor. Some of the spectators got a few hard kicks into his sternum as he writhed on the ground.

"How quick your beliefs are thrown away," Aric said, choking the words out.

"If you fidget, your end will not be quick," said the hangman.

Aric climbed the steps in front of him to his destiny. Cheers and curses rang out from the crowd. The executioner slung the rope around Aric's neck.

"Any last words?" Joseph asked. Aric wanted to plead for his life, though his pride wouldn't allow it.

"You condemn my family, and that's fine. We don't need your

love. Never forget this country survives because of us. I regret a great many things, but killing those that endangered my family aren't among them."

Aric gave one last look at Drake as the hood came down over his head. His life did not flash before his eyes. There were no happy memories. Darkness enveloped him, followed by sheer terror. The man beside him gave him a push. He floated for a moment until the rope cracked, and like a snake, it constricted around his neck. Aric kicked wildly. Choking and gurgling sounds followed muffled cries. Aric thrashed like a dying animal to the amusement of the onlookers.

"His neck didn't break?!" Joseph said with shock.

Silence fell over the crowd as Aric died slowly. His muffled cries echoed across the mountain. Urine ran down Aric's leg. A few in the crowd laughed.

"How hard is it to set up a fucking noose!" Joseph roared. Melvin and Thos didn't seem to care.

"Do we do something?" the hangman asked. Joseph shook his head. Zora and Drake refused to watch the spectacle any longer and walked away. Aric fought on trying to break free, dying to the sounds of rebel incompetence. He managed to get a single word out.

"Dad." Then Aric's movements began to slow until finally, they ceased.

DRAKE

Aric Blackthorne dangled over the southern wall of Fort Alexander beside his loyal knights to the sounds of jubilation all around. The executioner cut Aric's body loose from the gallows, the lifeless sack of meat crashing to the ground. Adding further insult to injury, the Red Devil mercs pissed on the corpse.

"His body will be returned to the capital and given a proper burial," Joseph said with a laugh, directing his comments towards Drake. "Not by you. You'll be staying with us for the time being."

The majority of the rebels tended to the bodies and the raging fires. After cleanup, the celebration lasted until the fort's stores of food and drink were depleted. The whole day made Drake begin to question his certainty. With Aric gone, he made plans to quell the rebel threat. Thos chatted up some soldiers over near the gallows, people finally laughing at his jokes. Zora stood by herself, looking at the forests below. Melvin stood on the gallows mocking Aric's corpse. *Should've let him get eaten*, Drake thought bitterly.

Drake wandered aimlessly while he waited for an opportunity to make his move. Drake sneaked around to Aric's tower, where Joseph took up residence. Drake planned to sneak in and kill Joseph. However, constant bodyguards and patrolmen kept him from getting close.

Drake studied the troop movements for lapses in their defenses. He saw an opportunity. Zora stopped her investigation of the mountainside and approached Drake, interrupting his assassination. A guard noticed him eyeing the tower and doubled Joseph's security. Drake slammed his fist into his thigh.

"Holding up?" Zora inquired.

"Not really," Drake said, internally cursing his plan's derailment.

"Must've been hard," she said, placing a hand on his shoulder. *I let my king's son die*, Drake thought.

"Harder than I thought," he said. He shifted uncomfortably. "I'll stay with you another night then head back to the capital as soon as I can sneak away."

"With me?" she said, smiling.

"Well, you know, with you people," he said, face reddening from embarrassment. He caught the soldiers glaring at him.

"Perhaps you can help me with that. They won't let me leave. I'll be a corpse soon if they have their way. I need to get out," Drake said.

"Actually—" she said. Her smile faded fast. A commotion from the tower interrupted things yet again. A collection of soldiers led by Joseph approached Drake with weapons drawn. The men surrounded Drake, separating him from Zora. Joseph pointed his gun at Drake's head.

"You had no intention of letting me go," Drake said. It wasn't a question. Thos made protests from behind the mob that fell on deaf ears.

"I'm sorry, son. I wanted to," Joseph said. Drake's hand inched for his gun. Thos's cries distracted Joseph for a second, just long enough for Drake to get his gun up. The rebels moved in to attack Drake.

"Stop! Don't harm him," Zora screamed. Joseph and Drake did not lower their guns.

"This doesn't concern you," Joseph snarled.

"Release him or our deal is off!" Zora replied with rising authority. Joseph ground his teeth.

"That isn't part of our arrangement!" he snapped back, sneering at her as lowered his weapon. Drake responded with a mocking smile. Joseph and the mob dissipated, leaving him alone with a relieved Zora and flabbergasted Thos.

"I owe you," Drake said.

"You do," Zora teased.

"What's this about an arrangement?" Drake asked.

"I'd like you two to accompany me back home," Zora said reluctantly.

"To the Fey?" Drake asked with bewilderment.

"I was to be escorted home with some of Joe's men, but I'd rather travel with people I like—more than armed strangers, at least. The forces we were promised can travel separately." Drake gripped his gun tight, not trusting Joseph. Drake stared back into her soulful eyes and went with the only plan that would get him out of here alive.

"I've had more than enough of this place," Drake said.

"Good," she smiled. Thos nodded before realizing exactly what Zora said.

"Wait, did you just rope me into this?" Thos interjected.

"I'll explain later," she said and quickly vanished amid the celebrators. Drake shook his head, bracing himself for a new mess.

GREGOR

"KINGSBURY: THE ASSHOLE of the world," Gregor muttered. Groveling for aid to the very same people that scattered his order to the four winds and assigned him to the middle of nowhere was the worst form of humiliation Gregor could imagine. He spent the better part of five days waiting for a meeting with Anselm and his Board of Directors. While he suffered government indignation, Gregor allowed the rest of the order to relish the downtime however they saw fit.

His temporary home smelled like peaches and was the only thing he liked in Kingsbury. Outside Gregor's residence, male and female streetwalkers lined the entrance to the city, giving the tourists and soldiers a profane welcome.

For days, officials apologized, thanked, and rescheduled Gregor's meeting with the king. Gregor grew restless, spending his time exploring the city in the hopes of finding a contract. The town hustled and bustled as it always had, though he sensed something different this time. Roaming through the districts, he noticed a growing decline in the capital: overworked electrical grid, closing businesses, and roads in desperate need of repair despite the constant influx of tax money. Judging from the state of the city, Gregor found in unlikely he'd receive any monetary aid.

He debated leaving for the White Woods to see his brother, but whenever he made the decision, impromptu meetings confined him to the city. Sometimes they went so far as to ask Gregor what the other delegates asked him. The complimentary fruit and cheese baskets delegates gave Gregor didn't soothe his mounting anger; cheese wasn't bad though.

Thick, smoky air from the industrial sector blanketed a large portion of the town under an oppressive cloud. The choking mess pushed him away from the town to the fields in the outer districts as far as the delegates would allow. He let out a series of deep breaths while watching the swaying grass of the rolling hills just outside the White Woods.

A caravan from Gloire left the city beginning the long journey back to their domain carrying their trademark white banners with golden chimeras. Some people greeted him warmly, especially the young children dazzled by his embellished adventures against monsters and machines. One little girl reminded him of his two nieces, fully-grown now. One street chef offered him roasted scorpions, claiming to come from the Empire of Toth in the west. The people of Toth didn't actually eat fried scorpions, but they were popular with inquisitive tourists, and Gregor enjoyed them well enough.

On the fourth day, Gregor bumped into Jerrick Hart, supreme commander of the nation's military forces. The gargantuan man almost knocked him off his feet, startling both of them. They grumbled and awkwardly apologized before recognizing each other. Jerrick was the only man that could refer to him as Gregory or Greg and get away with it. Jerrick's ceramic ivory armor glistened in the sun, creating a striking contrast with his dark skin. Wearing a helm with griffon wings only enhanced his frightening visage. Gregor apologized for his lack of awareness. With a firm handshake, the two parted ways.

Gregor tried to avoid any other military encounters, lest they get too interested in his business. Thoughts of his neglected family ate away at him. In the past twenty years, Gregor could count the times he had seen his brother on a hand missing several fingers. Sorrowful thoughts parched his throat. He strolled into the bar opposite the brothel, picking a spot in a poorly lit corner. An unexpected visitor barged in just three sips into Gregor's drink, none other than Percival Blackthorne. Gregor gave a quick comb over his beard and hair that stuck out in all directions. Percival greeted him with a lordly handshake.

He wore the ceremonial armor of the Blackthorne family, with a starry purple color trimmed with silver. The heavily engraved armor bore an image of Alexander taming the wild peoples two thousand years ago.

"Welcome Lord Sentinel Pavane. I apologize for the delay. It's been a long time since you've visited us," Percival said, with the practiced voice of a leader.

"Too long," Gregor replied, face contorting from a practiced smile that came off as insane. Percival brushed back his hair and tried not to get thrown off course by Gregor's maddeningly fake smile. Percival's guards kept the civilians away. Gregor chugged his beer, adding a layer of froth to his beard.

"To be honest, I prefer the monsters," Gregor said.

Percival made small talk with the Lord Sentinel, taking the opportunity to enjoy a meal while the two caught up on current events. Gregor, in a polite manner, hurried events along until gut-rumbling coerced him into a meal of his own.

"My father may support you," Percival began, "however, the Board will require far more coaxing. I'd say bring some of these whores with you," he added bluntly.

"If it takes another day I'll buy the whole damn brothel for them," Gregor said, honestly. Percival laughed and nodded, suggesting that may be the best option. The two had a simple meal of steak and potatoes and shared a pitcher of beer. After eating, Percival motioned Gregor to follow.

"We've been made aware of your situation and will discuss the terms of your assistance at the castle. In fact, we can go ahead now," Percival said. Cedric played cards outside with a dozen Blackthorne soldiers, the cards included demons, nude women, and Old World baseball cards. Leaving the bar, Percival got down to business. Gregor yelled at Cedric to follow.

Gregor and Cedric exchanged pleasantries with Percival all the way to the grand hall where Anselm sat on his gold and marble throne. The light from the windows illuminated Anselm, but he did not make a regal figure. Anselm sat hunched over with a disinterested stare. When he noticed Percival and Gregor, he immediately straightened up to an authoritative pose.

"You could have let me know you were bringing them early," Anselm said, clearing his throat. He brushed himself off and sat upright, now more fitting of his title.

"Sorry, father. I figured it be best not to alert the others," Percival said, embarrassed. His tough façade crumbled against his father.

The prince took his place at the king's side becoming no different than the display armors lining the walls. Gregor preemptively raised his hand to silence Cedric, lest ill-placed remarks got things off to a rocky and potentially dangerous start.

Gregor had a feeling that Anselm never liked him. The two had run-ins a every few years, going back to Anselm's youth when his father, Astor, pardoned the two extraordinarily successful killers that would be better serving the crown than feeding the worms. Vigilant itself also had a tumultuous relationship with the royal family. In centuries past, Vigilant threatened the Blackthorne line itself for overstepping, which resulted in the title of Grand Crusader that commanded all branches of Vigilant removed. Anselm bore an underlying anxiety that wore he wore like a second suit. With the words traitor and loyalist being thrown around, coupled with rising tensions and people taking sides, one statement could turn a man from an ally to a threat.

"I see the Board didn't even bother to show," Gregor said. The previous generation of the Board of Directors at least showed his order a shred of respect, when Mr. Derbin's mother ran things. Gregor blamed some childish political spat between them and king to be the culprit of this round of pussyfooting.

"I don't shirk my duties," Anselm said, his words chosen to separate himself from the Board. "How was your trip? Pay a visit to the haunted manor? Sounds like you had quite a time." Anselm's tone darkened. Gregor blushed.

"We're… we um… it was fine," Gregor replied. Anselm made a brushing gesture with his hand to show his lack of concern.

"At least they won't be asking for renovation funds anymore. Mayor was caught colluding with the traitors and burned along with the mansion, so I'm told. They might actually put something useful there now."

"A brothel," Gregor said.

"Make everyone happy," Anselm replied.

"You know why we're here?" Gregor cut to the chase.

"Yes. I thank you for eliminating these bothersome cults. Those fools who think they are following in Gideon's footsteps can do great harm. They've been little more than a nuisance so far, and I see no reason to believe that they pose a larger threat." Anselm brushed off the threat of the witches as any person would without the proper evidence, but something about Anselm's tone suggested he understood the threat to be quite real. *Is he hiding something?*

"I can assure you they're no idle threat. I've lost many men to them. Their numbers grow by the day. These aren't isolated incidents, something's going on," Gregor stressed. Cedric leaned in and whispered in Gregor's ear.

"He hears this shit a dozen times a day. Don't beat around

the bush," Cedric whispered. Anselm sat back in his chair clearly showcasing his lack of interest.

"Requesting troops and supplies is no small favor. The Board will give you nothing, nor will the merchants, hell the scholars don't even want you to access the library," Anselm said.

"Which means you won't help?" Gregor said bitterly. Gregor too proud to beg. That did not mean, however, he wasn't beneath lying for a good cause.

"We have reason to believe these cults are colluding with the rebels," Gregor said with false conviction. It was possible. Cedric played along. Anselm laughed heartily.

"You resort to lying very quickly," Anselm said. Anselm glanced out the windows at the sun peeking through.

"That was your plan? Show him the damn head," Cedric whispered.

"Don't be so quick to use technology to solve our problem. That's not what we do," Gregor chastised. Cedric frowned.

"Says the guy with a cyborg's head in a bag," Cedric retorted.

"Shhh," Gregor growled.

"You shh… fucker," Cedric replied. Gregor face darkened and he grabbed hold of Cedric.

"We'll be here until the next Dark Age while they dick around," Cedric reminded him.

"That's not what we do," Gregor reiterated.

"Bullshit. We use it when we need it," Cedric insisted. Gregor conceded the point from sheer lack of energy. The king cleared his throat and disrupted the private whispers.

"Gentlemen. King. Right here," Anselm said. "We're all firm believers in following the Compact as well as defending this country. Let it be said that I won't turn a blind eye to those in need. Vigilant will have access to my personal library. As for the soldiers… that will take a bit more work."

Anselm stood up and clapped his hands together. "I'm

famished. Let's discuss this over dinner. Tonight you shall feast with the Blackthornes!"

"That was too easy," Cedric said, making sure no one else heard the whisper. Gregor elbowed Cedric when Anselm looked away.

"What? Took a week to get a soft maybe," Gregor said, before shifting his attention back to Anselm. *That was too easy,* Gregor thought. "You honor us," Gregor said humble and with a bow.

The king muttered something to Percival and, with a nod, he bid the crusaders farewell before venturing off deeper into the castle.

"We'll prepare a fine feast for you and your men. Tonight you shall enjoy the life of luxury in my home. You can regale us with your stories. There is this dish the head chef makes, with cream cheese and crab, positively divine. You—" The doors to the throne room swung open, interrupting the regent, and a soldier sprinted down the long hall toward the king. Percival doubled back to his father's side. His heavy armor clanged horribly in the empty halls echoing like the sound of a kitchen caught in an earthquake. His demeanor changed instantly.

"What is it?" Anselm asked. The king grew pale and flushed. Gregor's instincts screamed louder than ever.

"Fuck me, what is it now?" Gregor blurted out. Cedric shot him a look equal in terror and anger.

"It's..." At once everyone in the room knew what the man was going to say. All the color drained from the king's weathered face.

"My son."

ANSELM

ANSELM STARED AT the body of Aric as it was prepared for its final journey to the mausoleum. Incense carried by funeral officials stifled the rancid pork smell from the alleyways. All in black, the royal family kept all eyes focused on the gold-lined casket of Aric Lucius Blackthorne. Anselm's three-piece suit choked him, while Edgar's suit clung to him. Abigail cast a ghostly visage behind her ebony veil. Percival showed no sign of emotion in the open, only stared emotionlessly at the body of his older brother. Anselm knew that Percival's burdens increased tenfold now that he was successor to the throne. With Aric gone it was Percival's responsibility to produce an heir, something Anselm wasn't convinced he even wanted to do.

The morticians had cleaned up the prince exceptionally well, covering bruises, rope marks, and cleaning off the stench of piss in places suggesting it wasn't his. The sun behind the castle bathed the city in shadow. Jerrick Hart and his honor guard lined the street leading from the courtyard to the city below. Scholars in front of Alexander's statue bellowed out the events of Aric's life. Anselm's vision blurred from tears. It took every ounce of his strength not to break down.

All the noble houses attended the funeral, offering half-hearted condolences. The entire city gathered outside the castle. Silently, Anselm cursed the warm blue sky. It felt like nature itself celebrated Aric's death. The cracked, rusty bell from the Hall of Epochs pealed incessantly behind them. Abigail wrapped her arms around Anselm and buried her head in his chest.

"I remember when he was ten," Anselm began. "We were out in the western fields at the start of summer. Aric was still so sad that damnable cat died. He wanted to be tough, slay a griffon like his father. We were chasing after some deer. Aric had his little bow with him. I almost gave him a rifle… good thing I didn't. He wanted to show me that he was the best archer in the world. We lost them and went to horseback. By dumb luck, we stumbled upon them again. He took the shot at the deer. The horse bucked him and somehow he shot my horse in the ass. Damn thing ran back to Kingsbury before I got it to calm down. My little warrior."

Abigail laughed, wiping the tears away. "He was the sweetest boy."

"I never should have let him go down there," Anselm replied.

"He would've gone regardless," she said.

Anselm bent over and kissed Aric's cold forehead, followed by Abigail.

He gave a nod, and soldiers closed the casket. They carried the casket down the street. Passing by the masses, a gold-masked man in white caught Anselm's attention. The man gave a solemn nod and walked down the alley towards the residences. He remembered the man's words and the horrifying truth to them. Anselm's attention returned to the casket.

The procession walked out onto the fields to the hallowed grounds of the enormous mausoleum housing generations of Blackthorne dead, at the heart of gargantuan cemetery. Cracks wrapped around the pillars like vines. Withered flowers diminished the beauty of the ones added today. The Kingsbury Hall of the Dead was a castle unto itself among a city-sized collection of graves. Statues of Blackthornes from the past two thousand years held eternal vigil, heads hung low in dejection. New Prosperity's first family entered the palace of death.

Mourning nobles waited outside the white walls as the Blackthorne family followed the pallbearers inside. The mausoleum's entrance was decorated with relics and personal belongings of the monarchs of old: crowns, swords, armor, writings from philosopher kings, and other testaments to the family that had rebuilt the world.

The whole facility consisted of twisting hallways connected to large rooms where Blackthorne dead lay. The structure was modeled after the tombs of Chinese emperors, all the while maintaining the European gothic beauty their ancestors loved. The back half of the original mausoleum was rebuilt after being destroyed by would-be usurpers a few centuries before. The replacement structure shined a bright pristine white compared to the dull putty color of the original structure currently in the middle of a restoration project. The largest rooms were adorned with black and gold coffins, the Blackthorne flag draped over each one. Each area contained many separate rooms, one for each generation of the bloodline.

The faint crackling of freshly lit torches provided barely enough light. Portraits of ancestors appeared in the firelight, ancient kings and queens with solemn frowns. The bleak, gelid atmosphere filled Anselm with dread. Abigail and his sons said nothing as the procession entered the room for Anselm's family at the bottom of the complex. Edgar sniffled and tried to keep up with his mother. The room contained space for twenty coffins for the king's descendants. Scraping sounds came from under the casket as it was pushed back into its hole where it would come to rest.

"You're in good company now," Anselm choked out.

The pallbearers walked out, leaving the family to say their goodbyes. After a few moments, Percival escorted Edgar out. Anselm and Abigail stayed in the darkness and wept by their son's side.

"It's too much to bear," Anselm said, sobbing. Her tears fell as freely as his.

"We have to bear it," Abigail reminded him. Anselm wiped the tears from her eyes and kissed her.

"I know. He never became man I wanted him to be, but he died trying to save this country," Anselm said, placing his hand of the casket. With a final goodbye, the Blackthorne family left the cemetery.

The procession marched back to the castle courtyard. Percival took Edgar back to his room. Members of the Board passed the king and queen, each giving one last round of condolences. Anselm found the apologies of Ben Campbell the most nauseatingly false, made worse because his father couldn't bother to attend. Anselm and Abigail quietly went to the elevator. The king's grief quickly turned to anger, the feeling ripped and clawed at his insides.

"They're celebrating his death," Anselm spat.

"Grieve for our son. All else can wait," she said. Anselm, chastened, tightened at the overbearing grief crashing down on him.

"They beat his corpse. They spat on him. Pissed on him. They *pissed* on our son. I will hunt them all down."

"As you should," Abigail agreed, "But you need some damning proof or all you'll do is turn everyone else against us."

"At least some of them are involved. No way the rebels pulled this off alone," he said.

"Let's not talk of this anymore. I want to lie down," she said.

Hand in hand, the two retreated to their private chambers, hoping to escape the oppression of the outside world. Abigail didn't eat that day, sitting quietly with Anselm and their two surviving sons while time crawled by. Percival absconded to grieve in his own way. Edgar stayed by mother's side. His physical condition had deteriorated by the month, leaving him a frail husk likely to soon join his late brother.

The lights burned blue outside the castle throughout the night in honor of the fallen prince. Anselm spent the next few days without sleep. The harder he tried to rest, the harder his mind resisted. His head ached from lack of sleep. Delicious foods lay strewn across the dining hall each day, but it was all tasteless gruel to him. He made his way to the royal bathhouse to alleviate his grief. Simone followed him in. The young serving girl kissed his back in the water. He paid it no mind, even as her breasts pressed up against his back and her hand went down around his cock. She fumbled around with the limp thing for a few minutes before giving up. "I told you, I'm loyal to my wife," he said in a menacing tone. His thoughts grew paranoid. *Did the Board put her up to this?*

"Don't mourn, my liege. You still have two children," she said, attempting to soothe his broken heart. Her gesture backfired.

"I'm still ahead in the numbers, is that it?!" His voice grew sinister. He spun around to face the young woman and grabbed her throat, stopping himself from strangling her in the nick of time. "Leave the city."

After a disappointing soak, Anselm dried off and returned to shambling around as the castle ghost. After shaving off his beard, he looked much older than his years. The skin no longer hidden beneath the beard sagged in thick pouches. Guards ignored him as he shuffled around in his robes.

The passing days were not kind. Lost in his own thoughts his paranoia deepened. Patrols intensified along the roads and across the cities. It grew easier for Anselm to convince himself of everyone's guilt. His newfound friend, the Grey Sister, proved more effective than any common spy. With her technical expertise, the cultist gave the king eyes on his foes in their own homes, using their own private security cameras against them. In exchange for her manipulation of the city's technology, he allowed her to take any downtrodden folk she deemed useful. Anselm did not relish the idea of disreputables roaming his city abducting people, however she became too useful to eliminate.

One night, the woman appeared before him yet again, in his study. The room smelled of wine, courtesy of a drunken fit earlier. Anselm thumbed through volumes on Greek myths, one of his prized possessions, allowing him a different world in which to dwell. He kept his personal collection away from the library he so generously offered to Vigilant. Though the woman did not make a sound, Anselm felt her presence.

"My security is alarmingly lacking," Anselm said.

"I have news. The forces plotting your death will attack tomorrow night," she said, providing no elaboration. Her right eye burned green, and Anselm saw blurry figures sitting at a dinner table. Anselm realized these events transpired this very moment. The vague information only furthered his mounting rage. The woman's green eye flickered and went dark.

"You tease me, these images give me nothing! Surely you can give me more than that," Anselm said. The woman grunted with pain. She strained under the pressure. She collapsed to the floor.

"I… cannot. Perhaps they do not will it so," she said. Anselm fists clenched, and he shook with uncontainable wrath.

"You provide no info. These system hacks you perform seem to fail when I need them. I tire of these games!" he pulled a pistol from beneath his robe and aimed it at the woman's head. He slid his finger over the safety mechanism and turned it.

"Do they will this?" he asked. He pulled the trigger and the gun fell apart.

"All is their will, our lives… and our deaths. We all have our part to play, though yours may be at its end. Farewell, Anselm, we'll not meet again." Anselm lunged at her. Before he wrapped his hands around her, a hard knee to the gut sent him backward into the table. His head swam. When the disorientation ebbed, the woman was gone. Soldiers outside rushed in at the sound, finding their sovereign standing confused over a three-centuries-old carpet, now speckled with wine.

"I'm fine. Drank too much," Anselm growled. The soldiers noticed the pieces of gun on the floor.

"I'm fine," Anselm repeated. The soldiers nodded and returned to their duties. Anselm had more pressing concerns to deal with than a missing witch. Despite the woman's vanishing act her information helped him tremendously the last few days. Anselm seldom approved of his son's methods however he understood now that more aggressive methods were necessary to protect the Blackthorne line. Somewhere in the city, Anselm's allies plotted his demise; his body tingled with excitement at the thought of showing them the error of their ways.

BEN CAMPBELL

Ben Campbell sat naked in the spacious bedroom of his family's palatial Estates. Glancing out the window, he saw the Wells girls sipping tea in the courtyard with his brother and niece. He looked out onto the world unable to do anything but smile. With Aric unable to sniff around his business anymore, his weapon and vehicle sales to the cartels in Mexico would proceed unfettered. Technically the weapon industry belonged to Mr. Derbin; however, Ben had slowly moved in on his territory as the man grew increasingly feeble. Ben's endeavors in the southernmost state of New Prosperity more than made up for his failed ventures in the automobile business. He basked in the blinding warmth of the sun and relished this hands-off victory.

Ben craned his neck, double-checking that his bedroom door was closed. He dreaded hearing the exasperated voice of father demanding unremitting care. As long as his father Adam lived, he ruled the household; as tradition dictated, the most senior living parent or parents of the noble houses served on the Board until abdication or death. Adam, rapidly approaching his ninety-first year, had grown increasingly senile. Ben loved his father, but he grew weary of tending Adam's every need and watching his mind deteriorate only salted the wound.

Ben learned long ago that age didn't always bring wisdom. The Board of Directors generally adopted a condescending attitude toward all others, including other members they viewed as lesser. Younger representatives often fought an uphill battle against senior members, only to end up as pompous when they gained influence. Ben Campbell learned a long time ago that no one respected him. Ben chomped at the bit to get the power and respect he deserved. For the time being, he would have to settle for carnal pleasures.

Ecstasy surged through every fiber of his being. He wiped the sweat off his overly broad forehead. He adjusted himself. "Careful," he said. The gagging sound halted. Ben ran his lanky fingers through the girl's raven hair. "How old are you, again?"

"Thirteen, milord," she said.

"Don't look it," Ben responded. He normally preferred his girls a bit younger, a dark vice for the Minister of Foreign Affairs who championed ending child prostitution. Condemning men to death for committing the same crimes he did three times a week used to be disgusting to him; however, he'd had seen such hypocritical behavior from his peers that it no longer fazed him. He remembered being an idealist once; idealists never got far. Ben rammed the girl's head back down onto his cock. "Keep goin'." He groaned louder until he finished and sent her on her way.

When their business concluded, Ben slipped on his charcoal suit and sauntered down to the dining hall where his father ate. His father turned from his afternoon soup, trying to ignore the girl exiting through the back door. Adam did not sit alone. Across from him sat fellow Board members, Thaddeus Whitehall and Richard Davidson. After months of plotting to bring down the Blackthornes, only two Board members bothered to follow through.

"Sorry for the delay," Ben said with a wry smile.

A freshly shaven Richard Davidson sat cross-armed in a teal suit. The Davidson family was the manufacturing giant in the country. Though Thaddeus Whitehall technically served as

Minister of the Treasury, he also had power over departments of finance, commerce, and general services. In short, Thaddeus held near absolute control of the nation's currency. Thaddeus, like every Board member, saw himself as the true ruler of New Prosperity. Even without Anselm, such egos meant dealings with the other members devolved into pissing contests. Ben luckily joined the conversation after the ego battle concluded.

"We've delayed long enough," said Richard.

"The conflict is brewing all around us now. I say we let the rebels play out their little war. We can survive this and not lift a finger," replied Adam, dumping the broth back into the bowl.

Ben took a seat beside his father. "It should be tonight," he declared. Ben ignored the stares at his Frankenstein forehead. Adam dropped his spoon in the bowl and cussed loudly. Ben ignored it.

"He just buried his son," Adam said, fishing for his spoon.

"He's vulnerable," Ben replied.

"This isn't a decision we come across lightly. All he has to do is nod and we're gone. We can't buy off everyone," Adam said.

Ben scoffed. Richard ran his fingers through his hair.

"You're on your own," came Richard's voice.

"Mr. Derbin and I do not consent. Mrs. Caan is still on the fence," Adam cautioned.

"Fuck Mr. Derbin. He would gladly sacrifice us all to sit on that throne himself—just like his mother. We don't need him or you," Richard Davidson said venomously. Ben kept the urge to slam a kitchen knife into Richard's skull at bay.

"You grow bold," Adam said in a frail voice that had long ago lost the ability to intimidate. "And don't count Mr. Derbin out. He can make things happen."

Richard yawned in response to the veiled threat.

"Then we'll move tonight?" asked John.

"Yes. Everything is already set," Richard said with elation.

"Brotherhood of Minos?" Adam inquired.

"Heavens no, they got too greedy," Richard replied. Ben laughed aloud at the irony of such a judgment from one of the most selfish people in country.

"When the deed is done, we'll meet in the throne room. I'll send word. Good day gentlemen," Ben said. Adam sighed. *If anything goes wrong they'll sell each other out*, Ben thought. When the others left, Ben snacked on a glass of white wine and some toasted bread drizzled with chocolate. He and his father sat and ate as the setting sun bathed the dining room in crimson light.

"You don't think they'll be able to pull this off, do you?" Ben asked.

"The king may be weak, but he is no fool. You might need to frame the others just in case," Adam said. After the light meal, Ben escorted his father back to bed.

With Adam napping, Ben strolled through the mansion and savored his domain. The house guards saluted him as he passed. Ben not only commanded respect from subordinates, he demanded it. Kitchen staff, servants, dog trainers, soldiers—he ran a tight ship. Though Adam held the title as head of the household, it was Ben that handled the bulk of the family's affairs. Entering the courtyard, Ben watched the daughter of his niece's friend running about without a care in the world. Ben's dark appetite had spiraled out of control over the past few years. Everyone knew his vice, though few could do anything to a powerful family like his. Ben no longer bothered to seek help for his problem. *Everyone else is worse than me*, he told himself.

Out in the street, patrols marched constantly in an attempt to ferret out any potential threats. The death of Anselm's son affected the king's personality much faster than anticipated, further wearing down the mentally exhausted ruler. Blackthorne troops held constant vigil over the city, fueling everyone's paranoia.

Knight Ambassadors on his payroll fed him information about rebel forces on the march toward forts on the outskirts of the state.

He admired the rebels—despite being a loose organization of various militias, they quickly evolved into regime-ending force. One of the Knight Ambassadors on his payroll admired his pups in the kennel, there were always weaselly types looking to do favors to gain the Campbell's influence. The huskies regarded him with sweetness. John made kissy noises at the sweet dogs. He prided himself on the nicest dogs in the region. Ben was one of the nation's top dog breeders. He raised dogs of every kind and sold them to anyone that could pay. He approached the Knight Ambassador wiping the dog slobber onto his right pant leg to salute the nobleman properly.

"Need a girl for the night?" he asked. Ben considered packing the family up and leaving town for a few days, but he figured he had time for one last thrill.

"Indeed. Fetch me one. Don't care who. Don't care how," Ben said.

"Understood," the knight replied. Ben glowed, positively giddy at the coming night. He looked down at his pets.

"Tonight is daddy's big night."

ANSELM

SHAMBLING THROUGH THE halls, Anselm popped a few more anxiety pills to ease the horrendous pressure on his chest. Emotional outbursts and perpetual numbness left the king a shadow of his former self. For hours, Anselm wandered through the castle when not thrashing around in bed from insomnia. Damp air from the open windows left him congested and constantly spitting out mucus. He had worn the same wrinkly grey suit for the past three days, no longer caring about his appearance.

Anselm walked past the security office and immediately sensed something amiss. No one guarded the door. The security office contained a CCTV system, monitors that gave him eyes in the castle and the city. Thanks to the witch, it now secretly connected to the private security systems of the Board of Directors. Slowly, Anselm pushed open the door and found the place desolate.

He moved through the offices, stumbling upon the dead bodies of the monitoring staff with gunshot holes between the eyes. Anselm rushed over to the nearest row of monitors. He pounded on the keyboards to no avail. The screens flashed; golden masks filled every screen. Anselm stepped back, questioning his sanity yet again. With another flash, the masks disappeared. On one of the screens, Anselm noticed four unidentified figures sneaking through the halls. *One for every Blackthorne*, Anselm realized.

The assassins left dead men in their wake. In other rooms, Blackthorne troops carried on, unaware of what transpired in the halls. One took out a camera with a silenced pistol. Anselm pulled the silent alarm. Through the camera, Anselm saw troops jump to their feet. In the screen at the top left corner, one assassin moved unopposed toward his family. Troops burst into the security office. Anselm got them up to speed. None made it to the family rooms yet. He ordered men to guard Percival and Abigail and sent others after the assassins.

Using secret passageways hidden throughout the castle, Anselm got ahead of the last assassin and dashed inside Edgar's room. At that moment, the king lost his wits, after years of inaction he decided not to wait for the guards. Pulling out the knife he carried on his hip belt, he ducked inside the room. Anselm hid in the dark, waiting for the man who would dare to kill his eight-year-old son. Silently, the door opened and a shadowy figure stepped in. The assassin closed the door and moved over to the slumbering Edgar, only to find large pillows under the blanket. The king maneuvered himself between the assassin and the door.

"I never realized how arrogant you people were," Anselm said. He flipped the light switch, revealing himself to the man.

"How did—" The assassin choked out the words, as Anselm slowly pushed the knife into his right breast. Anselm's voice became frighteningly cool. "Who authorized this?" Anselm pressed the sword further in.

"The Campbells, the Whitehalls, and the Davidsons," the assassin gurgled. Anselm squinted at him, taken aback by the ease of the interrogation. The rage boiled inside him. He could suppress it no longer. Anselm wished the man wasn't so loose lipped; the torture rooms had sat vacant since Aric's departure. He once condemned Aric for going too far, now he considered that maybe the prince hadn't gone far enough.

The assassin made a desperate stab at the king, but Anselm dodged the blow and stabbed the man repeatedly in the torso, leaving his son's room a bloody mess. The assassin whimpered on the floor. Anselm slowly ran the knife through the assassin's neck, savoring his last gurgles.

He calmly walked from the room to his bedroom where his family hid with a small army of personal guards. Guards apprehended the other assassins. With hands bound and mouths gagged, the assassins couldn't use suicide as an escape. Anselm ordered them to the dungeons. The king went to the master bedroom. Edgar slept on the master bed while Abigail sat beside him stroking his hair. Percival stood at attention, with his rifle at the ready. Anselm noticed Edgar's stirring and gave a loving smile.

"It's okay, son. Go back to sleep," he said, patting Edgar on the head.

"Did he talk?" Abigail cut right to the chase.

"Yes. Members of the Board have moved against us. I must remind them who holds power," Anselm said, voice turned to a beastly growl.

"What happens now?" Edgar asked.

"Not for you to worry about. Sleep," Anselm said. He smiled again and gave Edgar a hug, leaving him to his dreams. Exiting the room, the regent approached the guards outside while Percy and Abby kept vigil over Edgar.

"Remove the body from my son's room. Alert my guard. Tell them to await my arrival in the courtyard. Monitor the Whitehalls and Davidsons, make sure they don't leave the city." Acknowledging the order, they left with haste. The king noticed the flickering lights of the hallway.

In the courtyard, Anselm led the black-clad soldiers down the street toward the Campbell Estates, the easy family to eliminate. Soldiers enforced the curfew with loaded rifles. The black outfit chaffed him terribly and clearly wasn't designed for his aging body.

Anselm realized the stupidity in leading this attack himself, but he wanted to give this matter his personal attention. Only stray animals and the homeless wandered the roads during the nightly curfews. A few suspicious loiterers were arrested.

Anselm and his personal guard marched to Adam's doorstep with snipers covering the area just in case. With knowledge provided by the Grey Sister, Anselm disabled the Campbell's security devices. The guards picked the locked door and entered the living room, dispatching the butler caught in the wrong place at the wrong time.

Adam's family consisted of two children, Ben and Bryce, and Bryce's eighteen-year-old daughter Emilia. The entire Campbell family lived on the Estates. The house guards lay dead around the complex, already eliminated by the king's agents. The sound of creaking doors brought Bryce out of his room. From the dumbfounded, agape expression on his face, Bryce expected arrogant thieves. He was too bewildered to act, and the soldiers rushed him and threw him to the ground. He tried to scream, but one of the king's guards quickly covered his mouth with thick tape. The troops moved to slash his throat, only to be stopped by the king. Bryce glanced up to a smiling king, who had a worse fate in mind.

"Fetch some rope, and for Emilia too. I'll be back," Anselm said, with far too much joy in his voice. He motioned the rest of his guard to stay. The king ascended the marble staircase. At the end of the hallway, a door opened, and a young girl ran out. He crept silently down the hallway. The brunette girl appeared young, fourteen at the oldest. She stopped dead in her tracks at sight of the king and his troops. Anselm placed his pointer finger over his lips and the girl acknowledged.

The door on the right side of the hallway lay open, and Anselm crept in. In the procession of slipping on some pants, Ben paid no attention to the person in the doorway. "Can't get enough of me, can you?" Ben asked. Turning around, Ben received the butt of a sword to his face. The soldiers dragged the unconscious Ben back to his brother.

Anselm proceeded to the deal with the Campbell family patriarch in the master bedroom. The king snuck in unnoticed. Adam slept like the dead in his gargantuan bed.

A statuette was perched atop Adam's nightstand, a crystalline figure of a corpulent nude female Anselm recognized as a gift from a merchant of Toth. The transparent innards of the statuette shined as if it contained the very cosmos itself. Anselm smiled and wrapped his right hand around the statuette. Placing the other hand across Adam's drooling, agape mouth. Adam gasped for air. Anselm held his hand in place, allowing Adam to suffer for a little while.

"Time to retire," Anselm whispered, his voice dripping with malice. Anselm removed his hand from Adam's mouth, giving the old man one last chance to scream before the statute crashed down on his face. Over and over again the statue impacted Adam's head, turning it to red mush. Anselm callously tossed the face-covered statue onto the twitching corpse of Adam Campbell. He casually walked back down the hallway, wiping bits of Adam's shriveled grey matter off his clothes. Anselm had Adam's body dragged to the living room for his sons to see. Emilia sat on her knees, bloodied and bruised. The three surviving Campbells pleaded for mercy.

Anselm moved to Emilia and pulled a dagger from his belt. The soldiers forced the brothers to watch Anselm open Emilia's throat from ear to ear. The brothers screamed. Anselm's conscience begged him to stop; he let it wash away with the blood running down to the floor.

"Family for family," Anselm said, coldly. The Campbell brothers wept. The soldiers placed Adam's and Emilia's corpses in between the brothers and tied them all together forcing them to face each other. Anselm's troops moved through the spacious house carrying barrels of brown liquid. Throughout the city, his men exterminated the known spies of the Whitehalls and Davidsons.

With a quick light, flames greedily consumed the Campbell home. Ben spent his final moments staring into the mashed-in face of his father while Bryce stared into the lifeless eyes of his daughter. With the deed done Anselm made his way back to the castle. He shook nervously when the gravity of his actions finally hit him, a lump formed in his throat as he prepared for what he was about to do next.

Anselm entered his private elevator and pressed the secret code on the keypad. He waited patiently while the elevator descended down through tower and earth. Few knew about the vault buried three miles beneath Blackthorne Castle. The vault was one of the oldest structures in the kingdom. His father had told him that it served as a shelter during the last days of the Old World as a refuge beneath the megalopolis of Chicago, now it served as a private storehouse for illegal tech concocted by his grandfather's chief scientist, Gideon Grey.

Gideon was brilliant man whose machinations led him into violating the Compact, as did many like him seeking knowledge and power of ancestors that were once poised to conquer the stars. Gideon's genius devolved into madness during his final days in the capital, with ramblings about manmade gods and transcendence. Anslem once doubted some of the more outlandish rumors of what Gideon accomplished. At the very least, Gideon built a few things to bring the Blackthorne's foes to heel and maybe nothing more. After being thrown around by masked men and chatting with cybernetic cultists, however, he wondered if Gideon wasn't so crazy after all. On the other hand, Gideon fled the capital and disappeared somewhere in the White Woods, which meant even the nation's best mind couldn't outwit the Compact.

A clang heralded the descent's end, and the doors opened. A hallway lined with red lights led to a black door with a small indentation in its side. Anselm placed his hand inside the opening and groaned as a needle pierced his skin. The machine greedily sucked up the blood. It buzzed and the vault hissed as the ancient air poured forth. Before Anselm lay large room of metal filled with wall safes and large human-sized containers.

Anselm walked over the left wall and opened the middle container. The door pushed in and slid aside. White light shot forth. In the light, he saw his Gideon's custom-made armor in all its glory. Before Anselm lay the beauty of the New World and the function of the Old, Gideon's parting gift to the Blackthorne family. Anselm moved close enough to touch the armor. Pieced together to look like human muscle, it was emblazoned on with the fiery crest of the family. He stretched out his hand, and the armor hummed to life. The chest pulled back, and each limb opened up. The armor enveloped him, becoming a second skin.

It took a few minutes to adjust to his new armor. He picked up the blade that lay beside it, made from meteor rock dubbed "heavenstone." Words inside Anselm's head guided him. He walked to the center of the room and plunged the sword into a slot in the ground. Brilliant light formed three circles around him. The room shuddered. White light filled the lines of the walls around the vault. The walls slid down revealing rows upon rows of weapons, armors, chemicals, and various machines of every kind. Scowling faces adorned the walls. Anselm perused the contents of the vault. The Vault was bult during the beginning of his grandfather's reign. The decades of peace made the need to access the Vault nonexistent; however, his parents and grandparents always had the desire to see what Gideon left for them as a last resort. Anselm weighed the possible death from the Compact against the possible, and already plotted, death at the hands of the Board. With the power of the Vault, Anselm at least had a fighting chance.

Returning the to the central chamber, he turned the sword again in the keyhole to close off the chambers, and then turned it a third time. A pedestal rose from within the circles of light. On the pedestal lay a syringe of pulsating orange liquid, the darkest of the forbidden tech. The chemical compound enhanced a person's mental and physical abilities, remnants of the outlawed genetic engineering of the Old World. He knew this compound was what the masked figure wanted him to use. Anselm would test it on himself before sharing this gift with his family. He opened his hand. His heart thudded violently. He recalled the masked figure's words: salvation has a price. Anselm buried his doubts and fear. Anselm grabbed a syringe. He touched a small button on his right gauntlet. The gauntlet opened. Anselm smacked his arm until a vein popped up. He stuck the syringe in the vein and shot the compound inside.

Fire coursed through his body, charging every cell with forbidden power. The world swirled, causing him to stumble. The spinning became too much to bear, and the king hit the floor with a thunderous crash.

CASS

Cassandra Lewis fired a round from her rifle at the wild dogs scrambling away from the cow rotting in the southern field. It seemed to her that everything had stopped working the moment Thos stepped away. She sat down on the edge of the gazebo, taking heavy drags on a cigarette and listening to the insect chorus heralding the night. Night watchmen stirred in the cabins at the base of the hill; each one gave her a wave before starting the next shift. Cassandra went through two packs of cigarettes a day waiting on news of Thos.

The day after Thos departed, the Rancher Association swooped in to intimidate Cass. The RA was a powerful group that controlled the Badlands, a small country in between Toth and New Prosperity. The RA looked to expand into Heartland, seeing Averill Estates as the golden goose. Each showdown with the RA ended in thinly veiled threats.

This last visit from the RA had proven different. Their agents handed Cass a set of documents that put things in perspective for her. She examined the papers. The bank statements, stolen from Thos, showed the Averill Estates hemorrhaging money. She learned a long time ago not to trust strangers, but it warranted discussion upon Thos's return. She wondered if the RA would've helped the rebels take this place had Thos refused Joseph's offer.

The days without Thos were tedious, only smoking and hunting with the dogs helped pass the time. The families of the Estates had Pyrenees dogs, several cats, and a community of frogs that loved to swarm the ponds during the hot times.

The dogs chased a portly rabbit through the burnt fields. A legion of rebels patrolled the area turning the peaceful farmland into an impromptu military base. She followed the dogs out toward the southern end, after the chunky rabbits her dogs yearned to catch. Sniffing up and down every blade of grass gave her no confidence when she saw the little animal not two yards from them. The dogs abandoned the search as her tones sent them into affection mode. Cracking branches ahead interrupted the dog's love time. She pointed her rifle in the direction of the noise.

"I'll shoot," she said. The rustling ahead came to a sudden halt.

"You've been saying that for years. Starting to think you're all talk," a voice replied. A grinning Thos Averill stepped out from behind a tree.

"Day isn't over yet," Cass said. She immediately raced toward him, and the two locked lips. A wine bottle in his hand brushed her in the back when they embraced. The dogs jumped up, jealous of the affection not directed toward them. More crackling branches heralded Thos's rebel escort, breathing heavily and mumbling curses.

The rebel escorts left Thos and Cass out in the open fields. Thos gave Cass the rundown of his adventure and the mandatory trip next week that might leave her a widow.

The two of them made their way to the bedroom to spend quality time away from everyone else. An ensuing intimate encounter ended up in a snoring match that quickly roused her. Cass reached for more cigarettes while Thos slept, rolling one in between her fingers until she decided against it. Thos slept only for about a half hour before he jolted back awake, the kind of jolt from a falling dream.

"Was I asleep?" Thos asked in confusion.

"Yep. Barely after nightfall. We're getting old," she said.

"My back pills agree," he teased.

The following day, the two lounged in the bedroom, content doing nothing. The day after, a few business matters sent him off, leaving her alone again. Morning turned to afternoon, and his absence began to concern her. She threw on some clothes and hurried down the steps, hoping more people weren't here to claim the Averill Estates.

She searched high and low for him, farmhands and rebel soldiers all swearing they hadn't seen him. She maintained her composure trying not to worry. She worked her way around the house. It was a beautiful day, the kind of day on which they would picnic in other days. She walked out to their favorite spot. On the hill overlooking the property, under the two willow trees, she saw Thos waving at her with a bottle of champagne and his trademark grin. He summoned her on over to a large blanket with two pillows, a basket of peanut butter, raspberry jam sandwiches, and all the sweet tea they could drink. The dogs bounced around in fields below, creating a picturesque scene of bliss when they weren't laying balls up.

"All of my favorite things in one spot. And having you here is not so bad, either," Cass smiled.

"Take the good with the bad," he replied.

Thos took a seat and patted a spot on the blanket beside him. She sat down. Pouring her a glass of iced tea he made some small talk about the weather. Even when Thos wasn't trying to make her laugh he did, one of the many things about him she loved. After all these years, she never imagined that sad little boy from one happenstance encounter would be the love of her life. Cass had more on her mind than such niceties. She gave herself a little more time before they tackled the inevitable.

The two napped away a good chunk of the day under the trees, roused by the furious licks of happy dogs. They awoke to a blanket of stars. Stargazing had become something of a passion for them; some of her favorites memories involved nights under the stars. A quick brush of his hair signaled Thos adopting a serious disposition. He moved about as if it pained him to reveal his emotions. "You and I have been through some hellacious times. I don't know why you stayed honestly… lucky me, eh?"

"Most definitely," she teased.

"You saw something in me that no one else ever did, not even me. I was miserable until you showed up. All the adventures we've had, some have been real barn burners… literally that one time," he said.

The faint sound of music came from behind her. Cass turned around to find a few farmhands, one strumming a guitar, and the other singing. Her heart fluttered when she recognized the tune. It was "Kentucky Rain," an old bluegrass song she loved, hailing back from centuries before the fall of the UNA. She watched the musicians until she sensed Thos fumbling with something. When she looked back at him he held a shiny diamond ring, almost dropping it.

"I'd be totally lost without you, Cass. You have always been the center of my universe. No matter where am I or what I'm doin', I want you with me… well not the wars, but you know what I mean. I don't want to put this off any longer. Cassandra Lewis, will you marry me?" She kissed him. The kissing intensified. The musicians never missed a beat, playing the song in its entirety.

"That was a yes, by the way," she said. Thos waved and the band played more songs. After a few songs, the farmer band left the two cuddled beneath the stars. They pointed out the constellations, making a few up along the way. Thos's breathing suggested he had more to say, and she already knew what it was.

"I know we're losing money," Cass said. "I know the RA and Joe pushed you into this. I know we couldn't keep this going forever and I know you don't want to," Cass said. Thos sighed.

"Every time I see this place, I see my brother. It is a nice old place, but this was his life," Thos admitted.

"Your father just wanted you to be happy. This place is not what matters to me; you are. If it's time for us to leave then we leave," she said. His eyes teared up a bit. "Besides we can be lazy anywhere."

"I am glad you feel that way," Thos said.

"I'm with you 'til the end," she said. Cass finally brought up what had to be said.

"You realize we are in serious danger if Joe doesn't win. Or if these increasingly violent rebels decided that all businesses are evil and come after us," she said.

"I've been trying not to think about, but yes, if Joe loses you need to be prepared to flee the country with or without me," Thos said. "As for the rebel thing, just stay close to our friends; if they move on you, I will hand deliver them to the king myself." Cass thought on the idea of being an exile in the western neighboring country of Toth and the possibility of being executed should that fail. Cass and Thos made some plans to create some bug-out bags before he left.

"Don't worry about that now," he said. "Rebels are cropping up and winning all across the country, and we'll have plenty of time to flee while fight their way back down here." Cass accepted his words, knowing that all they could do was concoct a few plans and roll the dice.

"Let's enjoy this night. Everything else can wait 'til the morning," Thos said.

The two lay together under stars uttering no more words. This loveable man had a strange power over her, his whiskered face and buffoonish grin somehow always made everything right with the world. She rolled over onto to him and kissed his lips, his uneven patch of cactus whiskers tickled. He lay there at first, enjoying her affections. Her fingers entwined with his and the kissing turned white hot. Under the star-drenched night, Thos and Cass enjoyed each other.

"You know what happens when you poke the bear," he said, raising a mischievous eyebrow.

"My memory is a little fuzzy," she said. He tossed her onto the blanket, taking charge. The dogs lay curled up beside them, wild twitching suggested endless shenanigans even in their sleep. This perfect moment made all the toil and trouble worth it. Together, unmindful of princes and rebels, the two prepared for a bright future finally able to see their best days were ahead of them.

THOS

After a week recovery Thos, Drake, Zora, and against Zora's wishes, Melvin, regrouped and journeyed toward the Fey community south of Kingsbury. While the four recuperated from the assault on Fort Alexander, rebel forces seized control of Heartland and began expanding into the other states.

After a day of traveling on horseback, the group arrived at Calhoun. Calhoun was named after the city that stood in this very same spot during the Old World. The Green River cut through the two sections of town, connected by a metal bridge with an unappealing teal color. The foursome went over the rusty bridge, nearly knocked off by a speeding car. Thos rarely saw cars, except those owned by government officials. Cars required licenses from the capital and were taxed heavily; even then, acquiring one after extensive paperwork and inspections took years unless you knew the right people. Grey cars were available to anyone with the funds, whereas black and silver cars were given only to the elite. Thos had his automobile application denied seven times in seven years.

After nearly getting killed by what was possibly the only car in region, the group entered Calhoun. Thos imagined shimmering blues waters but was met with brown instead. Calhoun was a cozy riverside town of fifteen hundred people seldom involved in anything outside its borders. Thos and the others followed the cracked main street past brick and wooden buildings colored in plain whites, browns, and yellows to the Green River Inn.

"The name is not very accurate. The river is not green at all," Zora commented. Thos had no idea what to make of her words.

"Brown River is less enticing," Thos mused. He looked at Zora. "I think we should stay here and head out in the morning. May not find too many good stops the rest of the way. We'll press on if you'd rather, though."

"This place is fine," Zora said. All three men sighed with relief. She shook her head at them. "Whiners," she muttered.

After entering the reddish-brown building, the group found themselves in a decent sized pub with a few occupants. Thos approached the bartender methodically cleaning shot glasses.

"I don't reckon you have four rooms for a few weary travelers?" Thos said, showing off the shining silver crowns now resting in his palm.

"Three," said the innkeeper.

"It'll do," responded Thos. Thos threw four silver coins onto the table.

"Top floor. First two are on the left, and the other is second to last on the right. We're not responsible for any accidents that may befall your horses. One guy tried to eat one a few nights ago. Your valuables and lives are your own responsibility."

"There's the down home hospitality I like to hear," Thos replied. He accepted the three keys, jingling them wildly.

"I will warn you I'm a fierce cuddler," Thos joked.

"I don't plan on sleeping alone, but not with ya'll," Melvin said matter-of-factly. Thos doubted anyone would object to Melvin sleeping alone. *Sharing a room with his good friend Syphilis*, Thos thought.

"Drake and I can share," Zora said. Drake's eyes widened, turning the hardened soldier into a bumbling idiot.

"Yeah, no big thing," Drake stuttered.

"I'm not touching that one… and she probably won't either," Thos joked. Drake looked down at the floor. Thos and Melvin laughed.

"Let's revel," Melvin said, already heading to a corner table.

The four secured their belongings in their rooms and returned to the restaurant for a quality meal. Thos flicked the peanut shells littering the table, chugging down a beer while awaiting his meal. Thos and Melvin attempted to outdrink one another at first.

Drake took another sip of beer, leaving a frothy mustache across his upper lip. Zora pointed at her lip, and Drake self-consciously wiped his mouth. The two sat while Thos and Melvin engaged in the liquor battle with neither side gaining the upper hand. Several rounds later, the conversation was little more than badly tossed word salad.

Thos's head began to spin; he flicked a peanut shell directly at Melvin. Melvin yelled at the bartender for other illicit substances he might have on hand. The bartender brought over some hash. Melvin lit up, exacerbating his incoherence.

"My reputation will spread from here to the Specific Ocean," Melvin said.

"Not sure I know that one," Thos replied. Melvin laughed, and whiskey poured from his mouth like an amber waterfall. Melvin's behavior quickly began to lose its humor with Drake.

"Alright don't get too crazy. We're on a mission," Drake said.

"Yeah man, you are getting rather old for philandering. You need to find a special someone and settle down," Thos hiccupped.

"I had someone. I had a lot of things, but I cocked that up," Melvin said, his disposition turning sour.

"Sounds like a story coming on," Thos said. Melvin's face turned tomato red.

"Nope," Melvin responded. After some time blubbering over lost loves, Melvin thrust himself up from the chair and fumbled up the stairs towards his room. The rest of them turned their attention toward nourishment.

Following a hearty dinner of steak and butter-drowned asparagus, the group retired for the evening. Darkness just began to set in as Thos sat upright on the creaky, rigid bed. From his pocket, he removed a small leather-bound book entitled *In the Woods: Folklore of New Prosperity*. Thos carried the book with him everywhere, sneaking a read in his downtime. Out of all the gifts his father had given him, books were the ones that got the most mileage, primarily those on folklore.

Thos opened the weathered book to the section about the White Woods, his new destination. Once Cook County State Park in the Old World, it was now government protected land for the Fey. No highways or official roads cut through the dense forest, but it saw travelers report everything from metal men to bleeding trees to man-eating insects that snatched children. After sobering up, Thos read the entry.

From the journal of Jonathan Samson, squire to Ser Jean-Pierre Cadeaux of the Faucon Chevaliers:… In the darkest parts of the woods, we can see nothing. This damn forest is horrid, smelly, and way too hot. There are always strange sounds like buzzing and scraping. We came from the west sent to aid the Blackthornes against a group of raiders raping and killing travelers along our borders. Sir Cadeaux has taken it upon himself to deal with the problem. Lucky us. We entered the western side of the forest on the way to Kingsbury with no sign of any trouble. As we walked, the buzzing sound grew louder. We could not trace the sounds, and our lamps did little to help. We heard nothing from our companions since leaving the Fey.

The entire trip has been uneventful, and neither of us felt any danger, so we took the buzzing to be of little threat, Ser Cadeaux said he sensed movement beside of us. The buzzing became unbearable as I watched Ser Cadueax. He has killed nearly 200 men in his lifetime, fought off the barbarian tribes for the north and the west. He took the head of the Neo-Visigoth chief as his prize and his daughter for his slave. But the buzzing, I've never seen him like that before. The buzzing drove him crazy. He never let his guard down, not that it mattered in the end. The last thing I remember before I passed out was the sight of Ser Cadeaux, the top half of his head completely torn off. The magnificent Red Rider, slayer of a hundred men, died in an instant."

The tale captured Thos's imagination. The official accounts reported the knight as being murdered by raiders in hiding out in the woods. Thos understood that every bit of that story could be lies, but it didn't hurt to prepare for the worst.

DRAKE

Drake and Zora sat on the double bed in a perfectly average room, better than most he had stayed in. The lights were a little dim, but at least there were no stains on the wall. With nothing of interest going on in town, Drake struck up a conversation with Zora.

"I spend a lot of time traveling, but I never really get to enjoy it. Maybe I'm just a stick in the mud," he chuckled. Zora's glossed-over eyes filled with life upon hearing something from Drake besides duty.

"You're too busy solving everyone's problems. Take time off," she said, mustering a half smile.

"It is long overdue," Drake admitted. It was painfully obvious to Drake that Zora had not left her home entirely by choice. Drake, an experienced problem-solver, tried his hand at comforting Zora.

"This homecoming of yours isn't a heartwarming reunion, is it?" Drake asked, giving Zora his undivided attention. Drake sat down on the bed, his back straight, not the most relaxed posture.

"It's complicated," she sighed.

"Most things are," Drake said, thinking of the last few weeks.

"I don't want to go back," she said woefully.

"That bad?"

"I… there are… things I want to forget," Zora said. Drake's forehead wrinkled while he waited for her to clarify. "But a person can keep running forever." She stared into his eyes.

"I learned long ago that it's better to face these things head on because sooner or later they catch up to you. It may hurt and not go the way you want, but better to face it head on," Drake said. He looked at her as if he didn't want to believe the words himself.

"You think so?" she asked, also unconvinced.

Drake knew things had spiraled out of control and he prepared for the worst. Drake forced himself to maintain a glimmer of hope, but it vanished quickly at the rumors flying around of murders in capital pushing the king off the edge. Drake knew the kingdom would recover; however, he was unsure of the number of casualties between here and there. Anselm wasn't like his eldest son, though a part of him wouldn't deny that if backed into a corner, Anselm may resort to something desperate. Drake never put stock in the rumors of Gideon's weapon stash beneath the city, brushing it off given that had such a thing existed, someone in the capital would've used it by now. The more he thought about it, however, the deeper his heart sank.

Anselm managed to be even-tempered for most of his career, only showing the occasional flash of anger when obstructed by the Board at every turn. Drake visualized King Anselm racked by pain, cradling the body of his dead son. With the defiling of his son's corpse, rebels taking key locations around the nation, and assassination attempts on the rest of his family, Anselm may very well crack under the pressure of it all. Reports of Blackthrone supporters being attacked in the streets and their property burned made cities less than safe. Any man backed against the wall may resort to forbidden tech. With rumors of murder and the reputation of lost knowledge driving people mad, the idea became a frightening reality. One day Drake would have to face the king. *Am I willing to kill Anselm? Am I willing to let him die?*

Drake swallowed the doubts seeping in. Zora watched the chipped fan spin above them.

"I do," Drake said. They both smiled at each other, the mixture of silence and emotions grew uncomfortable. He continued his awkward smirk. Drake was attracted to her, though he hardly made time for romance or other things career knights saw as distractions. However, he wanted to get to know Zora better, another fish out of water sucked into the storm of civil war. He suddenly realized that talking to people wasn't part of his skill set. An unexpected cough only worsened his humiliation. Zora laughed. The double beds looked stiff and disagreeable. He moved over to the other bed.

Zora stood up and began to undress but stopped before revealing anything risqué.

"Oh! I'm so used to being alone. I didn't think—" she said, embarrassed. Drake felt his face go ablaze looking at her, internally kicking himself for not looking away as a gentleman should.

"I didn't think Fey were so… proper," he said, surprised.

"We may not have rules, but we're still decent. Outsiders like to paint us all as nymphomaniacs, I assure you, that's false," she said. Drake wasn't fond of letting others see his body either, though his issues came via scars from battle.

"People often make incorrect judgments about those they don't know and apparently I'm no different," Drake said. Drake turned to let Zora undress without an audience. When he heard the flick of the light he opened his eyes. In the dark, he saw her shape crawl under the covers of the other bed. He heard her suck in a breath.

"What's wrong?" Drake asked.

"Nervous," she said. He decided not to press the issue.

"Me, too," he said. He wished the same were true for him. It made it harder knowing his goal would lead him to battle against his newfound friends and possibly the king himself. Drake debated consulting the king and pleading for him not to follow in his son's footsteps while he still had the chance. Drake managed to gather intel on rebel plans to attack the forts on the state border, leaving the capital hopelessly surrounded by enemies. Though he feared the king's retaliation on the populace, he had the knowledge to crush the rebels and end the war. Drake couldn't bear to think of a plan that involved betraying the king, but he realized he would have to plan for the same just as he did with Aric. Drake got out of his own head and back to conversation with Zora.

"Whatever is bothering you, you no longer have to face it alone," Drake said.

"I appreciate that. Goodnight, Drake," she said.

"Goodnight," he replied. Drake closed his eyes.

Drake's thoughts again turned to the swinging corpse of Aric and the many soon to follow.

MELVIN

Melvin Shor lay on the bed watching the naked woman slumbering at his side, her sweat-beaded skin glistened in the apricot moonlight shining through the open window. He had her twice already that night, but instead of exhaustion he felt pure energy. From the position of the moon, he could tell it was after midnight. Melvin thrust himself up from the bed. Melvin smelled of sweaty sex and he couldn't care less.

Melvin threw on his clothes and crept out of the room to stretch his restless legs. He decided only to take his hunting knife, affectionately named Dainty, and a pistol with him as a precaution. The scented candles the woman brought with her were almost molten wax now, spilling out over the dresser. Melvin had a habit of leaving places a mess; he didn't see the big deal as an officer in the rebel army. He made great strides down to the bar. Downstairs a few men sat drinking; one of them shot him a sour look.

Melvin ignored the glares, there was another vice to satisfy this night. Rebelling against the king wasn't cheap. Or safe, especially with the news of Board attempt on the remaining Blackthornes, metamorphizing a grieving king more willing for a peace to a paranoid one willing to set fire to the world. With rebel groups massing around the globe, Melvin was confident that the king and the Board's arrogance would lead them to the same fate as Aric.

Joseph and his brother Abraham taxed the locals to maintain the war effort. His friendship with Joseph allowed Melvin a little inside knowledge. Every now and then he would sneak in the banks where the special war tax revenue was stored and skim a little off the top before the collector's arrived. A few coins light on payments was never that big a deal when Joseph ran things, but a few hundred every now and then did occasionally cause a problem.

Melvin shrugged off the pangs of guilt, taking advantage of his connection with the rebel leader. Melvin always had a knack for convincing himself he'd earned it, and for his efforts in the cause others might agree. Melvin used some of the earnings to help locals, so he figured it was better in his hands anyway. Melvin made an internal promise to lay off after this final collection

Melvin strode out of the inn and out to the cool night air, breathing in deep. He strolled cautiously through streets, making sure to stay in the well-lit areas in case the angry locals sought revenge for Joseph's tax. Melvin sensed a person following him. The man seemed familiar, someone from Joe's or Abraham's group. Abraham was far more authoritarian than his younger brother. Melvin pepped himself, walking on while maintaining an aura of confidence.

As he walked, he noticed little of interest in the small town. The edge of the city rapidly closed in on him. "The hero of Ellora doesn't run," Melvin told himself. Melvin promised himself he wouldn't let any more of his victories be accidental. He reached the edge of the town and worked his way around. He heard the man heading out of the city as he hid behind a corner. He waited for the man to come around. Melvin grabbed his pistol.

The man rounded the corner and aimed the pistol at Melvin. Melvin pointed his right back. The man was tall with jug-handle ears and a smashed-in nose sporting torn jeans and a button-up plaid shirt.

"You one of Joe's?" Melvin asked. The man sneered, suggesting Joe was beneath him. Melvin hated Abraham; he couldn't recall him doing much besides taking credit for the whole rebellion from halfway around the country. He only saw the man a few times before, but he had seen enough to know his type. The last he heard from Abraham, he'd murdered Emerald Coast's regent to prove that corrupt leaders aren't untouchable.

Melvin learned of Abraham's life on the Emerald Coast. Joseph said in the Old World the Emerald Coast was part of an area once called the "Tar Heel State," where mineral deposits like emeralds gave the place its name.

"I work for Abraham," the man said. "Been doing a little reconnaissance work down here. Heard a rumor the taxes have been coming up a tad short, and no surprise it happens to be everywhere you go. We figured since you and Joe was buddies he was letting it slide." Melvin regretted picking the alleyway that smelled of rotten fish on a hot summer day.

"So what? I've earned it, do more good with it than you. I led the charge while Abe twiddled his dick. You fellas do your fair share of stealing, too," Melvin snapped back. He smiled when he saw his words struck a nerve with his accuser. The agent smacked him in the face with his pistol. Melvin turned back and spit blood down on his boots. He burned with anger at this glorified raider talking down to him.

"I know all about you, Melvin. I know about your dirty little secrets, about your little dead wife. You stand here acting like you're the golden boy. Did it take the pain away from your failures? Did the brain pain make you like that? We know all about you. You're nobody now, just an idiot livin' in a cave." Someone bringing up his distant past took Melvin aback. The vein in Melvin's forehead throbbed, he felt a rash decision coming on.

"Fuck you. I was a damn good father and soldier. I paid for my mistakes. I'll be damned if I'm gonna be lectured by a child-killing shit like you," Melvin snarled.

"Careful what you say," the man said.

"Or you'll shoot me?" Melvin asked. He feared his friendship with Joseph didn't protect him as much as he believed.

"Joe wouldn't let that slide… but keep this up and I will," he said. The man lowered his gun. Melvin responded to the situation as he always did, acting without thinking. He had always struggled with gut reactions. He once had a great life, and certainly not that of some cave-dwelling idiot. He smiled with his gun still aimed at the man. Impulse got the better of him. Melvin pulled the trigger. Blood splattered on the wall behind him and the man crumpled to the ground. "Oh shit! Dumb, that was really dumb."

Men hollered and ran toward the sound of the gunshot. Melvin hastily looted the body. He ran down the alley and hopped over the chipped white fence at the end, bringing it down with him. He quickly jumped up, ran out into the forest, and worked his way back toward the town's entrance. His nerves were electric. There was no guilt in killing that man. Melvin felt good, better than good.

Returning to town, Melvin moved through the darkened streets. Only a handful of the streetlights worked. Melvin wished he had the chance to dump the body in the river, but he'd be gone by tomorrow. Melvin muttered to himself while he walked. "I don't take too much money. I'm a hero. I deserve a hero's reward," he said. A loud crash behind him caused Melvin to nearly jump out of his skin. A pivot maneuver left him pointing his gun at a kid in washed out overalls rummaging through the trash.

"What the fuck? Get out of here!" Melvin yelled, immediately throwing his hand over his mouth. The boy ran off with surprising haste. Melvin laughed nervously. Peering around the corner, he gave the city a once-over before strutting back to the inn.

Suspiciously he glanced back at the murder scene. In the distance, a crowd gathered around the man he'd killed. He dipped back inside the inn and fast walked up to his room. In his room the woman still asleep in bed, the covers tossed carelessly to the floor. He lightly licked her nipples, she responded with a groggy chuckle. He took her again as soon as she woke, fucking her hard and fast. The headboard of the bed bounced off the walls to the annoyance of the residents in the neighboring rooms. She moaned loudly, an exaggeration for her client's benefit, he knew. Melvin's thrusting grew harder and faster until he finished. "You are insatiable," she said.

The woman stretched beside him, fully awake again. Thoughts on his old life threatened to spoil his sunny disposition. Melvin fought hard to shed the darkness of his past. The thoughts of old misdeeds left him desiring more than just the usual carnal relations. Melvin walked into the bathroom and picked up a towel, tossing it to her.

"It's time for me to go," she said. The woman got up and made a move for her clothes.

"You don't have to go just yet, do you?" Melvin asked.

"Baby, I think you've had enough tonight," she said, while cleaning up his mess.

"Stay with me 'til sunup. I'd rather not be alone," he said, trying not to think about the family life he'd lost. The woman's brow wrinkled, and she gave him an expression of confusion.

"I really should be going," she said. Melvin fumbled for his wallet on the nightstand and threw a gold coin bearing the image of Anselm on the bed; the irony of using the king's money wasn't lost on him. The woman removed her bra back and went back to the bed.

Melvin lay down in the bed beside her and turned on his side, throwing his arm around the woman. It brought him back to the days before his life went to hell. He threw himself into drinking, fighting, drugs, and whoring to take his mind off a life he could never have back. As Melvin lay in the dark, he could tell by the way she moved that she didn't really care for him. It hurt at first, though after a time he found himself not caring. He'd done plenty of awful things in his days, yet he believed himself ahead in the numbers. Melvin rolled over and grabbed a cigar from a box in his nightstand and lighter on top. He lit the cigar and took a heavy drag. He knew good things were coming his way. He'd tell himself this incessantly until he believed it.

ANSELM

Anselm sat on his throne, glancing down at the newly downsized Board of Directors. His right arm throbbed, and he had no recollection of how he got back from the Vault. When he collected himself, Anselm headed to the throne room and called a meeting. Anselm smirked at Thaddeus Whitehall anxiously scouring the group for Adam and Ben Campbell after the fire that destroyed their home. The Board appeared vulnerable to Anselm now; he drew strength from that. Yellow streams of light poured into the room, shining a spotlight on the growing fear.

"For the life of me I cannot remember a time when we weren't at each other's throats," Anselm said with sinister calm.

"Why did you summon us? This better be important," Mr. Williamson grumbled.

"Oh, don't worry you'll appreciate this," Anselm's voice deepened to a growl. Mr. Davidson eyeballed the other members intently. Mr. Davidson's recent weight loss surgery left him looking like melted clay; after last night, he was now the ugliest member of the Board.

John Derbin remained icy calm. Anselm identified him long ago as the most dangerous of the group. It burned Anselm up to now. Mr. Derbin held more power and influence than he did, and he hoped this maneuver would remind the old man of his place.

"The last few days were, let's say taxing on me, to say the least. My oldest son is dead, my youngest son is sick, and Percival has yet to produce an heir. The country is shambles, and the people are making war on us. I was about ready to give up when last night something happened to me. I had a moment of clarity," Anselm said. Mr. Davidson sneered. The king sat up straight, and all except for Mr. Derbin stepped back. Anselm sat upright and proud, unlike the man he was so accustomed to being.

"Your assassins are dead," Anselm stated matter-of-factly. Anselm pushed himself off the throne and walked outside, motioning the Board members to follow. Anselm moved with a vigor not seen in years. The perplexed Board members whispered amongst themselves as they followed the king outside.

The royal guards herded them toward a wagon. Brown stains covered the wet blankets over some atrocious thing, while a few hungry flies zipped around. Anselm pulled the green cloth away from the wagon to reveal the charred bodies of the Campbell family. Mr. Beaumont slipped his mouth over his hand, failing to stop the vomit seeping through his fingers.

"The Campbell family has had its status revoked. They didn't act alone. Step forward and admit your guilt, and I'll show what little mercy is left in me," Anselm said. None of the Board members moved, a few quickly looked for the nearest exit. With a simple gesture from Anselm, two soldiers left the cart and approached Mr. Whitehall. The two soldiers grabbed Mr. Whitehall.

"You can't do this! Release me at once!" Mr. Whitehall squealed. Sweat began rolling off Mr. Whitehall's old brow; he struggled feebly against armed men. Anselm delighted in watching his foe cower. Anselm approached Mr. Whitehall, the king's hot breath rolled across his face. "I have fantasized about this day for such a long time," Anselm said, voice becoming a venomous whisper.

"My children will take your head," Mr. Whitehall barked.

"Well, the ones you didn't abandon to death," Anselm said. Anselm's jab referenced the one great commander, Victor Whitehall. Victor was a shining example of what the elite families were supposed to be. After suffering career-ending brain damage, Victor was disowned by his family and left to die in Heartland. Anselm took Mr. Whitehall's threat very seriously.

"But you bring up an excellent point, sergeant, round up his kids," Anselm commanded. Sheer terror fell over Mr. Whitehall's face. The guard hesitated. "Do it, soldier," Anselm growled. Anselm's predatory gaze froze Mr. Whitehall. The tough façade of Thaddeus Whitehall melted away.

"Please don't kill me! The Davidsons are the ones you want!" Mr. Davidson was overcome by a wide-eyed horror as his partner ratted him out. Anselm's evil eyes gave a quick look at Mr. Davidson. He focused on Mr. Whitehall first, it took him all of five seconds to decide the man's fate.

Profanities streamed from Mr. Whitehall's mouth as he was dragged across the courtyard. A crowd gathered in the courtyard, per the king's "request." Soldiers worked their way behind the rest of the Board. Gasps echoed down the sea of people that filled the streets. Anselm took the center stage, and instantaneously the crowd grew silent.

"People of New Prosperity, look upon this man. He's everything wrong with this nation. This man, along with others, tried to kill my family. This man used you from the day you were born. While you were struggling to live, his coffers grew fatter. He gambled away your money, bullied you off your property, bet against the substandard homes he sold you, and left in a debt you can never repay, and that is just his day job. The Whitehalls have lost their purpose. The rest of the Board, and the nation, must work with me—not against me."

The castle doors let out a rusty groan as Abigail ran out, along with her sons and a host of bodyguards. Abigail reached Anselm's side, immediately wrapping her arm around him. Mr. Whitehall's pleas rolled across silent courtyard,

"Let any who doubt me see that this is the fate of any who would harm my family. He nodded to the men holding Mr. Whitehall. The two soldiers tore Mr. Whitehall's clothes off as another soldier drove up in a black four-door car. The driver stepped out of the vehicle and grabbed a rope from the trunk. Anselm's voice became a thunderous and commanding.

"Tad fancied himself an automobile aficionado, having more than half the cars in the kingdom. So much so that he destroyed most of the manufacturers he wasn't invested in. He sure loved cars, being driven around the world he thought he owned. I guess if one has to die what better way than doing what you love."

Mr. Whitehall watched completely impotent while the ropes were tied around his wrists and attached to the reinforced bumper of the car. Soldiers cleared people from the road. Anselm gave the command and a soldier entered the car and fired up the engine. With a vicious jerk, Thaddeus flew forward and slammed against the uncaring road.

The terror from the citizens drowned out the man's screams. Some in the crowd cheered at the cruel spectacle. One older man attempted to spit on Mr. Whitehall. The citizens of Kingsbury watched as the car dragged the naked Mr. Whitehall down the street and out of sight. Anselm's empowered voice brought all attention to him.

"Soon Mr. Whitehall will return here vastly improved. He will be a reminder of the end those who threaten this land will suffer. Those loyal to the crown need not fret, for I am not your enemy. To prove to you my sincerity, the wealth of the traitors will be used to repair the nation's infrastructure that has been neglected for so long. This is the first step to healing this great nation. Stand proud citizens of New Prosperity. It's a new day!" Mr. Davidson gulped within earshot of the king. Anselm leaned over him, feeling invincible. He raised his hands up to the crowd, feeding off the energy.

With Mr. Whitehall on his farewell tour, the commoners returned to their lives. Mr. Davidson watched the empty street dumbfounded at the grisly end of Mr. Whitehall. Anselm walked by and placed a hand on Mr. Davidson's shoulder. Anselm looked at his soldiers.

"Hang him from the wall," Anselm said.

After concluding his business for the day, Anselm returned to the throne room with his family. Breathing heavily, he could hardly believe he what he had done. It was a fantastic feeling to remove the ticks embedded in the country's skin. With a monstrous stretch, he welcomed young Edgar onto his lap.

"Your old man did a good job today. I hope that didn't bother you, seeing that," Anselm said. Edgar's complexion appeared deathly pale for one so active.

"No, sir," he replied, clearly lying.

"Just dad," Anselm corrected. Anselm ran his fingers through Edgar's raven hair and kissed his forehead. Out of the corner of his eye, Anselm saw Abigail and noted her growing concern for him.

"I need to speak with your mother for a moment," Anselm said. Edgar hopped off Anselm's lap. The moment Edgar left Percival approached him, looking particularly haggard. Percival motioned and Edgar followed him. Abigail passed in front of him. As she approached, Anselm grabbed her arm, surprising her. He kissed her hand and pulled her onto his lap.

"If I spend my days grieving, things will only get worse. This country needs a strong leader. It's good to be me again," Anselm said with vigor. He reached in to kiss her, but she turned away.

"I... I need more time," she said. It brought Anselm added guilt to have any emotion other than grief. He rested his hand on the throne armrest and tapped his fingers to a deafening echo.

"Guess I got carried away," he admitted. Abigail smiled briefly.

"Perhaps now we can rein in this dissent," she said.

Anselm let out a bitter laugh. "If only. They're just looking for an excuse to move against us. I doubt there's anything we can do that won't inflame some group or another. And if we do nothing then we are weak, and they will move on us anyway."

"We need to tread carefully from here on out," she cautioned.

"Indeed. Killing Tad and using his money for good will gain me the public's favor." He tapped the fingers of his free hand on the throne in a different sequence now.

"Unless someone riles them up," she reminded him. Anselm massaged his right temple.

"All the more reason to remove them all. There are plenty of loyal men and women who'd eagerly fill the vacant board seats, like the Hales," Anselm said. Viciousness lined his voice, the same viciousness Aric possessed at the end. Abigail stepped out of kissing distance. "I have already contacted the Brotherhood of Minos—all I have to do is give the word and they are done," Anselm said.

"They aren't cheap," Abigail reminded him.

"Which is why I'm using some of Tad's money to foot the bill," Anselm said. Anselm hated owing people favors, but he needed some powerful friends now, a bitter pill for a man known as king. He lamented losing the Grey Sister, an ally who vanished just as quickly as she appeared.

"I've got things to do," she said. He worried he may have switched from acting too slow to far too much haste.

"Keep a weapon handy," Anselm said.

Without Abigail to lighten his mood, the gruesome images of Aric wormed in Anselm's mind. In his mind, he saw all of his family dead. Anselm started to believe the Board was unsalvageable. His arm ached and his temper flared. Anselm knew the bloodshed was just beginning.

PERCIVAL

Percival Blackthorne wiped the sweat from his eyes and parried the oncoming sword thrust. His sparring partner, James Dumas, cocked his head and thrust again.

Percival dodged the attacks with a dancer's grace. He had tried his best to teach Edgar the basics of fighting. Edgar only half watched, yawning as the sparring outlasted his attention span. Edgar kicked the unused training dummy with the growling expression.

"I'm trying to teach you how to fight, it might save your life one day," Percival said. Percival deflected the attacks with less grace, thanks to Edgar's distraction.

"I'm gonna die soon, anyway," Edgar said, kicking the nearby dummy again. Training came to a screeching halt.

"Why would you say something like that?" Percival asked. He tried not to get angry at his little brother, especially since the words were truer than he wanted to accept.

"I heard mom and dad talking," Edgar said.

"Just a few weeks ago you could barely walk. Look at you now," Percival said.

"There's always something wrong with me. If that man had

killed me, no one would have to worry," Edgar said. The words hurt Percival more than any blade. He knelt down by Edgar's side.

"Don't say that. Mom and dad need us," Percival said, his tone growing stern. James walked to the far corner and picked up a towel, clearly not wanting to be part of the conversation.

James was an up-and-coming soldier on the fast track to becoming a Knight-Ambassador thanks to an exceptional track record. He had been a childhood friend of Percival, whose friendship had developed into brotherhood like Drake and Aric once shared. James had become Percival's confidant and rock through all of the growing burdens of life as a member of the royal family and now heir to the throne. "You're going to live another two hundred years."

"People don't live that long," Edgar said.

"I don't know. I've heard some crazy stories," Percival replied. Edgar's mood picked up.

Percival walked to the center of the room. James toweled off and prepared for another round. The two clashed swords. Percival parried all incoming attacks, showcasing all the ways to dodge a blade. He then moved on to offensive attacks, the part of the training James did not enjoy. Percival circled James, never taking his eyes off his target.

Percival unleashed a flurry of attacks on James. James slipped up on the last deflection and received a slice across the forearm. Using real swords in practice had been an idea of Percival's, seeing it as necessary for the flawless performance required in all aspects of Blackthorne life. Percival dropped the sword and rushed over to James.

James covered the oozing cut. "It's fine, just need to get it wrapped up," James said. Percival wiped the sweat from his eyes.

"We'll take you down to the doctor. Come on, Eddy," Percival said.

"I can manage," James insisted.

James said a farewell and went off to the doctor alone, leaving Percival to dwell on the increase media attention on him as the new heir. Percival wanted not one shred of his personal life to go beyond the castle walls, even if his life was as exciting as a beige wall. Percival always put off the idea of having children being the second son, though he enjoyed the idea of being a father one day. With his older brother gone, Percival now felt the pressure of having a child, and the very real possibility of Edgar dying young. As the next king, the bloodline and the entire nation rested on Percival's shoulders with the very real possibility that more Blackthornes would die by the end of the conflict. Even if his father disapproved, he would not risk bringing another target into the world until the rebels were taken out. Percival got out of his own head and moved to his focus back to Edgar.

He escorted his brother back to the family bedroom where Anselm retreated after constant meetings. In the room, Anselm sat on the bed in a daze, cradling his right arm. The king sat in nothing but an old turquoise robe and black socks. All the windows were covered. Percival slammed the door to snap his father out of his trance. Anselm jumped up, nearly slipping in the process. Anselm gathered his wits and greeted them properly. "Sorry, I was in another world," Anselm laughed. Anselm's eyes were so bloodshot they looked solid red.

"It didn't look like a pleasant one," Percival replied.

"Spacing out is about the only peace I get anymore." Anselm played it off as no big deal, the behavior greatly concerned Percival. Anselm wrapped the fingers of his left hand around his right wrist.

"Something wrong with your arm?" Percival asked.

"Old man problems," Anselm said. Edgar walked over the bed and sat down, now to be babysat by his mother and father. He remained under constant supervision, never more than a few feet from his brother, parents, or trusted guards. Anselm enacted a much more thorough vetting process to make sure his family guards were both loyal and competent. With the near success of the assassins, Anselm tripled his guard.

Percival waved goodbye and headed back out. Percival loathed acting in his father's stead. Business came to a grinding halt despite his aptitude for it. Percival and Abigail picked up the slack during the king's increasing absences. Percival made his way to the throne. He sat in the absurd chair for the first time, instantly feeling the weight of the job. "I guess I better get used to this," he mumbled. Moments later, people entered the hall. Percival sat up straight and began his first step towards kingship.

GREGOR

Another week came and went, leaving Gregor no closer to his goal. "Of all the times for Aric to die, it would have to be now," Gregor said. He wandered the castle when permitted, always under the watchful eyes of the guards. In the meantime, Cedric poured over the books in the Blackthorne library.

The mood of the city changed drastically over the past week. Since Aric's death tension strangled the city. A citywide curfew only worsened the situation. Patrols intensified three times during his brief tenure here. Gregor and his men couldn't take a piss without Blackthorne agents monitoring the streams for suspicious contents. Gregor possessed all the time in the world for his family reunion, leaving him no excuse to put it off.

The sounds of spring from the fields echoed across the silent city that night. Gregor spied Minos agents sneaking around town wearing skull face paint and leathers rumored to be human skin, though he knew that was just something made up to scare people. He made note of the snipers in the towers. With the recent deaths, the nobles also had their own agents sneaking about. Gregor placed his hand over the sack containing the witch's head, now affectionately dubbed "Medusa."

"Just you and me tonight," he said. The city lights flickered to life the moment the sun went down. The stink of ass and mildew persuaded him to retreat to the castle.

Inside the castle, Gregor saw Anselm on his throne staring lifelessly at nothing in particular. Gregor was fully aware of the botched assassination and the king's murderous counterstrike. Gregor pitied him, catching the king snacking on anxiety meds on more than one occasion. Gregor walked by Anselm who only grit his teeth and cradled his right arm. Gregor shook off the notion of Anselm hiding something at first, however the attack on elite families that commanded resources equal to his own suggested he either was desperate or had a devilish ace up his sleeve. Gregor dealt with the scenarios like these throughout his career, he executed decent people that stooped to using forbidden tech in dire straits. Gregor's hunch saddled him with the secondary mission to ensure neither the king nor the Board dabbled in the same dark things Vigilant came here to seek their aid to fight.

Gregor went up to the library. He encountered numerous soldiers giving him the stink eye. The halls of the castle were disturbingly quiet, causing his old man grunts to echo throughout.

Gregor arrived at the Royal Library. Three floors with rows upon rows of books greeted him. A wall of glass provided Gregor a view of Lake Thaxter. The library contained books covering all topics and genres both Old World and New. He saw books about mythology, cookbooks, and political satires not about the Blackthorne family. Anselm proudly displayed his collection of fantasy and mythology that survived the collapse of the world twice over, including books he claimed dated back to the time of the Roman Empire.

Gregor cared little for Anselm's personal collection, desiring more practical items. The off-limits collection amassed by the scholars. The most valued of these works, he suspected, lay on the upper floor behind the protection of lock, key, and gun-wielding soldiers.

Moonlight washed the glass hallways a ghostly glow, more often reserved for the desolate places of the world that he knew well. At the top, the guards stepped aside and allowed him access. Bookcases and file cabinets filled to the brim with technical documents, historical records, and scientific journals meticulously lined the walls. He moved through the aisles without a single trace of Cedric. The absence of Gregor's second only furthered his concerns about events in the capital. Gregor moved through the aisle with haste.

A few volumes lay on a small desk in the corner prompting Gregor to investigate, three hefty books written by Gideon Grey. Though the man vanished before Gregor's time, he knew all about Gideon. A scientific genius, Gideon stood head and shoulders above his peers when it came to technology—everything from long distance communicators and surgery robots to the scrapped electric railroad system designed to connect to every major city in the country. Despite all his lofty accomplishments, Gideon's final years of genetic experiments on unwilling hosts would be his legacy, that and disappearing without a trace after King Aldous's death. Gideon became an idol of sorts to witches and warlocks. Grey Sisters and Grey Brothers believed Gideon achieved transcendence, and they intended to follow in his footsteps. Gregor fought these cults to ensure that they never succeeded.

Gregor picked up each book and skimmed the pages. The first two books concerned the technological state of the nation at the end of the previous century. They included Gideon's own founding of the ISA, portable electricity, firearms, food modification, musings on robotics, and his plans to establish an information network based on something called the "Internet."

Gregor made another sweep of the forbidden halls hoping to find anything to help him fight this menace. The search proved fruitless. After two walkthroughs, however, one plain musty tome caused him to do a double take. A piece of paper jutting out of an unassuming green book on automobiles warranted further investigation. Gregor pulled out the loose papers and sure enough instantly recognized Cedric's barely legible handwriting. Cedric wrote like a madman about faraday cages, hidden cities, and masked figures. The last few sentences told him everything he needed to know.

Find the Vault. Destroy it. Godseeds are the key. Medical Wing. Anselm's guest. He quickly stuffed the note in his pocket and left the library, adding a convincing grumble of frustration at the guards by the door. Gregor tread carefully while he debated how to investigate a castle full of soldiers and surveillance cameras to learn more of this Vault. He went to his room and waited for nightfall.

Unbeknownst to outsiders, members of Vigilant possessed small gadgets the size of pens called disrupters. Disrupters emitted a brief pulse that temporarily blocked electrical systems, designed by Cedric to combat pesky warlocks that set up cameras and sensors in their makeshift labs and fortresses. Of course, those fortresses paled in comparison to Blackthorne Castle. Gregor slipped the disrupter into his pocket and opted for a tried and true solution. He walked to the elevator at the end of the hall, clutching his stomach.

"State your business," the doorman said, irritated.

"Not feeling so hot," Gregor said, feigning nausea.

"Fine, but don't try anything stupid," the door replied, hitting the down button by the elevator. Gregor walked past and ascended to the medical wing. A skeleton crew operated the medical wing, which housed only a few patients at the moment. Gregor approached the receptionist and embellished his fake illness. He waited until a doctor led him into a room. Gregor went through the motions and received medicine for his faux illness. He was told the way out, so he hurried in case the doc realized he made a huge mistake letting the old man roam free.

Gregor pulled the disrupter from his pocket and clicked it. He zipped under the camera's cone of vision, knocked on doors, slipping inside the room with no response. He clicked his disrupter and moved from empty room to empty room, back toward lab area. Gregor ducked out of sight to gauge the sounds of people inside and heard an intriguing lack of sound.

He slowly pushed on the door, to find a lab technician asleep at the corner station. While two others stood around in a daze, Gregor recognized this behavior, confirming his fear. He walked past the oblivious technicians and clicked and snuck his way to an operating room. A few more technicians and nurses stood frozen in the halls. Gregor ignored them and went to his goal.

A lone woman hunched over a gurney in the center of the room. The woman wore a lab outfit. A black spine crawled into out from under her coat. The woman rolled up her sleeve and placed her arm on the table. A collection of parts lay on the table, including various custom plating, tubes, and a scalpel. The woman picked up the scalpel and lowered it to her forearm. The blade touched her flesh, and she stopped. Gregor realized he had been made.

"You need to brush up on your skills," she said. Attacking the witch was no longer an option with so many enthralled people waking up to find an intruder. "You are about to have way bigger problems than me," she said. Gregor cursed.

"The Vault?" he asked.

"Yes. The buried world re-remerging at last. Weapons of war unleashed. Ask the king, you'll see him soon enough. That's all I can say. So is their will," she said. The witch turned to face him; her green eyes began to dull. Gregor internally thanked the small victory of the witch's failing power to enthrall.

"No!" she gasped and vanished around the corner. The enthralled technicians began to stir. Gregor hurried out of the room and through the hall to the lobby. He went over to the stairs and rushed to his room. Gregor reduced his pace to a less conspicuous one and entered the room, sighing with relief that his weapon and witch head were not yet taken. Gregor picked them up. He had to contact his men, whose absence became all the more concerning.

Gregor left his room. He felt a presence quickly zeroing in on him. Around the corner approached the king himself.

"Good evening, Mr. Pavane. Any shocking revelations?"

Anselm asked. Something about the way Anselm carried himself alarmed Gregor. The stories of his growing paranoia encouraged Gregor to tread carefully.

"No," Gregor lied. The king adjusted his wrinkly charcoal suit and clenched his right fist.

"Your subordinate poured over books day and night and found nothing. Not sure where he went."

Gregor played along with the king's little game. "Probably wanted to get more time at the brothel," Gregor said.

"Can't blame him. Sometimes we need to forget." Anselm's words were filled with sorrow.

"I'm sorry about Aric. He was a… good man," Gregor said with false sincerity. Anselm looked at him, wearing an expression of a man trying not to cry.

"No, he wasn't," Anselm said with pain. "I loved him through it all, but he hadn't been a good man in a very long time." Gregor looked at him in confusion. "Follow me. I'd like to show you something," Anselm said.

Gregor nodded and followed, trying to hide the mounting trepidation. The two walked silently to a meeting room many floors below the library. Inside the room sat the table and chairs were the rulers of the country cajoled, postured, and lied in a never-ending scuffle for power.

"This is the most important place in the entire kingdom, where our fates are decided. There was a time when kings and advisors worked for the good of all. Now it's little more than a toilet." Anselm walked over to the window; a look of disgust washed over his face as he watched the neon world below.

"The most dangerous enemies are the ones from within. Not witches or monsters or demons but parasites that eat you from the inside." *Something is very wrong*, Gregor thought.

"Do you know the early days of your order?" Anselm asked. His passive-aggressive tone suggested it a rhetorical question. "Vigilant had a purpose: to keep the people from developing technologies capable of upsetting the established order, but somewhere along the way that devolved. All forms of technology deemed sufficiently dangerous were destroyed while others became heavily regulated. Every civilized nation on this continent obeys the Compact— or so they claim. We both know better. You silence, censor, and destroy… same as the Old World you hate with such fervor." He left the window and came back over to Gregor. Gregor saw the hatred burning in the king's eyes.

"Vigilant has been reduced to technophobic fools hunting monsters," Anselm pronounced. He unsheathed his blade and examined it. "Did you know that these blades are quite different from the ones wielded back in the first Dark Age? Hell, they are different than the ones of my grandfather's time, lighter, yet every bit as deadly." Gregor thought about it often, but was apprehensive of the king's odd speech.

"What is your point, my king?" he said politely. Anselm clenched his right fist as if in pain.

"A sham," Anselm began. "That's what your order has become. The swords you use, the equipment, the ability-enhancing drugs, then there is the matter of that head you are carrying around. Trust me, you are no Perseus. And now you are consorting with my enemies."

Gregor's eyes widened at the reference, letting him know Anselm had it all figured out. Two soldiers entered the room, dragging in the pummeled body of Cedric. Cedric smiled at Gregor before being thrown to the floor.

"I just can't seem to do anything right," Cedric laughed, although pained and winded.

"We caught your friend here consorting with agents of the Campbell family." Anselm placed his boot upon Cedric's back and pushed him down.

"You decided that if I wouldn't help they would, huh?" Anselm asked. Gregor lacked the strength to take out the king and his men, knowing it would be certain death even if he did. Anselm pointed the blade down at Cedric's neck.

"They were going to help you get in the Vault, weren't they? I can promise they will abuse it more than I ever would," Anselm assured.

"I have no idea—" Gregor said truthfully.

"Save the denials. I don't like interrogation; however, they can be useful."

"Cedric?! You didn't—" Gregor cried in disbelief.

"Never been tortured before. Hurt way more than I expected," Cedric said. "They offered to help us if we help them. I refused them, but some of our men didn't. Anselm, I beg you, don't do this. You will be the death of us all!" Cedric said.

"I do what I must to save our country. You can't fault me for that," Anselm said woefully.

"You are making a mistake," Gregor said. Anselm's skin went red and he slammed his foot down on Cedric.

"What would you have me do, let my family die!?" Anselm cried.

"Cedric is not my men, do not punish him," Gregor said. Anselm gritted his teeth as if in tremendous pain.

"Your men have already been dealt with. You have been declared enemies of the state. More reliable men will take your place," Anselm said matter-of-factly. Gregor gave one last attempt to convince the king.

"If you do this, you will become everything they say you are," Gregor pleaded. Anselm's expression darkened. With cultists in the castle, Gregor feared the witch's words were true and he may be too late. In his hunt to eliminate one threat, he had stumbled upon one far greater. Gregor had to time to dwell on the convenient timing and further implications. Anselm signed heavily.

"So be it," Anselm said. The king drove the blade down through

Cedric's neck, leaving him to spend his last few moments choking on his own blood.

"You crazy fucker!" Gregor screamed. The king came toward him with Cedric's blood fresh on his sword. One desperate idea popped in Gregor's mind. Gregor pulled the witch's head from the sack. The head's green eyes burned with power, stopping Anselm in his tracks. Anselm turned his head and ran from the room to avoid the enthrallment. The soldiers still inside stood motionless from the witch's enchantment. *Damn, that actually worked,* Gregor thought in disbelief. Anselm screamed for more guards.

With the severed head raised he charged into the incoming troops. Some managed to avoid the paralyzing gaze while the others were reduced to drooling imbeciles. Those that avoided the gaze fired blindly, hitting some of their own comrades. Gregor dashed down the hallway toward the stairs.

Running down half a dozen flights of stairs, he came into a blocked hallway with troops that fired the second he stepped out. Gregor dipped inside the nearest room. In the empty office, he had a chance to recuperate for a last stand. He ran to the window to see if how far of a fall he faced. When he turned around he stared down Anselm Blackthorne.

How did he move so fast?

"You and your ilk were always a proud lot. You know what they say about pride," Anselm said. Gunfire from Anselm's soldiers blew apart the witch's head before Gregor could turn it on them, leaving him defenseless. Anselm walked up to the shocked Gregor. Before Gregor could react Anselm gave him a hard push. With the sound of shattering glass, Gregor saw the beauty of the night sky before crashing to the ground below.

MR. WESTERFIELD

David Westerfield sat lackadaisically in his garden, frowning at his empty wine glass. The bronze griffon perched over the entrance proudly welcomed visitors to the Westerfield Estates. These days, the mighty griffon might as well symbolize the Blackthorne terror descending upon him. Mr. Westerfield served as the Minister of Crisis Management as well as transportation, veteran's affairs, and a dozen other departments in an ever-expanding bureaucracy. Sometimes he forgot all the things he lorded over. The actor once considered mentally feeble now held more power than anyone except Mr. Derbin with the Whitehalls out of the picture.

Some of his prized fish floated lifelessly at the top his pond, which was big enough to be classified as a small lake. He counted his two dragonfly koi, one shubunkin, and one shimmerskin fish. As a genetically engineered Old World fish designed to thrive in and clean the oceans, the blue-eyed, shimmerskins were the prize possession of any fish enthusiast. The living fish carelessly weaved through the roots and vegetation at the heart of his aquatic world. David blamed his wife for their deaths. She never cared for fish and was happy to let him know so.

David yelled out for one of the servants to solve the problem.

Almost instantly, his young servant, Rin, answered the call clad in a yellow-stained white shirt and tattered pants.

"Yes, milord?" Rin asked.

David pointed to the fish. "Remove them," David said. The servant walked to the storage building in the back and brought forth the green pole with a net and small black container Mr. Westerfield had designated for fish disposal. He noticed the ragged look of the young man. David groaned in disgust.

"Why are you dressed like that?" David asked.

"Mr. Williamson had a fit and tore my clothes. This was all I could find." David let out a heavy sigh.

"He's a petulant cunt, but most of his friends are dead now so I understand his duress," David said. Now more than ever, David had begun to distance himself from Anselm's enemies, in public at least. He turned his attention back to Rin, a man with a disturbing lack of ambition. "You don't have to be a servant your entire life," David said. The manservant didn't stop his task.

"I don't?" he asked.

"Of course not," David began, "There was a time when even my family was viewed as peons. 'Generic' they called us in the Old World. Back in the twenty-first century, genetic modification created entirely new factions of people: modded and generic. Modded people enhanced themselves with things like cybernetics and non-human DNA. For the longest time there was no problem, until it was made a problem for a few years. The cunning bred division as they had done throughout that century to pit the people against each other. Groups promoting equality, security, and all the useful buzzwords used fears to take absolute control of the continent. When one fear went away they created new demons to slay."

David often got sidetracked when speaking and never turned away an opportunity to give a history lesson. The servant looked at him the way most did, as an old windbag. David could see plainly that Rin didn't see where he was going with this speech.

"I don't follow," Rin said.

"Gaining power and influence is not always about hard work. Race, religion, money, politics, and other petty things can be weaponized. There was a time in the Old World where lives got ruined over silly comments and mild opinions on something called social media. It's always changing, but the results are the same. Half the Board families are here because of inciting conflict and little else. What I'm trying to tell you is if you can't make it the right way then divide and conquer. Create an enemy to slay and people will do anything to help you slay it, even surrender their own freedom. It worked on Aric. Half the stories about him were completely embellished by my people. Got everyone so riled up that violence was inevitable."

Rin grimaced at milky white eyes of rotting fish in the net. He tossed the dead fish into a small black container. He made sure he didn't splash any water on his employer. David's pants were also pulled up a way too high, making his front look like a giant ass. David unbuttoned the top button on his pink flannel shirt and wiped the sweat off of his neck. Rin wisely made no mention of the ridiculous appearance of his master. David called for wine, taking a seat on an ornate chair with griffon wings arms.

Rin finished tending the garden and then hurried off to meet Mrs. Davidson's laundry list of demands. David sat back down firmly in the lap of luxury. He nodded off a few times, leaving his sleep apnea to ruin things. The voice of another manservant pierced David's ears.

"Your guests are here, sir," said another servant. David sat up for his guests but made no effort beyond that. His guests approached: Mr. Williamson, Mr. Droullin, Mrs. Gordon, and Mr. Beaumont. He could sense the judgment on wrinkly labyrinth of Mr. Williamson's face, downright pleasant compared to Mr. Droullin. The most recent round of plastic surgery gave Arthur Droullin a permanent, smiling expression, like an oversized doll from David's worst nightmares. Rickard Beaumont kept his milquetoast appearance. Mrs. Gordon took her place as the silent observer. Mr. Westerfield did not see Mr. Derbin or Mrs. Caan among them, giving credence to reports they had fled the city.

"Tad's being scraped all across the countryside and you're just lying around?" Mr. Beaumont asked. David acted as if he missed the comment.

"Welcome to my home, gentlemen. It's customary to be invited in," David said, in a tone as dry as the martinis he suddenly craved.

"All of our heads are on the chopping block, damn it," Rickard Beaumont said in a nervous, twitchy manner of someone that partook in too much of his own thriving pharmaceutical business.

David languidly stood and made a quick glance over in the direction of his eldest daughter, Olivia, hoping she steered clear of this nasty business. She read a book out on the boat in his lagoon, her only sanctuary being the nation's most desired actress. Olivia would soon join David's other children, Kevyn and Mya, at his other home on the Emerald Coast. Arthur poked the nearby flowers.

"Anselm will move against us soon. Which means we need to act, more successfully than the Campbells," Arthur spoke wistfully. David wanted to slap the glazy look from Arthur's plastic face, though he did agree.

Everyone knew the Board thrived when dealing with weak kings, and David believed it was time to return to this standard. He believed Joseph Kerr to be the person to help move the balance of power into the hands of the Board.

"We are going about this the wrong way," David began. "We should work with the rebels—control them. These rebels want change so bad they'll take help from anyone that offers it." David and the others moved closer to the lagoon when Olivia left.

"You can arrange this?" Mr. Droullin asked.

"This very night, I will. Feel free to join me. My people will contact your people," David said with unshakeable confidence.

With no response, the men showed themselves out. David reached for the wine glass and took another sip. This bottle cost $4,000 gold crowns; he spat it on the floor like it was nothing. He flung the cup to the ground as the servant approached.

"Clean that up," David said. Rin gave him a sour look.

"I thought I didn't have to be a servant," Rin said.

"But today you are," David replied.

David sat around, waiting for night to fall. Tonight, spreading misinformation about a meeting near Lake Thaxter would allow the Board to avoid the king's agents. David's driver took his car to the docks to further cement the lie, not to mention bribing the night watchmen for good measure. David put on his best navy suit, regretting the choice when the pants cut into his waist. He kissed his wife goodbye and prepared to seal the fate of the Blackthorne family.

David forgot the last time he'd been outside Kingsbury, seeing the surroundings jogged his memory as to why. He joined the others at the meeting place. Mr. Williamson and Mr. Beaumont stood beside him nervously glancing at their surroundings. Mrs. Gordon and Mr. Droullin hid behind a gaggle of bodyguards. David rubbed his hands together, desperately craving sanitizer.

"Guns at the ready," David said, picking the lint off his suit.

The Board members and their guards waited on the outskirts of Worthington, a factory town southeast of Kingsbury. Worthington resembled more of a steelyard than a town, with rows of lodgings near the edge. Worthington provided the bulk of metal in the country. Plumes of smoke spewed constantly from its towering stacks leaving a cloud of smoke over the town.

Mr. Beaumont pulled out his glistening, tiger-engraved pistol and spoke to his men. "If we start running, you start killing." Lights from behind the group blinded them, light from two headlights belonging to a bronze car. Bronze-colored cars were only allow to New World governors, called regents.

In the distance, a mass approached under the nigh-impenetrable darkness. Stepping into the blinding white of the city lights, David saw a man with a small army. The rebel army surrounded the Board members.

"Finally you slither out of your holes," said the man. The man had no hair. Two wrinkles of his cheek went straight down his face like deep cuts. He was an older man, in his sixties. He wore a dark suit, no doubt to show he belonged among them.

"And you are?" David asked.

"Abraham Kerr. My friends tell me you're in serious distress—gotta be true if you're here groveling." Abraham looked at each and every person before him.

"Your brother killed Aric," Mr. Droullin said. David recalled a troublesome east coast official a decade back by the name of Abraham. It explained his ability to garner support.

"Under my advisement," Abraham said.

"Let's get to it, shall we? I believe we can come to an arrangement beneficial to us all," David said, fidgeting with his too-tight pants. "When all is said and done, this country will need strong leadership, a thing we know quite well."

"What makes you think we need you?" Abraham asked, smiling. Mrs. Gordon moved closer to her bodyguards, practically hugging them. David remained firm in an attempt to earn Abraham's respect.

"I suppose that you have experience governing an entire country. Creating public works projects? Maintaining roads, bridges, sewer systems, and schools? Defense? Economy? Keeping all regents under control?"

"About as much as you," Abraham retorted. David snorted, having to admit he set himself up for that.

"Can you finance the army? Where do you think all this money and all these resources come from? From us. That includes a military force far greater than yours, and control of all industries,"

David said. Abraham's expression shifted. "You seize power and plan to deal with the rest as it comes. Such a lackadaisical attitude will only get you the country's shortest reign. You need us." David pressed his verbal advantage. "If you need further convincing of our value then perhaps we can give you the layout of Blackthorne Castle and a few of its structural weaknesses, plus a few other things the king thinks we don't know. We have a man on the inside."

Abraham scratched the side of his face and nodded.

"That could make things easier," he said.

"We can be great enemies or greater friends," David said, throwing in a salesman-quality grin.

"I'll think on it," Abraham said. He turned away, hidden rebels emerging to escort their leader away.

The Board members huddled together their bodyguards forming a full circle around them. With the others out of range, Mrs. Gordon grew confident enough to voice her concerns.

"He could've killed us," Mrs. Gordon said.

"He knows better," David moved restlessly.

"We can't trust them," Mr. Beaumont said. He peeked over the bodyguards, trying to spy any unwanted eyes and ears.

"We don't need to trust them; we just need them to be our shield. Shields don't last very long, but just long enough," David said.

"If they decide not to work with us, our heads will still end up skewered," Mr. Beaumont said.

David shook his head. "We could reveal the rebel location to Anselm," David began, "or help the rebels destroy the castle, or let them kill each other. Don't forget half the country is on our payroll. One carefully placed shot and we'll own the rest."

"Helping them will put the people on our side. Give Mr. Kerr a little power and he'll fall in line," Mr. Droullin conceded. David considered this meeting a major victory. His men did not move until Abraham's forces left town.

"Let's head back to Kingsbury," David said. "Make sure that loyal men are watching your backs at all times. Buy off who you have to and start calling in favors." David had a feeling deep in his gut that soon there would no king, only the Board.

292

ZORA

An uneventful trip proved a relief to Zora. After another day's travel, Eddington leered over the hills on the horizon. Eddington was a more compact city than Greenfield, free of labyrinthine alleyways. Much of the residential areas consisted of multistory apartments, separated by the occasional shop or laundromat. Drake dished out the local history.

"Eddington, often called The Centenarian, has been around for nearly a thousand years. It's been burned down many times, overrun by marauders, and ground zero for a syphilis outbreak. Disaster hits this town every century or so, but it always comes back stronger."

"Does it have a whorehouse?" Melvin asked with childlike glee.

"Yes," Drake groaned.

"All I need to know," Melvin replied giddily.

"We'll be staying at the Woodsman Inn tonight. You can see the statue out front," Zora said.

Opposite the large central park, a giant hunk of metal blocked the sidewalk, a bipedal machine in the image of a human. The nine-footer commanded the scene.

"It's a robot," Drake began. "This one served as a logger in the Old World, so the locals claim. There were nearly a million of these active during the last days of the Great Empire, according to our records. Long after the Old World died it continued carrying out his duties until it one day, it just stopped."

"And he's been there ever since. That's sad," Zora said.

The companions hitched their horses and rented four separate rooms. After replenishing their supplies, they hit the town. Zora made note of the mounting animosity between Melvin and Drake, noticeably worse since Melvin's last talk with Joseph Kerr. The four headed off to the closest restaurant, but some commotion up ahead stopped them.

Coming from the north, three people were dragging what was left of a man towards the clinic. Much of his clothes and his skin had been shredded, hanging off the bone like gooey cheese. The word "fairies" flew from the lips of frightened locals. The term caused some confusion with outsiders, as her own people were referred to as Fey, which came to mean the same thing.

"I'll investigate and meet you at the hotel in about an hour," Drake said. Zora knew what he'd find, but she didn't bother to stop him.

"Oh well, I'm hungry anyway," Thos said, rubbing his belly.

"Yeah, I could eat a horse," Melvin said. Zora's hunger vanished at the thought of the fairies.

"If we hurry we can get that one," Thos jested, pointing at the largest one hitched in front of the diner.

Zora laughed nervously not knowing if there was any truth in his words. After an hour of truth-seeking, Drake returned to his companions. From the grim expression on his face, he came to validate Zora's fears.

"Find anything?" Zora asked.

"There have been numerous disappearances in the area and not just in the woods, either. People are being carried off or torn to shreds. The locals hired mercs to check it out. The gentlemen we saw being dragged through the street was the last of them," Drake said. A pit formed in Zora's stomach, and she could no longer hide her dread.

"You know what's going on up there, don't you?" Drake asked. Zora sighed, trying her best to ignore the growing inevitability.

"The fairies are real. We thought Vigilant wiped them out decades ago, but now they're back, and spreading," Zora said. "A day before you arrived in Greenfield, I received news from home. The attacks are getting worse. They killed people I cared about, people I failed to protect—so I left. We seek an alliance to rid us of them, I was to return home with aid since Kingsbury refused to help and there is no Vigilant presence in the state."

"Vigilant won't help you? I thought that was their job?" Thos asked.

"We've been unable to contact them for some time. My father was once in Vigilant and still he's found no one to help. We contacted Joseph's people. They offered to help us if we aid in them return."

"So that is why we're really here. To stop this at the source before either side learns how to use whatever is responsible," Drake said. Zora nodded. Zora wanted to drop the subject for now. The group wisely left her alone for the time being.

"We'll head out in the morning," Zora said. Melvin looked at Drake.

"When it's over will you rat us out?" Melvin spoke bluntly.

"I intend to keep this country from falling apart, that is my job. If some kind of deal can be reached between the rebels and the Blackthornes, I'm all for it. But it comes down to you or the king, after we help Zora you and I can settle things," Drake said. Melvin sneered.

"I suggest you join up with us, or just bug out before things turn to shit. I doubt the crown will be on your side now," Thos said.

Drake shrugged; the pain of the harsh fact plastered on his face. He ran his hand through his raven hair while dwelling on the matter. "I'll help Zora, and then I'm heading back home. I suggest you guys stay out of this war from here on," Drake said. Thos turned his gaze to the ground.

"I made my bed," Thos said bitterly. Zora ran her finger in her glass of water watching the ripples, concerned for both men grappling we the lesser of two evils.

"I think I'm going to go for a walk now," she said. Drake began to stand. "Alone." Zora braced herself to face her nightmares.

PERCIVAL

Percival and Edgar lounged on the grassy hills behind Blackthorne Castle that overlooked Lake Thaxter. Their countryside adventure provided a fleeting reprieve from the growing madness in the city. Fishing and sport boats cruised the waters under the blood-orange sky. It was a beautiful scene, marred by the three dozen bodyguards only a step away. "It's been a long time since we've been down on the lake." Percival missed having James by his side but understood his desire to withdraw from the world during the turmoil.

Percival recalled the days when his brothers sailed across the lake, spending as much time bonding as they did butting heads. It hurt Percival to know the kingdom was better off with his brother dead.

"I wanted the three of us to spend some time out on the lake, without mom and dad," Percival said with lament. He pulled blades of grass from the hill one at a time. Edgar sat cross-legged on the field.

"You okay?" Percival leaned in to draw Edgar's gaze—the lifeless stare disturbed him.

"Yeah," Edgar said, his mechanical state failed to convince.

"You can do better than that."

"Yeah," Edgar said, with the first smile Percival had seen from him all day.

"It's about time you smiled. Maybe we can go out on the lake tomorrow. That'll lift your spirits," Percival said. Percival doubted the chances of that, however, Edgar needed a morale boost. "We'll have to find a big enough boat to support four hundred bodyguards. Or maybe they could form up, and we can walk across them like a bridge," Percival laughed. Edgar looked back at the armored troops. Having a garrison of riflemen with guns pointed in every direction soured the mood. The sun dipped over the trees in the distance.

Relaxation gave way to sloth as Percival and Edgar lay in the grass while life went by. Fisherman on the shore moved too close to them and were shooed away at gunpoint. The ambiance of the surroundings threatened to lull Percival into a dream state, a welcome change from the grim hell of Kingsbury. Percival scheduled five different family get-togethers this week, getting only Edgar to join. Coughs and armor adjustments from bodyguards ruined the tranquil illusion.

"Are mom and dad okay?" Edgar's question brought the awful world back into focus.

"I don't think they'll be okay for a very long time," Percival said, perhaps being too honest. A few times during the family time, groups of sycophants attempted to do business with him. *I'll never have peace,* Percival thought.

"Sometimes when mom thinks she's alone, she cries. And dad is weird. I heard him mumbling about witches and masks," Edgar said. It took Percival a moment to respond. He lacked to heart to tell his brother of dad's failing mind.

"I… I'm supposed to cheer you up and tell you it's going to be alright, but it will take some time. That's why you need to chin up. If you're happy, it'll help mom and dad," Percival said. Percival still lacked the desire to move, so he came up with another reason for them to stay. More brownnosers interrupted him, wearing absurd silks that made them look like shower curtains.

"Leave us in peace for one fucking second!" Percival hollered, picking up a small rock and tossing it at the asslickers. Gunmen escorted the sycophants away from Percival. With Anselm mentally unable to lead, Percival stepped up in the meantime: handling trade agreements with frightened merchants, approving military strikes against rebels, and doling out justice to criminals. Acting in the king's stead proved debilitating. Ordering executions even for the deserving left a bad taste in his mouth. Percival forced the thoughts out and refused to let them sour his mood.

"Do you know the story of the Lady of the Lake?" Percival asked.

"She's the one that gave Arthur Excalibur."

"I always imagined it was like Lake Thaxter. Who knows, maybe there's a legendary sword down there?" Percival vividly imagined the famed blade rising from the mist-covered waters.

"No," Edgar said, cutting through Percival's waking dream. It hurt Percival to see his little brother without a sense of wonder.

"It's a nice thought. I think we could use a few magic swords and wizards on our side," Percival said. The final traces of the sun faded fast. Percival became drowsy lying in the grass. Nightfall increased the dangers the Blackthornes faced a dozen times over.

"We should get back," Percival said. He stretched out his arm and helped Edgar to his feet. The guards followed the princes back to the city, all the while giving Percival his requested personal space. As they traveled toward the closest entrance, Edgar lagged behind. Percival heard a loud thud from behind him. Turning around, a child-sized lump lay on the hillside. "Edgar!" Percival's sprinted as hard as he could, feeling his heart scraping against his rib. Edgar shook violently. Percival scooped up his brother without thinking of the consequences or his surroundings. "Get the doctors!"

With his brother dying in his arms, Percival lost his wits. A lone bodyguard followed the orders, leaving the young Blackthorne princes more vulnerable than ever. Percival ran, holding the convulsing body of his baby brother.

ANSELM

"He looks so peaceful," Anselm said, looking down at the frail body of his youngest son. Pain stabbed up and down Anselm's right arm, leaving him teetering on the verge of a rage. The pain and mood swings kept Anselm from focusing on anything, not even able to devote his full attention to his son. Edgar dozed soundly in a hospital bed. Abigail rested her head on Anselm's shoulder. Her eyes were dry as sand dunes now, unable to produce tears. On Anselm's other side, Percival held his emotions in check with disturbing control.

Edgar received round-the-clock care, a benefit of being the only patient in the Castle's medical wing. Doctor Malthus, a dwarfish, middle-aged man with a neatly trimmed black beard, came into the room. The doctor thumbed through some papers and tampered with the ancient medical machines, his mumbling echoed in the abyss of the white room. Doctor Malthus had only recently become his head doctor, after the previous one chose the life of a Grey Sister.

"He's stable now, Your Grace," Malthus said. Anselm knew better than to direct his anger at those trying to keep his son alive. He pressed the roiling anger back down. He had chewed on his lip, leaving it a bloody mess. He reached in his pocket for his container of anxiety pills and swallowed two.

"Will he recover?" Anselm asked.

The doctor's expression darkened. "Yes, but one of these days these spells will kill him. I fear operation is the only course of action now." Anselm cursed. Brain surgery was risky, even without the risk of violating the Compact.

"Is it really the only way?" Abigail said, sighing from exhaustion.

"From the looks of it, he'll be lucky to make it another year. I suggest we operate as soon as possible. If we can get rid of that, then we can deal with his other issues. It's my opinion that we shouldn't wait any longer. We can start in a few hours, sir."

"He'll survive," Anselm said, a command. The doctor looked over at the soldiers at the door. The two-dozen soldiers choking the halls and snipers perched outside the window ensured Edgar's safety from threats. Anselm picked tiny white strips of skin from his lip and flicked them to the floor.

"We'll be in the throne room, alert us when it's time," Anselm said.

The rest of the Blackthorne family sat in the frigid throne room, less inviting than ever. On the rare occasions, the king held court here and passed swift justice on enemies of the state: de-limbing thieves, executing murderers, gelding rapists, and expanding the prison population by leaps and bounds. Despite the throne room being empty, Anselm felt the stress of the meetings bearing down on him. Blood trickled from the gash in his lip. Anselm ran his tongue over the wound and swallowed the blood.

After an eternity, Doctor Malthus entered the throne room. "Ready," he said. Anselm poured himself a handful of stress pills from the bottle in his robe pocket. The Blackthorne family followed the doctor into the old elevator and back up to the lifeless white of the medical wing. "We ask that you wait outside the room during the procedure. Your son's awake right now if you want to say anything before we start," Malthus said.

The Blackthorne family entered the surgery room. The family approached and Edgar smiled, offsetting the sickly pale color of his skin. Abigail leaned in and kissed Edgar on the cheek.

"Stop it," Edgar said. Edgar's pale face turned a deep red.

"You'll be up in no time," Percival said. Anselm hid his doubts behind a warm smile. "When all this is over we are leaving this place, if only for a few days," Anselm decreed. Percival seized the opportunity to suggest one.

"Edgar wanted to go out on Lake Thaxter. Perhaps we could make a day of it," Percival said.

"I think that sounds lovely," Abigail said. Doctor Alan Malthus interrupted the family moment.

"This violates the Compact, you know," Malthus said.

Anselm nodded his approval.

"Time to fix you up, My Liege." Doctor Malthus hurried them out the door before any emotional outbursts occurred.

"We love you," Percival said. Abigail addressed the doctor one more time.

"If he dies, so do you," she said. The color vanished from the doctor's face. The door closed, and the nation's top medical doctors gathered around the frail prince. The mask went over his face and Edgar slumbered again, possibly for the last time. Malthus flipped a switch on a large metallic box, and it hummed to life. An assistant in a blue medical uniform walked over to the machine.

Doctor Malthus tapped on the small keyboard emerging from the torso region; a series of beeps followed, and four mechanical arms shot from the trash can-shaped body. The doctor entered a few more commands while the two of the arms positioned themselves around Edgar's shaved head. Assistants wrote on clipboards as the machine began its grisly operation. One arm opened up. A small beam shot from the arm, cutting into Edgar's skull. In anticipation, the doctors watched, like children opening a bone-encased present. The laser beam stopped, and the claw gently pulled the scalp back, exposing his skull. The medical staff monitored Edgar's vital stats on a beeping computer screen.

With scalp peeled back, the laser made another horizontal cut across the skull. A puttering sound came from the surgery robot caused momentary distress. The beam finished again, and another arm snaked out of the body, gently removing Edgar's skullcap. The doctors saw for the first time a tumor on a human brain. The abysmal growth perched atop the left hemisphere, a sickly yellowish bubble seeking to expand its territory.

"It's massive. This tumor is… very different. Even the primates we've tested never had one like this," Malthus said.

A few more taps on the keyboard and the arms buzzed again with newfound purpose. A few more precision cuts and the left claw gently grabbed hold of the red-blotched growth jutting from the young boy's brain. One of the doctors rushed forward with a glass jar in hand. The machine dropped the tumor into the jar. The medical staff applauded. The machine placed Edgar's skullcap back on. The machine's fourth arm stretched out, emitting a small blue beam to connect the skull, not unlike the task of a welder. One of the other arms quickly stitched Edgar up.

The operating room door opened, and the team of doctors poured out, beaming with joy. Anselm and Abigail instantly rose to their feet. "The operation was a success, better than we ever could have hoped," Doctor Malthus said, rattling the tumor jar. Anselm and Abigail glowed at the news. Percival let out a heavy sigh.

"Thank you, doctor," Anselm spoke with renewed vigor. His attention once again turned to the Board of Directors. "I have other tumors to cut out myself."

ZORA

IT HAD BEEN a few years since Zora witnessed the grandeur of the White Woods, so named for pale oaks that lined the southern edge. Normally inviting, this time it gave off an aura of dread. An unnatural heat poured out from within the dense forest. Zora peered into the thick wilderness with no signs of life, fearing the fairies wiped out all life in the region.

The one thing helping her through the darkness was Drake Hale. In her journey across the nation, Zora ended up gravitating toward the Knight-Ambassador. She enjoyed chatting with him, and he preferred her company over anyone else. It was clear he liked her, though she couldn't tell if it was some honor code or his awkwardness that got in the way. She seldom liked approaching men, but she considered making a move on him after she resolved the unfinished business that constantly hovered over her like an unceasing rain cloud. Without people like Drake at her side, she may never have returned. Thos broke her out of her thought and back to the oppressive woods.

"Doesn't appear very inviting," Thos muttered. Melvin anxiously monitored at the sea of trees.

"Looks can be deceiving. We've thrived inside the woods for decades. You'd be surprised how quickly Fey can mobilize," Zora said. Up ahead, a narrow trail barely wide enough for one horse at a time, winded through the oppressive growth.

Zora assumed the lead, followed by Thos and Drake, with nerve-wracked Melvin taking the rear. Vibrant green foliage coupled with large healthy albino trees and unknown flowers blooming gave off a feeling most might call "too good to be true." No one bothered to ask why the place was already so lush in the early days of spring, chalking it up to Old World tomfoolery.

The humidity of the woods assaulted them as soon as they entered, more the dog days of summer than early spring. Drake and Melvin boiled inside their armor. As Zora inched closer to home, her dread rose exponentially. Melvin fidgeted, the excess facial hair slick and wet.

"You'll get used to the heat. Our armors are made to be thin in every area except vitals. All those clothes and armors you people like to wear just make you slow, shiny targets," Zora said.

"Could've warned us," Thos replied, sneaking a drink of rationed water.

"I thought you were used to heat and hard work, Thos?" Drake chided.

"No, not at all," Thos replied.

The group bobbed and weaved around the ancient wooden titans. The deeper they went, the darker the woods became, the pale oaks took on a phantom quality in the darkness. Melvin's sword arm grew twitchy in the dark spots.

"Ever seen a fairy?" Melvin asked.

"No. Up until I left, they were always something of a rarity. People out scouting the darkest regions made numerous claims about buzzing shadows but nothing more."

The group trekked deeper into the White Woods to a new sight. Manmade structures clung to the treetops. "I'm home," Zora said.

The circular platforms winded around the trees like snakes.

Zora pointed out the viewing platforms in the forest canopy. A lone female figure appeared before them, brandishing a sleek emerald shortsword with a hilt chiseled in the form of a branch and leaves. The woman wore a leather tunic and boots all in the browns and greens of forest camo. Zora noticed a few other camouflaged snipers.

"Zora Rayntree returns to us," the woman said. The woman rested the ornate bow at her side. Zora recognized the woman—Aurora, head of the Fey's volunteer militia. Zora always suspected Aurora didn't like her, a dislike stemming from perceived favoritism she thought Zora benefited from due to her father being the founder of this community, even though he held no true authority.

"I came to let everyone know I've secured an alliance with Joseph Kerr," Zora said. Drake and Thos sat patiently on their horses, while Melvin squirmed nervously.

"We know. Most of this aid arrived a few days ago. I'm surprised you travel with others. I remember you being more solitary," Aurora said. Zora ignore the verbal jabs

"I'd like to speak with father, in private," Zora said.

"Very well," Aurora said bitterly.

"Rayntree? Taking the nature thing kinda far," Thos joked, trying to convey the friendliness of his jest. Zora ignored him.

"Don't worry, we're here with you," Drake said. Zora appreciated the support, but it didn't lessen her dread. Having Drake there with her provided a boost of strength, she found him creeping into her thoughts more than she anticipated.

Aurora talked as she led the four travelers past the thick trees adorned with houses connected via rope bridges. The thicker trees were whittled away to form spiral staircases winding up to the city above.

The deeper the travelers delved, the more treetop structures they found. Shops, hanging gardens, longhouse, a clinic, and every other type of building a city needed filled the woodland domain.

The man-made architecture carved with brilliant depictions of animals, nature, and the naked human form. Melvin pointed at the statues.

"Most of the figures are female," he said.

"Well yeah. No one, not even penis lovers, want to see 'em everywhere. They could call it 'the Unwanted Wood,'" Thos commented. Zora shook her head.

"It's true. There are enough dicks as is," Zora agreed, shooting looks at Thos and Melvin.

At the heart of the city, a statue caught the attention of the travelers. Carved from mighty pale oak trees, a woman hung above them nearly five times the size of a drake. The supple, naked figure had long, green hair and wore a crown of flowers with petals of crimson, aqua, tangerine, and violet. In the eye sockets were eyes of pure heavenstone, a refined meteorite ore that glowed with divine white light. Branches and vines stretched out from nearby trees giving the impression of it floating above. Thick branches wrapped around the arms and legs, providing the only covering for the naked form. Drake blushed at the level of detail that left nothing to the imagination. Beneath the mammoth statue, a circular pond glistened in the rays of sunlight.

"I ain't seen nothin' like it in my life," Thos said.

"This is the shrine of Gaia, an image depicting Earth in human form. We don't believe in nature goddesses or magic, but are fond of the aesthetic. Through artwork and architecture, we show our love of nature and living off the land. It's where our nickname came from, like the ones from European mythology. We are actually referred to as the Freemen. We live free of government and as true equals. Here, there is seldom crime. 'Live and let live' our only true law," Zora said.

Zora caught the sight of her childhood home and zipped up the stairs toward a two-story building near the suspended courtyard, her companions struggled to keep up.

"Why does the government let this place exist? Seems a place they'd want to stamp out," Thos said.

"I'm not really sure, but there is always the fear that their tolerance will run out," she said. Melvin constantly watched Zora and the other Fey; she no longer chalked up his glares to lust. *He's spying on us for Joseph*, Zora realized.

Zora stopped to greet old friends, striking up brief conversations about her time away from the Fey community. Drake touched one of the hanging flowerbeds, causing a piece to fall off. He casually looked around to ensure no one saw. When the missing piece hit Gaia's pool he sped up to Zora's side. Zora saw the whole thing out of the corner of her eye.

Outside the big house, Zora told her companions to wait while she spoke with her father.

"We'll hang here, see how much damage we can do," Thos said. Thos grinned at Drake, who instantly looked away.

The three men took a seat on a bench, leaving Zora to attend to her business alone. She pushed open one of the double doors. On large cushions, wearing silk robes sat her father. Once named Matthew Pavane, her father now lived as Kami Rayntree of the Freemen. His unkempt beard formed strands, like white tendrils. His snow-white hair reached down past his shoulders. He sipped on nectar, a hallucinogenic Fey cocktail. The stench of incense filled the room. When he saw Zora, he spat nectar in all directions.

"Some things never change," Zora said. Her father squinted his eyes and did a double take, not yet knowing if this was the real thing or a drug-induced hallucination. He jumped to his feet and did a quick once over to make sure he was presentable.

"Zora! That really you?" he asked in disbelief. Her anxiety vanished at seeing him again.

"I'm home," she replied. Kami approached her and wrapped his arms around her in a loving embrace.

"The outside world has been kind to you. How were your travels?" He asked.

"They've been, well, interesting," Zora admitted. Zora detailed her time traveling around the country as a nomad, her sojourn in Greenfield, and bloody events that led her back home.

"Hope you at least enjoyed some of it. Without a little fun, you'll end like your shithead uncle," he said.

"Can we not bad-mouth uncle right now?" Zora asked. Kami scowled and dropped his upcoming rant.

Zora informed her father of her travels throughout Heartland and of her three new companions. Kami breathed in some more incense to help cope with the rest of her news.

"Out of all the places and things you could get involved in, that?!" He sipped some more nectar to calm his nerves.

"Wasn't it you that wanted us to make an alliance? You were the one that said the kingdom will soon strip the place," she reminded him.

"Did I say that?"

"You don't use enough drugs to be that forgetful," Zora said. She gave him the look, the look that forced his confession.

"Fine. Yes, I remember. I still don't like it, though," he said. "It was going to hit us sooner or later, at least this way we have some say in it."

"I was really hoping it wouldn't have gone this far," Zora said.

"Me, too. But enough, we can discuss that later. The fairy attacks are growing more frequent. They must have a hive or something in the west. I've paid those damn mercenaries a small fortune to deal with this issue, unsuccessfully, I might add."

"I brought trustworthy warriors to take care of this problem. From what I've heard the rest are already here, as well," Zora said. Zora understood that despite being a capable fighter, a father would always be concerned.

"Your sister, please, don't follow in her footsteps. You have nothing to prove. Just stay here and be happy." He attempted to dissuade her.

"It's not about proving anything," she replied.

"I forbid it," Kami said. Fey elders held no real authority. The pure freedom of the community sometimes worked against them.

"That will not stop me, and you know it," Zora fired back.

"Worth a shot." Kami fanned the smoke away. "You will at least humor me by going with the mercenaries and some of our hunters. Just please be careful. You're the only daughter I have left," he said.

THOS

Something about the White Woods unnerved Thos, and it worsened with each step. Even surrounded by mercenaries and Fey hunters, Thos couldn't help thinking this was another in a long list of mistakes. Together, this newly created monster-hunting group moved toward the epicenter of the fairy attacks. Shadows danced through the thick canopy, intensifying Thos's desire to flee. A black blur swooped down in the distance enveloping something on the forest floor before vanishing behind a large tree. He rubbed his eyes and looked again.

"See something?" Drake asked. The mercenaries operated like a well-oiled machine with eyes on all directions the second Drake asked the question.

"Trees," Thos said, using humor to deflect his rising fear.

"Ass," Drake said. Thos didn't smile.

"You did see something?" Drake asked.

"Not sure," Thos replied.

A second shadowy mass dashed by up ahead. All the mercenaries instantly brandished guns to shoot any inbound threat. A scream pierced the eerie silence. A third shadow whizzed by the left side of the group. Thos looked around.

"What happened to the Fey?" Thos asked. More screams

reverberated through the sweltering forest. A final heart-stopping scream boomed up ahead. A small figure ran toward them. The figure drew closer with a clearly human shape.

"Help!" the voiced cried, gasping for breath. This girl didn't even look to be ten years old. Thos's blood ran cold when a deformed mass swooped down on her. In a split second, the top half of the girls head vanished, replaced by a fountain of gore. The shadow darted back up into the canopy with the dripping piece of head still in its gangly claws. The mercs wasted no time filling the woods full of holes. Thos and the others panicked.

"Stand your ground!" Zora yelled.

"Fuck you, I'm outta here!" a soldier yelped out while fleeing on horseback. A mass bore down on him, severing the front legs of his horse. The man flew from the saddle, his body rolled carelessly through the grass. The shape latched on to him and sliced through his armor like a can opener, flesh and blood spewed from his back. The mercs blasted the target, unsure if the bullets hit their mark. Another merc fled the battle.

The Fey hunters were reduced to a handful, faring not much better than the mercenaries. More blurry horrors fell upon them. One creature hit a merc near Drake causing him to spin and shoot Drake's horse. The wild thrashing of the horse knocked the gun from Drake's hand, and seconds later sent Drake right after it.

"We gotta help Drake!" Zora said.

Thos repelled a monster zipping toward him. Inhuman screeching signaled that some of his bullets hit their mark. Drake switched to his sword, keeping the monsters at bay with continuous slashing. Mercenaries fell like dominos. Downed men crawled away only to be sliced open like baked potatoes. Melvin's blind firing hit a panicked mercenary running into his line of fire. Thos looked down to see the upper half of a mercenary reaching out for him with a long red trail of intestines stretching across the ground.

One of the monstrosities made quick work of the man nearest

Thos, severing the head with one quick slice. The killer sped toward Thos. Thos managed to get off a single shot at the creature, resulting in a stream of rust-colored blood that splattered across his chest. The stink made him woozy, causing some impromptu gagging. The creature hit the ground and Thos fired again, only to hear the click of an empty barrel. Thos scrambled for an extra bullet. The creature stirred again, flapping its translucent, veiny wings. Thos saw far too many humanesque features on the monster, a mash of man and insect. The life faded from the bulbous eyes. The arms with hook-like claws twitched. Thos's disgusted curiosity distracted him long enough, he focused on the battle at hand.

Zora leaped from her horse and switched to daggers once out of bullets. Moving swiftly toward the monster, she pulled a dagger from her hilt and planted it inside the monster's forehead. It shrieked, and thick blood oozed from the wound. Drake drove his sword into the monster's bulbous left eye, ensuring its death. Melvin unloaded shell after shell from his shotgun, clipping a few of the monsters. The creatures sped away, providing them a temporary reprieve from the onslaught. Zora and the others saw one the buzzing nightmares slumped over at their feet.

Melvin kicked the corpse and wiped gallons of sweat from his brow. He rolled the corpse over with his foot to get a good look it. The creature appeared to be around normal human height with a hump in its back. Long slender arms and legs stretched from creature's torso. Tiny hairs covered the entire body. The top half looked human: ears, nose, and eyes. The eyes were mismatched and pale, roughly three times the size of a normal human and segmented like an insect. A few jagged teeth protruded from the top of the mouth. Instead of a bottom jaw, it had three sets of pincers and a sickly gray tongue. Melvin shot it in the head just to be safe.

"This is Old World devilry," Melvin grunted. Drake nodded.

"What exactly do you know about these things?" Thos asked.

"Little," Zora replied. "There was a strange man that dwelled out here around sixty years ago, called himself The Seer. When he appeared, so did they. Not sure why they reappeared."

"Seer—that is what Gideon Grey was once called," Drake said. That got everyone's attention.

"Then either he ain't dead, or someone else is cooking these up," Thos said.

"That's the theory, but we've never found any evidence of labs. But it's a big place, and not exactly to safe to explore," Zora said.

"Dammit," Drake said. Zora looked as if she had more to say. Melvin aimed at every passing shadow. Drake took a moment to collect himself. Thos examined the nearby trees, something in them caught his attention.

"Do some of these trees look off to you?" Thos asked, pointing at one of the lighter colored trees with the others in tow.

"Off?" Zora asked. Thos could hardly believe the words himself.

"Fake," he replied. Thos squinted, noticing only the faintest of differences.

"We should check them while we have a chance," Drake said, walking over to one of the trees. Drake slammed his sword into the tree, creating a metallic clang. Off in the distance came the sound of buzzing.

ANSELM

Anselm didn't know how he had reached the throne room, but there he was sitting in the darkened halls. He tasted blood from his raw, tattered lip. Pain shot through his body. His stomached roared for sustenance despite eating an hour ago. A voiced called to him from on the edge his perception, alerting him to the mob outside.

"Anselm!" He finally came to his senses realizing the world around him.

"I'm fine," Anselm replied.

"You must really be out of it if you think you can convince me of that," Abigail said.

He felt tightness across his entire body, not yet realizing he wore his new armor. The look she shot Anselm told him she knew he had opened the Vault.

"It had to be done," Anselm said.

His trusted scientists diligently examined the collection of Old World technology while he struggled to keep himself sane. Abigail sighed and placed her hand on his.

"I'm worried about you. Everyone that looks at you funny is hanging from the walls or rotting in the dungeons. And it seems that half the time you're here… you aren't," she said.

"I'm doing what I have to do; it's harder on me than I thought.

Posturing now will get us killed." Inexplicable anger welled up in him; the orange serum coursing through his veins forced his buried emotions to the surface.

"You're a good man," Abigail said.

"That's not enough!" Abigail jumped back at the king's outburst. Immediately he frowned and looked away with chagrin. "I'm sorry. This job, it's quicksand; the more I struggle, the faster I sink." His tone went for anger to exhaustion, eyes filled with tears. "It's all gone wrong," she said. They embraced, and Anselm wiped away her tears before wiping away his own.

"We'll make it right," he said. The screaming mob raged outside; soldiers rushed out to de-escalate the situation. An officer burst in the throne room.

"I know. Send more guards to the medical wing," Anselm cut him off. The officer nodded and carried out the king's command.

"Stay with me, Abby," Anselm said. He stretched out his hand and together they walked down the cold halls toward the doors to the courtyard.

"Are you sure about this?" Abigail said.

"Not in the slightest," he replied. The guards held the door open for the king. Anselm saw the Board of Directors huddled together under the statue of Alexander.

Everyone gawked in wonder at his second skin armor. The guards drew weapons while riflemen took positions on the walls above the courtyard.

Liar, bastard, and less flattering words filled the streets. The crowd smelled of fresh piss and not so fresh cheese. Anselm sensed the bloodlust in the mob. The elite guard awaited his word to attack. Anselm raised his hand in the air. Warning shots from his riflemen silenced the crowd.

"Good people of New Prosperity, why has it come to this?" Anselm asked. Everyone spoke at once, creating a mass of incomprehensible fury. A gunshot quelled the noise again. "I know why, it's because we have failed you." Anselm kept his steely gaze on the crowd.

A self-appointed mob spokesman stepped forward, an old man of no repute whatsoever. The man hunched over with a smattering of gray hair combed over his liver-spotted head. Anselm allowed him to speak.

"We work and suffer and die. You sit in your castle doing nothing. There is no work and no money," he said. Anselm heard the rhetoric before that ignored the fact that the unemployment and pay situation wasn't nearly as bad as dissenters believed. A younger man in a green jerkin pushed him aside and took center stage.

"You fucking cunt!" he said. That word always made Anselm cringe.

"Eloquent," Anselm replied. The king prepared to speak when Mrs. Gordon seized the opportunity, growing ever more brazen since the death of her comrades.

"We've only ever been your humble servants," Mrs. Gordon said. Anselm smirked when he heard someone call Mrs. Gordon out on her blatant lie.

"They've never loved you. They steal your homes, fuck your wives, sell your jobs, rape your children, and kill whoever suits their fancy. My ancestors gave them the power to run this country and they ran it right into the ground," Anselm said.

Anselm listed the numerous crimes committed by the families over the years. The plump Mrs. Gordon waddled to front of the Board wearing fine orange silk, giving her the appearance of a pumpkin with a frog stuck in the top.

"Liar!" Mrs. Gordon choked out the words. The other Board members nodded in agreement behind their own cadre of armed thugs. Anselm's body started to ache. Mr. Beaumont adjusted his charcoal suit and brought up an easy target.

"What of Aric? How many did he take? Just one rumor and to

the grave with you," Mr. Beaumont said. A man in tattered white shirt and brown shorts began to shout over the crowd.

"That devil raped my daughter," a man said. The king spoke over the accuser.

"My son was cruel but never did such a thing. Though it pains me to admit it, I know the type of man my son was. I'm truly sorry for the grief he caused," Anselm spoke woefully. The truth of Aric wounded the king almost as much as his son's death.

"The prince killed my brother!" another screamed. Not all of the accusations against his son were unwarranted, Anselm knew. Mrs. Gordon laughed silently; her enormous jowls bounced with each laugh. Anselm greatly desired to rip into her body. He could almost taste Mrs. Gordon's flesh.

"My son died for his crimes. More blood will not feed your bellies or warm your homes," Anselm said.

"No more Blackthornes! No more king!" yelled an old bald man. Anselm sneered. He had a glorious speech prepared, however, lost it in his roiling anger.

The screams grew louder. The crowd smashed against the courtyard door and trampled one of the soldiers guarding it. A man at the front pulled something from his pocket and smiled a nasty yellow smile. Anselm's heart stopped.

"He has a gate key!" Anselm cried. Sweat began to soak the clothes beneath Anselm's armor. The man jammed the key in the lock. Some of the man's comrades formed around him. The Board members cowered behind the armed guards. Soldiers shot the keyman dead, only to be replaced by another eager rioter. The second man grabbed the key and the gates flew open. Without giving it a second thought, Anselm ordered his troops to fire on the crowd. A tidal wave of infuriated masses flooded the courtyard, overwhelming the bodyguards. Off-duty soldiers rushed from the barracks and kitchens to clash with the rioters. The first line of Blackthorne defense fell under the stampeding horde.

The second wave of soldiers cut down the rioters assaulting their brothers. More waves trampled the corpses, reducing the downed soldiers to canned meat. The steady stream of rioters pushed the soldiers back. Instead of retreating, Anselm let his rage out. He drew his blade and began cutting down any that got close. Anselm slashed the throat of an older man, and the spraying blood filled his mouth. A mammoth of a man barreled into him. Anselm hit the ground hard.

He never dropped his sword and hacked away at the man's ankle. Adrenaline took over. Anselm jumped up and stabbed another man rushing him. In the chaos, Anselm forgot his wife. "Abigail!" Abigail fled to the castle gates, with no support left. A man tackled her to ground. The king's vision went red. He charged into his wife's attacker. He threw the man off her, his head making a sickening crack against the castle wall. Anselm fell upon him in an instant. His fingers dug deep into the man's eye sockets and tore the eyes from his head. Anselm thrust his sword, and with a single click, it engulfed in mesmerizing flame. Metal armor wrapped around his face. The mask shielded him from the flames, yet he still felt the intense heat. The flames turned a mesmerizing blue before cocooning around the blade. Anselm's stopped for a second to admire the strange hot energy wrapped around his blade, and the fact it hadn't burned him. He held the blade down by the man's face. The flesh became moist and ran down the man's face, exposing the bone and muscle beneath. The agonizing screams drew the attention of comrades. It was an impractical weapon; he doubted it was anything more than Gideon's tinkering and he couldn't wait to use it on the others.

A young man rushed him, with one the swipe the flaming blade went clean through the man, his top half fell backward as the legs continued forward a few seconds more.

The gunmen on the towers eliminated the middle ranks of the attackers, dividing their forces. Abigail pulled a pistol from the holster of the nearest officer and opened fire on oncoming foes. Abigail, the officer, and his men retreated to the safety of the throne room. Anselm's blade filled the courtyard with white light, seeing his charred and diced victims proved more than adequate at demoralizing his foes. The heat from his bizarre sword forced everyone back. The raging mob fizzled quickly as the guards mobilized. Anselm killed three more men attempting to flee. The survivors were rounded up.

Anselm roared in half-mad rage. A dying rioter lay at his feet, looking up at him. Anselm held his sword to the man's face. He adjusted a knob on the hilt of his sword. The sword energy went from blue to white. The downed man gurgled out a final cry before his face blistered and dripped off. Anselm turned off the blade and instantly his mask opened back up. The pain subsided and his senses hummed.

"I've let this game go on long enough. Hang them on the street corners so none forget," Anselm said. After years of impotence, he felt powerful again. Guards cried out in the distance, dragging two men toward the king. When Anselm recognized the pair, he experienced unbridled joy.

"We caught these two were trying to escape. The others have fled the city. We figured you'd like a word with 'em," one of the soldiers said. For the first time in Anselm's life, Mrs. Gordon and Mr. Beaumont cowered before him. Anselm looked at them and grinned.

"It's good to be king."

ZORA

Buzzing horrors darted towards Zora and her companions. Zora, Thos, Drake, and Melvin slashed at the fairies, conserving bullets for clear shots. The fairies circled them for the kill. Drake slammed his sword into the fake tree. A large piece of faux bark fell off, revealing the rusty metal underneath. Drake swung his sword repeatedly until the bark fell away, revealing what looked like a door.

"Hey, Paul Bunyan, hurry up!" Thos said in a high, panicky tone.

Melvin hacked away at anything that entered his kill zone, getting a few decent shotgun blasts in when things got too dicey. One fairy lost half an arm to Melvin, splattering him with hot blood. Zora snatched up the severed claw.

"Running out gas here!" Melvin yelled.

Zora sliced at the door with the fairy claw. Screeches of claw on metal defiled their eardrums. Melvin's sword cleaved through the creatures like butter when they connected. Suddenly, a bullet whizzed by. Arrows and bullets from the treetops provided the group with much-needed support. Fairies broke off their attack to deal with the new threat. Perfectly camouflaged warriors from all around scattered the fairies. The door began to give. Zora jammed the claw in the rusty metal with all her might and the old thing came loose.

"Come on!" she exclaimed

Together, they pushed open the door. Steps descended down into the earth far beyond their vision. Zora ran through, followed by Melvin, Drake, and Thos.

"If there weren't monsters behind us, I'd be against this," Thos commented. As Drake held the rear and pulled the newly made door closed. The group caught their breath before cautiously moving down the stone steps. Zora questioned the decision to descend into the darkness.

"How do we know them blighters aren't down here?" Melvin asked.

"We don't," Zora said. Drake pulled a flashlight from his travel pack. Silently the four walked down the steps. Gusts of cool air came up to greet them in waves, a spectral breath. At the bottom of the steps, a hall opened into a rectangular room. Long tables end on end filled the room, with several chairs at each table.

"What's all this?" Drake asked.

"Father believes there are pieces of Old World Chicago beneath the forest," Zora began. "They say the old city stretches all across the state, not just Kingsbury. We've tried to find access to them before, but only rubble. We abandoned our efforts when the fairies came back. The Seer came here wanting to learn more about the Great Empire's lost knowledge, as did my sister. When my sister… when this is all started."

"Sister?" Drake said. Zora didn't reply. Her silence answered Drake's question.

"I'm sorry," Drake said. She gave a pained smile and a nod.

"She wanted to explore, always too curious for her own good," Zora replied. She eyed the barren room. "This place should be overgrown. There's not a single vine or blade of grass," she said.

Together the foursome explored the facility, eventually

reaching a room with a massive screen on the back wall. In front of the screen, a large metal table and a single chair sat conspicuously. On the table were many buttons with odd labels. Drake read them aloud.

"This is a keyboard," Drake said.

A small green eye opened on the screen, and a barrage of words trickled down from it. A grid formed, taking the shape of a human face. Skin formed on the face, followed by eyes. A series of beeps followed. Melvin and Thos jumped back, ready for battle.

"If you smell piss it ain't me," Melvin said while checking his pants. The machine spoke to them.

"Hello," it said in a lifeless tone. "This console has not been accessed by the administrator in—" The machine paused to make a few more beeps. "Twenty-one years, two months, six days, and three seconds."

"That the monster button? Please don't be the monster button," Thos said, not joking.

"What are you?" Zora asked. The artificial eyes looked up at the ceiling, imitating human contemplation.

"I am Os; I run this facility. This is private property. If you do not have the authorization code you must remain here while I contact the administrator."

"Is that who was here last?" Zora asked. Os beeped.

"No. The last user is unknown. They did not know the password," it said.

"Who's the administrator? Gideon?" Drake asked. A nasty sounded beep suggested followed.

"The administrator is… the administrator," Os replied.

"Helpful," Drake said.

"What is this place?" Zora asked. Os replied with a series of musical beeps.

"This place was designed by the administrator to study and reverse engineer technologies from United North America, referred by your people as the 'Great Empire.' This research facility was constructed 103 years, two months, eight days, twenty-nine minutes, and fourteen seconds ago by the administrator. It was converted from an unused fallout shelter."

"Research facility? Can we see the labs?" Zora asked. Beeps of all kind shot forth from the machine, the louder, more ominous ones suggested some kind of error.

The walls on both sides of the screen sank into the ground revealing walls of glass and doors and a seemingly endless structure. Lights flickered on the other side of the glass. Collections of misshapen bones all jawless with large eye sockets littered the rooms. A glass tube lay in the center room, containing a half-rotten corpse covered in wires and a metal frame.

"Much of what the administrator created here has been discontinued. Operations were moved to other facilities," Os said. A lump developed in Zora's throat.

"There are other places like this?" Drake spoke with dread.

"Yes, but information not available." Sad musical notes followed, imitating emotion. *This machine is just a sad child missing its father*, Zora realized.

"Those bones, what made those people like that?" she asked.

More whimsical tones followed. A large vial of orange liquid rotated on the screen.

"GM-004, the fourth iteration of a human enhancement mutagen inspired by the UNA Science Division circa 2098 AD. GM004 bonded with a success rate of 45 percent to subjects from the local populace. Mixed with environmental variables, it created a homo sapiens offshoot, not the administrator's intended result," Os said. The voice beeped in disappointment as if the failure was its own.

"Those things outside were people?" Drake asked.

"Yes. I started up phase two of the project when I was

reactivated," Os said. A revelation hit Zora with enough force to knock the wind from her.

"My sister's friend, she woke you up!" Zora exclaimed.

"Mercy… the missing people were just some sick experiment," Drake said. The face disappeared, turning to one big red eye fixated on Drake. At that moment, Zora could almost hear their collective sphincters tightening.

"I don't think it likes what you're insinuating," Thos said.

"My apologies, Os. You did a… real bang-up job," Drake replied. Thos and Melvin quickly moved away from Drake and over to Zora.

"It's alright, Os. Please continue," Zora said. With a happy beep, the face returned.

"Most subjects died in captivity, however, some escaped. A lapse in my security prevents me from sealing all the vents, allowing them access to the forest. All efforts at colonization have failed. The imperfect cell mutation has rendered reproduction impossible. The new progenitor is not doing as expected." The room lowered to an area deep underground. Behind Os, a room with an organic mass in the center appeared. The mass quivered.

In the center of the room, lay a mountain of flesh, covered with dozens of human and insect appendages. The blob had two faces, one vaguely human and a second with a collection of pincers and eyes protruding from the side. A few strands of faded blue hair jutted out from the heads. A viscous yellow material oozed out from under the folds of flesh. A serpentine tail extended from the creature and up to a husk-like mass in the ceiling. Hundreds of dead fairies covered the ground around the monster.

"All babies are stillborn," Os continued, "Efforts to create more have proven fruitless. I have programmed some to bring me new subjects, more study is needed. Analysis suggests human and insect cells conflict. The current hypothesis is the attacks outside are not intentional, it is due to the trauma from the pre-life mind in conflict with the post-mutation brain." Zora felt knots in her stomach. She understood at once.

"These monsters are just trying to reach their families, but the mutation drives them crazy. Those poor souls," she said. Her sickness turned to sadness.

"The last subject from the new phase is trapped in the vent system above the cafeteria area, the vents were not big enough for transport. Many of the subjects injured themselves traveling through them. A subject blocks the main shaft, preventing the others from returning," Os said.

"Do you have any more information on these things? On anything," Zora pleaded.

The machine stopped speaking while they talked and resumed immediately after. "A few audio entries remain. Play audio entries?"

"Play what have," Zora replied.

Broken, disjointed audio journals narrated by a man detailed mutations, experiments, hypotheses, histories, and equations. The voice referenced America, Canada, and Mexico: the eastern half of these countries would become New Prosperity. The audio entries halted at the sounds of more fevered beeping indicating an error. Os played the most recent entry that comprised mostly of phrases and lone words that meant little without the full context. There was one word that caught their attention: godseeds. The word repeated over and over by a panicked voice. The journal entry ended with cryptic words and static, "Key to everything… Compact knows… my time grows short… coming for me. I must finish my work. So close now." Os ended the playback.

Zora found it odd this machine was so forthcoming; she wondered if something was wrong with it or if its designer intentionally left it this way for hopeful acolytes.

"My systems are corrupted. I can no longer continue the experiments," Os said.

"If the subject stuck in the vent is removed can you get the others to return and destroy this place?" Zora asked, in a sweet, almost motherly tone.

The machine beeped rapidly. Zora's father occasionally spoke to her about his time in Vigilant and the nature of old machines he'd encountered. Some old machines had minds of their own, and like human minds degenerated over time.

"Administrator authorization is required," Os replied. Zora's father told her old machines required some kind of password Os had lost over time. Whatever security this machine once had now appeared long gone. Zora learned machine password conventions from her father, who had cracked many ancient systems throughout his life.

"Do you remember what the administrator looked like? Height? Weight? Gender?" she asked.

"Visual recordings are corrupted." *Good. He doesn't remember,* Zora realized.

"I'm the administrator," she spoke with gentle yet firm authority. All turned at her, showcasing their fear.

"Enter the password," Os said. Zora approached the keyboard and typed the word "administrator" in. "Press enter," Os said. Zora complied. Os beeped wildly, musical tones flying forth in rapid succession. "Welcome, administrator," Os said, beeping happily.

"Nice trick," Thos said.

"Trick?" Os asked, returning to the form of a red eyeball.

"Ignore him. Thos, zip it," Zora said. "I will remove the subject, and then I will give you the okay to start the purge."

"Yes, administrator," Os replied. He beeped in delight; the door beside them slid open. "The lab entrance is unlocked."

The group drew weapons and proceeded to the labs. Only a single fluorescent light worked in the lab. They could see three other labs through the windows of Lab One, all devoid of life. Sticky yellow residue dripped from the man-sized honeycombs clinging to the room.

Drake kicked a piece of the honeycomb and it crumbled to yellow dust. Small monitors much like Os were present in the room, though broken. The silent vents loomed above. Zora couldn't see anything from the floor. She climbed up onto the nearby table. She held out her hand and Drake tossed her his flashlight. Zora aimed the light up at the blackened hole and fell back when she saw the creature trapped in the vent. She landed near misshapen bones on the floor, cutting her forearm on the broken pieces. The thrashing steadily grew louder.

"You just rang the dinner bell," Melvin said.

All stepped back. The monster crashed to the floor, breaking its weak limbs on impact. This fairy didn't have all the bony mandibles the others did, instead a single pincer protruded from a human jaw. The creature's wings were mangled, and its right ankle twisted and broken. This creature retained some of the feminine features of its past life, enough for Zora to recognize it. Zora didn't want to believe it, but her darkest nightmares were confirmed. The creature looked up at Zora, surprisingly docile. Zora's eyes welled up with tears.

"It's Sprout. I found you, just like I promised. I... I'm so sorry I couldn't save you. I should've fought harder. I should've—" The creature grunted back at her with a small semblance of humanity left. "Your pain is over now. I love you, sis." Zora drove her dagger into the monster's skull. It whimpered and fell limp.

Zora wept until thrashing sounds from a dozen more fairies above interrupted her. Zora quickly treated her wounds. The group sped out of the room, closing the door seconds before the first fairy crashed to the floor. Within seconds ten grotesque fairies filled the room, breaking limbs in an effort to get to the lab.

"All subjects present. Initiate purge?" Os asked. Zora nodded. A huge red light in the corner of the room flashed repeatedly. Metal shutters came down, covering the lab windows. Os counted down from thirty. None could see, but all could hear the buzzing growing ever more ferocious. When the countdown ended came the sounds of intense flame and shrieking. Os beeped whimsically. "Purge complete." The walls came back down, revealing only ash and bone.

"Thank you, Os. We're leaving. Shut down this facility. Do not allow anyone but me access it," Zora said, trying to keep her sorrow under control. Os beeped its feelings of sadness. "I'll return again soon. I promise," Zora said. *I will return and destroy this place,* she thought.

Os beeped his content. "Goodbye," Os said. The screen went black and the green eye above flickered off.

ANSELM

With his family by his side, Anselm monitored the citizens of Kingsbury from the safety of the castle balcony. He glanced down at the lower castle wall, at the impaled bodies of Mrs. Gordon and Mr. Beaumont that served as his new lawn ornaments. Rioters dangled from the streetlights creating grim warnings to those strolling down the main street. People showing even a smidgeon of support for the crown had their homes and business burned to the ground across the nation. News of rebel victories within the state disturbed Anselm; he withheld this information from the public lest more rallied to their cause. Anselm cleared his throat.

"People of Kingsbury, the Board of Directors has been permanently dissolved. You can see two of them dissolving right there." A protester in the crowd attempted to incite the others. The king pointed to the riflemen and they aimed at the man's head, coercing him to relent. Down below an executioner stood cross-armed, waiting for the cue to execute a prisoner. With a lethargic wave, Anselm ordered the man's death. The executioner in the courtyard below bore his massive ax down on the last member of the Beaumont family. A simple bullet to head would've sufficed, yet Anselm deemed this a more effective deterrent against treason. Reginald Beaumont, second cousin to Edward Beaumont, endured three vicious chops before his self-important head detached from his shoulders. "Reginald avoided paying for his crimes in Mexico for nearly thirteen years thanks to his family's position. That ended today," Anselm said. The king stood proud, feeling a sense of accomplishment.

"Certain individuals of this nation, *my* nation, have proven themselves to be gullible tools for men like this. Patrols will increase. A curfew is now in effect until further notice. The old order has been re-established. You would do well to know your place in it. This will be your one and only warning." Thousands of soldiers filled the courtyard and the streets, and dozens of riflemen lined the castle walls.

Anselm's new armor pressed tightly against his chest, tight as the constant stress to which he had grown so accustomed. Though nerves were frayed, and muscles ached, Anselm never felt more alive. His trusted officers and scientists were hard at work, studying and preparing Gideon's stockpile of weapons. Troops on leave were being called into action to bolster numbers of the forts and cities in the warpath. Forces were gathering large enough to oppose the rebel groups in both Heartland and Emerald Coast. With the balance of power shifting from the Board to him, a united front was more than capable of stamping out the rebel threat.

Rain gently fell upon his heavy brow. Together, the Blackthorne family left the balcony for the security of their private quarters. It warmed Anselm's heart to have his family here with him. He picked Edgar up and swung him around.

Anselm finally believed things were changing for the better. The dull ache in his right arm still distracted him. Anselm threw off his suit jacket, and with family in tow, headed to the dining hall for a family meal. In the private dining hall, the Blackthornes feasted on butter-drenched lobster, chocolate-covered strawberries, and a dozen foods Anselm couldn't identify. Amid soft candlelight, they laughed and talked of the pleasant days to come.

After an hour, Percival took Edgar to bed. The nigh grew late, but Anselm and Abigail lingered in the dining hall. They sat together, sipping from the last of his collection of Verdant wine. Sipping turned to drinking and, after more than a few bottles, the king and Abigail became truly inebriated. Anselm moved close to Abigail and regaled her among the firelight. "With a single stroke, I brought down the mighty griffon! Hya! Ha!" Abigail laughed at his sword noises. "And that's how its head ended up here." He pointed at the elk head on the wall. Abigail pushed his hand to the griffon head on the other side of the room.

"Life was simpler then," she spoke softly, stroking the whiskers of his returning beard.

"Because we were fools," he laughed, choking on wine. "The world is made for fools. Fools are happy," Anselm said.

"Then let's be fools again," she said. Abigail moved in closer to Anselm and wrapped her arms around his shoulders. Anselm kissed her forehead. The faint thumping of his heart became the fierce beating of a war drum. His nerves became electric. She looked into his eyes and kissed him. Slowly, he unzipped her dress, using ghost-soft touches on her back that made her flesh shiver. He kissed her neck. She unbuttoned his shirt, his feelings of self-loathing because of his aged body melted away beneath her grace. The passion threatened to swallow him whole. The animal side of Anselm's long forgotten youth soared to life. He threw the dishes to the floor and tossed Abigail onto the table. She moaned with excitement and grabbed his hard manhood through his pants. She kissed his neck. "Take me now," she whispered.

She moaned loudly as he went inside her slowly. He felt her warmth, and gently ran his teeth across her nipples. They continued looking into each other's eyes, smiling and laughing. His thrusting became rough and hard. He picked her up and pushed her against the wall. He bit her neck. Abigail screamed with delight as she climaxed, her body quivering uncontrollably. A guard coughed uncomfortably from outside the hall, Abigail laughed only half-aware of her surroundings.

"Let the whole world hear," Anselm said.

Anselm bit her again, harder. She grunted her displeasure. The animal became a monster. Passion became rage. He felt an urge to bite her again, to draw blood. He heard a voice in his head. *Bite her. Hurt her. Tear her flesh.* He fought against such dark impulses, knowing it to be a side effect of Gideon's "gift." Anselm came, and his wild, bestial scream thundered down the hall. Both were drenched with sweat and nearly all of Abigail's clothes lay in tatters. He picked up the naked Abigail and carried her out of the dining hall to the royal bedchambers, to the dismay of the guards. Anselm laid her onto the bed and took his place beside her.

"I wish this could last forever," she said before drifting off to sleep. Not long after she fell asleep, fiery pain shot through Anselm's body. There was scratching in his head, a scratching that turned to words.

"Dungeon. Now," it commanded.

He quietly threw on some clothes and crept down to the chambers now full of unwilling guests. Dozens of people were chained to the walls, covered with cuts and bruises. He didn't even remember sentencing some of these men, though he assured himself of their guilt. By the torchlight, the dungeons resembled the old tales of Hell, a stark contrast to the heavenly décor above.

Prisoners cried out in all corners of the winding halls of torment, proclaiming innocence. Doubt gnawed away at him, but he ignored it. The voice in Anselm's head directed him to the crematorium. The crematorium was a massive room with a singular pit in the center. Huge slides from the upper complex fed a constant stream of bodies down to the unquenchable fires of the incinerator pit. The smell of roasting flesh repulsed Anselm less and less these days. He bent over and stared into the flames reaching out for him. His arm tingled. A body came sliding down past the king sending the flames up higher. The tingling pain stabbed inside his arm forcing him back. He recoiled to find a familiar figure standing before him: Aric. The king stumbled back from the shock, dangerously close to the incineration pit. A pile of corpses caught his attention, as well as the lack of anyone in the area to throw the bodies onto the chute.

Wordless, the figure walked toward him. It shuffled closer, pushing Anselm toward the pit. Anselm blinked, and he saw this was just some commoner. He jumped out of the way, turning to watch the man fall down into the burning pit. Anselm looked down into the fire to find the gold-masked man staring up at him.

"Good to see you again, ant-king," the masked man said. Anselm blinked and the figure disappeared. He turned to find the masked man behind him.

"What do you want?" Anselm asked. He felt other masked figures watching him through the flames.

"You are conflicted over this gift we've given. We wanted you to see your true potential." The masked man pointed at a pile of bodies that had fallen off the slide. The corpses began to stir. Mechanically, the dead rose to their feet. Anselm watched, dumbfounded.

"The power of the vault can raise the dead?" Anselm asked. The masked man laugh's was like a hellish scraping in the king's brain.

"And so much more," the masked man replied. The dead twisted and broke, taking on unnatural shapes. The masked man lowered his hand and the dead collapsed instantly. He snapped his fingers and the bodies bubbled and blistered before falling apart. *Power over life and death*, Anselm realized.

"You didn't have to drag me down for magic tricks," Anselm growled.

"All this suffering and death, it won't stop here. Not for them and not for you. You will have to walk through your own fire in the days to come. We just came to keep you motivated." the masked man said. Anselm turned back from the disintegrated corpse pile to face the masked man.

"More pain! Have I not suffered enough?" Anselm asked. Anselm struck the masked man with superhuman force. The masked man's head snapped back with a sickening crunch, breaking his neck. Anselm marveled at his own newfound power, but only for a moment. The masked man's broken bones snapped back into place. His head shot forward, his mask now sporting a wicked grin. Pain surged through Anselm's body, stronger than ever before. He fell to the ground, clutching his chest. Anselm looked up again. All the masked figures now surrounded him, grinning wickedly. The female figures held hands up to their mouths, imitating laughter.

"My dear ant-king, your hell is just starting," the masked man said. Anselm's pain intensified. His consciousness faded. Suddenly, Anselm found himself alone. He struggled to his feet. He looked around for more surprises and found only the dead sliding toward an unceasing flame. Anslem headed back up to the bedroom, no longer facing the future with hope, but dread.

DRAKE

THE SAPPHIRE LIGHTS around the Fey community swayed to and fro in the night wind like fireflies. Drake smoked cannabis given to him by Zora's father, it soothed his exhausted nerves.

Loathing crowds, Drake watched the celebratory bacchanal from a distance. He saw Zora grieving alone on a treetop platform. Over by the elders' huts sat a group of old men and women that partook in a variety of drugs unknown to Drake. Melvin joined a group of revelers with a frenzied giddiness.

Word of rebel victories around the nation flew from the lips of the few travelers passing through. Tomorrow, Drake would slip away from the others and return to Kingsbury. The moment he left the forest, his Fey protection would end. Drake suspected the rebels would move against him then. He also knew the information he relayed to the king might bring down his wrath upon the Fey.

Drake always feared, if the rumors of Anselm's rage were true, that the king would hold him personally responsible for failing to save Aric. Drake feared he couldn't stand up to the king, but he told himself it may be necessary lest the whole kingdom fall apart. If Anselm or the Board were a threat, he would have to act. He was once excited to see the king, now he dreaded the day. He kept thinking about the rumors of long-dead tech built by Gideon and if true the possibility Anselm would use it to fight back. Drake wanted to believe the king wasn't spiraling into madness, however from the sound of things he feared it to be true. Again Drake was stuck with a dozen decisions each with a dozen consequences. Despite willing to die for his country, Drake couldn't help but worry about his fate. He took a few more heavy drags to erase his thoughts for the night.

Beneath trees and light, the people danced, sang, and made love. Melvin approached Thos and Drake. The boastful warrior reeked of sweat and an unknown concoction of recreational herbs. He grinned widely.

"You guys are no fun hanging out all by yourselves. You guys need to enjoy yourself. It took a lot of convincing, but I'm gonna be part of an orgy!" Melvin proclaimed. "I've never done that before. Despite what Zora told me, it looks like some of the Fey do like to get freaky. This place is somethin' else."

"Expand your horizons, just not in front of me," Thos said. Melvin grunted with delight.

"You should grab you some girls or guys or whatever and have fun. It may be our last chance," Melvin said. "That one over there is built like a tree." Thos looked. Drake also caught a glimpse and both men did a double take.

"Damn you really are fried. That *is* a tree, a wooden statue of a woman," Drake said. Melvin turned around with squinting eyes to the trees and then back to Thos.

"So that's why she was starin'," Melvin said.

"It seems to me you belong here, not down in some cave," Thos said.

Melvin nodded. "Eh, but Ellora is my home," he replied. "They took me in when my own family left me to die and after... I'd be dead if not for them."

"You feel you owe them?" Drake asked, trying a get some insight on his companion.

"It's the only place I've ever really mattered. I was nothing until Joe recruited me."

"That's why you like to be the big hero?" Thos said.

"Joseph says I like to overcompensate, calls the warrior my 'public face.' Perhaps he's right. I am more than that, just so you know," Melvin said. Melvin fell over, catching a face full of dirt.

"Aspiring plant too," Thos joked. Melvin laughed. Drake stared Melvin down.

"Enough of that shit. I wanna enjoy my time. Goodnight," Melvin said. Melvin casually stood, popped his fingers, and ran to the crowd of dancers. Thos turned his attention to Drake. Drake pulled out his gun and inspected it. He ran his fingers along the Blackthorne emblem on the gun.

"I'm restless. See ya later," he said. He jumped up and took off, giving Thos a wave.

After aimlessly wandering through the treetop world, Drake headed toward Zora. She was hunched over the wooden railing carved with phoenixes, staring at nothing in particular. Drake delayed approaching her. He couldn't deny his attraction to her, but now was not the time for that. He felt shame for dwelling on such things at a time like this, especially for someone he barely knew. Eventually, he climbed the winding stair and approached her.

"It's a different place now," Drake said. She didn't look back at him. Drake could tell she did not want others to see her tears, he preferred to hide his as well. "I'm not sure if anything I say can help you… or what to even say after what happened. You've been through something most people never will, and you survived. Most could not carry on. You have a strength that few possess. In time, the grief will fade. I think your sister would be proud of the woman you've become. I hope that makes it a little easier." Drake stopped and rubbed the back of his head.

"Oh boy, got a bit sappy, didn't I?" Drake asked. Drake tired not to be flustered by Zora, and he had an inkling from the occasional glimpse in his direction that Zora's interest purely business related.

"You did, but I appreciate it," she said. She kept looking out at the forest. "I don't think she would be proud of me. I never cared for honor or duty. All I wanted was to explore the world. I've never been one to stick around for too long," she said.

"Me either," Drake said. "I go wherever there is trouble and hope I put down more than I create. Nothing wrong with being a nomad from time to time." Drake moved beside her, placing his hands on the railing. He fought to maintain his composure while fumbling about like an idiot.

"What will you do now?" Drake asked.

"I'd like to travel the country, maybe go to Mexico when things're settled. There are Fey communities all way down there. There are still existing structures from the BC era out there to, maybe destroy more of these labs while I'm at it." Drake found the life of a traveling adventurer charming, the true appeal of being a Knight-Ambassador.

"Finding ruins and old world cities, if they are real, sounds appealing. I've half a mind go with you," he blurted out. Zora's eyebrows rose.

"Do you?" Zora asked. Drake's hand slipped the rails, knocking a small wooden figure down to the forest floor.

"I mean, if I knew you. I would. If I knew you. Better, you know?" *I should throw myself off the balcony*, he thought. She giggled seeing the battle-hardened warrior reduced to a klutz.

"What about you? Really going back to the capital?" she asked. Drake braced for his confrontation with the king and to kill the rebels when they inevitably made a move on him.

"And I'm going to end this war. Mercy help me."

GREGOR

In Gregor's world, there was only pain. After his fall from Blackthorne Castle, he crawled on broken legs until agony left him unconscious. Gregor woke to find himself on a bed in a small room, still very much alive.

He remembered falling from the castle window. Gregor had managed to grab one the flags hanging from the tower, preventing his splatter in the courtyard. Bullets whizzed by, nearly ending his life a dozen times. Gregor landed legs first in the corner of the courtyard, inches from the massive tubs of soft laundry left by servants fleeing the rain of glass, bullets, and crabby old men. Broken but living, Gregor considered himself the luckiest man in the world. Gregor wanted to see who aided him in the desperate escape. The room smelled of incense, honey, and what he believed was cannabis.

Though not the most comfortable of beds, Gregor lacked any desire to leave it. He sighed with relief that his body remained mostly intact. An arm reached out to him holding a cup of nectar.

"Drink," said a male voice. Gregor drank it down, and the arm snatched the cup away for a refill. His senses dulled little by little with each sip.

"I hate this shit," Gregor said. The dulling pain encouraged him to keep drinking. "Give me more."

The brain fog made Gregor's recovery infinitely more tolerable. Gregor lay inside a dome-shaped hut made of thick animal hide. Such tents were constructs of forest-dwelling Fey from the White Woods.

"You jumped from the tower. *The* tower. Crazy old coot." The male voice spoke with amazement.

"Fastest way down," Gregor replied. The man helped Gregor sit up. The crusader appeared to be in his mid-twenties with stringy red-brown hair. He didn't recognize the young man.

"Yeah, remember, me? My name is Patrick Sims, I saved your life," he said. The camaraderie in the Northern Frontier turned vicious at times.

"I… don't. In any case, I owe you," Gregor said. Gregor tried to stand. Excruciating pain forced him back down flat on the bed. "We the only ones left?"

"I think so," Patrick said. Patrick brought Gregor up to speed on current events: the bounty placed on Gregor's branch of Vigilant, Anselm's attack on the Board, the loss of Blackthorne forts to Joe Kerr's men, and the rebel gathering in these very same woods. Gregor sipped on nectar, contemplating his next move.

"There is someone who has been waiting to see you." Patrick interrupted his thoughts. An elderly man shambled his way inside the tent, with long shaggy hair and ghostly white beard.

"I never thought I'd see Gregory Lynn stumble back through my door," the old man said. Gregor got to his feet but fell back down onto the bed. Gregor always considered himself a tough, grizzled old man with no more tears to shed. The tears began to flow freely at the sight of his little brother, Matthew. The two embraced.

"It has been too long," Gregor said, overjoyed.

"It took you falling out of the king's castle to come back here. You should fall more often," Matthew said.

"Think I've done that enough," Gregor replied with a smile. Patrick stood awkwardly while supporting his injured commander.

"So the famous Matthew Pavane is protecting the Fey people," Patrick said.

"No one told me I was famous," Matthew said, surprised.

"You're being modest. You were what we always strived to be. I can't believe you're standing right here," Patrick said.

"Here I am, decrepit and content as can be as Kami Rayntree of the Fey." Matthew shifted his attention back to Gregor. Gregor raised an eyebrow and smirked.

"You were baked when you came up with that, weren't you?" Gregor asked.

"Probably," Matthew began, "Anyway, you can mock me later. Things are dark indeed in the world these days. I knew Vigilant's days were numbered, but I didn't think we'd go out like that."

"We aren't gone yet," Gregor said.

"You gonna to take on the government by yourself? Your glorified monster killers," Matthew reminded.

"Monster killers? You shortsighted—" Gregor said with a flash of anger. He took a deep breath. "Sorry. Maybe that is all we really are." Matthew's eyes widened.

"What was that? Say that in my good ear," Matthew said, flabbergasted.

"I'm sorry dammit!" Gregor snarled. "I'm sorry for… for everything." Patrick took the opportunity to leave the two men to a long overdue conversation. Gregor cursed under his breath not being able to walk around on his own.

"You do realize this is the first place they'll come looking for you?" Matthew asked.

"They barely know anything about me, much less you. I had my subordinate tamper with their records," Gregor said. He scratched the back of his head, considering the words. "And to be honest, I wanted to see you," Gregor admitted.

"It's good to see you again, brother," Matthew said. "Don't worry, we have the extra scouts out, not to mention the rebel army camped here. The rebels march to the capital in the morning, matter of fact."

"Supporting the rebellion?" Gregor asked.

"They'll win. Even if the king is colluding with Grey Sisters his days are numbered," Matthew said convincingly. Cults, tyrants, civil war, and an order under the gun: it made Gregor despair.

"I could use some air," Gregor said.

Matthew had a wheelchair brought in and led his brother out to the cool evening air. Gregor followed his brother around the outskirts of the town. Fey reveled off in the distance along with rebel fighters preparing for the final leg of their journey. Gregor and Matthew shied away from the crowds.

"I can't believe you jumped from the top of Blackthorne Castle. You should be dead," Matthew reminded him. Gregor knew what Matthew was referring to.

"Doesn't mean I gotta like it," Gregor said.

"A little genetic modification never hurt anyone. Technically speaking, all humans have some. We use the weapons of the enemy against them, just like everyone in history." Matthew tried to show his brother the good in it, but Gregor would have none of it.

Gregor changed the subject. "How are your daughters doing? Elena must be grown by now," he said. He didn't remember the last time he saw his nieces.

"Zora is fine. She never goes by Elena. She is over there right now," Matthew said. Matthew pointed up to one of the tree houses where she chatted with a Knight-Ambassador. Gregor was confused by such a development and consulted his brother on the story of the noble hostage swept up in the shitstorm and could sympathize with the young man. Gregor advised Matthew to sway the knight to remain the woods, or he would likely die with the king in the days ahead. *Anselm may kill him if he's not careful,* Gregor thought.

The mixture of fire and electric light illuminated Zora's skin, giving her an almost angelic quality. Gregor had clearly been away longer than he remembered. She had grown into a strong woman. Both men were amazed that a monster killer turned drug-loving peacenik helped bring such a person into the world.

"What about Ashley, or Sunbeam, or whatever the fuck you call her?" Gregor inquired. The question brought pain to Matthew's face. Matthew moved farther towards the edge of the community.

"She died," Matthew said. Gregor bowed his head and tried in vain to remember his niece.

"How?" Gregor asked.

"Those goddamn fairies came back. It turns out there is a lab beneath the forest, right on my damn doorstep.., thought we got 'em all. We reached out for aid, but no one helped until now, not even Vigilant."

"I'm sorry. Had I known I would've come here immediately. I'm not sure why word never reached us," Gregor said.

"Over now. The next time a caravan comes through maybe we can get what we need to blow the damn place up. I'll see if the rebels have anything we can use. I'll make some excuse about it being for defense. No one else can know about the labs," Matthew said.

Gregor placed his hand on his brother's shoulder. Away from the bacchanalia, the sounds of crickets, owls, and the other forest dwellers rang out. The sounds of nature calmed his spirit. "I'm glad you're here," Matthew said, wiping tears from his eyes.

The two spent the majority of the evening reminiscing about the glory days of Vigilant. Gregor filled his belly with the finest food and wine in the community. For the rest of the night, the two brothers forgot their troubles and enjoyed their well-earned reunion. Neither man realized the wee hours of the morning crept up on them. Gregor anticipated the looming question Matthew waited to ask.

"You don't have to leave. Let new blood be spilled for a change. You've paid your dues," Matthew said. It was an undeniable truth. Gregor found the option of leaving the order more and more tempting as his brother talked. *I'm a liability to them now,* Gregor thought.

"It does sound nice, maybe it's time. In any case, I have plenty of time to think about it while I heal." Gregor wasn't convinced yet, though he was in no condition to be doing much of anything from a wheelchair.

"I think we'll be able to win you over in the end." Matthew beamed with confidence.

"You may," Gregor said.

"You should speak with Zora; she barely remembers you. Naia's death weighs heavy on her, on all of us. She needs more family in her life. I think it'll give you both a reason to stay. But don't you go recruiting her," Matthew warned. Tired, broken, and reunited with his family, Gregor thought hard on Matthew's words. He realized that he wanted this, but would not accept it.

"I wish you could stay," Matthew said, knowing Gregor's response.

"So do I, but you know I can't. There is still too much to do. The Grey Sisters are still out there. Who knows what they got working with Anselm? Even if I have to run them over with this fucking wheelchair, I'll stop them," Gregor said. Matthew nodded and laughed at the thought.

"Damn you and your honor," Matthew said. Gregor pushed himself up out of wheelchair only to fall back in it again. Gregor would accomplish none of his goals anytime soon.

"I suppose I can stay for a little while," Gregor said. Matthew gave his brother a pat on the back. A sensation washed over Gregor that he'd long forgotten. Sitting beside his brother and watching his niece, Gregor suspected that new feeling inside might very well be happiness.

ZORA

Drake and Zora watched the festivities below in awkward silence. They walked through the hanging courtyard to the Gaia statue now displaying ribbon-like butterfly orchids. The genetically engineered flowers descended from Old World science and shimmered with a neon radiance.

Despite the serenity around her, Zora couldn't stop thinking about her sister. Every time she closed her eyes, her sister was there.

"My sister," Zora began. Drake immediately shifted all of his focus to her. "She didn't vanish by chance; she was a Grey Sister." Drake had heard the term several times in the past. Everyone with an ear to the ground knew they were targets of Vigilant and were more often referred to as witches.

"She yearned to experience the world, like me. She grew bored being away from 'everything that mattered.' We always talked about traveling across the country, and the lands beyond. We even made plans… before a stranger showed up." The day came back to her as it was yesterday, clashing steel and gunfire, followed by blood.

"About five years ago, a group came to destroy us. Never found out why or who. They burned down some of our homes, killed many of us. My sister had been in the area at the time." Zora saw herself stabbing them mercilessly. Drake put his hand on hers as a gesture of comfort.

"The things they did to her," she said. To this day, there was no pity in Zora for what she did. Naked, caked with blood, and half-comatose, her sister was forever changed. "We lived in peace for decades, and they ended that. Naia avoided outsiders from then on, particularly any in large groups. After a few years she met an older woman who called herself a Grey Sister. The name meant nothing back then. They developed a friendship. The woman began living in the woods a few miles out, and the two spent most of their days together. The woman was part of a larger group. She wanted my sister to join them. Eventually she won my sister over. Of course, my sister wanted me to come along. I refused, but my sister didn't; she left before I could stop her. I managed to find out where she was going."

As the words flowed, Zora again returned to that moment two years ago. She slinked through the trees toward the stranger's home. The small hut the woman had built lay bare save for a few trinkets. Lingering aromas of roasted beef suggested they hadn't left that long before.

Zora sped toward the grove, certain they'd be there. Judging by the trampled grass, she had just missed them. She followed their trail to where no Fey lived. She heard chanting. Strange flashes surged through the woods, brilliant greens flashing like surges of alien sunlight. Zora followed the light. She saw twelve cloaked figures looking off in the direction of the otherworldly brightness. The deeper Zora dug into the memory, the more her head hurt.

Zora didn't see her sister among them. She suspected her to be hidden beneath one of the thick cloaks. The chanting ceased from all the hooded figures, save for one. The leader pulled back her hood, revealing her neon blue hair and rose-colored eyes. Zora identified her as Naia's new love. Zora moved closer, nearly breaking a small branch off in her haste. She maintained her composure.

The heat of the forest intensified, sweat formed on Zora's forehead and under her clothes.

The cult leader walked toward the light. The light formed into a large mass in a tattered robe. Zora's blood turned to ice. The black mass floated toward the women. "You've grown bold to summon us," it said. A sense of vertigo overcame Zora with each word.

"We seek your transcendence, great Gideon," the leader said. The hulking shadow stared down at the leader and her followers. Zora had revisited this memory a hundred times before. Tears ran down her face, knowing she would not be able to alter the result.

"Gideon?" it laughed. "You insult us. We are not here to bestow anything to you. You are all unworthy." The women took a step backward; a few of them drew curved daggers. Zora shimmied down the tree to rescue her sister from impending doom. Zora failed to save her sister every single time she relived this memory, but she would not stop trying. The cloaked monstrosity spoke again.

"Your part in the equation is over; however, we have other uses for you. A test, so to speak," it said. Two of the hooded figures were pulled off their feet. The sisters screamed as unseen forces tore at them. Clawing at the earth did nothing to stop the magnetic power. The sisters disappeared to the darkest reaches of the forest.

Zora hit the forest floor sprinting. Each step brought her closer to her goal. Two more sisters cried out before slipping into the void. The scraping voice of the monster came again. The leader of the sisters watched in horror as her followers were all dragged away. The leader vanished next. Zora knew her sister would soon be taken. Her fingers brushed against her sister's robes for an all-too-brief second. Naia flew from Zora's grasp and vanished in the darkness. Normally, the dream ended here, but this time she remained standing in the dead forest. The cloaked figure turned its attention to Zora.

"This isn't real!" Zora said in disbelief. She couldn't wake from this dream.

"Oh, it most certainly is. You should not remember this," it said. The unholy mass floated toward her. Searing pain set her brain alight. Zora grabbed her head, now throbbing with pain. Blood ran from her nose, ears, and eyes. "Rejoice little one, a grand future awaits!" She threw a dagger at the fiend. Out from the darkness came a golden mask with a gaping maw like an abyss that threatened to pull her in. Zora fell forward. At the moment she returned to the present, nearly falling over the balcony. Drake grabbed her in the nick of time.

"Zora! What happened? You all right?" Drake asked. Her head swam.

"I… I'm not sure," she said. Drake began to help her to a nearby medical tent, but she stopped him. Her maladies vanished like they were never there. Zora wiped the blood from her nose. Drake looked at her, perplexed.

"I don't think there is help for this. This requires Vigilant," Zora said. Drake scowled at the notion.

"I'll stay and help," Drake replied.

"Can you really stay here and not do anything about the world outside? I will consult with father on this," she said. He hated to agree with her on this matter.

"Dammit," Drake said.

"Thank you for helping me, but you have your own path to walk now," she said.

"Helping people is what I do," he said. He smiled awkwardly, and she found the battle-hardened warrior fumbling for the right words rather cute. Drake hid behind a gentlemen's code that prevented him from making moves he clearly wanted to make. Zora hoped this wouldn't be their last meeting. She quickly found her own smile became awkward, too. Zora's cheeks turn a faint shade of tomato red.

"I like you," Zora said. She knew he wouldn't make a move, so she took the initiative. She moved close to Drake and kissed him on the mouth. She felt the nervous energy shoot through his body. The delectable sweetness from fruits at the gathering wafted up to her, especially the strawberries. The pent-up emotions burst forth from Drake.

"Strawberries!" he blurted out. Zora could not contain her laughter. "It smells… like strawberries. Strawberries are nice," he said, with an embarrassed grin.

"You better say goodbye to me tomorrow… and make a move next time," she said. Drake grabbed her and pulled her toward him. He kissed her, unleashing passion and bottled-up emotion. She felt Drake let go of the shackles of endless duty. The two kissed among the firelight. Her heart fluttered. When the kiss ended, she found herself almost swept away by it.

"Like that?" he asked, no longer the awkward man fumbling for the right words.

"Like that," she replied. The two held each other for a while. Zora at last broke away, leaving Drake to prepare for his trip to the capital. Zora had a hunch Drake would not only survive the coming war and not be so guarded in the future.

Blue fires roared into the night from the nonstop celebrating, now coupled with fires of purple and green. Zora prepared to walk home when she noticed her father waving her over. Beside her father sat an old man in chair. Zora went down to them. Something about the second man was familiar to her.

"My how you've grown," the man said. Her mind shifted through memories, vaguely recalling such a man when she was a child. The man bore a resemblance to her father.

"Uncle Gregor?" she asked, floored by his sudden appearance.

"I've missed you so much," he said, sniffling. Gregor pushed himself up and embrace her, before falling back down in the chair.

"Why? How?" Zora said.

"Doesn't matter. What matters is that we're here together, and

I have so much to make up for." Matthew placed his hand on Gregor's shoulder and smiled.

"Then let's not waste any more time."

354

THOS

THE SOFT PURPLES of the dawn sky came sooner than anyone wanted, especially Thos. His nerves tingled. He emerged from the tent to Melvin standing around while Zora and Drake had their final chat. Melvin hollered incessantly for Thos to hurry. "Let me tinkle first," Thos replied.

He took an excruciatingly long piss. A group of men sat on horseback in the distance, the patchwork of leather and metal announcing their rebel affiliation. They all waited on him.

"We got places to be!" Melvin hollered.

"Looks like your escort is here," Drake said as he cast his own hateful glare at them. Zora turned to Melvin. "Hurt Drake and the deal is off," Zora said.

"Time for me to go," Drake said. He hugged Zora, gave Thos a firm handshake, and nodded to Melvin.

"We'll have to have strawberries sometime," Zora said. Drake smirked.

"It's been quite the adventure, Thos. I hope to see you all again when this business is over," Drake said.

"Don't die out there," Thos said.

Drake adjusted his pack and hopped onto the chestnut horse Zora's father bequeathed him and quickly faded from sight.

"Well, guess this is it. Take care," Thos said to Zora.

"I will," she replied. Thos gave Zora an intentionally awkward hug, trying to embarrass her. Melvin simply waved. As Thos and Melvin walked toward the caravan, Thos squinted curiously.

"Weren't there more men just a second ago?" Thos asked. The two looked around their vanished escort.

"Yeah they were just here," Melvin said. "Something about that seems a little—"

"Fishy." A rebel finished his sentence.

"Where the hell have you been?" Melvin asked while picking biscuit crumbs from his beard.

"Scoutin' around. Rest of the group went on ahead. Word on the grapevine is you had quite the experience out here in woods," the agent said.

"It's handled," Melvin said, shutting down the conversation. Melvin pulled some crushed leaf from his pocket and shoved it in his mouth. "We best be getting." Thos worried about the Knight-Ambassador with the conspicuous absence of the rebel soldiers.

"You didn't kill the boy," the agent snarled. Thos's eye widened to the size of saucers.

"What! You were going to kill Drake the second you secured the Fey deal," Thos said. He grimaced at the thought.

"But I didn't," Melvin replied.

"I knew you didn't have stones. I've sent people to deal with it. You are becoming more trouble than you are worth, Mel." The agent eyed both Thos and Melvin.

"You can't be serious?" Thos choked out. Melvin avoided the accusatory glare. Thos felt to urge to run after Drake, unfortunately, the agent's gun pointed at his stomach dissuaded him.

"Them thoughts you're having, forget 'em," the agent warned.

"What happened to being the great hero? I reckon you gotta keep me fat 'n' happy," Thos stated.

"That's for the public, ain't no public here," the agent reminded.

The agent holstered his gun and rammed his fist, hard, into Thos's gut. Thos fell to his hands and knees, muttering curses. He looked up and noticed the bloody emblem of a Red Devil mercenary.

"You are just our little dancing monkey, and it's almost show-time," the agent said. Melvin helped Thos to his feet.

"I told Joe it was a mistake to hire those twats," Melvin said.

The merc laughed in their faces, showing gold and silver teeth. The more Thos saw of these mercenaries, the more he grew to despise them. He shuddered to think of what Heartland's fate now that Joseph gave them Fort Alexander and the funds to rebuild it.

"Greater good, eh?" Thos mocked. Melvin didn't respond. The agent grew tired of waiting.

"Come. Time we get this over with."

DRAKE

DRAKE SIGHED WITH relief to be free of forests. On the horizon, he saw Blackthorne Castle. From here it looked like nature's way of flipping him the bird. He breathed deep in the open air. The grass glistened with fresh dewdrops.

Passing over a big hill, Drake spied a man on the highway. Sitting atop a horse wearing a boiled leather outfit and a dented breastplate. Drake's instincts told him to be wary. He casually looked off to the capital, all the while using his peripheral vision to espy unwanted company approaching from the sides: first one rider, then two. Within a few yards of the man, he waved at Drake.

"Mornin'," exclaimed the man with an overly kind tone. The man had close-cropped hair and teeth far too white for a marauder.

"Waiting on me?" Drake asked.

"I've heard reports of a traitor skulking 'round these parts," he said.

"A traitor, you say? He should be dealt with accordingly," Drake said. The man laughed at him.

"None pass through here much these days, save suspicious folk, and you have a queer look about ya." Drake had killed numerous arrogant fools like this throughout his career.

"Do your two friends back there feel the same? Bandits hang," Drake said.

"We ain't bandits, and I have more friends than that," he said.

Drake realized these men were rebel agents. An arrow clipped Drake's shoulder. Drake rushed the horse-bound man, effortlessly pulling his sword from the hilt and through the man's mouth. "Should've worn a helmet," Drake said.

With a sideways jerk, Drake's blade slid out of the man's jaw. The man fell off his horse. Drake turned his horse around, galloping towards another man preparing to fire. Drake ran his horse straight over the man, who failed to completely dive out of the way. The man crumpled under the horse. More arrows whizzed by Drake, he deflected one with his blade. The other man drew a pistol; no longer caring if nearby troops heard. Drake stopped his horse as quickly as he could and dove to the ground. A gunshot rang out across the fields and Drake's horse fell dead. Drake slithered through the wet grass toward his next target.

The shooter cursed repeatedly while scouring the grass for Drake. Birds flying up from the grass distracted the gunman who instinctively fired at the sound. Drake seized the opportunity and jumped up, stabbing the man under his breastplate and through his heart. The archer turned at the other man's screams and fired wildly. Drake again dove to the ground. The archer panicked. An arrow pierced the ground to his left then another to the right. Drake jumped up again as the man fumbled for another arrow. Drake pulled out his pistol and fired. With a red splash, the bullet zipped through the man's left eye and out the back of the skull. Drake noted another man concealed in the grass. The second he poked his head out, Drake shot him through the bridge of his nose. Drake heard the trampled man gurgling out curses through the pain.

"Pretty clever idea you guys had. Keeping me as a hostage to retain honor, then letting 'bandits' do the dirty work. These aren't the actions of men fighting for justice," Drake shouted.

"Wars aren't won by the just," the man said.

"Maybe you're right," Drake said coldly. Drake swung his sword and cut deep into the man's right hand. The golden grass turned red. A hidden attacker jumped out of the grass, forcing Drake to sidestep. A bullet clipped his bicep instead of his chest thanks to the well-timed dodge. Drake fired again, catching the sneak right between the eyes.

He had no more medical supplies with him, so he doubled his efforts to the capital. All the horses fled to battle, forcing Drake to travel on foot. As Drake rushed home, he hoped Zora and Thos could forgive what he was about to do. He heard a sound like scratching inside his own head. He became disoriented and nauseated. Something spoke to him in his head, the sound like scraping metal.

Drake did not see the gunman on the far hill. Before he knew it, a bullet lodged in his shoulder and he grimaced with pain. He collapsed into the wet grass.

Drake did not recall reaching Kingsbury, yet somehow he did. It was nightfall; he had lost an entire day. The streets lay almost bare, quite strange for the normally bustling city. A few people wandered around. A small crowd gathered around the entrance to the whorehouse, laughing and haggling with prostitutes.

Few paid mind to the Knight-Ambassador lying on the street corner. A drunken man slept beside him, his arm draped across Drake. Drake stumbled to his feet and headed for the Blessed Lady, a hospital for active and retired soldiers.

The hospital stood six floors high in a gated section of the city. Above the main entrance, a large statue of a woman clad in white with outstretched arms greeted him. The doors slid open. A woman in a plain white outfit and black hair with gold highlights sat at the front desk.

"Nice to see you again, Judy," Drake said, stumbling about in a vain attempt to be nonchalant. He had come to know Judith well throughout the years, and injuries.

"Drake! Good to see you again," she said. She gave him a once-over.

"Been one of those days," he said. Dizziness and exhaustion still hounded him. "I'm about to fall over. Would you be so kind—"

A nurse assisted Drake to the nearest room. Once inside, Drake plopped down on the bed. The woman pulled the bloody clothes off of him.

"Bless me! How long ago?" the nurse said.

"Not sure," Drake replied. The nurse gave him a sour look.

"Drinking again?" she said accusingly.

"Actually, an arrow, some bullets, a few cuts, a giant lizard attack, oh and other stuff," he said.

"Drugs, huh?" the nurse replied. Drake frowned.

The nurse cleaned his wounds. Drake growled at the stinging pain. She gave him three pea-sized red pills and a glass of water. The medicine worked quickly. Drake sat blissfully in his medicated delirium while the nurse patched him up and ran the necessary tests.

"The wound has been treated," she said. "The cut on your arm will not require stitches. Do you remember any of it? Be serious this time," she said. He omitted the exotic aspects of the story this time.

"Rebels ambushed me. They shot me. One minute I'm in the fields outside the city and the next I'm at the front gate. I heard sounds in my head, like a voice, but not in any language I know. Was I poisoned?"

"Oh my, that's… disturbing. We've found no toxins in your blood but we'll check again," she said. Drake looked at her, confused. *Was this what happened to Zora?* Drake chose to get a rundown of happenings in the city.

"Place go to hell in my absence?" Drake asked. Judith's pleasant smile curled into a frown.

"A lot has happened, Ser Hale. We have sent word to Lord Hart of your return. He'll be here shortly." She took the empty cup of water from him and left the room. The nurses periodically checked on him for the next few hours. Drake faded in and out of consciousness until a booming voice caused him to sit straight up.

In walked Jerrick Hart, supreme commander of New Prosperity's military. Jerrick stood thick and brawny, larger and stronger than any man Drake knew. Jerrick was the fiercest and most respected person in the country. He prided himself on being slow to anger, luckily for everyone else. Most jokingly referred to him as the Black Death for his dark skin, a nickname Jerrick seemed fond of. Jerrick was bald with slate-gray beard, quite different from the last time Drake saw him. Drake shot to his feet. The men locked forearms in a sign of respect.

"Good to see you again, Drake," Jerrick said with a smile that still managed to intimidated.

"Happy to be home, sir," Drake said wearily.

"We both know that isn't true," Hart jested. Drake scratched the back of his head, verifying Jerrick's statement. Drake feared Jerrick and the rest of Kingsbury believed him go be Aric's killer.

"How're the kids?" Drake asked.

"Mary's well, finally started walking. Jaren finally became a Knight-Ambassador, and he was deployed to the frontier last month. I wish that were the only news I had," he said, quickly turning grim.

Drake sat back down on the soft bed and listened as Jerrick recounted the degenerating situation in Kingsbury. It took a few minutes for Drake to collect himself after Jerrick's tale.

"I must see the king at once," Drake began. "I know of the rebels attack plans. I was a hostage for a time. I got free of them in the wood outside the capital. The Fey and Thos Averill are being coerced to aid them." In his time as Knight-Ambassador, Drake Hale learned how to bend the truth quite well. *All for the good of the nation*, he incessantly reminded himself.

"We'll deal with them if we can stop the infighting, however, our spies tell otherwise on Mr. Averill. True or not, you will have to lobby hard to save Thos's life. There is one other thing I have to ask about. Were you involved in Aric's death?" Jerrick asked. Everyone north of Heartland was well versed in the constant butting of heads potential spilling over to violence.

"No, sir," Drake replied, a true statement since the rebels beat him to the punch.

"We are all aware you openly condemned his actions; there is talk of you actively interfering with his mission." Jerrick looked Drake over. Jerrick had an uncanny ability to glean truth from a man's movements, mannerisms, and demeanor. Drake looked Jerrick Hart square in the eye.

"It is true I interfered… to stop him from slaughtering innocents, but I did not kill him, sir," Drake said. Drake tensed up to the point of shattering. Jerrick nodded his head, respecting Drake's honesty.

"Good. That matches with our intel," Jerrick said. Jerrick liked and respected Drake, yet was also willing to end him without hesitation. Drake's heart fell into his churning stomach. Jerrick gave Drake a pat on the back.

"The king will be overjoyed to see you. He does not blame you for Aric's death, but he will want to discuss that matter with you," Jerrick said. "I will set up an appointment for tomorrow morning. He needs friends now more than ever. Everything that's happened, it's taking a toll on him."

Jerrick's voice grew soft. Drake heard the uneasiness and felt his own will dissolving. Drowsiness hit him full force. He let out a loud yawn. His body melted down onto the bed.

"Sorry, sir. It's been one hell of a trip. A rest seems lovely right now," Drake said.

"Rest up, you'll need it," Jerrick said. As soon as Jerrick left, the nurse walked in with more pills. Drake swallowed the meds and laid down for a proper rest. Anselm may be delighted to see Drake after such a long time, but joy was the one emotion not present in the maelstrom within him. Before drifting off to sleep, one thing occupied his thoughts: tomorrow he would face the king.

365

THOS

Thos Averill cradled his sore gut amid thousands of armed, angry, and famished rebel warriors. Thos squinted at the capital, a lone prick illuminated by the setting sun. It seemed arrogant to Thos that the rebels were hiding in the town where anyone from the capital with decent binoculars could see.

"How much to keep the locals quiet?" Thos said as he nudged Joseph.

"Quite a bit," Joseph said.

Thos wanted to make a quip but instead bit his tongue. The town of Worthington was bent and rusty, an ominous sight under the blood-orange dusk sky. The hole-riddled towers groaned with metallic woe. Joseph climbed onto one of the dinner tables. Melvin moved closer to Thos and explained Joseph's plan to create a document that would serve as the framework for the new system of government. Melvin said it was based on something called the "Decoration of Independence," which didn't sound right but Thos didn't argue. Joseph cleared his throat for a speech.

"We've come a long way. Our nation has grown sick and we will cure it. Far too long have we let armchair leaders piss away our fortunes and our lives. We've all lost something in this war.

Soon we can have lives again. Good, decent lives free of tyranny. Tomorrow we make history!"

Joseph hopped off the table, nearly slipping as he did. The banquet of food distracted the troops from his demoralizing blunder. A hearty feast sprawled out across the tables. Delicious pots of roasted venison, potatoes, mushrooms, honey biscuits, soda, and watered-down ale covered each table. All the food provided was courtesy of Averill Estates. Thos hated growing food, but he sure loved eating it. Pots were quickly stripped of food. More rose to take their place like heads on a hydra. Too full to move, Thos did the only thing he could: people watch.

Soldiers young and old occupied every nook and cranny of the decaying town. Farmers, stable hands, cooks, bakers—Thos even recognized a few Greenfield prostitutes in the ranks, each fighting for the chance at a better life. Some went to and fro the houses now serving as their quarters for the night. Thos downed a second glass of ale before being cut off per the drink limitations imposed by Joseph.

He breathed in the night air until his body cried out for sleep. Thos passed the guards in the lobby and entered the main room. Inside the mansion, locals cleaned the abandoned building for their rebel host. Dust flew off the nooks and crannies like thick grey clouds, an eager trigger for Thos's allergies. Joseph sat in a soft red-leather chair with a large cloth map rolled up in his hand. Five other men sat at the table in front of him. One older gentleman sat cleaning out his pipe, looking disturbingly similar to Joseph. A man whispered something into Joseph's ear. Joseph looked up at his guest. On the floor above Melvin wandered back and forth, examining the old paintings on the walls.

"Mr. Averill, welcome. My name is Abraham Kerr," he said, with a voice as cold as steel. Thos wanted to throw up knowing another Kerr ran around. Abraham had a demeanor vastly more intimidating than his mustachioed brother. Melvin waved at Thos, who did not wave back.

"Ready for the big day?" Joseph asked, running fingers along the sagging neck.

"Hell, no," Thos said. Smells of aged tobacco and books permeated the room.

"You won't see much combat," Joseph said, not assuring Thos in the least. Thos stopped, feeling another caveat coming on.

"Much?" Thos asked, more than a little annoyed.

"There are no guarantees. Anselm will not be prepared for us tomorrow, however, that doesn't mean it won't get dicey," Joseph beamed. The other men nodded with agreement.

"Tomorrow? I thought you were attacking the forts?" Thos nearly choked. "Maybe the kid really can put a stop to this."

"Are you serious? Drake won't betray the king, and you know it," Melvin replied. Thos shot Melvin an angry look. Abraham whispered something to his brother. Joseph nodded.

"He helped us get here and saved you too, if I recall," Thos reminded. Melvin blushed.

"Melvin's right," Joseph interrupted. "Likely he's telling Anselm this very moment—if he made it, that is. We gave him and the other spies false information, just in case."

Melvin shifted uncomfortably on a bookshelf he was leaning on, knocking a bottle off the nearby table. He left the bottle where it lay and walked the other side of the room.

"If Drake survives, he can keep his position. I made that deal, out of respect for you and Zora," Melvin added.

"Makes me feel warm inside. So how do you plan to win, inside job?" Thos asked.

"We learned a few things from Prince Ar-dick," Melvin said.

"Don't worry about that. You'll know what you need in the morning" Joseph said. Abraham watched him without speaking.

"Go rest. Won't be long now." Joseph stood, giving Thos a pat on the back, and returned to his brother's side.

"Oh, before I forget. Some of your men were forcing themselves on a local woman. You need to stamp that shit out if you want to keep me involved in this," Thos said. Thos gave a description of the men to Joseph. Joseph grit his teeth, suggesting this wasn't the first occurrence.

"I'll take care it. Goodnight, Thos," Joseph said. A soldier escorted Thos to his room on the second floor of the old house.

After hours of tossing and turning, Thos scrounged up a few hours of sleep. The next thing he knew, the town readied for war. Rubbing the sleep from his eyes, Thos ran headfirst into Joseph waiting outside his room. Joseph no longer wore the plain drab clothes of a failed businessman, instead sporting the engraved armor of a royal officer. Thos looked at the armor, and then looked at Joseph's face numerous times until he got the message of its absurdity.

"Walk with me," Joseph ordered.

Thos followed Joseph down the stairs to the old study room. In the center of the room lay a table with a full set of thick plated armor. Beside the armor was a flag. The blue flag depicted a griffon holding a bent crown in its talons.

"This is the symbol of our new nation, inspired by the old. You will carry it into battle," Joseph said. Thos wondered if this was his punishment for being so sassy all the time.

"I'm the fucking flag boy?" Thos sighed.

"Hurry up and eat, it's almost time," Joseph said.

Thos consumed what remained of the bacon and grits, cursing his luck for missing out on the biscuits. He chugged down a glass of water and returned to the mansion, where troops helped Thos don his armor. Others brought him a shiny new sword, pistol, and a surplus of armor-piercing bullets. Thos stumbled about in an awkward, jerky fashion at first. After a few minutes, however, he adapted to the armor.

He slowly walked toward the town exit where a man waited for him with a charcoal horse. Out in the fields, the rebel army amassed: a patchwork of foot swordsman, horseback troops, snipers, riflemen, and dozens of trucks. By the looks of it, Thos estimated their forces to be in the thousands, a terrifying sight to behold. Melvin, brandishing the flag, galloped over to Thos and handed it to him.

"Wave it high," Melvin said. Thos and Melvin took their place alongside Joseph at the head of the army. Thos leaned over to Joseph, who wore a ghastly helmet in the shape of an eagle. "These people have faith in you, remember that," Thos said. Joseph raised his hand to silence the rebel army.

"I'll save the speeches for when we win!" Joseph exclaimed. The rebel army began its final march. Thos squirmed on his horse holding the pole with the flaccid symbol of a new nation. The capital city came into view. Thos stared in awe at the sprawling metropolis of Kingsbury. He marveled at its towering buildings peeking from behind the thick walls.

Thos wiped the sweat from his neck. Upon reaching the front gate, the army surrounded the outer walls, carrying large metal containers. Snipers lining the outer walls saw them clear as day, yet only nodded at their presence before abandoning their posts.

"Is anyone loyal?" Thos asked.

The iron gates of the city rose. The violent hawking of an alarm rang from all corners of the city. Joseph pulled a small device from his pocket, not unlike the one Aric once possessed. He counted to three and pushed the red button on the device. A series of flashes came from the city walls, followed by explosions.

Thos raised the flag.

DRAKE

Blackthorne Castle loomed over Drake with a menace he'd never known. Flies swarmed around bloated, rotting corpses hanging from the walls. Internally, Drake panicked. The oppressive dread threatened to knock him off his feet and swallow him whole. Facing princes, monsters, and certain death paled in comparison to what he felt now. He let out one more deep breath and pushed the door open.

Drake's heart pounded with monstrous force when he stepped inside the mighty throne room. Today, it seemed to stretch on for miles. Anselm languished in a hunched-over position on his throne. Guards lined the bloodstained carpet that led up to the king. Drake's name reverberated through the hall when the crier belted out his name, snapping Anselm out of his comatose state. He reached the feet of King Anselm and knelt. The king sat clad in exquisite armor with detailed musculature, unlike any Drake had ever seen before. A silver-blue sword propped up against the side of his throne. Drake could no longer deny the rumors of buried tech to be painfully true.

"Rise, son," Anselm said, in a warm tone. When Drake rose, so did Anselm. The king embraced Drake with a lordly hug. Drake never grew accustomed to hugs, one of the many things his own family never gave him.

"It's good you're home," Anselm said.

"Glad to be back, Your Grace. It has been a rather dark time," Drake replied. Anselm greeted him with the same amount of love as he would offer one of his own. Despite the warmness, something about the king seemed off. Through the smile, Drake felt Anselm sizing him up. Whether Anselm thought him innocent or not, Drake feared that he'd be forever associated with Aric's death.

"Unfortunately, but dark times are the only ones in which men show their worth. Time and again you have shown yours. I hope you can maintain this standard because I fear things will only grow darker from here," Anselm said. The king's composure had changed drastically since Drake's last visit. He now conveyed the soul of a man distant and disturbed. Sunlight poured in from the mighty stained-glass windows, leaving brilliant images of the country's history emblazoned on the floor. Drake feared the fall of the nation might be the next image to fill these halls.

"I remember when you and Aric were pups," Anselm began, "swinging little wooden swords through these same halls. You were good to him when no one else was, even when he didn't deserve it. If only things had turned out different, you two might have conquered the world."

"I'm sorry for your loss," Drake said.

"My son was a hard man to love. You suffered his wrath more than most. I know he brought his fate upon himself, but that does not stop a father from loving his son. The things they did to him, and the others in their crosshairs, are beyond forgiveness. Their punishment will be tenfold. Things have been… difficult since then." Drake lowered his head in shame. He bore the guilt of Aric's demise almost as if he was the killer.

"It is not your fault, son. I know you did what you could,"

Anselm said. The words came out and failed to convince, each in a pained rage from a man barely holding on.

"Are the rumors true? Is the Board gone?" Drake asked.

"They moved against me and I responded, as necessary. They're snakes, all. Their poison is already in the nation's blood. I'm still drawing it out."

"You killed them all?" Drake asked, still reeling from the news.

"Regrettably, no." Anselm favored his right arm as if it pained him. Anselm noticed Drake's concern. "Your concern is appreciated, few care about the Blackthornes anymore."

"Kings are seldom loved," Drake replied.

Anselm squinted, giving a confused look at someone behind Drake. Drake turned around to find nothing. "Sorry. The job has gotten to me," Anselm laughed. "Lord Hart tells me you have news about the rebels. From what I hear, you've had quite the adventure. I would like to hear it."

Drake told the story of his journey, making sure to let Anselm know Thos Averill and Zora Rayntree pawns in a grand game. Anselm tapped the fingers of his right hand on the arm of the throne.

"Quite the adventure," Anselm mused. "When the war is over, I will pardon this lady you are sweet on. You will have to work much harder to convince me the Averills deserve anything but bullets." Anselm's words told him that Thos's fiancée was also a target. Drake tried to calm his heart pounding hard enough to crack ribs.

"Now, tell me of your findings," Anselm commanded. The king's face scrunched up like an invisible knife diced up his insides. The tapping ceased.

"The rebels are going to attack Fort Aldous, Stonehaven, and the Redhand. After that, they will attack here." Anselm's brow wrinkled up.

"How did you manage to escape them?" Anselm asked,

bewildered. Drake realized his tale left his survival seeming nothing short of a miracle or an egregious lie.

"Zora secured my release. When I left the woods, they ambushed me just outside the city so the Fey wouldn't see." Anselm scratched his head with his left hand, his right twitching.

"Quite the tale indeed. That seems to match up with my intel, however there is something that is bothering me," Anselm said with a darkening tone. Anselm's tone was on the verge of accusatory. His gaze turned predatory. Drake could see the man fighting the whirlwind of emotions threatening to tear him apart. Without warning, the screeching of alarms filled the stoic corridors of the castle. The castle trembled as explosions rocked the city. Anselm thrust himself up from the chair. A soldier burst in the room, screaming.

"They broke through the walls!" he said.

The guards all rushed to the door. Sounds of death raged outside. Drake looked in the king's eyes and saw a man he no longer recognized. In a split second, Anselm's personality changed. A madness filled the king's eyes.

"What is this! How did they get through our defense?" Anselm cried.

"I'm… I don't know," Drake said. Drake feared the rage flowing through Anselm, tearing away sense and reason.

"Someone helped them out. Someone let them in!" Anselm snarled. Anselm focused his maddening inferno on Drake.

"Are you are working for them?!" Anselm cried.

"I would never betray you!" Drake exclaimed. Anselm winced from unknown pains.

"I should've known the Hales would turn against me. They'll finally get a seat at the table." Anselm's hurt quickly spiraled into rage. "You were like a son to me!"

"It's not what you think!" Drake pleaded.

"Enough!" Anselm roared. Two metallic wings burst from the back of his armor and a mask wrapped around his face. A second later, he fell upon Drake, knocking him back into the statue of Old Aldous. Pain shot through Drake's back. He moved quickly as Anselm flew at him again, his sword now engulfed in flame.

"Please stop!" Drake said, trying his best to distance himself from the feral king. Troops entered into the hall, clashing with rebel forces pouring in.

"They're scaling the castle!" one guard screamed right before a warhammer crushed his helmet, reducing his head to a pulp. Anselm slashed at Drake in a relentless assault. Drake narrowly dodged attack after attack, not fighting back. Rebels came down from the second floor. Anselm and his knights were slowly driven into the throne room. Nearby, Blackthorne soldiers moved in on Drake. Anselm called out to a man at his side. "Use it!"

Drake drew his blade in defense. As Drake prepared for his final, stand the soldiers began attacking each other. The enemies surrounding him fell quickly to soldiers wearing purple sashes. *Betrayed by our own at a time like this… pitiful*, Drake thought.

The traitorous guard closed ranks, using the king's own training to dismantle his battalion. Black-clad fighters stormed up from the dungeons brandishing gray high-powered rifles with what appeared to be two barrels, one on top of the other. The troops pulled the triggers.

Magnetized bullets flew from between the barrels riding blue-colored beams. Drake had heard of railgun technology, the last form of Old World weaponry before the failed attempts at laser guns. The honor guard avoided the beams, leaving their newfound allies to take the brunt of the assault. More troops stormed up from the dungeons brandishing railgun weaponry. Rounds shredded limbs from torsos leaving a few strands of stringy meat. Missed shots blew apart the decorative armor suits, shattered glass, and put indentions in the walls.

"You're doing more damage to us!" Anselm screamed.

The rebels countered with assault rifles of their own. Neither the rebel soldiers nor the traitors defended Drake.

Canisters of gas came hurdling through the broken windows, pouring smoke into the room, forcing the battle out into the courtyard. Anselm fought with inhuman ferocity, slaying five men as he was pushed out to the courtyard. He cleaved through everyone in his path, driving back the invaders almost single-handedly. New batches of rebels attempted to kill Anselm, only to be sliced to ribbons.

More royal troops pointed guns at Drake, forcing him to fire back. Everyone Drake slew only caused him pain. Anselm fought in the distance. The king desperately tried to reach the stairs to the upper floors, only to be pushed further back by enemy forces coming through the windows. Drake realized Anselm's family fought for their lives above him. The soldiers slowly wore down Anselm's forces. A few of the rebels wrestled away railgun weapons from Anselm's forces. The sight paralyzed Drake. Sorrow overcame him as he watched the final moments of the Blackthorne family.

THOS

The rebel army burst through the front gate like an erupting dam, trampling Blackthorne soldiers caught in the ambush. Thos, Joseph, and Melvin led the charge. Patrols in the city attacked as they became aware of the situation. Civilians fled in all directions to escape the chaos. Bullets screamed all around them.

"Look out!" Joseph pointed upward. A rifleman beside Thos shot the sniper in the cheek, sending him sliding down the roof along with some shingles. A large group of armed men stormed the whorehouse. They went from room to room killing the helpless and unaware Blackthorne supporters. Workers ran screaming from the building, still wearing corsets, stockings, and in some cases, nothing at all. A few of the male and female prostitutes fought back, only to be cut down. The whorehouse went up in flames.

"Whoever did that is getting strung up!" Joseph said.

"Losing control of our people?" Thos asked.

"Just wave the flag!" Joseph snapped.

Thos waved the flag, heralding the rebel charge through the city. Rebels slaughtered the troops massing in the streets. Up ahead, Blackthorne soldiers with tower shields and rifles blocked off the main road leading to the castle.

"Alley on the left!" Melvin yelled. Thos turned without thinking down the nearest alley. He dropped the flag while escaping the hail of bullets. The rebels crashed headfirst into the roadblock. Joseph and the factions of his troops broke off the advance and split down the alleyways. Gunmen failed to keep up with the diverging group.

Thos, Joseph, and Melvin sped down the cramped alleyway. Cannons and armored trucks with mounted guns mobilized back on the main street, shredding up rebel forces. Thos wanted to close his ears to the symphony of death raging all around him.

He heard stirrings above them and grabbed the reins, forcing a hard stop. Thos jerked back, almost being thrown off his horse in the process. "Shooters above!" he cried. Joseph gained too much ground on them to hear. Arrows and bullets rained down, transforming the alley full of people ahead into a meaty pincushion. Nearly a dozen arrows skewered Joseph, though none proved fatal. A few bullets pierced his horse, causing it to thrash, violently throwing him off.

"Turn!" Melvin screamed.

"What about—" Thos said.

"Leave him!"

Melvin reluctantly took charge. Thos heard Joseph screaming for help, but they kept going. The gunners above noticed the escape and scrambled after them. Thos turned back to see a soldier tear off Joseph's helmet and splattered his brains on the walls.

Melvin and Thos used what little space available within the alley to bob and weave through the rain of death. Thos and Melvin worked their way down the alley and around the roadblock. Passing the openings, they could see the rebel forces advancing toward enemy cannons with their mounted trucks.

As the Blackthorne troops retreated to the Fountain of the Holy Queen, the tide of battle turned to the rebels favor. Thos and Melvin returned to the main street, joining the rebel advancement through the town square.

Melvin caught up with other officers and relayed news of

Joseph's death. A wounded soldier hiding among dead shot the temporary rebel flag bearer. Melvin's shotgun blasted off the top of his skull for his troubles. Thos snatched up the flag and the rebel army surrounded him for protection.

"Don't drop it this time!" Melvin roared. Soldiers charged down the hill firing strange new rifles. The rebels moved farther back down the street, away from Blackthorne Castle. The band protecting Thos held its own. Farther back down the street, the royal battalion rejoiced at seeing the small rebel bands separated from the main group massacred in the alleys.

"Wave that fucking flag!" Melvin barked. Thos spent less time on flag waving and more on shooting. Carrying the flag made Thos the focal point of the royal army's offensive. The bizarre new weapons made short work of the nearby rebels, blasting pieces of them into the fountain and pretty much everywhere else. The two forces clashed up and down the main street in a grisly tug-of-war.

Thos's flag-waving revitalized battle-worn comrades. Enemy forces mobilized ahead of them, the rebel shield men absorbed most of the gunfire. Ambushers beset the rebels on all sides, whittling down their numbers. Rebels scaled the sides of the houses, trying to get the jump on the enemy. Civilians aided both sides in the battle, using whatever killing tools available: knives, rakes, and even scalding hot soup. A potato bounced off the helmet of one Blackthorne soldier, distracting him just long enough for a group on angry civilians to swarm him.

Melvin swung his massive sword, knocking down armored troops. His blade sank deep in the soft leather and flesh of lightly armored foes. Groups that rushed him met a grisly demise from the business end of his shotgun.

A soldier cried out, and all watched what appeared to be a man taking to the sky with a glowing sword. The winged figure jetted off toward the castle. "The fuck? Is that the king? Shoot him down,"

Melvin said. The cannon spewed forth, shattering one of the wings and sending the man crashing back down to the courtyard.

The Blackthorne forces, overwhelmed, still didn't flee. The town square now belonged to the rebels. Thos raised the flag again. He and a few others climbed the fountain. Melvin acquired one of the rail rifles and fired upon the Holy Queen, obliterating the 500 year old statue. All forces were steadily pushed to the town square.

The cries of surrender sounded from multiple directions as the Blackthorne army lay down arms. Up the road, Anselm and a handful of loyal warriors fought valiantly despite being continuously pushed back. Anselm turned his blade on those that chose to surrender, causing him to lose even more support. Anselm again fought his way up the hill to the castle, only to be forced back down to the fountain. The king reached out to the castle, screaming out as he fought his way back to his family. Thos knew the king's time was up.

PERCIVAL

Abigail, Percival, and Edgar watched from the bedroom window in horror as the enemy breached the castle walls. The high-pitched shrill of sirens echoed from every corner of the castle. They could hear the guards outside shouting, followed by dozens of them hastily scampering by. Percival snatched up his pistol while Abigail pulled a dagger out from the leg strap under her dress and sprinted to the gun safe in her room. Percival rushed to the emergency elevator in the royal chambers that led to the garage, punching the button to no avail.

"They've taken out the elevator!" Percival screamed, throwing one last punch into the dead buttons.

Edgar peered out the window. "There are men climbing up!" he shrieked. Abigail ran over to see for herself. Forty men scaled the right side of the tower, bursting through the windows of the first few floors. Percy spied a hundred more, preparing to climb. The invaders wore black ceramic armor and orange-eyed gas masks, looking like bipedal cockroaches.

"Anselm," Abigail muttered.

"Dad's not dead!" Edgar screamed back. Percival paced with sword drawn, contemplating a way out.

"We need to get to the garage," Abigail said. The bottom of

the tower was thick with enemy soldiers, crawling up like ants on a picnic basket. The enemy reached the tenth floor; others ran through the lower levels to divide the amassing Blackthorne force. Castle gunmen shot rebels off the ropes; however, returning gunfire only slowed their advancement. Below them, the city burned. Guards threw open the door and escorted the Blackthorne family down the hall. They could hear fighting on the floor just below them. The hallway lights flickered before giving out.

A gunshot rang out from the main stairway. Percival turned to flee to the trophy room. He flattened himself against the wall beside the door and fired when able. Bullets shredded the griffons, bears, and snallygasters in the room. The rebel's ceramic torsoplates absorbed Percival's bullets. Percival jumped out, aiming for the soft lenses of the gas mask. The first few shots hit nothing. His heart raced fast enough to burst as other men came up the steps, blocking the path to the hidden stairs.

The remaining Blackthorne guard made it to the emergency stairs. He pushed open the false wall and fumbled at the door behind it. The locked clicked, and he ran through, abandoning the Blackthornes to their fate. Edgar cried. Abigail pulled Edgar to her breast and cradled him. Percival shot a man dead running up on them, however, more took his place. Bullets peppered the area, keeping Percival behind cover. Percival blind-fired to force the enemy back.

"You and Edgar need to go! I'll cover you. Don't worry, I'll be right behind you," Percival said. Abigail grabbed Edgar and ran down the hall. Percival fired at the men to cover his family. Percival braced to engage the attackers up close, unsheathing his sword. He slashed at the men; his blade did little damage to the ceramic plating, forcing him to attack the unprotected spots. Percival kicked one man down the stairs and shot another through the eye. The man rolled down the stairs knocking two other men off their feet. Percy lifted the corpse of the first man he shot, using him as a shield. The other attackers continued to fire, slowly eating away at the armor and flesh of the human shield. Percival picked them off before they obliterated his meat shield.

A woman screamed from within the dining hall. Percival dropped two approaching attackers and ran to help. Another tackled him to the ground. Instinctively, he rammed his blade through the man's waist and slid it horizontally through his stomach. Percival pushed the man and his dangling guts off. During his outburst, he lost sight of Abigail and Edgar. He picked up the rifle of one fallen man and followed the trail of his family.

More enemies burst through the window down the hall, firing the instant they came through. Percival dipped into the kitchen to avoid heavy arms fire. A man inside ran up to knife him. Percival heard him a mile away, spinning around to blast him in the chest. In the dining hall, a serving girl lay on the table with her throat opened ear to ear.

The killers laughed as Percival approached them. Percival moved toward them. "Someone save me!" one rebel mocked. The men goaded Percival, yet made no moves against him.

The sounds of fighting ended behind him. Three other invaders rushed Percival from behind and kicked him to the floor, effectively cutting him off from his mother and brother. The rebels formed a circle around him. Each time Percival rose, a man kicked him down. Percival got a good look at the last man and his heart broke at the sight.

"James? No, not you, too," Percival said. This was not the James Dumas that Percival knew, the man's once loving demeanor was cold and pitiless.

"Way of the world," James said, showcasing a previously unforeseen viciousness. James held a small object Percival knew well: a detonator. At once Percival realized the horrible truth. He held back the tears as long as he could.

"You've been using me from the start!" Percival said. It hurt to see a man he'd known for most of his life saw Percival only as a means of advancement. James nodded.

"What did you expect? I thank you for showing me around the place. I learned everything I need." One of the men beside James gave Percival a hard kick to the stomach.

"Why? You were family! Was… was it for money?" Percival asked.

"I told you that I had big dreams, this place will run better with me as Regent. I'm sorry, Percy. When your family is gone, I will be part of the new order," James said.

"All this for power," Percival said, hurt and confused. Percival realized the most successful enemy to his family was the one he had willingly let in.

Percival pushed himself to his feet only to receive another hard kick in the gut. Though James didn't seem to revel in his pain, the other men didn't bother to hide their joy. Percival no longer saw a caring, thoughtful knight; in that man's place was cold, ravenous ambition held together by skin and bone.

"I can't die like this! I can't!" Percival cried.

The men allowed Percival to stand. Percival picked up his blade and slashed at the man in front of him, but his attack was deflected by the man's sword. One by one the men jumped in, slashing at him, making his execution a sadistic game. Percival burned with shame trying to fight them off.

"Sorry, but I have places to be," James said, shaking the detonator. "Goodbye Percy, sorry it had to end this way." James, with detonator in hand, walked away, leaving to others to execute the prince. Percival made one last desperate attempt to kill the defilers. Wearing no armor, Percival's clothes and flesh were shredded to ribbons. Blood seeped from cuts all over Percival's body, however, he fought on. Percival sprinted past the attackers only to be caught by one waiting just outside the door. When his vision returned, he saw the man wore the armor of a Blackthorne officer.

"Traitor!" Percival growled. The Blackthorne soldier shrugged before pushing him back towards the others.

"Don't you worry about mommy. I'll take good care of her," he gloated.

"My mother is not easy prey," Percival warned.

"Good," the man said with a wicked smile. Percival recognized more Blackthorne soldiers joining the group to savor Percival's final moments. "You may kill me, but you won't kill them," Percy said assuredly.

Exhaustion took control, resulting in his attacks growing sloppy. The cuts on Percival's body grew ever deeper and more numerous. He lunged again, this time the attacker's sword went through his stomach. Percival slashed one last time before the man kicked him off. He fell forward and the men huddled over him. With all swords drawn, they stabbed Percival with reckless abandon.

ABIGAIL

Abigail gasped with every breath as she hurried down the stair-case holding Edgar tightly to her breast. Edgar proved easy to carry, still being gaunt. She wanted to laugh at herself for thinking such things at a time as this. Distracting thoughts made it easier to fight her way to safety while her other son fought for his life. She kept the gunfire to a minimum, taking shots only when drown out by loud noises echoing through her home. The backup elevator lead-ing to the garage was accessed from behind the armory. Enemies blocked her way back to Percival, giving her no choice but to focus on getting Edgar out alive. She heard frantic footsteps behind her, the numbers suggesting someone other than friendly.

"They will beg for death when I get ahold of them," she mut-tered. Whenever possible, she stopped to put Edgar down and silently dispatch any invaders separated from the main groups. Each time she put down her son, she gave him the look that told him to close his eyes. Edgar abhorred violence and blood. He eagerly followed his mother's advice. Splashes of blood decorated her dress and hair creating a grim visage straight from one of the city's 'bargain bin horror' novels. Abigail heard the sounds of what she assumed were tear-gas canisters. She ripped a mask from a dead rebel and placed it on Edgar's head. Armed with a dagger and pistol she prayed that no enemies awaited her. She tried not to think of Percival as she moved down the tower.

The sounds of battle grew louder when descended to the lower floors. Gunshots rang out in the halls. From the sounds, many threats lay between her and escape; she would need to clear the area. She reached the bottom floor of Blackthorne's private residence and stopped to catch her breath, not letting go of Edgar. Hatred urged her to kill every invader defiling her home; she buried the urge, knowing it was best to kill only when necessary. Edgar cried.

"I need you to be strong now," Abigail said, trying not to break down at the thought.

"Yes, mom," he sniffled.

"Hide in the stairwell. I'll make sure it's safe. Don't make a sound." She handed him the gun. He shook his head.

"Take it!" she said, mustering the sternest tone she could. "You know how to use this. Don't you hesitate to shoot." She removed his mask to wipe away his tears and pushed the mask back down. He nodded and took the gun. Abigail taught him many times of the false walls scattered through the castle he could use for hiding in just such situations.

"Mommy loves you. I'll be back soon," she said.

"I love you," he said, with eyes red and soggy from tears.

Abigail glanced from out of the bullet holes in the wall to get a view of the hall. There were six massive rooms on the third floor of the Blackthorne section of the tower: a training room, a study room stuffed with books, and the personal armory. Faint traces of tear gas forced her to cover her mouth and eyes every few minutes. The armory was the center room on the left side. A few dead invaders lay on the floor, though none wore a mask for her to steal. The Blackthorne family banner once displayed above the study lay tattered on the floor. She gently opened the door, closing it behind her as if vanishing from the world completely.

A lone man in the study threw books to the floor. She snuck

up behind him and cut his throat, spitting on him when he hit the floor. A guard heard him hit the floor and ran in, but not before Abigail pressed herself against the wall. She buried her dagger in the back of his unarmored skull. Waiting a moment, she snuck from the room, carefully eyeing the others as she walked. Three men talked and laughed, confident in their looming victory. The black-haired man with flecks of grey in the center wore a different set of armor, white with a large eagle holding a crown. She peeked out again. Something about the man was familiar to her.

"We done?" he asked.

"Yup, the whole place is rigged," the other man replied. "They are going to detonate it tomorrow for some ceremony. James gave me the detonator. He told me to blow the place if I had no choice, but I'm not dying for this… that asshole already hightailed it outta here. Anyway, we have more work to do. A few people got through tunnels, better not have been the royal family."

"We have people down there already. They'll take care of it." Their chances of getting out of the city decreased with each passing second, Abigail thought.

"They can't escape. I have a score to settle," the leader replied. Abigail gripped the blade tight in her left hand a pistol in her right, biding her time. These were all that remained between her and freedom. At once she recognized the leader: Hektor Droullin, son of the late, frozen-faced Arthur.

"All the other survivors are imprisoned in the castle right now. I say we lock 'em in and blow the thing now. Joe won't care."

"No. He wanted to make a big deal of it. Demonstrate his power," Hektor said.

"His power?" the guard asked.

"Idiot thinks he and his brother are calling the shots. I doubt he'll reach the tower. He'll die a hero at least," Hektor said with a laugh

The men stole what they could carry. Hektor stood around

deciding which pieces to keep for himself. He picked up the original armor worn by Alexander IV and threw it to carelessly to the floor. Abigail rounded the corner as his fellow looters rushed out, the name James made her furious and she knew Percival's closest friend was the enemy right beneath their nose. She would hunt him down when Edgar was safe. Hektor was the only thing standing between her and the hidden elevator. Abigail's emotions got the best of her as she snuck up behind him.

"I can see you in the armor," Hektor said. She shot at him. He dodged the attacks and backhanded her, knocking the gun from her hand. Hektor picked up the gun and dismantled it. "Your family's dead, you got nothing left. The Blackthorne reign ends today. We will seize full control, do all the same things we always do, and those shits down there will love us for it. The peasants always fight for the authority, and that authority will be us and us alone."

Abigail kneed Hektor in the groin and he stumbled backward, chuckling. "We've already won, you stupid twat. Your husband's dead. Your kids are dead. You got no friends left. Die with dignity." His smile was glistening thanks to his veneers. Hektor took a step forward and Abigail lashed out, her weapon inches away from his cheek. "Best be quick, my lady, because I won't be." He made a lunging motion but jumped back, luring her in.

It was almost as if he knew her thoughts. "You think Edgar is safe? My men have him. Don't you, boys?" She turned toward the door and Trevor hit her in the mouth with the butt of his blade causing it to fill with the metallic taste of blood. The dagger fell from her hand.

"I saw you sneaking around out there. We know all about your cameras," Hektor said, lips curling into a malicious smile.

She pursed her lips and spat her blood in Hektor's face. He hit her hard again, cracking Abigail's jaw. She kicked him repeatedly, getting a few shots in on his face. He wiped the blood from his face and pummeled her. She reached for his holstered gun.

A young boy's scream brought her back to the world. "Edgar!" she cried. Two maskless soldiers brought in the broken, bloody body of her youngest son. "Mommy," Edgar said through broken teeth.

Abigail had no more tears left. She accepted her death; fighting and crying would not delay it. One of the men holding Edgar pulled out a knife with his free arm. *I can at least end it as a Blackthorne*, she thought.

Seizing the opportunity, Abigail grabbed the small detonator hanging from Hektor's belt. Throughout the years Abigail, like all other members of the royal family, learned enough of weapons technology to use it should the need arise. She flipped the switch on the side. "It'll be over soon," she said to Edgar.

Hektor stabbed her, but not before she pushed the button. The tower shook and buckled. The floors cracked open. Flames burst forth all around them. The man holding Edgar threw him to the ground and dashed to the window. Abigail lay dying, watching the terrified look on Trevor's face as Blackthorne Castle collapsed. Edgar looked at her. Abigail gave one him last motherly look before the ceiling crashed down.

DRAKE

"Lay down your arms, king!" Melvin yelled, mocking Anselm. Cheers erupted from the rebel conquerors. The heat from Anselm's bizarre sword melted parts of his own armor. He tore the dripping gauntlet off and tossed it at Melvin. Anselm howled in pain as the armor burned him. The king threw the rest of his half melted armor off. Surrounded and alone, Anselm knelt to the deafening cheers of the crowd. Drake found Thos in the crowd.

"It wasn't supposed to go down like this, Thos," Drake said.

"Trust me, I've been in the dark this whole time too," Thos replied.

"You chose the right side, Drake," Melvin said.

"Wasn't my choice," Drake replied. Drake knew better than say anything more about his true feelings.

"The city is ours!" Melvin said. When the cheers died, Melvin hopped on the fountain and addressed the troops. "On behalf of the people of the United Republic of Allied States I strip you, Anselm Blackthorne, of all authority!"

Anselm's voice cut through the rising cheers. Anselm looked at the men surrounding him, making sure to stare down Drake too. "You're not free. You think these men you die for are liberators?

Ignorant brutes the lot of you! The ones you label as heroes will be far worse kings than I ever was," Anselm said.

Anselm scanned the crowd, seeing faces of trusted friends already joining the new order. A man Drake identified as James Dumas approached Melvin and spoke loud enough for Anselm to hear. Drake knew James was a close friend of Percival, and from the look on Anselm's face, this was another crushing blow to the king. James addressed Melvin.

"We received word from Commander Droullin, Abigail and the brat are trapped in the castle along with the other prisoners. Percival's dead," he said. Melvin smiled at the news. Anselm lunged at James, but the rebels pushed him back.

"Have you forgotten who saved you? It was my family that saved this damned world! Without us, you would be nothing but apes in caves!" The king singled out James Dumas. "And you, James, if I get free so help me I will flay you alive!" Anselm roared.

A rock hit Anselm in the forehead and he fell down, hitting the cold stones of his beloved city. A couple of rays of sunlight poked out from the oppressive smoke blanketing the land. Anselm stumbled back to his feet. Cheers gave way to gasps of horror when a series of explosions rocked the base of the castle. A hellish groaning sound bellowed from deep within the structure. Anselm rose instantly and watched as the castle fell, each floor shattering beneath the weight of the next. Anselm's scream pierced the heavens.

Anselm sobbed. Unable to speak, he fell back down to his knees. Within moments, nothing remained of the mighty castle but rubble. Drake tackled Melvin and punched him with reckless abandon.

"There were innocent people in there!" Drake roared. Two soldiers subdued the Knight-Ambassador.

"The bombs were… there must've been a malfunction. We were to demolish the building tomorrow," Melvin said. Drake broke free of his captors and struck Melvin again. This time a soldier hit Drake in the face with the butt of his gun.

"What did you think was going to happen you dumb shit? No Blackthornes are getting out alive," Drake's attacker said. Another man struck him repeatedly in the stomach when he jumped back to his feet. Rifles pointed at Drake to deter him from further assaults.

"Stop!" Melvin boomed. The men left Drake doubled over on the ground. Anselm rocked back and forth, unable to process this grim new reality.

"My world is dead," Anselm said, as the tears ran down his cheeks.

"All for nothing," he said. Anselm spoke to the smoldering ruin once called home. Drake felt tears welling in his own eyes, witnessing the agony of the man that had raised him. A rebel officer approached Melvin and whispered something in his ear.

"We must deal with him," Melvin said.

The crowd yelled out their verdict, almost unanimously for execution. Cries for shooting, hanging, and burning rang out. The crowd took a liking to one verdict, it became a singular cry.

"Burn him!" Anselm did not look back at them. Drake could see the man had no life left in him. Drake would not watch the closest thing he had to a father suffer such an end.

"Seems a little extreme," Melvin replied.

"For fuck's sake, don't torture him. Just put him out of his misery," Thos said.

"The people have spoken. We burn him," James said. Drake approached Anselm as all watched nervously.

"What are you doing?" Melvin said. Anselm sobbed. Drake hovered over Anselm. The king stared up at him with eyes dead and bloodshot.

"Forgive me," Drake said. Anselm closed his eyes.

"Abby," he said. Before anyone could react, Drake drew his

sword and drove it down through Anselm's neck and into his chest. Anselm fell dead. The soldiers grabbed hold of Drake.

"Detain him for now. Perhaps we'll roast this one instead," the commander said. Thos interjected.

"Is this really necessary?" he asked.

"You forget your place, Mr. Averill," James threatened. Some of the rebels did not respond well to Thos disrespected in such a manner. Melvin muttered some words under his breath and motioned for Drake's release.

"We'll remember this," the officer said. *As will I*, Drake thought.

GREGOR

Violent shaking and the familiar mumbles of human speech awoke Gregory Pavane from a pleasant slumber about a strawberry pie so good it might violate the Compact. Gregor liked his sleep; it was the only time he separated himself from his work. Gregor paid little attention to the outside world during his recovery, though he couldn't deny the news of Anselm's death brought him some joy. Patrick Sims said something, but Gregor's drowsiness blocked it from his ears. He dozed off again and felt the impact of a hand going across his face.

"I'm up, dammit!" Gregor said with drowsiness. The side of his face burned. "Did you slap me?"

"I... didn't know what else to do. You've been out for almost a day. We were starting to worry." Light poured in the room, blinding him just as his eyes fully opened, he winced and cursed.

Gregor slowly opened his eyes and rose to his feet, wearing the Fey-provided clothing he forgot to take off last night.

"Better have a good reason for waking me," Gregor said between yawns.

"I do. I've found a few other members of Vigilant, and they claim to have found another Hell Gate," Patrick said. Gregor reached for his sword out of habit. Patrick pushed Gregor to a glade outside the community once inaccessible due to the fairies. Gregor saw Zora near. She waved at him, and he responded. He had only spent a few hours with his niece so far, when not resting to mend his shattered body.

Gregor spied the occasional sniper in the treetops, keeping nefarious sorts at bay until the lab beneath their feet could be destroyed. Patrick wheeled Gregor to the glade. Electricity rippled through the air, the kind Gregor came to associate with imminent danger.

Since his confinement to what he dubbed a "roller jail," Gregor carried a jet-black pistol bought off a traveling gunrunner. He reached down for the gun and took it in his hand for the inevitable trouble. Metal fragments littered the ground. Patrick looked around nervously.

"What? Looks like they destroyed it already but where did they go?" he said, spinning around frantically.

A monstrous crunch boomed off to the right of the men. Before Gregor could even mutter a curse a white-robed body collided with Patrick. Upon Patrick lay a dead crusader, head twisted around. Patrick squealed while pushing the mangled body off. Gregor pointed his gun in the direction of the flying body. Patrick stumbled to his feet.

A thick tree crashed behind them. Patrick spun around in time to witness his chest being hollowed out by a metal fist. Gregor thrust himself out of the wheelchair; only to receive a metallic foot to the gut that knocked him back down. A humanoid female stood in front of him, bearing the unmistakable cybernetic enhancements of a Grey Sister. She was machine from head to toe, save for the nose and mouth section of a human skull. Two rows of four green eyes crawled up the side of the head, thankfully lacking the power to enthrall Gregor like those of other witches. Reinforced plates replaced the breasts, abdomen, and major muscles, and a thick black spine reinforced a greying synthetic skin. Thick, tube-like hair glowing a neon pink ran down the back of her head. Just a little too thin and standing just a little too tall, this horror was the crowning achievement of body modification.

The long black fingers of the sister's hand pulled Gregor up and tossed him with the ease of a newborn babe. Gregor rolled across the ground, breaking a few new bones in the process. When Gregor came to a stop he saw another crusader, contorted like a pretzel.

"Why can't you just leave me alone? Do you not see, I have failed!" she screamed. Gregor crawled over to the pistol a few yards away, she did not try to stop him. His bullets bounced off her.

"What the hell are you babbling about?" Gregor yelled, throwing his gun at her in one last fit of rage.

"I was rejected. We've all been rejected," she said. The woman looked down at her metallic figure. "I gave them my body and my mind and still they rejected me. They chose a weak king. I never should've helped them. Their savior is now rotting in the ground." Gregor raised an eyebrow.

"King... Anselm?" Gregor asked. He gauged his foe, though unrecognizable he knew her from the castle.

"I knew I'd run in to you again, makes this easier," he said. With his foe still lacking the ability to enthrall, Gregor had a sliver of a chance.

"They cast me aside. For their betrayal, I'll destroy all of their works," she said. Gregor lay helpless in the grass, awaiting a killing blow that never came.

"Wait, you've destroyed the Hell Gate?! Why? What are they?" Gregor asked. The woman cocked her head. He took it as a condescending glare.

"It is their connection to the land. They can move through them. These cylinders stretch across the world. Without the gates they are weaker now," she said.

Using just her hand she chopped wildly at another tree, cutting through with the efficiency of a chainsaw. Gregor didn't relish the idea of talking with a cultist, however, this proved too valuable a source of information.

"Who is this 'they' you keep referring to? Perhaps we can help each other," Gregor said.

Asking from help from a witch caused him near as much pain as the broken bones. Though lacking human expression, he followed the green eyes examining his crippled body.

"I think I can manage," she said. Gregor scoffed. *Fuck me… insulted and murdered,* Gregor thought.

"If you won't leave me be then you have to die. Trust me it will be a mercy compared to what's coming," she said. The figure walked over to Gregor. He dug his hands into the soft earth and tried to crawl away.

"Leave him alone!" a voice cried out. Two more feet appeared from nowhere beside Gregor on the right side this time, belonging to his brother. Matthew carried a sword at his hip and a black-green meshed pattern assault rifle in his right hand.

"You sure picked the wrong family," Matthew said.

"Woe is me, I am no match for Dopey and Wheels!" she cried. Gregor and Matthew looked at each other.

"Damn, that's unnecessary," Matthew said.

"I know, right? Bitch," Gregor said. Matthew helped Gregor over to the wheelchair and handed him the assault rifle. Another figure rushed to Gregor's side, his niece, Zora. Matthew drew his sword.

"Make your shots count, don't hit me," Matthew said. Zora fired shots from a pistol. Matthew charged at the woman. Matthew's blade precision-sliced through the thinner sections of the witch's synthetic flesh. Armor-piercing rounds from Matthew's custom-made rifle chipped away at the stronger pieces of her frame. The witch swatted at Matthew. Dodging the attacks, Matthew wedged his sword under her left breast and slowly pried it off. The armor plate, disconnected, fell away, sticky and red on the underside. Without the plating, the witch's soft, organics became exposed.

Zora moved closer with each shot, preparing to deliver a killing stroke. She jumped back just in time to avoid a fatal strike from the revitalized witch. Matthew plunged his sword down through the muscle in the witch's open wound, receiving a rib-snapping kick to the sternum for his efforts.

"Don't you get it? We're all just part of the equation, slaves to It's will. I thought I was going to be different, but I was wrong. I'm doomed… same as you," the witch said.

Gregor fired round after round at the witch, tearing through her open wound and blasting off her two left eyes. Thick red blood seeped out from her wounds, signaling there was still plenty of vulnerable human inside. Wounded and angry, the metal woman approached Gregor with no signs of slowing down. Gregor turned his fire to her legs, blasting away bits and pieces of her right ankle. A downed Matthew joined in, chopping while still lying on the ground. Blood and metal showered forth, and the woman fell to one knee.

Gregor got a few more shots on her right hand, taking off some of her fingers. Zora chopped at the tree the witch had intended for her weapon, finishing what she started. Matthew hobbled to his feet, seeing the plan formulating around him. He gave the witch a hard push, lining her up, and then jumped out of the way. The unmistakable sound of a toppling tree caught the witch's attention, just in time to see it crashing down on her. One last desperate attempt to catch the falling behemoth proved in vain, folding her up like a lawn chair under it.

The metallic remains stirred from underneath the tree. Zora rushed forward to end this battle for good. Gregor rolled to her side. The witch pushed the tree up enough to expose her dented head, now leaking streams of red. Cracks in the metallic cranium exposed a fatal weakness. Zora raised her sword high.

"I just wanted to be fr—" the witch said before a sword pierced her organic brain. The color from her artificial hair and eye flickered before going grey. They hum of her internal parts ceased. Gregor let out a pained sigh of triumphant relief. He looked at his brother and his niece, smiling at the notion of the Pavane family vanquishing a foe together.

"Any clue what the hell she was yammering about?" Matthew asked between gasps for air.

"Not the foggiest, but I intend to find out," Gregor said. Matthew shook his head.

"So much for settling down," he said. Zora responded with a look of hurt that stung Gregor worse than his injuries, he dreaded leaving Zora and Matthew for what might be the last time.

"You just came back," Zora said. Gregor forced himself out of the chair. Nearly toppling back over he was caught by Zora, which didn't bode well for his return to Vigilant.

"I think I might be here a while longer, but you know I can't stay. There is some weird shit going on, and someone needs to do something about it. We need to find out who this ominous 'they' are, what happened with the king, what's in that Vault, and whatever 'they' are planning next." Gregor formulated a mission, quickly forgetting those around him. He felt the sadness of his brother and niece.

"Don't grieve, Elena; you'll be seeing a lot more of me. I neglected my family for too long and I won't make that mistake again. I like you two shits," Gregor said.

"You sure you can keep that promise?" Matthew asked.

"Not a promise, a mission. And I see my missions through, to the end."

DRAKE

Drake retreated to the outskirts of Kingsbury, still reeling from the death of the Blackthorne family. Watching the victors have their way with the city became more than he could bear. He spent the next few days holed up in his parent's Estates, the only place in the city where he wasn't under constant surveillance. Drake was eventually pardoned when his father ended up joining the ranks of the new Board of Directors. After a few days in isolation, Drake needed to escape the madness. He decided to go to the one other place he could be alone.

The pale half-moon peeked out behind the clouds above when Drake entered the Blackthorne mausoleum. Anselm had no funeral and was quickly tossed in a sarcophagus and shoved in the mausoleum, done as "an act of respect and decency" by Abraham Kerr. He wondered how long the tomb would stand before the new rulers decided to tear it down or let it suffer an unfortunate accident. The tomb held a particularly frigid chill when Drake stepped in. The dying flames in the tomb hallways cast wild shadows on the monuments of kings and queens. Drake followed the hall to the resting place of Anselm at the end of the enormous complex. The rest of Anselm's family lay buried beneath the ruins of Blackthorne Castle, except for the king and his oldest son.

No heat could drive out the cold haunting every step down the long dark corridors. His hand gripped the hilt of his blade tighter as he went ever deeper in the Blackthorne tomb. Drake reached the large alcove that housed the former king. The headless, unfinished monument held vigil over Anselm's sarcophagus. Placing his hand on top of the ornate stone hand of the visage of the king, Drake mourned the loss of Anselm Blackthorne.

"You raised me, taught me, loved me as your own, and I… killed you. I couldn't end this war. I wish you could hear me. I wish… please forgive me," Drake said. For the first time in his life, despair took hold of him. "I tried to do the right thing. All I ever wanted was to make you proud. I spent my whole life doing what I could to hold this country together… and it was all for nothing." Cold wisps of air were his only replies.

Drake felt uneasy in the halls of the dead. He feared the new rulers had eyes on him even here. Even with his father on the new Board, he was told not to leave the city for the time being. Drake had a few contacts in the capital, trusted friends not yet on the government's shit list. The contacts told him that given his reputation, and the murder of the king so desired, the Board would allow him to continue his work like nothing ever happened.

"These are dark times, the only time in which we can truly be called men. I won't run. The country will need me in the days to come. I will protect this nation, from itself if need be." He vowed to fight any that would do harm to the people of the nation. Drake searched for resolve within himself. The flames from torches slowly began to die out for the last time. Drake spoke to the slab housing the closest thing to a father he had ever had.

"You told me once long ago that nothing matters more than people: not codes, not honor, not even blood. If we don't fight for people, then we are worth nothing. I will protect the people until my dying day," Drake said.

Deep within the winding hallways of the great Blackthorne

tomb, Drake considered himself an outsider, because technically, he had been.

He knelt down in front of Anselm's sarcophagus and repeated the Oath of Prosperity. "I, Drake Hale, pledge my life to my country. To destroy all who would threaten it, enemies both foreign and domestic. From this day until my last, I am no longer a man, but ideals made flesh. I am the protector of the people, their weapon and their voice. I am honor. I am duty. I am the sword of the nation. I am the shield against corruption. I am a Son of Prosperity."

Drake rose. Exiting the halls of the dead, Drake Hale emerged a man with renewed purpose. Renewing his vows made the bleak world seemed a little less dark.

THOS

THOS AVERILL SPENT the better part of the week feasting and enjoying the spoils of war. In just a few short weeks, Thos went from Heartland businessman to national hero and soon to be CEO and owner of Averill Estates Farms, the largest farming conglomerate in the country. For the first time since this whole mess started, he relished being at the center of everything. With the war over, he had turned his attention to wedding plans and forgetting the horrors he had witnessed.

Thos lived in the vacant Beaumont house for the duration of his stay in the city. Though he stayed there alone, he often found Melvin skulking about. Just that morning, he had found Melvin there, outside. Melvin shook his head and walked toward Thos Averill. Melvin wore a slate grey suit, a new pompadourish haircut, and slightly more groomed caveman beard. Thos gathered Melvin was now a spokesmen for the new order.

"Helluva week," Thos said.

"Yup," Melvin replied.

"A lot of people died, people died that had nothing to do with any of this," Thos said with disgust.

Melvin looked down. "We did the right thing," he said, not sounding wholly convinced.

"I sincerely hope so. You staying?" Thos asked. Melvin nodded.

"Yup. Loyalists will strike at us, bandits will attack, and Mexico might try to secede. It'll be a hard road, but one worth taking. You?"

"The bosses offered me a shit ton of property out by the lake. A few men came to me earlier about expanding the Averill farm into a nationwide business, buying out the other farms and become one big supercorp. Got a wedding to plan, too."

"Big plans," Melvin said.

"Thos Averill, family man and *retired* war hero," Thos said.

"Don't worry, no more fighting for you, probably," Melvin laughed. A group of stern-faced men and women in suits hollered for him. "Well, duty calls. See you around."

"Yeah," Thos replied. Thos spied Drake near the castle ruins, now returned after vanishing for days. He walked over to Drake, who stared up at the clouds with his trademark brooding frown.

"I appreciate your concern, but words won't help," Drake said with a tortured look.

"Worth a shot," Thos replied. Another silence followed. He began to walk away.

Thos knew Drake had a lot on his mind, so he took a seat on the steps beside him and listened.

"I betrayed my king. I considered betraying all of you. I tried to, in fact. I wanted all this infighting to end. This country is broken, and I don't think we can put it back together again."

"For what's it's worth, I'm sorry this happened," Thos said. "The new government probably won't turn out as well as anyone plans, but I have hope things'll get better."

"I doubt it. Democracy is not freedom, its mob rule… if the leaders even allow that," Drake replied.

"In that case we need people like you more than ever."

"That's exactly why I'm staying. People still need help, and that's what I intend to do," Drake said. Thos wore heart on his sleeve, and Drake noticed.

"Doubts?" Drake asked.

"Of course. I was just a pawn in all this. If Aric wasn't trying to kill me, it might've been Joe burning my house down. I doubt there was a good side this time; hell, maybe there never is. I only hope the suffering of the people will force the new leadership to honor their promises," Thos replied.

"Maybe the Fey have it right. Maybe we are better off without leaders," Drake said.

"Perhaps. Our leaders may stumble and fall off the wagon, all the time it seems. Until then we need people to show them the way. Sometimes the world needs a swift kick in the ass. Hey, maybe you're the boot."

Drake smiled. "I like it even more when you put it that way," he said.

"Something tells me you have a large role in how this whole big mess plays out," Thos said.

"You, too, I'd wager," Drake said.

"That's why I said mess. In any case, stay in touch," Thos said. He extended his hand and Drake gripped it firmly.

"I will. See you around."

"See you around, Ser Knight. My door is always open, well, when I get one, it will be. I mean it'll be locked so you'll have to knock." Drake laughed.

"Can't turn it off, can you?" Drake asked.

"My burden to bear," Thos smiled.

As Drake left, an older man approached Thos, and sat down beside him. The man coughed, shaking Thos from his pleasant daydreams of a happy marriage.

"Help you?" The man smiled at him. The old man's face had pronounced features and bulbous eyes, giving him the appearance of a sharply dressed vulture. The man was freakishly thin, almost skeletal. He had waxen skin and sunken eyes, adding vampiric qualities to his already macabre visage.

"You've helped us a great deal, Mr. Averill," he said. He placed a bony hand on Thos's back. Thos's spine tingled at the touch of a man one hood away from being Death.

"You're about to rope me into something, aren't you?" Thos asked, with an expectant frown. "And who might you be?"

"A friend. You looked like you were having second thoughts. You and your Averill Estates will play an important part of the new world, the world you helped build. Big things are coming your way." The pit in Thos's stomach became a chasm.

"Trust me, you'll feel better after a nice vacation. I do believe you've earned it." He gave Thos a pat on the back. The old man rose, adjusting his wrinkly charcoal suit. He walked away, stopping to face Thos Averill one more time.

"Seriously, who are you?" Thos asked again.

"John Derbin. I look forward to doing business with you. Welcome to the future, Mr. Averill."

MELVIN

MELVIN ADJUSTED HIS jacket and tie before throwing open the back doors of First Prosperity Bank, the current meeting spot of the rulers the new government.

Melvin entered the stuffy back room that had only a single window, an odd choice given the size of a bank with plenty of bigger and better rooms. He smelled fresh paper. In the room sat David Westerfield, John Derbin, Katonah Hale, Janice Caan, Abraham Kerr, James Dumas, and another woman Melvin was unsure of. Melvin knew David, John, and Janice to be members of the former Board of Directors. Melvin was also quite shocked to see Drake's father in the mix. Mr. Westerfield kept eyeballing Melvin as if he knew him, but quickly dismissed it.

"About time," John grumbled between puffs on his cigar. A young female in the group stood out. She wore a black suit and thick web of gold around her neck. She matched Joseph's description of Toth immigrant Yadira Khouri, a rising star in the political arena. A conversation resumed as Melvin pulled up a seat.

"I need to stop by the cobbler," David said. Melvin chimed in before anyone else could speak.

"Cobbler, yeah, I could really go for a peach one right now,"

Melvin said. All sound was instantly sucked out of the room. After a moment David cleared his throat and spoke.

"It's time we established a working government. New leadership is needed—compliant leadership. Should we hold elections?" David asked. They all grunted in confusion. A few in the room chuckled, including Joseph's own brother. Melvin decided not to speak up. From Melvin's point of view, things were off to a terrible start.

"Have you forgotten that the people despise you? If you place yourselves in charge, the people will just rebel again. We need to restore faith in our system," Yadira said. The others groaned at her suggestion. Melvin spoke up, trying not to sound intimidated or stupid.

"The end goal is for the people to live free. That is what your brother died for," Melvin said, singling out Abraham.

"It's not so simple. They always want more. They need someone to guide them. Pure freedom will not work," Abraham said. The hypocrisy of Abraham's words floored Melvin. Melvin couldn't bear to hear anymore and tuned out the rest of the conversation. He daydreamed for the rest of conversation, nearly falling asleep in plain view of everyone. After the long drawn out plans for the next few months, he interjected.

"What was the point of summoning me here?" Melvin blurted out. Mr. Derbin shot him a hateful look. Something about John scared Melvin more than any of the monsters he'd encountered. He immediately shut up.

"You have a role in this, would you like to hear it?" John asked.

"Yes, sir," Melvin said.

"You're going to be the Minister of Internal Affairs, we'll make sure of it," John replied. Melvin did not like the way he said it. Melvin also didn't really know the position entailed, so he decided to ask.

"Like, head of the Knights? What about Lord Whatever?"

"Not head of the knights, but a similar job. As for Jerrick… he was a loyalist and has been dealt with," John said. There was a finality to John's words that made things painfully clear. The temptation of rewards quieted his discontent. Melvin liked the idea of being Minister of Internal Affairs. The more he heard the title in his head the more he liked it. *Lord Shor… hot damn,* he thought.

"We will help you select a cabinet," John said.

"I don't even have a kitchen yet," Melvin said.

"Advisors," Abraham replied irritably. The others groaned.

"Is that acceptable?" Mr. Derbin asked.

"Hell, yes," Melvin said with a wide grin. Melvin listened while the others hashed out plans for the new government. Melvin didn't want his mood ruined, so he bid farewell to his new masters.

"I've always wanted to run the bank," David Westerfield said, laughing as Melvin walked out.

Melvin left the bank, not sticking around to hear the rest of the news. He strolled up to the hill where Blackthorne Castle once stood, now a pile of rubble. Workers slowly cleared the ruins, chomping at the bit to get at the forbidden technology of the Blackthorne Vault. With Vigilant pardoned but currently banned from entering the city, it allowed the new government to obtain these dangerous items unfettered. The lack of grisly deaths from violating the Compact made Melvin wonder if it was hogwash after all. Effigies of Anselm burned in the streets the first few nights after the king's death. The new government considered adding effigy burnings to the fireworks of the Blackthorne's "Prosperity Day."

Over the next few weeks, Melvin watched the new Board of Directors set the groundwork for a new government, including drafting documents based off the Constitution, Amendments, and Bill of Rights from the time of the United States. Melvin forced himself to turn a blind eye to the glaring corruption of the regime. The kinglike power the Board exerted proved hard to swallow. James Dumas took his place as Regent of New Prosperity, second only to the Board. The new leadership quickly destroyed the Black-thorne mausoleum despite the respect they had shown for Anselm's body, the respectable act used to win over more hearts and mind of those not loyal to the crown or the new regime. The new leaders did mention some good things, however: veteran care, improved power grid, tax reductions, and enough other items to lift his spirits.

Out of all the leadership, Melvin found Yadira to be one of the few good ones, he hoped she could help keep the country on track. She discussed her plans expand the role of Vigilant, includ-ing appointing a man named Mathias Rehnquist as the supreme commander of all branches. Few liked the idea, as Vigilant lacked a supreme commander since it tried to destroy the government's attempts to violate the Compact some three hundred years ago. It took the influence of Regent Dumas to convince them. Katonah Hale immediately pardoned his son for any and all crimes.

Melvin reflected on the new life that awaited him as the Min-ister of Internal Affairs. Melvin saw Joseph's scowling face in his mind. He told himself it would all be worth it. He headed down to the Droullin house, now serving as the new brothel. Melvin forgot his troubles in the arms of Madame Dehar, who often wore gold body paint as frequently requested by her clientele. After taking care of business there, Melvin sat down by the ruined Fountain of the Holy Queen he had demolished. The world passed him by as he thought about all the good that he could accomplish with his newfound authority. He imagined the cheering crowds gathered to celebrate all of his good deeds. The early spring always brought change, and this year spring brought unprecedented change to New Prosperity. The acts leading to this moment left him feeling dirty, but he knew there were great things to come.

He had noticed joy returning to the nation. The people spent many years suffering with little hope for a better future. The most powerful nation on the continent and first established after the end of the Old World declined further and further each day, in desperate need of change. Joseph never doubted this day would come, and his conviction never faltered. Melvin couldn't afford to falter either.

Thoughts of money, power, freedom, and sex flashed before his eyes. The sun beamed down brightly upon him. He celebrated the dawning of a glorious new age. He saw New Prosperity once again living up to the name. Like the blooming sweet peas growing outside the bank, he could breathe in the seductive fragrance of victory. Melvin psyched himself up, desperately trying to bury his growing doubts about the future A stranger walked by and greeted him.

"It's a good day, is it not, sir?" she asked. Melvin looked up at the woman and grinned from ear to ear.

"Yes, ma'am. Yes, it is."

ZORA

Even a week later, Fey talked about the end of the 2000-year-old Blackthorne dynasty. Having her wheelchair bound uncle show up for the first time in over a decade, followed by a witch attack, only added to the surreal nature of these days. Zora meditated silently and hoped her friends had survived the war. Her uncle rolled around in a wheelchair, grumbling most of the time about his limited nobility. Zora's company brought her uncle of out his perpetual sourness. Though Gregor promised to stay and heal, mentally he was already waging another crusade.

Zora made numerous trips to see Os, gleaning information from the corrupted computer while her father and uncle prepared to destroy it before the new government found out. She asked Os time and time again about the masked entity, receiving only beeps for her efforts. The masked faces appeared to her clear as ever; she had a gut feeling from the Vigilant training provided by her father that this masked thing wasn't only connected to the cults, but Gideon Grey, the labs, and these godseeds. She continued grilling Os for useful information.

Kami made frequent trips to the labs, helping Gregor to them as well. Zora and Kami made numerous sweeps through the labs to ensure no traces of Old World monstrosities remained. With their combined efforts they were able to access more of Os's files, including Gideon's electronic journal. Gideon's journal entries became increasingly erratic, his tone declined into terrified ramblings about what he uncovered. Zora, with her father and uncle's help, sifted through what they found. Little made sense, while the rest only detailed the things of which they were already aware. Kami and Zora made one last trip to the lab before they were ready to destroy it. One entry stood out among the others, dated a few years before Zora's birth.

"That's interesting. Wonder who left this one?" Matthew asked. The voice was familiar yet different. Zora listened while trying to decipher the man's identity.

"To think I feared this life. In my quest for knowledge I risk death upon death," he said.

"I think that's Gideon," Zora said. "He sounds like a completely new person."

"That is very odd. In the other records he was terrified," Kami said. Zora and her father listened to the recording.

"I am one with It now, like the others. We become less ourselves and more of It. The Compact is so much more than anyone knew. I was but a fumbling child beneath It's glory. When you arrive here you will know. From here you will be set on a new path. The information is scattered across facilities like this all across the country, by the enlightened ones that came before me. So many have been groomed or altered themselves for this task, pretenders to be consumed and repurposed. Your bloodline has been cultivated to stand above the others. You are what the Compact requires."

Gideon's tone sent icy fingers up Zora's spine. Kami, slack jawed, listened to the words.

"This recording was meant for someone else," Zora said. Kami ran his fingers through his beard, the tried and true thought processing move of the Pavane brothers.

"That person may have already been here," Kami said. "Which

could mean we could be far behind in stopping whatever has been set in motion."

A map appeared on the screen with dots in northern corner of the frontier and the southwestern area of Mexico. Other blips appeared all over the map. The map turned to static.

"Shit. Did you get those locations?" Kami asked. Zora shook her head.

"Some," she said.

The machine let out deep, long beeps. Os's face appeared on the screen. It's eyes and mouth went black, the mouth curved into a wicked smile. Zora felt a presence other than Os, the one that haunted her dreams. The image vanished.

"Did you see that?" Zora asked.

"I did," Kami nodded. A red light flashed above the keyboard. Matthew cursed and frantically hit keys on the keyboard. The journal stopped and returned to the main screen. Folders disappeared.

"Dammit, everything is being wiped," Kami said, unable to stop it. The screen went black. Kami tapped on the keyboard. The machine did not respond.

Os stopped speaking altogether.

"Whatever that is, it seems to be well aware of what we're doing," Zora said. Zora and Kami left the underground lab and discussed the findings with the chairbound Gregor. Gregor and Kami developed plans to investigate the matter further. Gregor planned to contact the Mexico branch of Vigilant and return to the Northern Frontier branch if pardoned by the new government. With Os unresponsive, she spent her days in a pond a mile from town per her father and uncle's advice.

"There will be time for that. There is always crazy shit going on, take your rest when you can," Gregor told her. Judging how weary and grumpy her uncle always was, she realized Gregor should heed his own advice. Zora relaxed in the shimmering waters and forgot the days when monsters haunted the woods. Commotion back home interrupted her meditation.

Zora returned home. She noticed an unprecedented number of outsiders sizing up the community. A few men emerged from her father's home, giving the hanging courtyard a once-over. Zora dipped into the house the instant they left.

Kami sat cross-legged amid the incense he loved so much. The room smelled of incense and wax. Her father anticipated her question with a scowl.

"Delegates from the new government," he said with passive aggression.

"Are they forcing us out?" she asked. With news of the attempt on Drake's life, Zora watched them carefully.

"No, or so they say," Kami began. "They came to officially welcome us to the new government and to let us be so long as we pledge our allegiance. Brought us gifts, too. Guess they wanted to get back here before someone steals a page from their book and hides out here." *A community that must pledge allegiance is not free,* Zora thought. Zora picked up on Kami's fear.

"We must destroy the lab immediately," she said.

"I've acquired some explosives. We'll blow the place as soon as our guests leave. Hunters are setting it up as we speak," Kami said.

"If there are other places like that, we need to destroy them," Zora replied.

"I agree, as does your uncle," he said. "Though I'm not sure there is much we can do about it right now, but at least the bounty on him has been called off. You don't need to be worrying about that, anyway." The incense began to grow thick and the elder breathed deep, dulling his uncertainty.

"You and uncle are in no shape to care for anything, and I can't just forget what I saw. You heard what the woman said, what we saw in the lab. Something else is going on, this war was just the start," Zora said. Kami ground his teeth in frustration.

"Dammit. Of course you'd have that Pavane bullheadedness," Kami said, shaking his head in irritation.

"We must do something!" she said.

"We will, but right now we have to deal with keeping the new government happy and away. That will keep us occupied for some time, and you too. We will reach out to the rest of Vigilant and get the ball rolling." Kami closed his eyes and went into a meditative state. Zora waved the gathering vapors from her face, needing a clear head for this new assignment. "I'd like you to go the capital, for a job." Zora experienced excitement, joy, dread, and confusion all at once; she regretted waving away the vapors.

"Job? Me?" she asked.

"We want someone to represent our people. You'll be something of an ambassador like that Drake boy. Chance to travel, keep the peace, and contact the other Fey should we need them. If you still feel the need aid Vigilant, then your uncle can help with that."

At the moment, all thoughts escaped Zora. She knew this assignment wasn't just something for her benefit, yet it made her happy all the same.

"It won't happen till next week, so you have some time to think it over." As the incense slowly filled the room, this time she didn't fight it. The tingling nerves dulled as she breathed deep. Her father spoke no more as the smoke carried him off to blissful meditation.

Without a word, she left the house. She made her way to a collection of pale oaks where the dead lay buried. No personal markers of identification of any kind were found here, only small wooden figurines representing the departed. Grass covered the older unmarked graves leaving only a few open plots for the recent casualties. She approached the grave where her sister's ashes rested and sat beside it.

"Sprout misses you. Don't worry, I'll look after father and uncle," she said. Zora sat beside her sister's grave until the outsiders left the forest. She shed no more tears feeling the weight of this burden finally lifted.

Much to Zora's relief, the outsiders left without a fuss, for today at least. Her favorite spot lay far in the woods, one of the old mediation points seldom used by others. With the threat of the fairies gone, Zora headed to the old watchtower in the heart of their territory. Like most of the structures in the woods, the watchtower was built from a mighty white oak. A spiral staircase carved in the tree wrapped all the way up to the top of the ancient tree.

Zora climbed with ease, remembering the times of her youth when she'd be exhausted not halfway up. She reflected on the training that enabled her to accomplish exceptional feats of agility, tests created by her father inspired by his training days in Vigilant.

From the top of the watchtower, Zora saw for miles. The tower-less Kingsbury seemed completely different even from here. Nearly two millennia of Blackthorne rule undone in a single day. It was hard for Zora to fathom. She heard the Fey gathering near the secret lab not far from her location. From the watchtower, she watched fire spew from false trees. The ground rumbled below signaling the destruction of Gideon's lab. She wanted to know more about the place but felt relieved to see it burn. Fire shot up from the fake trees. The ground shuddered. She thought about similar labs across the country, something to add to her to-do list in her new job.

Zora reached a state of thoughtless serenity. When the peace washed over her, she sat until night turned to day. Something about her dreams still nagged at her, like memories under lock and key. She decided to speak with Gregor more about this masked figure when she returned home.

In the forest below, Fey began to break off from the main community to build homes in the now fairy-less areas of the forest. After everything she'd been through and all the lingering questions, Zora felt hopeful for the future. She spent the next week traveling to Kingsbury and securing the Fey's place in the new world, all the while spending time with Drake in her off hours.

She developed a connection with the Knight-Ambassador and wanted to see if it would become something more, and he seemed more than eager to spend his free time with her. The two of them also found themselves running into Thos Averill quite frequently, finding him a true friend. When not busy, her thoughts turned to less pleasant things. Zora knew the masked figures and their cults still lurked out in the darkness, not to mention inevitable clashes with the new government and its foes. There was much do in the days to come. Soon Zora would get to the truth of masked villains and dark designs. For now, Zora decided to enjoy her time, realizing how quickly things could change.

EPILOGUE

He awoke to madness and confusion. Cool, dark air swirled all around him. Ice cold sweat ran down his brow. The man came to his senses in a dead sprint. Large pieces of broken stone lay on the floor. He remembered blood, fire, and tearing flesh. There was no time to stop and think about the past. He ran as fast as his body allowed. His heart pounded with thunderous terror. A voice spoke to him. "Run!" Images flashed through his mind firing one after another: stone faces, piles of dead, smoke, and a collapsing tower. He remembered killing three men, their blood spilling onto the cold stones. The building crumbled all around him. He dashed from the structure into the brisk night air.

The world swirled around him in a murky haze. Colors blurred as he ran, making him nauseated. But he kept running. Wolves howled too close for comfort. He could run no longer and collapsed. The man lay in the wet grass under the supermoon. The wolves grew closer, and he could hear the hunger in their cries. He rose to his feet. Reaching for a weapon, he came to the realization he was naked and defenseless.

Teeth clamped around his ankle and he fell back down. He flipped over and brought his hands up, catching the jaws of a second wolf. Pain and hatred surged in his body. With unknown strength, he pulled at the wolf's jaws until they cracked. He kept on pulling with the ease of ripping paper. The wolf's jawbone split followed by the neck. Tendons and muscles stretched and ripped. He tore the animal in half, the wolf's bloody entrails washing over him.

The other wolf gnawed at his ankle. He kicked it fiercely, yet the jaws remained clamped. Four more wolves circled him for the kill. He kicked the wolf off his ankle and jumped to his feet. His fist came down on a wolf hurdling towards him. It hit the ground with a whimper. A second punch obliterated the wolf's skull, flattening its head. He picked up the other downed animal and threw it into a tree. The surviving pack members darted off in all directions. The broken wolf whimpered. He pitied the wolf and snapped its neck to end its suffering. After catching his breath, the man pressed on.

His heart slowed as he walked through the night woods. Firebugs hovered in the distance, brilliant white light flickering from them. He wanted to claw at his scratchy, dry throat. He could he hear far-off waters from deeper in the woods.

The man's ankle throbbed, raw and bloody. In the pitch dark that would impede any other man he could see all. Deer lounged in a small grove. A large indigo worm hung in a tree a dozen yards away. He turned west. Traces of humanity littered the trees above. He came upon a stream.

He cupped his hands and gulped down the cool water. He drank more than his fill, excess water sloshing around in his gut like an ocean storm. Four corpses shambled toward him, a woman and her three sons. Three of the corpses were charred whole the other rotten body wore roped burns on his neck. The man cowered from the dead, whimpering like a helpless pup.

"Go away! Please," he sobbed. The voices rang in a horrifying chorus.

"You still have a purpose in this world," they said. The images flickered; the man swore he saw the dead wearing masks.

"There is no purpose!" he screamed back.

"You can end it. Break the cycle," the dead wailed.

"How? Tell me!" he pleaded.

"You know how. Right beneath your feet," they said. The voices guided the man toward Gideon's long-rumored labs. His body ached. He needed rest. The man made his way deeper into the forest. One of the old Fey houses rested up in an elder tree, thicker and taller than all other trees in sight. A circular platform rested on its peak, branches and leaves wrapping around a modest house resembling a three-room cottage. A half tattered rope ladder extended down to the forest floor. He climbed the ladder. Tearing aside the flimsy door, and he collapsed on to the sunken bed with no sheets.

"Only for a minute," he said. Slowly his eyes opened to the warm light of day and voices new to him. He closed his eyes and pretended to still be slumbering.

"He's lucky to be alive," the female voice said. "He looks kind of like the king, though way younger and pale as death."

"Please think about this," came the voice of a man. "We don't know what he brings with him. He might be a survivor from the battle, likely one of the king's men. We can't harbor the king's men."

"The war is over, and he needs help," she said.

"I can't stop you, just be careful." The male voice grew agitated. The man left the building in a huff. The woman turned back to the man in the bed treated his wounds. She applied pressure to his tender ankle, causing him to curse in pain.

"You're terrible at eavesdropping," she said. The man shut his eyes for a second until he realized the jig was up.

"Out of practice," he said.

"My name's Zora. And you?" The man looked at the floor.

"Doesn't matter anymore," he replied.

"How long have you been up here?" she questioned.

"Not a clue," he replied. Zora looked him over. He knew she didn't buy his story; he needed to leave.

"Your wounds have been treated, should heal up soon. We have provided you clothes," she said. On the floor beside him laid well-worn clothes. Rising from the soft wool bed, the man dressed in a brown jacket, undershirt with only one sleeve, dark cotton pants, and hide boots.

"Aren't you going to ask me where I come from?" he asked.

"The only thing I care about is that you leave soon as you can," Zora said. Zora pointed to the table beside her. "There's a hunting knife, feel free to take it. We have also provided you a backpack with enough provisions for a few days."

"Thank you," he said.

Zora stared at him, waiting for him to speak; it took him a second to get the hint. The man left the truth a secret for now. He was confused and relieved no one recognized him. He ran his fingers over his face, finding fewer wrinkles than he remembered. He attempted to hide his shock at this realization.

"I'm no threat to you," he emphasized.

"That remains to be seen," she replied dryly.

"I will trouble you no longer. Just a little information and I'll be on my way," he said. "I'm searching for a man that used to live here, Gideon Grey." The color vanished from her skin at the mention of that name.

"Abandon whatever it is you plan to do," she said.

"I cannot, my life is at stake."

"Then I'm sorry for you. Nothing good comes from seeking Gideon," Zora said.

"I beg you—"

"What do you plan to accomplish?" she asked.

"That man destroyed everything I loved. I seek revenge. Will you not show me?" he asked. His response was a half-truth.

"I don't trust you." Zora looked him over, trying to discern his true nature.

"Can't say I blame you. Trusting people got me in this mess.

Men from the capital approached you this week, didn't they? You are right not to trust them. They're villains and will use Gideon's power. They've already found a great deal of it beneath the castle and won't tolerate free cities like this any longer. I intend to fight them, alone, if necessary," he said with voice ringing conviction.

"Are you Vigilant?" Zora appeared to stop herself from saying more. The man continued with the lie, trying to not scowl at the mention of that name.

"Only one left, I think. With the city plundered, it's only a matter of time before they find the other hidden caches and exploit them. They must all be destroyed." He was prepared to kill this woman if he deemed it necessary.

"Gideon's lab has already been destroyed, but I can show you where it was," she said.

"Are you sure? I've heard such structures run deep. There's a whole world under our feet. I suppose it's a start at least," he responded. Zora looked him over one more time.

"I don't trust you, but more than them," Zora said. The man sensed the tautness of her muscles and elevated heart rate, he realized she didn't buy a word of his story. He needed to give her the slip and find the masked man on his own.

"Let's not waste any more time," he said.

Zora escorted him past a mishmash of tents, houses, and walkways. He had time to admire the hanging courtyard as Zora made a quick trip to a wheelchair-bound man. Upon speaking with the man, her body language grew even more hostile, though she was unaware he knew it. There was something familiar about the wheelchair man, the kind of familiar that made him angry. After speaking with the man, she returned, giving him a polite smile. She was lured away from the people. He pretended not to notice the archers tailing him. *I can hear them breathe*, he thought.

She pointed up ahead and approached a large, discolored tree. As he grew closer, he saw a large section of pulled-apart bark resembling a collapsed door. A voice rang out inside his head. A trap, it said. Out of the corner of his eye, he saw her hand moving to her dagger as he drew close. He did not let on he saw the other Fey waiting to shoot the moment he moved. He turned around and saw a man in a white suit sporting a golden mask. He knew it was time to act.

The man heard Zora's attacks the instant they occurred. He anticipated her strikes with frightening accuracy. He parried her attacks and gave her a hard punch to the face with his right hand. The blow knocked her out cold. The archers wasted little time firing on him. He avoided every attack. The archers jumped down from their perches and drew swords. He wasted no time dispatching them. Three slashes severed three heads. He closed in on the next two men, splitting the skull of one and crushing the neck of the other. He could feel the masked man analyzing him.

The last Fey archer turned to flee, only to receive a hunting knife in the back. Stepping over the corpses, the man saw Zora lying in the grass. He raised his blade to finish her off, but stayed his hand.

"She doesn't deserve to die like this. Just a kid defending her home, just like…" The masked man entered his field of vision and pointed to the left. He followed the trail. The masked man guided him to his goal: one of the half-melted trees. He tore apart the faux tree and descended down the stairs inside.

His body tingled with anticipation when he entered the underground lab. Cutting a path through the middle of the facility, he stumbled upon a smashed-in black screen. Broken and burnt equipment littered the rooms. Piles of ash, bone, and glass lay strewn across rooms. The masked man told him what to do. He stepped on the small platform in front of the broken screen. With a hum the floor lowered, taking him even deeper underground.

At the bottom, the platform stopped with a jerk, nearly knocking the man off his feet. A door in front of him opened. An endless facility stretched as far as the eye could see with massive black towers glowing with blue lights, larger versions of the "Hell Gates" described to him in his former life. Tunnels went off in all directions, connecting to other areas all across the state.

In front of the towers stood a single man, wearing a white suit and smiling gold mask with a long, pointed nose. He approached the man, wanting answers to all his burning questions.

"Here you are at last, ant-king," the masked man said. He stepped back.

"I'm sick of your games!" Anselm roared. The towers hummed with electric life in the background. The masked man cocked his head.

"The reward for your pain," the masked man said.

"Reward?! My family is dead! *I* should be dead!" he screamed. In the blink of an eye, the figure appeared directly in front of him.

"Again such limited thinking. You can accomplish so much more now. You're the variable to the great equation." Anselm's head began to ache. Six well-dressed men and women wearing silver masks now encircled him.

"I don't understand," Anselm said. His vision blurred.

"We will show you," the masked figures said in unison. Anselm found himself on the ground outside Blackthorne Castle, though not how he remembered. The city sprawled out far, exponentially larger than during his reign. Skyscrapers reached up to the heavens. Neon lights of all colors illuminated every corner of the megalopolis. Seconds later, the buildings quickly decayed around him. Flames engulfed the city. Buildings collapsed. Flying machines fell from the sky. Millions of artificial humans stopped dead in their tracks.

Anselm witnessed the final decades of the Old World. The bright, shiny city became a desolate wasteland. Children ran from the lone tower left standing in the city. A young couple ran straight through Anselm towards the Northern Frontier. Anselm watched the couple birth a son. That boy grew into a man. The man led an assault on that same tower. The man crowned himself Alexander Blackthorne, dubbed "Alexander the Great" like the conqueror of ancient times. Anselm watched the children and grandchildren of this man forge his kingdom into what it became today. Anselm watched the deaths of his wife and three sons and felt his heart break all over again.

The visions turned to a middle-aged man communing with an unseen presence in this very spot, a man named Gideon Grey. A fog enveloped Gideon, breaking him down into nothing. Time went in reverse. Anselm grew nauseated. He now stood in front of an unknown location with floating towers and an orb at its heart. Thousands gathered in front of it and a gold-masked man took center stage. Among the masses gathered, he noticed crowns and jewels signaling some of these individuals were the kings and queens of the New World. He witnessed the first Compact.

"You... you created the Compact!?" Anselm exclaimed. Like ghosts, the figures flew toward each other, becoming a singular black mass sporting masked faces. A haunting chorus of male and female voices spoke in unison. Even with his new life and superhuman power, this entity filled him with unbridled dread.

"We *are* the Compact. We have kept the world alive. It lives and dies by our design," it said.

"Why did you appear to me?" Anselm asked.

"You are what we seek, a change in the algorithm. You're the template for the new. It is time to begin the next phase of the Great Equation. You have been... altered for this purpose and accepted these changes even better than predicted. You're a product of many centuries of genetics, mutations, and events. We have been guiding your family for a very long time. At last, our labors have borne fruit." Locations appeared out of thin air in front of Anselm, places found all across the country teasing forbidden knowledge.

"Don't fret, ant-king. You will have all that you desire, but not yet. Head north," it said. The voices ceased and the lights died, leaving him alone in the cavernous ruins of Chicago. Armed with the new knowledge, he found his purpose restored. He blocked out the pain gnawing at him. Crumbling and rotting towers of metal and cracked asphalt stretched out like a metal sea in the dark underworld. Rebels tried to kill him. Vigilant tried to kill him. Fey tried to kill him. Drake succeeded in killing him, yet here he stood. Anselm headed deeper into the ruins with a new life and a chance to set things right.

"I have work to do."

The End

Thank you so much for reading my book.

Did you enjoy it? Spread the word! Please share your thoughts and leave a review on Goodreads and Amazon. Your feedback is greatly appreciated. Follow me on social media or on my website, www.aaroncolewilliams.com.